ALSO BY TIMOTHY EGAN

Lasso the Wind

The Good Rain

Breaking Blue

THE WINEMAKER'S DAUGHTER

—THE—
WINEMAKER'S DAUGHTER

A NOVEL

TIMOTHY EGAN

ALFRED A. KNOPF, NEW YORK 2004

THIS IS A BORZOI BOOK
PUBLISHED BY ALFRED A. KNOPF

Copyright © 2004 by Timothy Egan
All rights reserved under International and Pan-American
Copyright Conventions. Published in the United States by
Alfred A. Knopf, a division of Random House, Inc.,
New York, and simultaneously in Canada by Random
House of Canada Limited, Toronto.
Distributed by Random House, Inc., New York.
www.aaknopf.com

Knopf, Borzoi Books, and the colophon are
registered trademarks of Random House, Inc.

Grateful acknowledgment is made to the Hal Leonard Corporation for permission
to reprint an excerpt from "Brass in Pocket," words and music by Chrissie Hynde
and James Honeyman-Scott. Copyright © 1979 EMI Music Publishing Ltd., trading
as Clive Banks Songs. All rights for the United States and Canada controlled and
administered by EMI April Music, Inc. All rights for the world excluding the United
States and Canada controlled and administered by EMI Music Publishing. All
rights reserved. International copyright secured. Reprinted by permission of the Hal
Leonard Corporation.

ISBN: 1-4000-4099-X
LCCN: 2003112114

Manufactured in the United States of America
First Edition

To Sophie and Casey, for light, love,
and drama every day, and a persistent request:
Tell me a story.

A people without history is like the wind on the buffalo grass.

—attributed to the Teton Sioux

THE WINEMAKER'S DAUGHTER

PROLOGUE

WHEN THE COLUMBIA RIVER cut through layered rock in the greatest flood of all time, it left a cleft in the earth where the children of Chief Moses feared to play. In that coulee, nothing grew until the waters were dammed and the Indians gone and the land terraced to face the sun at all hours.

During the winter before irrigation a young man walked the length of the coulee, sleeping three nights on hard ground. He built a two-story house of timber and stone, bolted it to the basalt shoulders of the little ravine, and trimmed it out with fine-grained planks from the ghost barns of homesteaders who thought rain would follow the plow but never dreamed water from the big river could be brought to their doorstep. Then, at midcentury, the Biggest Thing Ever Built by Man lifted the Columbia River uphill and filled the cavities from the ancient flood until the wrinkled ground was fertile like the newcomer's family home in the Italian Piemonte.

In the moist weave of this new land, the man planted Nebbiolo grapes from the Old World, tended the vines through a troubled early life, and crafted a red wine that became one of the most sought-after products of the Pacific Northwest. His house stood through two earthquakes, though it became out of plumb to anyone who could see with a carpenter's eye. He was married late to a woman from the East who always missed the city and did not want her children to live in the coulee when they came of age. She died after the children moved away, leaving the aging man alone in a slightly listing house. Once a year he held a party, a gathering of people who believed in the transformative miracle of wine-making but had little idea that water, the base nutrient of this miracle, would be to the new century what oil had been to the last.

CHAPTER ONE

R IDING A MEMORY, hot air floats up from the river and slides through an open door, finding Brunella Cartolano with her eyes closed. She takes a deep breath, feels lighter. Eight months of limited play and fitful sleep have passed under a cloud cover on the other side of the mountains, and now this—the air tickling the insides of her legs, a thermal tease. She orders black coffee and ice in a cup from the roadside caffeine hut and kicks off her shoes. She feels liquid.

"Let's go sit on the rock."

"Are there rattlesnakes?"

"Yes, but they usually warn you. Follow me, Ethan. I'll show you something—"

"What if I see one?"

"You'll feel alive."

"And how long will that last?"

"As long as you dare."

Crossing the Cascade Range, Brunella and Ethan Winthrop have stopped just east of the pass, an hour from the Cartolano family home, in a canyon lit by slices of sunlight. Though she lives in Seattle, barely two hundred miles from her father's coulee, Brunella has not seen a summer in the land of her birth for three years. She is the middle child, the only girl. As they left thickets of salal and salmonberry and the mist of the maritime pelt of the Cascades behind, she felt the tug of home. She was a different person—she could feel the change coming on, mile by mile—

5

whenever she crossed the divide from the wet west side of the Cascades to the desert east.

"I've never seen the river this low," she says. As she leads Ethan around a boulder he stumbles a bit, the hesitant walk of an indoor man. "But look . . . see where it turns there? That's where we used to go tubing. They say it's class three: a few bumps but it won't kill you. Not this year. Water's too flat."

"I'm hot."

"It's dry heat. Don't you love it?"

"I hate the sun. Why live in the meteorological equivalent of a smiley face?"

"You're such a stiff, Ethan."

Here the big summits have given up their snow and the meadows are aflame with Indian paintbrush and columbine, brushed back by the thermal. She presses her feet into the sand and spells out N-E-L-L-A with her big toe. Two days removed from ice holds in the highest reaches of the mountains, the water slides over stones and pools up just downstream. Brunella takes off her top and wiggles out of her shorts.

"Hold this." She hands him her clothes. Ethan glances back at the road, frowning.

"And you can look if you want."

"I'd rather not."

"Now listen." She cups her hand to her ear, near the froth of a small channel of white water. *Zeee-eeet! Zeee-eeet!*

"You hear that?"

He shakes his head.

"Dippers. These dinky birds that live in the shade of mountain streams and love white water."

She plunges into a deep pool just below the riffles and, when she is fully submerged, opens her eyes. The rocks are a polished blur, the river grass sashaying. Brunella lets herself go limp in the arms of the current, riding the water downstream until she is out of sight and her laughter bounces against the canyon walls.

.   .   .

They drive through a faux Bavarian village, the hotels, restaurants, and supermarket framed in costumes of alpine Tudor. At the town's lone stoplight, she looks away at the crowded balconies of the town structures and wonders if they would hold up if this part of the Cascades went into a shudder. It is the kind of trance she has fallen into of late—staring at brick warehouses or the stilts of the bridges that stitch one hill to another and thinking *tectonic thrust:* ocean plates pushing up against continental ones, shaking off the urban attachments like fleas on a dog.

She pulls into the liquor store, buys scotch, gin, and a squat bottle of gold tequila for the party. "Is this going to be enough?"

"You know I don't drink."

She gives him a straight-on look, one eyebrow arched. "But you've seen people do it." Her black hair is still damp from the swim, face primed for a laugh.

"It's never enough, from what I can tell. Get another bottle. Get another half dozen, for all I care. I'll pay."

"Your millions are worth nothing on this side of the mountains, Ethan. Close your wallet and open your senses."

"Then how will I sleep?"

Ethan has narrow fingers and hair as thin as spider webbing. He seems afraid to be out of the city, troubled by his sudden dependence on Brunella in unknown territory. In the city, he is master; without him, Brunella would never have made her name. She had been working nearly a year—for him—on their latest project when he told her he wanted to "see the West." Not Arizona or Texas but the big brown land on the other side of the Cascade curtain. It surprised her. Ethan Winthrop, the Great Indoorsman? She promised to show him salmon in the desert, Indians at a rodeo, and sunrise over the North Cascades.

Driving east, the pull on Brunella is like gravity now, orchards all around, heat still rising, the land burnished in wraparound brown. At a fruit stand, she stops the car and rushes to a bin overflowing with peaches as if greeting a lost friend. "My God! Look at these Red Havens!"

She fondles a piece of the fruit and bites deep; the syrupy juice dribbles past her lips and onto her chin. She wipes it clean and shivers in joy. "Wars could be fought over a peach like this. Here . . . try it."

A teenage girl sits at the cash register, fanning herself under a tarp. A sign, in bold colors, is hung just behind her:

SAVE OUR DAMS

She wears a button with the same message. Brunella sorts through the fruit, whistling a tune. "Oh . . . and cherries!" The Rainier cherries are nearly as big as plums, have the color of flushed cheeks, and taste like candy. She plucks one from a pile and tosses it to Ethan. "There is certainly nothing wrong with a garden-variety Bing cherry. But this—here—*this* is a cherry. And wait till you see our place. It's mostly grapes, but my father grows a white apricot that is better than sex."

She slips away to the bathroom. A sign over the toilet reads DON'T FLUSH UNLESS YOU HAVE TO. When she turns on the faucet in the sink to wash her hands, a putrid coffee-colored liquid dribbles from the tap.

"What's up with the water around here?" she asks the clerk.

The road levels out, the land losing its green except for the orchards. A few homes are planted in the foothills behind windbreaks of Lombardy poplars and cottonwoods. And here is the Columbia River, bulked up and sluggish, the flat water holding the sky of late afternoon, dimpled by little whorls. The high walls of the old river channel rise hundreds of feet above the surface, tiers of the ages bleeding minerals. Brunella turns down a rutted side road to a rusted fence, gets out, and opens a gate with a NO TRESPASSING sign shot through with bullet holes.

They pass an arthritic homestead, roof caved in, the wood sun-bleached and perforated. In front are lilac bushes, domesticated orphans now left to their own in the raw basin heat. The road ends suddenly at a cliff above the Columbia. They walk through dried brush, raising a clatter of hoppers, to the edge, where they can see what the river has done, consuming bluff and rock in steady gulps during its epochal mood swings. She picks a handful of olive-colored leaves from a scablands bush, crumbles them, smells the release, and offers Ethan a sample: sage.

"The scent of the West," she says, with a proprietary hand sweep through the air, "and its biggest river."

In a crease of beige rock, a petroglyph stands out: three human figures, floating and legless, with horned heads, following animals, next to a swirl—all of it scratched onto the desert varnish of oxidized stone. When Brunella presses the palm of her hand on the head of the rock image, it makes her tremble, as if she has just tapped into a current in the stone.

"This glyph is so simple. They're hunting elk—"

"What's with the antennas on their heads?"

"I think they're horns. Like the elk."

"I find these petroglyphs to be rather banal and overly romanticized," says Ethan. "Is there really any difference between that rock sketch and an e-mail about what you had for dinner last night?"

"There's no mystery to an e-mail. It's a word fart."

She moves closer to the cliff, crab-walks over a section, and is gone. Ethan pales, falls to his knees. "Brunella . . . ?"

She stands on a ledge barely wide enough to hold her feet, face to the desert wind, an eagle-beaked hood ornament out of Ethan's sight. She fears nothing at this moment. She leaps from the ledge over a deep crack in the high cliff, to a landing closer to Ethan. As she comes down, she laughs, but a twitching muscle above her knee betrays her true feelings. The drop, had she missed, is several hundred feet.

Ethan stares at her. "Why would anyone build a house this high up from the water?"

"You've been to France, Ethan—"

"Every other year since I turned twenty-two."

"I forgot: You're a Francophile in addition to being scared of snakes, water, and sun. Or maybe that's why you're a Francophile."

"Could you at least pretend to suck up to me?"

"This river gets its water from an area about the size of France, so they say. Think of the power. This old place was built high because those homesteaders were afraid of the river. They knew enough to stay out of its way in the spring."

"Then why did they leave?"

"Our national impulse. Why do tumbleweeds roll?"

"What's a tumbleweed?" Ethan says, but this time he winks at her.

They head north, following the river, Brunella still at the wheel, the window down to let the oven air on her face. Above, the walls of the canyon are lined with irrigation pipes, the coronary veins of the basin. Brunella steers away from the river and onto a gravel road, a steep switchback that contours along a streambed. She gets out and leads him by the hand to a ravine where a bare trickle of water flows toward the river. She crouches down and examines the ground.

"This is the stream I told you about."

"Are you sure?"

"Yes. Except I've seen puddles in the city with more water."

"Where are the fish?" He mimics her. " 'Salmon the size of toddlers in the middle of the desert basin.' "

"There's nothing here."

"What's that?" He points to a fish dried crisp by the sun, its eyes pecked out.

"We used to come here at night, me and my little brother Niccolo. You'd hear them thrash around, splashing up through this little canyon. It's one of the things that made this place so magical for me, Ethan. And look at my little stream now: It's been killed somehow. I don't even hear a mosquito."

"So this is the end of that run of fish?"

"Not if they can get water back in here."

Up higher, groves of aspen and tamarack huddle in deep shade. Larch trees, their needles usually a velvety green in midsummer, are bare and sick, as if the tops and outer branches have been singed by a flame. Just inside the coulee, Brunella stops at an apple orchard overrun by dandelions gone to seed. The trees have not been pruned for some time; their tops are shaggy-headed, the trunks fountains of leggy sprouts. The fruit is sun-mottled and moth-eaten. Many of the leaves are chewed to the base, consumed by fibrous nests of tent caterpillars. A FOR SALE sign is hammered to the base of one of the bigger trees. And beneath that: ANY OFFER WELCOMED.

She touches the hardened sap of the tree with her fingers, stepping around an anthill at the base. "My God. This is the Flax farm. You've seen those stickers on the polished apples at the store, Flax in Wax? This was their first orchard. I can't believe the Flax family, of all people, gave up on apples."

They drive through a natural portal of enormous stone; on the other side is a valley of near-perfect proportions, the granite walls of the north Cascades at the distant end, well beyond the coulee.

"*È bello da mozzare il fiato!*" says Brunella.

"Is that a curse?"

"That's what my father says whenever he gives directions to our place. When you can say, 'It's so beautiful it takes your breath away'—*È bello da mozzare il fiato*—then you're here." She finishes the sentence with her hands, unbound again as she nears the refuge of northern Italy her father has built in the interior Northwest. "The mountains look like the Dolomites, don't you think?"

"I've never been east of Nice."

Sunflowers nod in the early evening breeze, their big heads lining the road. They follow the only road in the coulee, a single lane of rust-colored earth. It veers through a sentinel row of thick-waisted pine and then opens to a place where the coulee fans out into an amphitheater of vines, lavender, and fruit trees. The ages have worked orange and gold coatings into the big rock walls, slow-fading monuments to the epic flood that covered parts of three states, carrying water equal to ten times the flow of all the world's rivers. This edge of the coulee, a tilted bowl facing south, catches more than thirteen hours of sunlight in midsummer. The last rays glance off clusters of red grapes from old vines trellised along galvanized wire. A river rock wall encircles a cream-colored farmhouse with a wraparound porch painted baby blue. Brunella stops just short of the house and jumps out of the car, leaving the door open and the keys inside.

"Have you ever seen a more beautiful place?" She pulls him toward the house. "Have you ever smelled a more fragrant garden? Look here"— she points to a row of fruited bushes in large terra-cotta vases, wheels at the base—"oranges, from my father's *limonaia*. My God, how could I have stayed away? Have you ever seen such poetry in the land?"

"I'm soft-sentiment-impaired," he says. "Don't let that stop you."

She pinches a sprig of rosemary and hurries up the steps. Opening the screen door, she calls out for her father.

"Babbo-oh!"

Nothing.

She calls out again, using the Tuscan word for father favored by her long-dead *nonna*. She walks to the edge of the stairway but goes no farther. Since the death of her own mother three years ago, Brunella has been afraid to see the little landmarks of the house, the nooks and corners where her mother used to read or sing, the window seat where she looked off to the east, faraway east, a three-thousand-mile stare. These places will never be neutral. And she cannot imagine her father roaming the two-story five-bedroom farmhouse without becoming a haunt who speaks to himself as he shambles past the rooms given life by thirty-seven years of marriage.

She leads Ethan back outside through the rose garden. Every few steps, a new wisp of floral perfume envelops them. Hummingbirds buzz in the last angled light of the day. A small fountain circulates water from a big earthen pond. She skips ahead, uphill, following the sound of a base-ball game coming from a paint-splattered radio in the back rows of the vineyard. She spots her father from a distance, a Mariners cap on his head, wielding a pair of pruning shears like a conductor's baton.

"Babbo!"

Angelo Cartolano is in cutoff jeans and high-top baseball cleats; he has winged eyebrows and a face of untrained honesty, wearing the years with a proper fit. He stares down the hill, squinting in the last sunlight. They hug and twirl around. She kisses his nose, spins the cap backward, and holds him tight. The sweat runs through his shirt, and his hair is moist and askew. She resembles her father in one striking way: They have the same green eyes, though most of the color has gone out of Angelo's.

"You need some sun," he says.

"I have three full days here to catch up, and then we're going hiking in the Methow. Babbo, you look healthy. Let me feel your muscle." He makes a fist with his good hand and bends his arm the way he used to do when Brunella was a little girl and he was Popeye.

"Strong man. How's the fruit?"

"The grapes are stressed, Nella." He cups a bunch of velvet-colored fruit. "You know how this Nebbiolo likes to cluster. This year it's different. Everything is different. I'm not sure what kind of wine I can make with these conditions." Brunella notices his quivering left hand. "Every day, hot, hot, hot all the time, *tutti giorni*. Everybody's complaining about the water, and I must tell you I am very afraid."

"It can't be that bad. You still made wine last year."

"That was last year. I had—you can say—some help."

"How so?"

"Nothing. But this year, fourth year of the drought, and guess what? They are giving us less water than any time since the Grand Coulee Dam was finished. Thank God I have my pond. But listen, I still have so much hope, Nella—we're less than two months from October, and the Mariners are three games ahead of Texas."

"They have no immortals, Babbo, since A-Rod and Griffey left."

"But they have magic again this year. And look at you—you've been away too long. You smell like the city." He points to Ethan, who is finally making his way up to the vineyard, a panting willow of a man with a pallor like milky tea.

"That's our guest from Seattle, Ethan Winthrop. I'm working for him on my latest project. He wanted to see the other side of the state."

"He's your boss?"

"Sort of."

Angelo grins. *"Fare l'amore?"*

"With him?" She giggles. "No! I mean, look at him, he can hardly walk. I'm fascinated by his mind but I think he's asexual. Neutered or something. I've never felt any—I mean I've never asked him. And he's never said."

"Un castrato?"

"Not that. He's just not a physical man. He pocketed more than seventy million dollars on a dot-com that he sold two years before it went out of business."

"What did they make?"

"Some kind of virtual thing that nobody needed. Now obsolete. Imagine being forty years old and not knowing what to do with the rest of your life. He's helping this billionaire remake the old Ballard section of Seattle. Ethan is the conceptual brain behind the project. But first they have to pass a hurdle that won't allow you to knock down a city block if there might be something worth holding on to. That's where I come in. They hired me to do the cultural impact statement, freeing up the space. How many are you expecting for the party tomorrow?"

"A big crowd this year. I think they love the wine more than me. *Va bene*. Niccolo will try to make it by tonight, but I've heard nothing from your other brother."

"Did you expect to?"

"No. And I should thank you for coming before I start complaining. Some days, I think you look down on the little place where you grew up; you're such a big shot now you can't come home—"

"Stop it, Babbo. It's not that at all. Who else?"

"Some of your friends from growing up. Everyone from the Last Man's Club has promised to show. We're down to five of us, you know."

"The Last Men could almost fit in one tent."

"And there'd be one big symphony of farting, wheezing, snoring, and belching. From the coulee, the Flax family."

"I saw their orchard today. It's in horrible shape."

"They had to give up most of their water for the fish. Solvan Flax could not take it. He got drunk one night and shot up the construction hut that the Indians are operating out of, down by the river. Solvan says the Indians are behind all the water take-aways. Says they put it in the government's head to take back our water and—if they get their way— maybe even tear down one of the dams."

"But the Indians . . . my God, a more broken band of people does not exist in this county. How could that ragged little cluster of welfare cases have anything to do with it?"

"They've got a treaty promising them salmon for all time. If there's no water, there's no salmon. They use the treaty to get the water, you see. Thank God nobody was inside when Solvan went crazy with a twelve-gauge, but it's terrible. I tell you something, Nella: I no longer recognize my oldest neighbor. The man is sick with hatred."

"Who else?"

"Some two-oh-sixers may come down from on high to join us," he says, using the nickname for people from the Seattle area code who maintain homes in the coulee. "Look at Stuart right now."

They turn to the west. The summit of Mount Stuart is in plum-colored silhouette against a burning sky, gold trim on the edges, nearly ten thousand feet high.

"You must promise me, Nella, that when you plant me in the ground here it will be high enough in the vineyard so that on Judgment Day the first thing I see will be Mount Stuart."

"I will, Babbo, I will. You have my promise. But you have another twenty years left in you, so shush."

In the kitchen, Angelo Cartolano is ready to cook. He has picked zucchini flowers, filled a basket with three kinds of tomatoes, and brought wine up from the cellar. The cutthroat trout are cleaned and iced. Lamb shanks are marinating in Zinfandel, rosemary, brown sugar, garlic, and lemon. He pours wine and offers a simple toast.

"Beviam, beviam, beviam!"

Brunella holds the wine in her mouth before taking a longer sip. Ethan sets his glass to the side. "Wonderful," she says. "It tastes like . . . heaven without a dress code."

"Very good," says Angelo. "Truth is, it tastes like 1989. A mild winter. Early spring. Rain at just the right time after the bud. Then around Memorial Day—*poof!*—I never saw a cloud for the entire summer. Cooled off enough in August to keep the acid up in the grapes. The harvest was flawless. Stems and skins loved each other. Oh, God, what a blend! A *vino rosso* for all time. Strong tannins gave it enough backbone, and now it's starting to smooth out. I'm worried about this year, though. It's been too goddamn hot."

"Global warming, Mr. Cartolano?" Ethan asks. "Or do you distrust the science?"

"No one alive has ever seen such a time in this coulee. Up in the meadow, the ground is like bread crust from last month. The trees are spooked, no life left inside 'em. Nature answers only to its own rules, so we'll see what follows, yes? Try the wine, please."

"He doesn't drink, Babbo."

"I'm . . . so sorry," Angelo says in a hushed tone, funereal. To the Cartolano family, the only thing worse than someone who does not drink wine with food is the person who cannot laugh.

Angelo retreats down a hallway to a side pantry, where he keeps drawers full of flour and dried herbs, the ceiling draped in twined garlic and strips of oregano hanging overhead.

"What do you think of my father?" Brunella says, when he is out of earshot.

"Rustic," says Ethan. "I can see where you get your passion. Is there anything you two do not get excited about?"

"Is that so bad?"

Angelo returns, white flour dust trailing behind him. He mixes the flour with eggs and water in a bowl and adds olive oil. He takes moist balls of mozzarella and cuts them into one-inch sections, and dries the anchovies on a paper towel. His left hand is badly gnarled and knotted, and it shakes uncontrollably, making it hard for him to finish. Brunella folds her hand around his; it feels like a bag of marbles. She helps him open the petals of each flower and pinch out the filaments. They fill the insides with mozzarella and anchovies, add a dollop of honey, and press the petals until they are closed up again. The zucchini blossoms are dipped in the batter and pan-fried until golden brown.

"*Alora—fiori di zucchini fritti*," he says, with a jack-o'-lantern smile, turning to Ethan, sweat dripping from his brow. "My uncle used to make these in the camp in Missoula. The highlight of the summer. The guards thought we were crazy—look at the stupid dagos eating flowers. Hah! You do eat, don't you, Mr. Winthrop?"

They are just sitting down to dinner—grilled lamb and trout, potatoes quartered and roasted above the coals, a salad of Cartolano tomatoes with basil—when a car pulls up and Niccolo Cartolano bounds into the house. He has a deep mahogany tan, short hair dyed blond on top, broad shoulders, and Jason Giambi arms. This summer he has added a branded mark of a grape above his elbow. He is wearing shorts, sandals, and a UC Davis T-shirt. Angelo is ecstatic; his younger son is his favorite, something he has given up trying to hide. Niccolo sets his backpack down and pours himself a glass of wine in a single motion. He kisses his sister, shakes hands with Ethan, and winks at Brunella as he raises the glass.

"*Pancia mia, fatti capanna.*"

Brunella translates for Ethan the old ritual blessing before a big meal: "O belly of mine, make a storehouse of yourself."

Niccolo has finished his third year of college and is in his fourth summer as a smoke jumper for the Forest Service, which has a regional headquarters not too far from the Cartolano family home.

"This fire in Colorado: We dug breaks to the south, breaks to the north, backburned on another flank—no go. Finally, all we could do was spit on it and walk away. Some people were bitching 'cause we couldn't save all the trophy homes. Like, Hello? Jesus H. You're living in a fire zone. These are people who hate government and want us to save 'em. I'm in the Methow for the month, if I'm lucky. You did the trout just right, Dad. Haven't lost the touch. But the lamb needs something."

He helps himself to a second mound of food, pours another glass of wine from a different bottle, gulps it halfway down, then fills it to the brim. He pops the potato quarters into his mouth, five in a row. Watching the spectacle of three thousand calories vanish in a few minutes, Ethan is mesmerized.

"I'm not sure, but I think the '89 is better," Niccolo says. "This *is* the '89, isn't it?"

His father beams. "Niccolo, you have the nose of the Cartolano family, eight centuries in the making."

"And what am I," Brunella says, "a truffle pig?"

Niccolo always said he wanted to be a winemaker. He talked of Sonoma and Napa, as did nearly every aspiring vintner at UC Davis, but the frontier had long ago left those valleys and they were off-limits to anyone who had not amassed a fortune during the late gilded age.

"Moisture content in the Rockies is under ten percent," Niccolo says now. "They're starving for rain. Those pinyons were opening like popcorn. Parts of the Cascades aren't much better off. The Okanogan is one big bundle of upright kindling right now. You gonna eat all that?" When three seconds pass without a response, he scoops up Ethan's well-trimmed lamb. "So I'm here for the Last Men bash and whoever else straggles in for the party tomorrow. Maybe get a day of fishing in with the master here before another round of ground pounding and extra H-pay."

He separates the backbone from the trout and swallows the entire fish.

When everyone is asleep, Brunella throws on a nightshirt that just covers her underpants and strolls outside to feel the warm breeze against her body and the grass under her toes. Overhead, stars undimmed by city light and the high eroded walls of the other side of the coulee make her feel alone in a big place. The fragrance is stronger at night, or at least more distinct: sage and honeysuckle. She wants to stretch the moment and tries to remember why she turned away from her desert home.

CHAPTER TWO

O N SATURDAY MORNING, Brunella rises early and goes for a run in the hills where she used to play, up among the cheat grass that flames red in June and then fades to beige in the desert summer. She follows a faint road that passes by the second-oldest house in the coulee. There once was a 1952 pickup truck out front, left to die on the spot where the owner abandoned it in defiance of the Arab oil embargo thirty years earlier; now the car has vanished. She passes a small reservoir, full to the brim in the midst of the drought. She runs along the ditch that delivers water from the distant lake created by Grand Coulee Dam. She can see where bulldozers are moving rock and earth for a project down below, about five miles away. She remembers the abandoned mining village hidden nearby, a clot of cinnamon-colored cabins slowly vaporizing in the basin winds. Inside one of the cabins was a 1915 Marvel stove, walls covered by painted oilcloth, a heavily lacquered wood sink. It smelled of mice turds and dry rot, but it told a story frozen in its tracks, as if all life had been petrified on a single day. She used to spend afternoons inside the shack, reading books from a dust-covered shelf, and brought friends into this lost world, one at time, making them take an oath to keep the secret. On the day the village disappeared, knocked down in an afternoon, Brunella discovered how quickly this part of the world can erase itself.

Running back toward the vineyard, pleasantly numb on her fourth mile, her mind drifts, floating above the land. At seventeen, flying home from a school soccer competition in Denver, she looked down and saw the coulee from the air for the first time. She was horrified. It looked so lost and inconsequential, a trench in the ground removed from everything, the world passing it by. She knew then she would flee, she had no choice; maybe she was her mother's child.

Back at the house now she swims in her pond, a familiar embrace. Drying off, she rushes inside to kiss her father. "I'm glad to be home. Really, Babbo. I love you. Don't ever doubt that."

She picks flowers for the party. The Cartolanos put linen and wine on each of the tables, position a keg of beer in a garbage can of ice. By the brick oven outside, cherry- and apple-wood branches from winter pruning are stacked for fuel. Miguel brings mescal and little clay tequila cups that his daughter has made. Each cup bears the chiseled name of one of the five old men who climbed Mount Stuart more than sixty years earlier.

"You're home."

She turns to face Teddy Flax. The curious boy of her youth has filled out in his shoulders and arms, and his face is lean, with a soul patch of facial hair on his chin. When he smiles his eyes lead the rest of his face in a welcoming accordion. She is stirred and surprised by her reaction. As she walks toward him, he holds out his hand. "Oh, screw it," she says, and wraps her arms around him. His body is warm from the walk up the coulee.

"I heard you were teaching," she says.

"English—sophomores and seniors. Coaching baseball too. We play our first games in snow squalls and the play-offs in hundred-degree heat. That's why I moved to the Flathead Valley. No end to the drama. And you can nearly make a living. You can put gas in a beater car. You can housesit, because there's no shortage of big empty log mansions. And then, like they say, you get this other paycheck: big rainbows rising to a mayfly hatch just a few steps from where you live, that sort of thing."

"It sounds wonderful."

"The winters are long. Lotta people can't take that."

"What are your kids reading, Teddy?"

"Stegner. They liked *Angle of Repose,* once they gave it a chance, the little shits. My seniors will start *Sometimes a Great Notion* next year, after a fight with the curriculum committee. Somebody in Iowa doesn't think it's literature."

"I'm sorry about your father."

He fills a plastic cup with beer. "I'm chasing fires close to home this week. With OT and hazard pay, I can make almost half my teacher's salary in two months as a smoke jumper."

"With Niccolo?"

"I wish. Got posted to Murkowski's crew. Guy's an idiot with ambition—dangerous."

"I can get you on Niccolo's crew. It's not a problem."

"You went away. What, New York? Someplace in California? Or was it Europe?"

"The wandering architect's tour. In Manhattan I designed shoe closets for Martha Stewart acolytes. In California, it was strip malls that were supposed to look like quaint little villages in Vermont. And Europe . . . I went there to feel to inferior, and it worked. So I'm home."

"Which is where?"

"I'm not sure."

"But you got a job in Seattle?"

"Consulting."

"Is that the same as working?"

"Of course not." She laughs. "They pay you to be their conscience. You'd be surprised how big the market is for such a thing. I'm on contract with Waddy Kornflint's group."

"The zillionaire?"

"A mere multibillionaire. And another guy—Ethan Winthrop. I'll introduce you to him today. We're doing a thing at Salmon Bay in Seattle. It used to be its own little city, full of Norskis peddling lutefisk and that sailor's drink that tastes like paint thinner, you know. . . ."

"Aquavit?"

"That's it, the drink that has to cross the equator in oak barrels in a ship's hold before they can release it. How weird is that? But all the old Sons of Knute are gone. The place is a pit, nothing to look at. It could use a face-lift. Thank God Kornflint has some taste and a sense of history."

"And your job is—what?—making sure nothing's lost in the makeover?"

"The legal term is a finding that the new project would have 'no significant impact' on the culture. Without an NSI seal, you can't move forward with the development. Six years in the school of architecture, followed by a decade of shoe closet designs, faux villages, and Euro-treks have led me to this: I'm the NSI ace of the West Coast."

"Can you fit that on a business card?"

"The way I look at it is that I'm ensuring nothing of real value is lost. I would never sign off on an NSI if something really cool were at risk. Never."

She moves closer to him, curls her hand around one of his fingers.

"Are you free tomorrow?"

"As in unattached?"

"I didn't mean it that way, but if you want to volunteer." She tightens her grip.

"I came this close to marrying a girl from the city—this babe—looking for something in Montana. You meet a fair amount of people like that in Kalispell, always in the summer. Good combo: sense of humor, way smarter'n me, pretty hot. Hey, you talk about authenticity and trying to hold on to the past, get this: Her breasts were real."

"The rarest American woman, and there are more than two of us. So what was the problem?"

"Money. She had it, I didn't. And I don't care how much we had in common, I could not be her equal. You know how some people have these personal trainers to show 'em how to do sit-ups and keep their shoes tied? I woulda been her designated book reader–slash–river rat." He laughs at the thought. "Not a bad job, being that it came with gymnastic sex and an open account at Barnes and Noble. But then what? Waiting on her moods with white gloves? God, this beer tastes good today. It's hotter'n snot out here. I'm sorry; I dodged your question."

"No, you answered it."

"I have an itch to hit baseballs tomorrow afternoon. Friend of mine in Chelan has a pitching machine. You set it at ninety-plus mph and you're up against Pedro Martinez. A guy has about one third of a second to make up his mind whether to swing or not when that machine's throwing heat. Where's Angelo? I bet he could still hit the fastball."

She points to the deck. Teddy walks away, stopping to drain his beer, his back to Brunella. "Some guy from Omak wants to buy our orchard. I think what he's really after are the water rights."

"The water's worth more than the land now?"

"Yep."

"And you're going to sell?"

"I don't know what to tell the folks. They don't listen to me anyway. The orchard's almost dead. Nobody wants to buy a Red Delicious apple anymore. Has no taste and the skin's too hard. These irrigators—shit— they bred themselves out of business, even if they hadn't been side-whacked by four years of little water and high heat. So maybe it's time to fold the tent and stuff their pockets while they can. The old man's eligible for market-loss relief money, even after shooting up the Indian shack. And from what I hear, there's more on the way."

"A big bailout?"

"Something's brewing, Brunella, otherwise people wouldn't be so stirred up. You grew up here: You ever seen people clawing one another's eyes out over water, like they're doing now?"

"I guess you're right. I haven't been paying that much attention."

"Look at what happened with all those farms in the Midwest. There's big money to be made doing nothing, long as it's the right kind of nothing."

"I can't see Solvan Flax taking a check from the government for the rest of his life."

"I know you've been away for a while, Brunella, but outside of your old man and couple of hobbyists up on the bench, everybody in this coulee is going under. For that matter, the whole Columbia basin is on edge. If my folks sell, I'll get a piece of it, and that'll give me a cushion in Montana. Might even buy a house. My mother's here, if you want to talk to her."

"I do."

"Just don't set her off."

"Teddy, I've known her all my life."

"You think you have. Think again. Have you talked to her lately?"

"No, but—"

"Her boiling point's gotten pretty low."

. . .

The bristled edge of Louis Armstrong plays over the voices of old friends gathering on the big cedar deck of the Cartolano family home. The air is still and hot. Brunella and Niccolo mix it up with the old men from the climbing club, who poke each other in the ribs. They are all robust drinkers. One of the men, Alden Kosbleau, cannot stop talking about a climb he recently made in the Sierra.

"Brunella, I lost twenty years on that peak," he says.

She treats Alden like a favorite uncle. His family was the third to settle in the coulee and the first to move out. Alden Kosbleau always looks ten years down the road and he has yet to miscalculate. While other irrigators were still trying to create the ideal apple, Alden tore out his Red Delicious trees and planted Rainier cherries. He made a fortune in the Japanese market, where a single piece of fruit could sell for three dollars. When the ditches were complete and Grand Coulee reclamation water was in such great supply that the biggest problem farmers had was trying to drain off the excess before it saturated the ground, Alden proceeded to buy up more, using surrogates to get around the rules designed to give water only to small-acreage family farmers. When he left the coulee for a mansion on a hill above Lake Chelan, he owned enough water rights to determine the fate of a midsize city.

"So you're one of the pioneers?" Ethan asks.

"Yes, sir, it was just me, Flax, and the dago. You've seen the picture inside the house of what this dustbowl used to look like?"

"The transformation is remarkable."

"Remarkable? It's a goddamn miracle, what we've done here. Just look around, get the sweep of this place, for Chrissakes. We showed everyone we could bring life to a dead land. And if these goddamn Indians would back off, we could do a thing or two even more amazing. I come from a generation with no limits—me, Flax, and the dago, same deal."

He takes a long sip of his drink.

"What's left for me now," says Alden Kosbleau, "is the blue rose. You don't look horticulturally inclined, but I will tell you something about the blue rose: It's the unobtainable hybrid, the rarest of rose colors." He waits for a reaction.

"And why would you want to grow a blue rose?" Brunella says.

"To show I can do it."

"Hubris."

"What's that, a ten-dollar word for dreamin' big? Isn't that what your old man is all about?"

Angelo Cartolano had left Alba at the age of ten, a boy with not enough of a waist to hold up his pants, brown curly hair, and front teeth that looked like they belonged in a much bigger head. All his possessions fit into one rectangular suitcase, and he wore three sweaters as he boarded the ship out of Genoa. Sewn inside one of the sweaters was a pouch containing tomato seeds from the family farm in the Piemonte. Angelo's mother, a feisty Tuscan who insisted that the true Italian dialect of Dante be spoken at home, died in the flu epidemic. Angelo's father lost two of his brothers in the first year of the Great War, 1915, when more than 60,000 Italians died fighting in the mountains on the northeast border with Austria. They were killed in the Dolomites: One was shot in the head; the other died of gangrene from a shrapnel wound.

Twenty years later, when Mussolini upped the price of buying draft deferments for all but the best-connected sons of the north, the elder Cartolano could see there was no future in Italy for his family. Angelo was sent to America to live with an uncle in the Bushwick section of Brooklyn. He slept on a cot by the dining table of a third-floor apartment with a single window, facing north. His uncle was a sometime merchant marine, whose ambition ebbed during afternoons of grappa-laced espresso. While his uncle drank his *espresso corretto* and read *Il Progresso,* Angelo learned to play baseball in the tiny park just off Knickerbocker Avenue, two blocks from the café, becoming a catcher. He broke three fingers in his left hand before his thirteenth birthday.

Mussolini's alliance with Hitler kept Angelo's father from coming to Brooklyn and in a curious twist was responsible for the boy's introduction to the American West. More than ten thousand Italians were classified by the FBI as enemy aliens, rounded up for questioning, and detained for an indefinite period. The authorities swept through Bushwick, seizing radios, guns, cameras, flashlights—anything that could aid the Italian war effort. In the spring of 1941, twenty-nine Italian ships were impounded in American ports. Angelo's uncle was on a list of sailors assigned to one of them, and they traced him to the tiny apartment in Brooklyn. His English was poor and he could not prove that he was nothing more than a loafer in Bushwick. He and young Angelo were sent away to Montana, joining fifteen hundred other Italians interned at Camp Missoula, an old army base at a bend on the Bitterroot River. For Angelo, internment was his best break in America. He loved Bella Vista, the nickname given the big-timbered lodge and barracks in Montana, with wildflowers rolling to the high snowfields, herons and osprey diving for trout on the river, ten-o'clock sunsets on summer nights.

It was at Camp Missoula that Angelo learned to cook. He played a game with the Italian chefs, who were astonished by his instinctive but undeveloped palate. By smell alone, he could tell whether a *ragu* was short of even a single ingredient or if a *pecorino* had come from inferior sheep. The only trouble at Camp Missoula came when the cooks were presented one day with beef fat for frying instead of the olive oil that usually came on the train from California. Infuriated, a chef smacked the supplier over the head with a large steel pan. Guards were called, a smoke grenade was accidentally set off, and in the burst of excitement a watchtower sentry shot himself in the foot.

The talk of Missoula was all about the biggest public works project in the country, the Grand Coulee Dam, just a half day's drive to the west. Even before the war, Angelo had heard President Roosevelt sketch his dream of the Planned Promised Land in the sunbaked midsection of Washington State, where the river carried to the sea enough water to put all of Italy under nearly two feet. Roosevelt's design was to back up the Columbia and bring nearly a million acres of leathered ground to agricultural life. The dam, often compared to the pharaohs' pyramids or China's Great Wall, was called the Eighth Wonder of the World. Young men just out of college and drifters one step from starvation flocked to the sage and dust of the Columbia basin to build the largest concrete structure ever known, a noble cause, they all said.

The internees were released from Camp Missoula just before the Allied invasion of Sicily. Angelo had barely turned sixteen and was too young for service, but he decided to stay in the West. He had seen enough of the men in the smoky café near Knickerbocker and heard enough of their vaporous dreams. Grand Coulee was a cement palace of magic and industry. Angelo hired on to a cleanup unit, making eighty cents an hour. Later, he was assigned to a crew whose job was to dig up Indian graves in land that would soon be buried under more than a hundred feet of expanded reservoir water from the just finished dam. He found this work distasteful, scraping away hardpan at the edge of the swift river, looking for skeletons of people who had lived prosperous lives on the bounty of big chinook salmon that returned to the desert every year. Angelo knew nothing of salmon and very little of the Indians clustered in bands along the Columbia, except he was told that they went mad when they drank alcohol. Every day at the riverbank old men in braided ponytails stared wordlessly at the government gravediggers; their shadow seemed to lengthen day by day.

On his days off, Angelo discovered the North Cascades, which reminded him of home and gave him an escape from the haunted eyes of the Indians. He would follow the Methow River until it flanked into Early Winters Creek and hike to the high country of glaciers, pink-heathered meadows, and granite flanks polished by retreating ice. Roaming the south side of Silver Star Mountain, he was footloose again in the Valle d'Aosta. He joined an alpine club based in Yakima, mostly teenage boys too young for the draft, too inexperienced to have a proper fear of the nubs of rock and ice that had scared off the adults. Angelo and his friends told a reporter from Yakima that they were going to take Mount Stuart's north ridge, which had never been climbed. The mountain looked like Grand Teton; on the rare days when the wind did not kick up the dust in the Columbia Basin, it was visible from a hundred miles to the east. Stuart is the greatest mass of exposed granite in the United States; the north ridge is sheer vertical in parts. It was a terra incognita of fear and legend. The reporter prepared to write a dozen obituaries. But on the first day of August, the Yakima climbing club put ten people on the summit. Afterward, at their base at Ingalls Lake, the young climbers made a pact. They took a vow that no matter what happened the rest of their lives, they would come together once a year to commemorate the ascent of Mount Stuart. Angelo had hauled up a liter of wine that an Italian home vintner who worked with him at the dam had given him, a full-bodied red made from grapes near Walla Walla. He removed the wine from a sweater wrap inside the tent and held it above the fire.

"To the last man alive shall go this bottle," he said, and the boys all agreed. To seal the pact, each climber cut himself with the serrated edge of an ice ax and let droplets of blood fall onto the top of the cork and a primitive label.

After the war, Angelo took classes at Gonzaga University in Spokane. He struggled at the Jesuit college, and if he had not been the leading hitter on the Bulldog baseball team—his average was .421 and he was the best catcher on a team of wild pitchers—he probably would have dropped out after a semester. Each year he was on the team, he broke another finger, playing one season alone with a mummified left thumb that was fractured multiple times. After his junior year, he left school for good, taking a job on another dam construction project on the Columbia.

While working on this dam, the Chief Joseph, Angelo found the coulee that he would try to remake into a swath of the Italian Piemonte. There were a few old mine shafts up beyond the ridge left over from the random pokings of pioneer prospectors, and a couple of petroglyphs scratched on the walls of the coulee, but otherwise no evidence that human beings had spent time there. Once, he found a big bone in the dry soil, the ball joint of a mastodon. Angelo loved the high walls on one side of the coulee, a kind of antiquity he seldom saw in America. And he felt sheltered, felt he belonged, felt he could let the rest of the world spin on a nervous nuclear voyage while he hunkered down and started his own American story.

Angelo bought six hundred acres for $5,000, virtually his entire savings. There was no water in the coulee. It had coyotes and quail, mule deer in the spring and red hawks circling for field mice in the summer. A yellow wildflower, balsamwort, sprang from little holds in April, but then the coulee went brown and crusted as it baked through the long days. Just below the rock portal into the coulee, a perennial spring-fed stream that flowed into the Columbia served as home to a small run of spring chinook, a salmon that traveled nearly to Siberia before returning to its birthing waters in the inland desert.

The first thing Angelo did was dig a deep broad hole at the steep edge of the coulee. It rained just seven inches a year, but that was enough to fill

the hole after running downhill, providing Angelo with a pond and his own primitive irrigation system. It was a simple trick of making the contour of the land and what water fell from the sky work for you, as Italians had done for centuries with their catch-basin ponds. Angelo used the pond to grow his first vines. Then, when Grand Coulee irrigation water came, he was told he would no longer have to look to the sky for life, nor would he need his little pond. The weather could be random and stingy with its moisture and the farmers in the Planned Promised Land should not care; they had arrived at a new point in history—they controlled creation. The effort to siphon water more than three hundred feet up from the Columbia's channel and send it through a tangle of ditches, reservoirs, and canals brought the equivalent of forty inches a year, and it was almost free for the asking. But Angelo never drained his pond, even as he accepted the irrigation water.

The orchards thrived. The apples looked like Christmas tree ornaments, the apricots wore the soft fuzz of a baby's head, and the figs could match the taste of old-country fruits. But his pride was wrapped up in his grapes, for winemaking was a master art. In the late nineteenth century, Calabrese immigrants put *Vitis vinifera* in the ground at Walla Walla before their homes even had roofs overhead; they knew, in hard times, wine was much more than pleasure—it was caloric sustenance. They had been forced by the powers of Walla Walla to settle at the edge of town, out of sight near the sweet onion fields, and it proved to be a fortuitous snub, for the land was perfect for wine grapes.

In the 1950s, Angelo tried something that had never been done, planting noble grapes from the heart of Piemonte, the Nebbiolo used in making some of Italy's greatest wines: the delicate Barbaresco, the peppery Gattinara, and the muscular but tricky Barolo—known in Europe as the King of Wines and the Wine of Kings. Everybody said a deep freeze would kill the vines to the ground; the slopes he hoped to cultivate with the most storied of grapes were too far north, the soil too volcanic, the precipitation too sparse.

But the coulee had its own microclimate, protected from harsh northerly winds in winter and insulated at times by fog that drifted in from the Columbia. During the early part of the growing season, warm winds kept the vines free of mold. In early winter, Angelo buried the vines

that grew in the cold upper part of the coulee, as protection against killer frost. Like the hills around Alba, the land was walled off from incessant rain by a vast mountain curtain. The coulee was a big bowl of cobblestones and silty loam. To reach moisture in this poor soil, the roots went deep, picking up a taste of stone that was evident in the grapes. As it turned out, the great flood had created a little notch in the far corner of America that could produce fat, intensely flavored Nebbiolo grapes from a soil—*terroir*—of the ages. Plus, he had the sun. Angelo kept a wooden globe in his kitchen, with a line drawn from the Old World to the New, showing that the Columbia basin and his native Piemonte shared the same general latitude. Nebbiolo needs a long growing season, and as the Bureau of Reclamation men were always pointing out, the basin basked in two more hours of light than did California, which meant Angelo could get twelve more growing days in a season than Napa.

What Angelo had as a winemaker was his remarkable palate, which he followed instinctively. While still in college, he sampled wine from an ancient southern Italian grape, made by his friend in Walla Walla. "I can taste some cherry, some spice, and there's raspberry in there as well," Angelo said.

"My God!" said the older winemaker. "You have just described the essence of Primitivo."

Three years after planting the vines, Angelo harvested his first crop. At the same time, he finished building a small stone chapel at the crest of the coulee and painted frescoes on the inside. Surely, his God, the one who changed water into wine to keep a wedding party going, would get to know Bacchus in this edge-of-the-world setting. Given the divine interest in wine, Angelo had no doubts that he would succeed. He started out making sixty gallons of wine a year from a bit more than half a ton of grapes—enough to give him a bottle a day. Virtually all the water for those first vintages came from the pond.

"You can tell this wine is going somewhere," Angelo liked to say.

On advice from his Calabrese friend in Walla Walla, Angelo started experimenting, following the direction of his palate. During the crush, he did not remove stems from the grapes, nor did he wash them. His friend said he should use the powdery mildew for yeast and fermentation. At the same time, he aged the wine in small oak barrels, or *barriques*. After bot-

tling, the wine had to spend years laid down before Angelo would let it go. The Wine of Kings was no match for the ephemeral American attention span, but Angelo waited, confident that he could create something extraordinary in his little coulee.

For another decade, he worked night shifts at the dam, sold his apples and figs at harvest, and dreamed of the day when his own version of Barolo would grow up and free him. The result, when he finally started to release his wine, tasted like nothing that had ever been produced in the New World; it was an original American showing of the Nebbiolo grape. A person with open taste buds would find ripe berries and other red fruit, but it was also layered, with a bit of licorice and a finish you could still taste a day after drinking the wine. There was a mystery and tease about the Cartolano Nebbiolo, a blend of coulee soil and ancient grape. The wild tannins were tamed just right, but they foretold a long life.

Angelo had stored the first vintages in his basement—the smell never far from the floorboards of the house—but as the fame of his red wine grew, he had to build a large cellar away from the house. His basement Barolo became the toast of the Pacific Northwest, attracting oenophiles from Sonoma and Napa, from Bordeaux and Burgundy, and from his native land. Angelo named his only daughter for the Brunello di Montalcino that one of these visitors brought to the coulee. He rejected every offer to sell; a Cartolano would cut off his foot before he would give up family land, he explained, and two of his three children understood what he was saying.

But now Angelo heard the clock; he felt he had no more than five years of winemaking left in him, with no one to take his place. He could barely make a fist out of his crumbled left hand. The water withdrawals deeply troubled him at a time when drought was calcifying the land. As a precaution last year, after much agonizing, he overwatered his grapes. At harvest, it showed; the grapes still had considerable flavor, but something was missing. He sensed the vintage would have no staying power, and when he sampled it from the barrel at Christmas he was heartbroken. No wine made from Angelo Cartolano's hands had ever tasted so thin, with so little promise. Sadly, he concluded the worst thing he could ever think about a wine: "This has no story."

Angelo spent that night in the cellar, shivering and sleepless. When he awoke, he knew he had given in to a corruption of the soul. But he felt he had no choice; a bad vintage would surely outlive him, erasing the magnificence of what he had done with his American Barolo. Immortality, for a winemaker, was what went into the bottle. So for the first time in his life Angelo took shortcuts. Not only had he overwatered the grapes, he now tried to rush the wine. He added sugar to raise the alcohol level slightly, trying to enrich it, to make it bigger. And he filtered the wine with oak chips, which would make it taste as if it had legitimately absorbed the skin of the barrel, though he knew in his heart it would be just another tarted-up oaky fruit bomb of the type preferred by the wine press. These practices were permitted in some parts of the winemaking world; only true connoisseurs of Nebbiolo would notice. But to Angelo, and certainly to any Barolo vintner, it was cheating. He could taste and smell the difference, and he hated himself for doing it.

At the party, Brunella is distracted by a pinch-faced man with thin orange hair. He is aggressively sniffing the wine, as if trying to clean the inside of the glass with his nose. On impulse, she scolds him. "Don't park your snout in the wine. Just enjoy it."

"It's not a true Barolo," the man says. "The tannins are still a bit unsettled. The nose is off. But superficially, at least, it's quite close. You must be the vintner's daughter. I'm your neighbor."

Gregory Gorton explains that he lives part-time in one of the new houses on the far ridge above the coulee.

"What happened to the old cars in front of the Pickens home?" Brunella asks. "There was a '52 Ford up there—"

"Those eyesores. Gone forever. We got an ordinance passed last fall. No more than two cars to a property can be visible at any one time. Which means your father is just barely within the standards of the law. Somebody tried to call them lawn ornaments, in defiance. Quaint, these locals. I don't know if your father has informed you yet, but I put some cuttings in last year and expect fruit in two summers. I plan to make a Bordeaux-style *meritage*."

"Where's your water coming from?"

"Same place as yours. But instead of taking it from the Feds, for pen-nies, we're taking it from the aboriginal inhabitants, for which they will be paid extravagantly—by their standards—and then returning the excess to them, for whatever it is these Indians do with water. Frankly, I'm puzzled. What do these Indians do with water?"

She grabs Ethan by the arm as a way to escape her conversation with pinch-faced Gregory Gorton. Brunella whispers an Italian word to Ethan: "*Attaccabottoni.*" He shrugs. "We need a word like that in English—a bore who buttonholes people with pointless stories."

All eyes turn to one part of the garden, where Teddy's mother is causing a stir. She appears to be drunk: red-faced and shouting, with spittle on her lips, screaming to the sky.

"The apple trees—gone! The peach orchard—dead! My husband—in jail! What did we do to deserve this?"

She looks possessed. Brunella rushes over, trying to soothe her, fixing the strap on her print dress and pulling back her long white hair. Mrs. Flax pushes Brunella back. Her screed gets louder, disrupting the entire party.

"They say it's for . . . for . . . salmon. Salmon! That's a goddamn lie. You want salmon, go to the grocery store. These fish are just a goddamn ruse. The Indians are lying. The government's covering up for them. This is not about salmon. It's about getting even. It's about power. The Indians want the water back, so they're driving all of us out of here!"

She turns to face the entire party, nearly a hundred people. She flaps her arms, shouting into the listless heat. She takes a bottle and throws it against a stone wall. It shatters, splattering wine all over the deck.

"Listen to me, you people: Do something!" she says. "This is the finest orchard country in the world, and it's all going to die! You think it's just us—the poor damnable Flax family. It's not. They will drive every one of you out until this land is a desert again. Until it's dust. Until it's the way it was, nothin' but scrub and rattlers."

Brunella leads her into the house and upstairs to her mother's reading room. She sits Mrs. Flax down on a couch and brings her a glass of iced tea. Mrs. Flax knocks the tea out of her hand.

"This is war," she says, her thin lips quivering as she lights a cigarette. "Don't they see what's coming?"

Brunella goes down to the liquor cabinet and returns with a three-finger shot of bourbon. She strokes Mrs. Flax, nursing her with the drink, this brittle woman who had once shown Brunella how to cross the snow on skinny skis, who made oatmeal cookies for her and Teddy, who climbed to the top of a cottonwood to retrieve a kite.

At dusk, Angelo announces that dinner is ready—a feast cooked over apple wood. The pork loin has marinated in ginger, rosemary, garlic, wine, and diced pears. Angelo went to his big basement freezer two days earlier and retrieved venison steaks. He has panfried them with mushrooms and sweet onions. The red and white potatoes that Angelo has always grown— his reserve food, in case the world collapses—have become *gnocchi di patate,* doused in fresh-made pesto. The Yakima corn is crisp and slightly charred, licked by fire. And there are fist-sized Cartolano family tomatoes, bleeding juice, covered with basil, olive oil poured over them. Louis Armstrong is still playing. Angelo loves jazz, which he heard first in Bushwick and then in the camp at Missoula. His uncle would never let anyone play Verdi, because it was what Mussolini liked.

"You see all this, Brunella," he says to his daughter, as they watch people load up on food, "and you wonder why I have to beg you to come home."

"You don't have to beg me, Babbo. Stop with the guilt."

"What's wrong with our home, Miss Bigshot? You tell me, and I will stop."

Midway through dinner, Niccolo stands to make an announcement. He clanks his glass, but after so many toasts it is hard to get everyone's attention. Finally, he puts his fingers to his mouth and lets out a stadium whistle. Brunella, Teddy, and Ethan are seated together. Brunella's leg rubs against Teddy's; he doesn't flinch. She keeps her leg against Teddy as Niccolo makes his toast.

"My dad will be eighty years old in October—"

"Bravo, Angelo!"

"A better-preserved old fart does not exist," says Alden Kosbleau, a bit tipsy. Niccolo whistles again to regain control of the party.

"And my father's journey from Alba in Piemonte, to Bushwick in Brooklyn, to Missoula, Montana, and to this valley is the great journey of the Cartolano family. Take a moment, please, everyone, and look around. Look at what he has created in this coulee. Look at the vines, the grapes, the fruit trees, the garden; all of this my dad . . . my dad made from scratch. He built the pond, which started it all, and gave the first vines their lifeblood. He built this house. He trellised every . . . last . . . one of these vines. He—"

"The fence," Brunella says in a low voice. "The rock fence."

"Oh, yeah, the river rocks that line the road, that fence—he did that by hand. Moved every one of those stones. All of this came from him. And it should not end here. So"—he takes a breath—"I have decided to stay." He turns to his father. "When I graduate next spring, I will return and try to learn the ways of the Nebbiolo grape from you, Dad. And I will do it with humility."

Locked on his father, Niccolo raises his glass. A hundred or more glasses come together. Angelo puts his right hand on his boy's cheek and kisses him. His eyes are clouded by tears.

"Why didn't you let me know?"

"I wanted to surprise you."

Angelo turns to the crowd, voice quavering, his knotted left hand shaking badly. "Wine is . . . a living thing, a companion. With Niccolo's promise just now, we will not be without our companion for another sixty years."

"Hear, hear!"

Gregory Gorton, the pinch-faced orange-haired neighbor, rises with an announcement of his own. "This is excellent news about Cartolano Junior following in the footsteps of his father. And we may soon know exactly what we've got going in this coulee, for I have entered last year's Cartolano Nebbiolo—a sizable sampling that Angelo was kind enough to give me well before its release—in VinFaire in Bordeaux. I know it's young, but by God I think that wine you made last year is world-class, with a frightful load of potential. So here's to our entry in VinFaire."

Through the cheers and toasting, Angelo frets. "What's wrong, Babbo?" says Brunella.

"He never asked me," says Angelo, shaking his head, the color gone from his face. "I don't want that vintage released."

After dinner, the five climbers from the Last Man's Club resume their poker game, which has been going on for nearly sixty years, started by fireside in the shadow of Mount Stuart. Distant thunder bounces against the high granite walls of the North Cascades. Alden Kosbleau wins a pile of money, threatens to walk away, and then stays to let the others pick at his earnings.

"They're playing for real money," Brunella tells Teddy. "But the ultimate prize is in the cellar. You want to see?"

She pulls Teddy Flax inside the house and down a narrow flight of stairs to the Cartolano library of wine. Her skin tingles in the chill of the cellar, where the temperature never rises above 57 degrees. Several thousand dust-covered bottles line the walls, marked by year, going back to Angelo's first vintages in the early 1950s. Stumbling to find a light, Brunella brushes away a pile of fine-shredded bits of oak.

"What's with the wood chips?" Teddy asks.

"I have no idea. Babbo still makes his *riserva* in this cellar."

He points to a faded painting on the stone-and-concrete wall, depicting a grape harvest. "Frescoes?"

"He started here, but his best work is in the little chapel up on the ridge. Didn't I ever show you this as a kid?"

"You ought to see the frescoes in Saint Ignatius, not too far from where I've been living. People come from all over the world to stare at the ceiling of this little mission church in Montana. Some Franciscan dude spent thirty years on his back drawing 'em, so it's not the usual bleeding Jesuses and haloed Marys looking like they just got out of the dry cleaner's."

She goes to a locker, tries a combination. Inside is a single bottle.

"This is what they're holding on for," she says. "I'm sure it went south a long time ago."

Teddy holds the wine up to the light, studying the faded droplets of blood from the ten boys who made it up the north side of Mount Stuart.

"Immortality in a bottle," she says.

Close to him, she feels a gush of warmth as her skin touches his, the nipples of her breasts hard. She slips her tongue in his ear, whispers, and pulls back, wetting her lips. He turns his head slowly, and she does not move. Her body is charged; she bites her lip, looks into his eyes.

Upstairs, the poker game is suspended while everyone moves to the edge of the deck to look at the western sky. An electrical storm clanks through the Cascades, dry lightning, five-pronged forks thrown against the mountains. Some of the strikes are close enough to light entire mountainsides behind the coulee at one end. With each lightning strike, people count in unison—one, two, three—timing the thunder that always follows, applauding its arrival.

CHAPTER THREE

Sleepless night. Dawn is at the door, the banana-colored light of August. Brunella makes coffee and returns to her room. Two images had followed her to bed: the broken woman who shrieked at the party, and the son with the silken face. She had kissed Teddy in the cellar, nipped at his ear, licked his neck, and wanted to spend the night with her legs wrapped around him. She cannot corral the impulse. He is a pretty boy, familiar and bighearted; maybe it's nothing more than the lust that comes on like a sweet tooth. Morning reveals a bit of haze and still no breeze. She goes to the window, drawn by low voices below. The poker game has not ended; Niccolo is dealing, but her father has dropped out. She smells smoke, the air heavy with a tardy stench.

Brunella helps her father cook breakfast. He looks fresh, renewed by the party and Niccolo's announcement. They slice up cantaloupes, mix the fruit with blackberries and cream, cook *huevos rancheros* slathered in salsa. Angelo wants Brunella and Niccolo to spend the day with him in the vineyard.

"We're going to the Omak Stampede," she says. "Ethan's never been to a rodeo before."

"Ah, yes, he wants to see the West."

"I was afraid for Mrs. Flax last night, Babbo."

"She is falling apart."

"You've tried to help her?"

"I don't know what to say, Nella. I can't bring the water back. I'm more concerned about Gorton entering my wine in that contest. It's going to destroy my reputation."

At the call of breakfast, Niccolo suspends the card game for the year. He scarfs down a plate of eggs and some sausage and leaves the table for bed. While he is sleeping, his father goes into his room and stares at him, something he has not done since Niccolo was a baby. He is enraptured by the grown son at rest; even unshaven, smelly, snoring, with a dirty size-thirteen foot hanging over the bed and those Jason Giambi arms, the sight of Niccolo in repose nearly brings Angelo to tears. It bothers him still that too many Americans see Italians as gangsters. The Cartolanos are a family of artisans, and looking at Niccolo just now Angelo feels the pride of the Piemonte poised to assume greatness in another generation.

A beige car with the government emblem of the Fish and Wildlife Service pulls into the Cartolano driveway. A man with a full beard knocks on the door. Angelo welcomes him inside and offers him coffee.

"That creek outside your place, Mr. Cartolano. Have you taken a look at it lately?"

"I saw it when we pulled up," Brunella says, jumping in. "It's dewatered."

"That's what it looks like. Without water, we will lose one of the last runs of spring chinook left in the upper basin. We intend to find out what happened. And we intend to prosecute."

"Drought," says Angelo, with a shrug.

"Not likely," says the government man. "That stream came from water that's been in the ground for centuries. It's spring-fed. And now—where did it go?"

"The water table's down," says Angelo.

"Not enough to dry up a spring-fed stream that has been here since the first hydraulic maps were drawn."

"Look around the basin," says Angelo. "The land is turning itself inside out."

Shortly after noon, Niccolo pops awake and pronounces himself ready for reheated venison steaks, leftover peach pie, and the Omak Stampede. He gulps down the pie while the venison warms in the oven.

"You eat the peach pie before the meat?" Ethan asks him, horrified.

"You can do it either way. Same result."

"That was a beautiful toast last night," Brunella says.

"Yeah—what'd I say? Nothing stupid, I hope."

"You were channeling the poet, little brother. It was sweet."

They pile into the car and head north. Brunella tells her brother to pause for a look at the Indian construction site, a hive of workers, bulldozers, and cranes. An immense dust cloud rises from sprouts of rebar and cement pilings.

"The hell are these Indians building here?" says Niccolo.

Following the Columbia River, they drive through patches of rectangular green set on disorderly land. Canals line the upper and lower parts of the canyon, two tiers of irrigation water that keep everything alive. They enter a canyon crowded with sickly apple trees and rusted mobile homes that look like tin cans in a discard pile. The road leads to Lake Chelan, deep and clear, the inland fjord that snakes nearly sixty miles from the desert hills to the cloud-scraping peaks of the North Cascades. The Cartolano family always took relatives from Italy there because it was so much like Lake Como, a wild version with glaciers at the edge and mountains nearly eight thousand feet above the water.

Brunella has promised her father to return Alden Kosbleau's watch, which he put aside as collateral for a cash infusion late in the poker game. His home is a three-story manse atop a hill above the lake, surrounded by a forest of lanky sprinklers for the exotic trees, shrubs, and plants on the Kosbleau grounds—the water king and his empire. They find Alden Kosbleau cradling a rifle and sweating. He is straining, a twitch in one eye, a finger still on the trigger of the gun, a different man from the one at the party.

"My God, Alden, what happened here?" Brunella asks.

"Isn't it obvious?"

He is crouched over the body of a cougar, its almond eyes still open. Fresh blood has drained out of an ear of the big cat, though it appears to have been shot in the belly, the tan fur matted and red. The paws are worn like sandpaper with a sheen, a sign that the animal has spent much of its time on hot pavement. Brunella notices the partially eaten remains of a pile of meat nearby.

"This son of a bitch has scared its last family," Alden Kosbleau says.

"It's the third one we've had to kill this month. I'm gong to hang the carcass from a tree."

"That sounds barbaric," Brunella says. "Why would you want to do that?"

"To send a message. These cats don't belong here. They kill pets. They threaten kids. They have no respect for man."

"Ah, c'mon, Alden," Niccolo says, biting into an apple. "A cougar hasn't killed anybody in this state for a long time."

"But something has changed, Nick, or haven't you noticed? These animals have lost their fear of man. They're staking out this territory as their habitat. And it's not theirs for the staking. It's ours. Something is seriously out of whack."

"So you baited him?" Brunella says, pointing to the pile of meat.

"I took preemptive action. He's a trophy now. Hey, do you kids want to see where I'm planning to grow the blue rose?"

"Here's your watch."

On the north shore of the lake, Niccolo stops at El Hombre Grande for afternoon enchiladas. At the city park, Teddy Flax is hitting fast balls from a pitching machine, trying to clear the fence and land one in the lake. He wears his baggy bathing suit and nothing else. His friend feeds hardballs into the machine. Teddy lines shots to left field and grounders up the middle. He lifts two near the end but cannot clear the fence. Niccolo, half an enchilada in his mouth, takes a turn and hits the first ball over the fence.

"See the ball, hit the ball," says Niccolo. "By the way, you're on my crew, Teddy. You can thank big sister here for pulling strings."

Brunella is distracted by the view across the lake, the copper-colored flanks of the mountains, nearly a mile above the water, a sheer vertical wall. Staring at the mismatch of water and land, she wonders if the uplift had been incremental, a swollen crust rising as the young planet took shape, or if it had been sudden and violent. She decided on her last trip to Italy that she was genetically predisposed to see the fracture lines of the earth where others saw only a mall or a highway. The old peninsula of the Cartolano family was alive, not unlike the Pacific Northwest, with volcanoes that had never settled down and cliffs that could fall away in a random lurch. She had even come to accept some of the ancient superstitions about the land, after seeing how Neapolitans wept with joy when the dried blood of their patron saint, Gennaro, liquefied on cue on the first Saturday in May, a failure to do so being a harbinger of disaster.

They arrive at the Omak Stampede in the hottest part of the day, the sky white. Ethan looks more pale than usual, as if he is going to faint. They find a place in the shade of the old wooden stands and settle in to listen to a mariachi band. A blond rodeo queen prances and preens for the crowd, her crimson underpants matching the short skirt that bounces during her high-stepping promenade. Indians in Columbia Plateau regalia parade from a tribal encampment next to the grounds.

"Real Indians?" Ethan asks.

"Yes and no," Niccolo says. "They do this for the tourists, and the rodeo gives them a cut of the gate. You want to see a real Indian, go to the reservation, just across the river. It's not on any tourist maps."

Niccolo inhales two hot dogs and washes them down with a beer. He points to the sandy hill behind the rodeo stands, high above the river, as he explains the Suicide Race, the highlight of the rodeo.

"About twenty riders enter, sometimes less. It's a straight drop down that humongoloid steep hill to the river. Half the horses won't make it to the water without a sprain or a broken bone. They swim across the river and make a final dash to the stands."

"Will the horses actually go off that cliff?"

"They will and they do. Don't ask me why."

Brunella and Teddy slip away to a patch of dried grass in the shade behind the stands. She asks him to join her and Ethan on their hiking trip.

"Depends on whether the United States Forest Service pulls on my leash," Teddy says. "Last night's lightning started some spot fires. Plus I don't want to break anything up."

"Oh, no, you'd be perfect. I think you and Ethan would like each other. I'm working for him; there's nothing else between us. Just be nice. How's your mother?"

"Hungover. Pissed off at the world."

"Did she say anything?"

"About what?"

"The orchard. The water. Her hysterical appeal to the party last night."

"She asked for tea instead of coffee. And she wanted me to spike it with Yukon Jack."

Brunella moves closer to Teddy and runs her hand through his hair. "You looked good trying to hit Pedro Martinez today."

"Are you going to lick the inside of my ear again?"

"I don't know. Should I?"

"I'm getting kind of excited thinking about it."

"I can see that," she says, a glance at his shorts.

"Don't remember you this way as a kid, Brunella. You didn't like me much then, did you?"

"What makes you think I like you now?"

"I don't. I mean, yeah, that's presumptive, isn't it? Even in Montana, I would never assume a thing unless . . ."

"Unless what?"

"Forget it. At least dogs are honest."

"Dogs? What do you mean by that, Teddy?"

"The sniffing. The whole ritual." He's blushing, starting to sweat. "Forget it. I'm just . . . stupid."

"Teddy, relax. Are you hungry?"

"I can wait."

"I'm starved. Let's . . . find someplace to wrestle."

"Wrestle?" He laughs.

"I meant eat."

"Did you?"

When the sky darkens, the horses mill at the top of the hill in a lather even before the start of the race. Sheriff's deputies try to hold the crowd back, but it's futile. People are drinking and shouting, jostling to get close. Only a handful of bettors and the best riders care who wins the race. The reason people come from all over the world to the top of a steep hill outside one of the lost towns of the West is to see how far a human can push a horse. Somebody might die or break a neck. A horse or two will surely get injured. It's the thrill of being so close to risk in fast motion, like watching someone drop over Niagara Falls in a barrel, that keeps the Omak Stampede alive while other rodeos have died. Time has given the race the gloss of Western tradition, of custom and culture in a part of the world where such things are usually artificial in origin and then no sooner endangered.

The Cartolanos and their two guests have a prime viewing spot on the edge of the cliff, thanks to their long relationship with a county sheriff who has developed a taste for Nebbiolo. Niccolo tries to catch the attention of one of the riders, his friend Tozzie Cresthawk. The rider ignores him at first, then nods in his direction.

"Kick some butt, Toz."

"They're all Indians in this race?" Ethan asks Niccolo.

"It's an Indian race," Brunella says.

"White men can't fall off cliffs nearly as good as Indians can," says Niccolo.

Ethan cannot take his eyes off Tozzie Cresthawk. "I think your friend on the horse is drunk. Look at him! Brunella, Niccolo. He's wobbly. He's got to be drunk."

"Happens every year," Teddy says.

"No, this is seriously negligent. They can't let him ride a horse in that condition."

"He's Nez Perce," Niccolo says. "They're the best horsemen in the West. They beat Lewis and Clark in races two hundred years ago."

"But he's drunk! And, and . . . smell that? I think *all* these boys have been drinking!"

"They're going to do what they do," Brunella says. "You can't know them."

"So you're saying this is some sacred ritual: Drunken Indians plunge over a two-hundred-foot cliff for the amusement of forty thousand tourists."

"They're not all tourists."

"You wouldn't let a drunken race car driver take the wheel."

"They have a race in Siena twice a year, a mad dash around a tight cobblestone oval that isn't a decent enough track for a *passeggiata*, let alone a horse race."

"You don't have to lecture me about the Palio," Ethan says.

"Are you going to tell the people of Siena to give up their race after four hundred years so you can sleep better?"

The horses are anxious, dropping turds as their riders reassure them. Tozzie Cresthawk mounts an Appaloosa without a saddle. As he talks quietly into the horse's ear, he loses his grip and falls to the ground, a painful splat, met by laughter from the crowd.

"Riders, take your marks"—Tozzie scrambles to remount his horse— "set . . ." The judge fires the gun. The sprint to the edge of the cliff is short. One animal balks at the precipice, falling back on its haunches, causing another horse to skid and tumble in front of it. Two horses down, and here is the drop. They plunge off the cliff, disappearing into the night, kicking up an enormous cloud of dust in the spotlight that provides a view for the spectators back in the rodeo stands. Near the bottom, a mass pileup. Most horses are off their feet in the clump of adrenaline-fired sweat, shit, and dust. The better horses spring from the pile, popping up like foldouts in a children's book, and swim. Tozzie's Appaloosa has taken the hill well, holding back just enough to avoid the jam. Attempting to jump over the others, the horse makes a magnificent leap to the edge of the river. It falls just short, slamming into the gravel at the bank, a headfirst snap. The horse rolls over once and is pounded into the water by other horses just behind it. The animal comes back to the surface, floating unconscious in the current. Tozzie swims to join his horse. He strokes the eyes, which are still blinking, and the forehead. He does not weep. On the other side of the river, four riders emerge from the water and surge into the arena to the finish line. The crowd is on its feet, screaming, the announcer calling out the riders. At the finish, a Nez Perce rider edges out a Flathead from Montana. He tears off his shirt and circles the track in a victory lap.

When the rodeo stands empty and a hazy darkness covers Suicide Hill, Tozzie Cresthawk shoots his brain-dead horse. He has sobered up enough to kill him right, with a single shot to the temple. And then he weeps.

The smell of smoke has intensified. Angelo walks his two children through the vineyard in midmorning, bluish plumes to the west. Last night, a message was waiting for Niccolo: Lightning brought fires to the Cascades, and the smoke jumpers will chase the critical ones. Niccolo has half a day at home before he must report to base, and he wants to spend it going through the vineyard.

Angelo says he has a bad feeling about the next two months. Because of the water withdrawals, he has switched to drip irrigation this year, giving the vines less than half the usual water for summer and relying on the original pond once again for the oldest of the vines. The big mystery is what sort of grapes will come. The fruit could be small and raisiny. It could be concentrated with flavor. It could be more prone to disease, weakened, vulnerable. He thinks about the fruit all day; often he dreams about it as well. After filtering last year's vintage with oak chips, he still feels shamed by the self-betrayal, as if he has violated his family.

During the growing season, Angelo goes through three stages of rolling anxiety. In the spring, when the vines bloom and the fruit sets, he fears prolonged rain and cold, which would result in a bad set and much less fruit. In the summer, as the grapes fatten, he talks excessively about his heat units; premium red-wine grapes need a high amount of sunlight for conversion of the sugars. And in the fall during the harvest, when timing is everything, Angelo waits, trying to stretch out the start of picking until the last warm days, when the temperature goes from 80 degrees in the day to near freezing at night. Nebbiolo grapes are the last to be picked.

"We should get some new oak for this vintage," Niccolo says. "Start fresh with barrels from the Allier forest in France."

"And I could pay for it," Brunella says. "It's not a problem."

"What's wrong with the oak I've been using?"

"The grain, Dad. You know that. You get much tighter grain with Allier oak. It makes for an explosion of fruit."

"*Basta!* Wine should not be a loudmouth, Niccolo. It should taste like the grape and the earth that produced it. And Brunella, you can't buy that with French oak or anything else. You can't buy a story from the earth. Here. Put your hands into this ground of ours. Both of you, go ahead."

Niccolo scoops up a handful of small dry stones; Brunella does the same.

"Smell that. Go ahead. You cannot find them anywhere else in the world, these pebbles from the great flood. Our wine is a child of this land. Wine should never—how did you put it?—explode. Everybody wants a shortcut in this country."

"Now look where Mount Stuart should be," says Brunella, pointing to the west. "Nothing but haze."

"I don't think we should bottle last year's vintage," Angelo says. "We should kill it."

"But you haven't missed a year since '54, Dad."

Angelo stops, plants a worn-out baseball cleat in the uphill side of the slope, spins to look at his children, and falls on his back. Brunella reaches down to him.

"I'm all right. Would you lie next to me? One child on each side. *Vieni qui. Vieni.*"

Niccolo and Brunella share a look; the old man's heart needs to soak up just enough sentiment every year, like the grapes and their sun. Of late, his appetite has grown large. They lie on the ground, shaded by Nebbiolo vines, looking skyward.

"You go through your years, you start out thinking of just getting by. Then it gets better, and you start to think beyond your daily needs. And after a while, you think you can do something great."

He makes a sweeping motion with his atrophied left hand, pointing to the arena of red-tiered rock, his life's work at the center. "Try to imagine what this land used to be like a hundred years ago. Greasewood and sage, the ground so hard the only way you could break it was with an ax."

Angelo closes his eyes, as if in prayer.

"Have I ever told you children about the Ladin? They were the last Roman soldiers, the people who never made it home after the empire collapsed. They wandered for a long time. They hid in the forests and mountains. They stole food and hunted on land that was not theirs. And then they found a valley in the Dolomites, in the Alto Adige. They found a home. My father took me there when I was—I must have been ten, eleven years old, just before I came to America. He lost two brothers in the war and wanted me to see where they died. These people, they spoke a language in that valley, a kind of Latin I did not understand. They dressed funny. The Ladin were part of the mountains. And when I first wandered through America, this big land did not have a place for me until

I came here. I saw this coulee, and I felt like a Ladin. I knew the Cartolanos had found a home. And now . . . we have to defend it."

"We have our water allotment," Niccolo says. "If the drip irrigation works, we'll be fine. If not, we'll punch in a couple of new wells. I'm sure the water table is in semidecent shape."

"You always have so much hope, Niccolo. You're the American. Nella, you're different. You are the Italian. You have my mother's old-country fears in you."

Brunella knows it's time to escape to the high country, near the eternal ice of the North Cascades. The coulee heat makes Ethan cranky; he has been complaining about wanting to get back to Seattle, in the comfort beneath his cloud cover. They pick up Teddy Flax Monday afternoon and drive to the east flank of the mountains, just outside the national park. Brunella has chosen one of the highest lakes in the range, a deep pool of snowmelt cradled by granite, nearly a mile and a half above sea level. At the trailhead, Ethan slips away to a Forest Service toilet shed. When he emerges, he looks as if he has just stepped from a catalog, wearing purple plastic boots, stiff and unscuffed.

"They're supposed to be breathable," he says. "Whatever that is."

His legs are covered with pants made of a billowy odd-looking fabric, and he has a matching top with full-length sleeves, the price tag still attached.

"The sun protection is built right into the fabric—an SPF factor of forty-five, even when it's soaked with sweat," says Ethan. "So while you're risking malignant melanoma with your skimpy little tank top, I have protection."

"You look like a walking condom," Teddy says.

"You're not so pure yourself," Brunella says to Teddy. "What's that?"

"My beeper—the long arm of the Forest Service. It's the only way I can get away."

"And this book?" She fingers a tattered leather-bound volume sticking out of one pocket of his pack. "Couldn't you take a paperback?"

"I'll chuck my sleeping bag before I throw out this book," says Teddy.

The trail is eight miles, gaining nearly four thousand vertical feet.

They start in a valley of big cedars and Douglas firs along the Twisp River, then rise through ponderosa pines, following the switchback of the trail along a flank of the mountain. At two miles they reach a waterfall, a torrent of several hundred feet that levels into a narrow canyon of deep green and moss. Brunella takes off her pack and puts her face in the froth at the edge of the falls.

"This feels wonderful," she says.

"Ethan, my man, put your head in that waterfall and take a long sip," says Teddy. "That'll give you the baptism of the Cascades."

"Drink that water? Are you crazy? I've got one of these."

He takes out a pump and filter from the side of his pack.

"Every sip of this waterfall contains millions of microscopic bacteria from the feces of who knows what, and I for one am not going to let the collective sewage of the animal kingdom put me at risk of five to seven days of hospitaliza—"

Brunella cups her ear. *Zeee-eeet. Zeee-eeet.* "Do you hear that?" she says. "Dippers. God, what a life."

They enter a place of water and extravagant color, a meadow ringed by larch trees and wildflowers of lupine and Indian paintbrush. Big firs and perpetual shade give way to smaller alpine trees. In an opening from an old burn, the flowers are waist high, asters and daisies, fireweed of deep lavender color, and the breeze is stronger at every switchback. With the pack rubbing against her shoulder blades, her boots blistering heels, cramping toes, Brunella has slipped beyond the pain barrier, using a technique she has been working on for years, a way to transcend the cries of her body during long hikes or runs. It is also a way to get closer to God, she explains to Teddy. He says it is the endorphins, the body's natural morphine.

The last two miles are brutal, as if the trail builders had run out of patience and simply carved a path straight up, with no back and forth. She is thinking about what Teddy said of the woman from Manhattan he nearly married. We could never be equals, he said. Women marry for money, security, and a gene pool. Matches born of pure love are doomed. Brunella did not believe it, did not believe people were prisoners of encoded natural history, even as evidence mounted that there were biological reasons for selecting the richest man in the cave—survival, the oldest imperative. She could love a teacher because she would love a man first. That's what she told herself.

A slight breeze blows from the waterfalls. The jays follow them up, cawking, hovering close. The trail levels, just at timberline, and opens to a turquoise-colored lake fed by a small glacier in the shade on the side of the mountain. The water is dimpled by fish, just starting to feed as shadows move over the surface. Ethan looks drained, his face gaunt. He walks very slowly, lifting his legs in an awkward, deliberate fashion, as if he were forcing the muscles to contract. He stops and retrieves a small device from his backpack. He never looks at the glacier, or the deep blue-green of the lake, or the distant brown hills to the east, or the haze from the fires to the north. He punches in some numbers on his device; the result—flashing on a small screen—confounds him.

"Where are we?"

"We are at a jewel of a lake in the American Alps," says Brunella.

"No, but where *are* we?" says Ethan. "My GPS says we're seven thousand feet above sea level."

"Your GPS?"

"I didn't want to get lost."

"I wouldn't let that happen."

"This isn't right. I knew it. I probably shouldn't have come with you. I should not be socializing with the help."

"The help?" says Brunella. "Is that what I am?"

"Well, technically I could fire you."

Brunella grabs the Global Positioning System from Ethan and spins him around. "That ridge just above us is the Cascade Crest. One side drains to Puget Sound, the other to the Columbia River. That's all you need to know. Cut the tether to the wireless world for a second. Breathe, Ethan. Open your eyes."

In the evening, Brunella and Teddy go fishing. The water is clear to the bottom, in the deep center of the lake, so they have to keep their distance, crouching as they approach to avoid scaring the fish. They are not sure what bugs are hatching, but Teddy catches a few insects and suggests several matches. They can see smoke now coming from the east, in the direction of the Cartolano home, but their attention is on the lake. Brunella does not bother to match her fly to the emerging hatches. She does not care for all the fetish bundle iconography of fly-fishing. She fishes for the company. It has been her experience that the best men are fly fishermen. Brunella ties on a hardy caddis, claiming it has always worked for her in the past. Teddy decides on something smaller. The lake is full of cutthroats rising, as if the dinner bell has just been rung in the high Cascades and the trout sense the brevity of the feeding season. Stripped to his shorts, Teddy wades into the lake. His initial casts are quick, in a sidearm fashion.

A large trout jumps from the center of the lake, and they watch the fish dart back down to shallows beneath a rock.

"He's yours," Teddy says. "But first I have a gift for you." He presents her with a royal coachman made of fine strands of elk hair, four colors. "Take it and prosper, Brunella Cartolano."

Brunella's casts are old-school, in the arc between ten o'clock and two o'clock. Her line stretches out like a lizard's tongue. She waits only a few seconds before pulling the rod up in response to a bite. The fish shakes her fly loose.

Teddy sidearms a short delicate cast, ahead of the rock where the fish has gone for cover, and waits. The trout makes a line from beneath the rock to Teddy's fly, and the surface breaks with a splash. The fish hits the fly so quick, Teddy does not have time to set the hook. But the fish is on, swimming to the other side of the lake, Teddy's reel singing with the action. Brunella pulls her rod back and winks at Teddy as he brings his fish in. She has on a fighter, which jumps above the surface in mid-struggle, something cutts rarely do after taking a fly. She strips in her line slowly, keeping the tension just right, and lands the fish. It must be twelve inches, large for a high alpine lake.

"I'll let mine go," she says, "if you cook yours."

A breeze riffles the water, making it hard to fish. Brunella motions for Teddy to come sit next to her on a flat rock at the edge of the lake.

"You know why I fish?" she says. "That connection to the other side. Most of the time, we're little more than observers of nature. We watch. When you get a fish on, you're pulled into the world."

"And eating fresh trout instead of freeze-dried crap has nothing to do with it."

"Listen, Teddy boy." She rolls over on top of him, pinning him, licking his nose, his smooth face. God, he's pretty. She wants all of him.

"Hey, let me read to you," he says.

"Now?"

He dashes to his pack and returns with the weathered leather enclosure of an old man's prose. She tilts her head to catch the title. "Norman's book," she says. "I should have suspected."

He begins reading: " 'My father was very sure about certain things relating to the universe. To him all good things—trout as well as eternal salvation—come by grace and grace comes by art and art does not come easy.' "

She rests her head on his chest as he continues. After he reads the opening chapter, she feels roused in the way that a man and literature and alpenglow in the Cascades—this convergence of indigenous passions— can cause. "You know I come from a long line of dark-haired women who feel better with their clothes off."

"Then don't let me stop you from following the genetic impulse."

She reaches into his wet pants. "This needs to dry," she says. He is stiff. She runs her tongue down the front his body and tickles the top of his belly button. She feels her own body start to loosen.

"Didn't you used to have an inny?" she says.

"How do you remember that?"

"I was jealous. I had an outie."

She pulls his shorts down and licks him all over, around the edges, up and down, taking his penis in her mouth and giving him a long massage. The sun disappears from the rock. She keeps him wet, sucking softly, running her tongue all around, then stopping abruptly.

"What?" he says, looking down.

"This." She is laughing as she points to something on the inside of his leg. "The scar—it's the Nike swoosh."

"Oh, that. I cut myself four years ago on a hiking trip in the Mission Range. I know, I know, it looks exactly like the goddamn Nike logo."

"It does!"

"I'm the only guy in the world branded with a swoosh who isn't getting paid for it."

The shadow of the mountain covers the valley below, an outline of dark shade all the way down to where the Twisp River cuts through the cedar grove. They remain on the rock until they are both chilled, neither wanting to move. They keep each other warm as fish jump at the last chance for flies before dark.

At dinnertime, Brunella breads the cutthroat in flour and readies the pan with oil.

"Use butter," Teddy says. "This trout has given up its mountain lake for you. The least you can do is let him leave the world with a decent bath."

They make a pot of rice, flavored with saffron and bits of dried shrimp. They drink ice-cold white wine with the dinner, and it tastes clean—a perfect match.

"I'm sorry, Ethan," Brunella says. "I left you alone."

"I'm perfectly fine."

"I haven't been a very good guide. Are you upset?"

"You've been occupied."

"Tomorrow we'll find a little perch with a view you won't forget. Once you're up there, you'll never look at the world the same way."

"I doubt that."

After swatting at mosquitoes, Ethan sets his food down and goes inside his tent. He returns with a box the size of a small matchbox, sets it nearby, and turns it on. A low zzzzzz sound comes from the box. He smiles at Brunella and Teddy.

"It simulates the sound of a dragonfly," Ethan says. "That scares mosquitoes."

"And this came with the GPS?" Teddy says.

"It was extra."

Brunella puts water on the small stove for tea, just as a beeper goes off in the tent. It is Teddy's call from the Forest Service. He says he will be gone before dawn and tries to convince them how lucky they are to stay another day in the high Cascades without having to look at the mountains as the enemy.

CHAPTER FOUR

T HEY FALL OUT of the plane at first light, the ride so bumpy on the
convection currents that the jump is a relief. On the way to the fire,
the boxy Sherpa has been rattling more than usual; it's like white-water
rafting without advance notice of the rapids. A dozen and one smoke
jumpers—each loaded down with seventy pounds of chute, food, rope,
radio, and padding for the most vulnerable areas of the body, all wrapped
in Kevlar skin—want out. Tozzie Cresthawk looks sick. Teddy tosses his
copy of *The New Yorker*. Niccolo tries to stand, working the bounce in his
legs. When Teddy rises he is slammed against the ceiling, and Niccolo
calls him a "Ned," the jumper word for rookie.

Teddy clips into the line and jumps. Tozzie and four other Indians follow, and then comes the Old Man, two veteran women jumpers from
Pendleton, Oregon, three Neds, and finally Niccolo, the crew boss. Floating, his legs bent at a slight angle, his head against the big collar that protects his neck from a snap, staring through the caged mesh of the face
shield, Niccolo feels the surge that always comes with a jump—a minute,
rarely more, of descent into this small crowded world. Look out for the
trees, avoid the snags, angle-angle-angle away from the cliff, make the
currents work for you, and beware the downdraft, the squeeze of air that
could slam you hard. Now here's the smoke, heavy like a tangle of witch's
hair over the ground.

It is that time of year when a mountain range that normally bleeds
water turns to the opposite extreme. Fires are burning throughout the

Cascades. The ground pounders with their Pulaskis and chain saws are trying to contain the biggest of them, the Johnny Blackjack. The fire has skipped over ridges, hopping from crown to crown, spreading ten miles or more in a day, blotting out the sun. They say it is not a normal beast and does not behave as it should; it is hotter, faster, with an oversize appetite. The smoke jumpers are deployed strategically. Their job is to contain a fresh small fire that could join the Johnny Blackjack and open a flank through a valley with cabins, orchards, and summer homes in the lower elevations. Last night, somebody had written on the chalkboard WE ARE FIRE GODS.

Down, down, down, seventeen feet a second: Watch for rocks, aim for the small dried-out meadow at the edge of a grove of towering larches, watch for holes in the ground burrowed by marmots and rocks covered by bramble. Legs flexed, loose, Niccolo hits the ground—no give from this baked earth—rolls over, and springs up to corral his chute. The Indians make it, same with the Neds, the women from Pendleton. The Old Man's landing is formulaic. Head count. Six, a dozen . . . one missing: Tozzie Cresthawk.

"He's in the tree," says Teddy.

Tozzie radios Niccolo that he won't need help. He can manage. He reaches into his leg pocket and removes his let-down rope, rigs the rope to the tree, and cuts his chute. He breaks loose from the high canopy and falls, hitting a lower branch hard, a hot sting felt through the thick padding in his seat. He tumbles another twenty feet and drops headfirst, hands scraping bark, banging against the sharp ends of tree limbs snapped in storms, no sound coming from him but the *phfflmmp, phffllmmmp* of branches slipping away. His front gear bag, draped like an apron above his knees, snags in midfall, catching him head down about thirty feet above the ground. He swings back and forth. Two of the Indians climb the tree and help him down. His face is bleeding; part of his Kevlar suit is ripped.

"Big Ernie nearly got me," he says to Niccolo.

"Big Ernie ain't coming to the Cascades this year," says Niccolo.

.   .   .

By late afternoon, the jumpers have hiked two miles over scree to the edge of a spot fire—their target. It is burning the nubs of decapitated trees, heather shrubs, and some stubby high-alpine larches and moving like a sea tossed by cross-current winds. Niccolo's orders are to backburn just ahead of the fire's front line, starving it of fuel. Then they plan to traverse to the advancing high edge of the Johnny Blackjack fire and lay down another buffer line. The yellow-shirted jumpers go quickly about the backburn, splashing the brush with flaming diesel from their portable fusees. They have a good fire going when they retreat to watch it come together. As planned, the other fire dies when it meets up with fresh-burned area. The jumpers feel triumphant. Teddy is full of bluster and high energy, slapping Niccolo's gloved hand.

"We *are* the fire gods."

Niccolo takes out a stack of topo maps, each showing a square mile in the high eastern edge of the Cascades. He's a soldier. Choke the fire, stay out of Big Ernie's way, demobe, and go home. No other thoughts are allowed.

They walk downhill at a slight traverse until they come to a broad flat area atop a series of cliffs. The smoke, carrying the smell of boiled pine sap, is too thick to allow them to see much below. Every few minutes, they hear loud pops—the cannon fire of trees as they break open, the superheated sap swelling up fast and furious. At the rest stop, they eat nut-filled candy bars to bring their blood-sugar levels back up and drink electrolyte-replacement liquid to prevent cramping. The sweat never stops pouring out of them, and the ash never stops raining down. Niccolo takes a vacuum-wrapped hunk of dried meat and sets it on the rock. He cuts it with his knife, spreads little puddles of ketchup and mustard from small packets, and sprinkles sesame seeds on the side.

"Chinese pork," he announces, sweat dripping off his nose. "Everybody dig in. C'mon, you Neds."

The jumpers welcome the taste of something salty to go with their drinks. Everybody eats but Tozzie; he stares upward, beyond the ridge where they jumped at dawn.

"I want it back," Tozzie Cresthawk says to Niccolo. "Want my jump back."

"Got your native honor on the line?"

"I'm on a losing streak. Feels like Big Ernie's following me."

"It's down below where we gotta worry about Big Ernie. In the orchards."

In the evening the sun is a plum-colored splotch through the dirtied sheet of the sky. Niccolo talks with the Incident Commander at base camp, and the IC has one bit of good news: The humidity is up, a harbinger of possible rain. The winds have died as well. The jumpers will rest for a few hours, then get up around three in order to hit the Johnny Blackjack flank in first light. They try to sleep, some of them using the folded rectangle of their fire shelters for pillows. The shelters are a last-ditch cover designed to withstand flames and heat up to 600 degrees, with straps for handles and footholds, no floor. Jumpers call them shake-and-bakes. The moon appears through the smoke, lighting the edge of the trees. The fire seems groggy now, somewhat distant. Two nights ago, when Teddy took in the view at his high camp with Brunella—dew-coated wildflowers, dwarfed firs, and heather—it looked like a Japanese garden, serene and bent by the wind. Now everything that pokes from the ground is fuel.

When the jumpers rise the winds are still down, the fire still slumbering out of sight. They use their headlamps to pack out. The smoke is thicker, and it does not move, hanging in their hair, their nostrils, their eyes. The jumpers strap on masks and aim for the direction of a roar that grows louder with each step. The word from the IC is that a low-pressure system is moving in from the northwest, bringing some rain. Teddy asks if they can wait it out, in the hope that a storm will do their job. No chance. A new advance of the fire is too close to homes and property—the urban interface, they call it—which does not give them any choice. People in the valleys are sitting on their roofs with hoses, the IC says. Talk radio is a clatter of panic, blame, and invective, like Mrs. Flax at the party: Do something! The rumor is that somebody is trying to drive the irrigators out, using fire as the knockout blow after the long drought.

Niccolo still has his confidence, but now he is edgy. The soldier should not think. It is not a summer adventure anymore but a wet bag of thoughts on how many things can go wrong. He asks the IC to patch him through to Angelo. The phone rings for several minutes before Niccolo's father comes on the line. His voice sounds wan, out of breath.

"I've been up on the roof," Angelo says to Niccolo, "and we dug a line around the vineyard."

"How close, Dad?"

"It sounds like it's here now."

"*What?*"

"Sounds like jet engines on every side of me."

"You have to evacuate."

"I'll never leave. You know that. A Cartolano does not desert his land. I have some help. Miguel's here. We have other water."

"Stay off the roof. You're going to fall. How close is the fire?"

"I told you."

"How close?"

"The Flax orchard."

"Get out!"

"You know what, Niccolo? I'm scared. *Ho paura.* But I feel very . . . calm. I like my chances, Niccolo. I'm more worried about the grapes."

They stumble through an oven of haze to the edge of the Johnny Black-jack. Niccolo radios base camp: change of plans. They are ordered into a draw on another side of the fire, the one closest to a bench of new homes above the coulee. They trudge forward in a wordless march led by Niccolo.

"Think like a dipper," Teddy says to Niccolo.

"Fucking dippers. They know better than to walk into a fire."

They arrive at an unburned forest of brown needles, branches dry as potato chips, huckleberry bushes so barren of leaves they could have been in winter dormancy, the grass long dead. Everything looks spent. They can hear the main fire well before they see it; it is the Johnny Black-jack's own storm system—fierce gusts, the roar of crackling wood, limbs and tops falling away, and a constant *pop-pop-pop.*

"We start our burn here," Niccolo says. "Take advantage of the winds being down, and then get the hell out."

"This sucker's gonna go up like a pile of tires," says the Old Man. "You sure you wanna start it here?"

"We burn this strip and we choke off the Johnny Blackjack right here and now. Otherwise it runs through this firetrap of a fucking forest and charges right into the coulee."

Niccolo gathers his crew around a map. They can't see more than a few feet one way or another, which makes it hard to get grounded. They test small mikes on their shoulders, so that everyone is part of an audio link, and attach compasses to their fire shirts.

"Take a reading . . . northwest, thirty-five degrees. If you need cover, follow that direction and you'll find an old burn. If you don't find it, reverse course and go to the fresh black."

"Which way's the fresh black?" says Tozzie. "Can't see anything."

"Black is due west. The ground's gonna be hot, still smoking, but the fire will have gone."

A grouse hops around in a spiral near the jumpers, the feathers on one wing burned off and a foot severed. Niccolo reaches for the bird and it bites him. The Old Man puts his hand on Niccolo's shoulder and looks him in the eyes.

"I trust you, kid, you know that. But we've been going over the various scenarios, Suzanne, Laura, and me, and we don't think we should burn here, Nick. Not without pumps."

"You want pumps?" says Niccolo, unblinking. "Using what water? This basin is sucked dry. Look at the way everything is burning. There can't be any groundwater left."

"Let's get the pumps, Nick. For insurance."

"A fucking orchard is on fire below, dude!" Niccolo shouts. "My father is trapped!" He turns, mumbling to himself, fall-away words, and radios the IC to patch him through to Angelo again.

"Dad," he says, after a long delay. "You still on the roof?"

"Not going anywhere. I told you, son, I intend to die in this place. That's been my wish since I first put in the grapes."

"Gotta ask you something, and then I want you to get out. We got a guy here, wants us to get some pumps dropped in. But I'll be honest with you, I'm kinda confused. I don't think there's any water left in this basin."

"*Dovè stai?*"

"Dad, you gotta speak English to me here."

"Where you at?"

"We're at thirty-six hundred feet. You know where the old mine shafts are, where the canyon walls—"

"Should be plenty of water in that basin."

"You sure?"

"Plenty of water!"

"How do you know?"

"Trust me."

"Okay. Stay off the roof, Dad. Get outta there now. G-to-G. I'll see you in a couple of days."

He reconnects with the IC, telling him he wants an airlift of pumps. The IC says it will take two hours, which is too much time, given the pressure he is under.

"Then I think I'm just going to sit," Niccolo tells him. "I haven't had breakfast yet."

"You're insubordinate."

"Why don't you give us a couple of bucket drops while we're waiting for the pumps? Should be a reservoir just above the coulee. It's close enough to the fire to get a few dumps on the Johnny before we go in."

The IC agrees to send a helicopter with a bucketload of water and to airlift three small pumps to the jumpers. Each of the two-cycle engines can draw seventy gallons a minute, enough to have three strong hoses pouring water on the line, and a fallback position that makes everyone feel they have a true firewall. The jumpers sit in a circle and wait, all but Niccolo. He can't get his heart to settle. He paces and looks skyward.

The sky wrings out a mist that barely falls. Still, it's a relief. Heads back, the jumpers let the drizzle coat their faces. Teddy lights a cigar and opens his talisman, the leather-bound book that goes everywhere he goes. One of the Indians offers a prayer of thanks.

"Probably won't even need the pumps now, huh, Teddy?" Tozzie says. "Gonna rain this fire out. We're done. We're home."

"Let me see what the IC's got in mind."

When he calls the base, he is told there is no rain, no drizzle even, in the lower elevations.

"But we got a steady mist up here," says Niccolo.

"It's vapor. It'll be gone in minutes. There's no rain coming your way, Cartolano. Nothing. The forecast was wrong. The humidity's going the other way now."

"Where the hell's our bucket drop?"

"The pilot couldn't find that reservoir."

"What do you mean he couldn't find it?"

"Smoke is real thick on the ground. We got a dry cold front down here. Winds'll be picking up soon."

The pumps land in midmorning, three engines at the end of small chutes, each weighing under twenty pounds. Niccolo makes sure they are gassed and oiled before he caches them around a small spring. Then the crew advances on the Johnny Blackjack, unable to see more than a few feet ahead, moving in the direction of the heat, soldiers on the attack.

"I'm not going any closer," Tozzie shouts into his radio collar.

"Get your fusees out and let's start the burn."

Niccolo pees his pants. His eyes tear and blur. His hands are wet in the gloves, and his legs cramp. Ahead of him, he sees maroon and purple balls seeking oxygen. He smells burning hair. It is raining fire, a storm of embers. It takes only a few seconds to ignite the backburn, and only a few seconds to realize it is a mistake. For an instant, the dead forest just ahead of them is still, and then it blows up. The backburn was supposed to take off from the ground up until it met the advance of the Johnny Blackjack, but the old forest blows up as if it had been coated with kerosene. It blows up and sucks out all the oxygen from where the jumpers stand, and then reaches inside for the big fire and grabs it, pulls it along, until the backburn is engulfed, and the two fires are one, stampeding for fuel. The upwelling flames are higher than the oldest pines, the trees at the edge of the coulee. Flames jump sideways, reaching at anything. Burning branches and bursting cones shower down on them, and white ashes fall like a blizzard. Even boulders look like they are on fire, their coatings of dry lichen orange in flame. The jumpers drop their fusees and sprint in retreat to the base of the springs, against the slope. Nobody looks back. They are trapped at the point where the canyon wall meets the springs, but they have their pumps, their hydraulic fortress. Niccolo, Teddy, and

Tozzie unspool hoses. Laura and Suzanne place the suction end of the pumps in the fetid seeps of the springs. The Old Man looks around for other water sources. Niccolo is worried that the embers falling from the sky will cause the pumps to explode before they can put them to work. They start the engines and face the oncoming firestorm, ready to pour more than two hundred gallons a minute on the ground just ahead of them.

The jumpers hold tight to their flaccid hoses, desperate to feel the pulse of water as the fire closes in against them. The heat sears the exposed skin of their noses, and embers catch their hair and necks.

"The pumps!" Niccolo shouts. "Goddammit, what's holding 'em up?"

"They're on!" says Laura.

"Can't hold this hose anymore," says Tozzie. "My gloves are burning."

"Just wait another second. The water's gotta come."

Niccolo can hear the whine of the pump engines, and he checks the connection of the hoses. Everything is in place, but only a bare trickle of water comes forth. His crew will be dead from asphyxiation or overcome by the heat or burned alive if they do not abandon the line now and crawl for cover. Do you die two times—choked by the gas, then burned—or three, in anticipation? How many times have they asked the old jumper question?

"Head for the black!" Niccolo shouts, ordering the jumpers to the part of the forest that has just been burned. To get there, they will have to dash into the flames, running through the heart of the fire to reach uncertain deliverance on the other side. Nobody moves.

"Get to the black!" The Old Man bolts forward, disappears, and then reappears in a stagger, the reflector on his hard hat melted.

Only Teddy still clutches a hose, waiting for it to fill, trusting a machine over a gamble. "I can't get through the wall, Nick! I'm afraid. I just won't make it."

"Fire shelters!" Niccolo shouts. "Grab your shelters and get inside!" The jumpers scramble for a piece of ground to claim as a last hope, a place to dig in. Dying a first time. Fire gusts knock several jumpers down as soon as they unfurl the shelters. They stumble, jittery hot hands trying to shake out shelters, find the hand straps, and face the shake-and-bake into the oncoming fire. If they can get inside quick enough, the fire should bounce over them. The wind takes the Old Man's fire shelter as he tries to unfold it. He's defenseless.

"Come with me!" Niccolo shouts, but the Old Man is lost. Only Teddy stays on the fireline, still holding the flat hose, even as Niccolo yells at him to give it up. Now he screams; his face has caught fire, the flesh peeling back like tissue paper set to a torch. His nose blackens. Teddy falls down in a spasm of pain, rolling and flopping, trying to snuff out the blaze that is eating away his face. He jumps up and runs through the flames and into the gut of the Johnny Blackjack.

The jumpers who are able to get inside their shake-and-bakes have trouble keeping the covers over them, wrestling with the winds, and now the fire is upon them. The temptation is to get up rather than cook, to run. One of the shelters explodes; the jumper inside never removed his backpack, which held the fusee. Niccolo clutches his flapping foil roof and burrows into the dirt, trying to dig a small airhole with his nose, to corner a pocket of hot oxygen to keep him alive for the few minutes he needs until the storm passes. The shelter is pounded with embers and flaming branches. He knows that a fire hot enough to blow up, quickly exceeding 1,000 degrees, is hot enough to vaporize the glue of the shelter's seams. Face to the ground, he cringes at the heat that penetrates his fire shirt and his pants, scalding his skin. With his nose and chin, he scrapes away at the hardpan and keeps digging, digging, even though the ground is impenetrable. Every breath is a lungful of hot gas, burning the inside of his chest. His skin bubbles, blisters, and he chokes and coughs and cries, a weak human sound against a fire that runs up the ridge, and beyond, and burns for two more weeks.

CHAPTER FIVE

WHEN THE PUGET SOUND fog has thinned to a pale broth, the city comes out for the day. The fishing pier is crowded with rusting hulks that have not faced an ocean swell in decades, small wooden boats fresh-oiled to a shine like that of a horse saddle, and other boats topped by wind-shredded blue tarps. The oddest vessel, listing to starboard, is a long-retired ferry, once considered the most daring maritime design of its time. She looks like a bar of soap with little portholes and served in her final years as headquarters of the Fishing Sons of Norway. When the last Son of Norway died, the ferry was condemned. Brunella has two hours to kill before the press conference, and she wants to see once more what Waddy Kornflint's vision will replace. She has already written *No Significant Impact* on the consultant's report that Kornflint will use to clear any objections based on city preservation laws. She feels she has been deliberate and honest, passing judgment on five generations of American life on this small piece of real estate. Yes, it was once something mighty and industrious, a home port for a salmon fleet that roamed the Pacific, bringing to canneries a bounty that fed the American army in the Great War. But what is it now? Rust, hardened oil, dry rot, and wet rot. Memories, barely.

She drops into the small deli, Svenson's, where she skips the pickled herring on special today and orders a meal-sized helping of lefse, potato flatbread. If only the Scandinavians had discovered garlic, maybe this place would have been able to hang on. The walls are covered with pictures of John Olerud, and that's all anyone can talk about—Ole, Ole, Ole, the great first baseman for the Mariners, a local kid who hit .400 going into August one year, and too bad he always seemed to lose his swing against the Yanks. But what a sweet swing. Eat up, says Svenson, it'll soon be gone. For the final six months of his lease, he plans a new menu, getting rid of the lefse and herring and offering pocket pitas and frappacinos. Brunella likes Svenson and made a personal appeal in her report for Waddy Kornflint to accommodate him. Ethan has assured her they will. Outside, she watches the live-aboards, the squatters in long-retired tugs, hanging their clothes and basking like seals in the weak sun. A flock of gulls hops from towline to dock, the low growl of engines in the distance. A clump of sagging cedar shacks, each about the size of a large bedroom, cling to the edge of the water, next to a closed-up fabricating plant and warehouses where crab pots, nets, and flotation balls are piled to the rafters. The most vibrant color is at the entrance of the Purple Door Tavern, which has been drawing a crowd of regulars, usually around breakfast, since World War II—Greeks, Sicilians, Croats, Finns, Swedes, Norwegians, a community of people once tied to the sea, now bound to nothing but bar stools.

There will still be salmon fishermen, Brunella wrote in her report, just not here, on this broken-down pier. Kornflint has taken care of that, and he has been rather generous. The contrast between this decaying heap of fishing detritus and the gleaming new pier on the other side of the bay is stark. Across the water, the new pier is full of pleasure craft and yachts, spotless and without nicks. The old pier is only a slouch with no purpose. Of course, if it did not stand in the way of the biggest waterfront development in half a century, nobody would care how many slugs nested in old Salmon Bay.

Brunella walks up to a boat she has never seen, truant from a good coat of paint, smelling of something five days old and getting riper by the hour, perhaps not even seaworthy. She looks on the side and makes out a name: *SoundGardener*. Well, at least the owner has decent taste in local rock 'n' roll. She hears a brisk mumbling from the engine room, looks down, and spots a lanky figure with linguini strings of hair under a cap.

"You the part lady?" he says.

"Who are you?"

"Duff Almvik. You got my part?"

"No, I'm—you have the wrong person."

"Fucking-A. I'm leaking oil like a grease monkey with a kidney condition, and you got nothing for me. Bad enough, I counted fourteen restaurants today before I came to a place 'long the water where somebody knew ahi from aft."

"Where you from?"

"Here, open seas, and then here, always here. I got a run of chinook to chase in a few weeks, and my girl's gone to shit on me."

"Here?" Brunella hops aboard his boat. "You mean you live here, on this side of Salmon Bay?"

He crawls out of the engine room and wipes his hands on his SPAWN TILL YOU DIE T-shirt. "Living free and living large, but yeah, I've parked the *SoundGardener* here, more or less, going on twenty-two years."

"But that's impossible. I looked at all the records. I've been over the fishing licenses, talked to the archivists at the Nordic Heritage Museum, scanned every city houseboat permit. This pier does not have a working fisherman."

"Working's a relative term, lady." He lifts his cap, which has a stylized fishhook and the line BITE ME. "My gramps came to Seattle from Oslo, place that's full of blondies showing their titties this time of year, in case you never been. He came here 'cause the North Sea was fished out. Came here to Salmon Bay and felt like he'd never left Oslo. People used to hang codfish on clotheslines in their backyards and nobody looked at 'em funny. Now I get too close to somebody on land, and the yups are on me with their lawyers. Like their shit don't stink. My gramps started catching chinook—a very special run of fish, oiled and fat with just the right color—started catching 'em and kept doing it till he croaked on the boat. My old man picked it up, and then he handed the license down to me. If you're not the part lady, who are you?"

When Brunella explains that she is working on contract for Waddy Kornflint to ensure that his project will not erase a community of cultural significance, Duff starts to laugh. He has a cackle, horsey and deep, honed from solo laughs on the high seas.

"I'm not significant?"

"You could move across the bay, join the people at the new pier."

"Think they'd let me in?"

"They would have to. Mr. Kornflint has made space for fishing boats."

"If I don't fit on this side of Salmon Bay, I don't fit anywhere."

"Oh, that's nonsense. You can adapt."

"Adapt? And then what? I'm probably the last gill-netter chasing those big spring chinook. Get rid of me, what're you left with?"

"There are other runs of fish."

"Not like this one. You got a minute? Let me show you something." He retreats to a locker in the rear of the cabin, rustles through some papers, and returns with a large stained map, big enough to cover a kitchen table. The map shows the Pacific Northwest, its major rivers and streams, the islands of Puget Sound, the Strait of Juan de Fuca, and the Pacific shore. There are colored lines, like arteries, running from different parts of the sound and ocean, up the rivers to inland destinations.

"See here? Each of these lines is a run of fish," Duff says. "They're genetically extinct, going back to the Ice Age—"

"Distinct. You mean *distinct*."

"Now follow me without interrupting, wouldja, please? Hey, you got kind of a nice rack there, you know? Firm little pair—"

"A nice . . . ?"

"Nothing. I catch my chinookies off the northern tip of Whidbey. They're on their way home after a long life in the Pacific. They dip through the sound to gorge on food before heading out and south again, along the coast, to the Columbia River. They take a left at the Columbia, see, and swim past—oh, shit—half a dozen dams, climbing those worthless fish ladders they got, and then, inland, higher still to the desert, 'bout twelve thousand miles round trip. You following this on the map?"

"Let me see that." Brunella moves closer. "Oh, my God. This can't be."

"Yeah, it's a goddamn miracle. Every time I explain what a good bunch of hikers these chinookies are, I get the same reaction."

"I know this run of fish," says Brunella. "I know it well."

"Then you know they hang a left just after Wenatchee and crawl up a creek to their final spawning ground, here next to a little coulee. You can't see it on the map, but that's where they end up, near this little desert coulee. Spawn. Die. Then, come spring, my meal ticket heads out to sea."

"Are you sure?"

"Guy at the U-Dub fisheries school tagged a bunch of 'em. That's my run of fish, the Coulee Kings. You know anything about the desert in eastern Washington?"

"Yes, I grew up there. This coulee . . . what if the creek were dry?"

"Impossible. It's a spring-fed stream. I been there myself."

"But what if? I mean, what if the creek were dry when the fish came back, what then?"

"I'd be done. End of the line for me and my Coulee Kings. Why, you know somethin'?"

On the top floor of the oldest skyscraper on the West Coast, Brunella steps outside to the observation deck. She had written her speech weeks ago, before going east of the mountains, but it looks like pablum now, like somebody else wrote it, somebody she doesn't like. People are crowding into the showcase room in the Smith Tower, and she is five minutes away from feeding them—this? Remember now to keep the hands down, she reminds herself, hide the Italian and don't talk with your hands, the refrain she heard time and again when she first moved to this city of Asian and Scandinavian reserve. Of course, a livable city needs a past, *blah-blah,* and what's more we have a tradition of not erasing our heritage, *blah-blah,* and Waddy Kornflint's project will keep that tradition alive because it will have No Significant Impact on anything of lasting cultural value, and don't forget to staple the hands and pander and tell three jokes before the serious stuff.

She has invited the press, the mayor, the city council, and a few philanthropists and professional goo-goos to the Smith Tower to announce the finding of No Significant Impact. Kornflint is the fourth richest person on earth, an anorexic-looking tycoon given to elliptic non sequiturs that are overinterpreted by aides in sweatshirts, a man who does not have a community-minded thought that he does not inflict on the community through the filter of his sycophants. But to his credit, Brunella believes, Kornflint has both good taste and a sense of restraint, a rare combination for somebody who likes his money to be visible. The Salmon Bay development is her biggest project, and she was surprised at how little opposition there was. Not a peep from the museum boards, the arts councils, the self-appointed cultural watchdogs. It wasn't because they didn't care about Salmon Bay. They cared, at least in the abstract; it was funky and quirky in the Seattle tradition, if nothing else. But Kornflint is a Medici in a plaid shirt; the concerns of nonprofit boards for old piers and diminished rituals does not extend to those coveted by the city's biggest benefactor.

Brunella's reputation is gold. She has fought on behalf of the city's public market and waged several high-profile campaigns against Kornflint in the International District. When they hired her, she was given an unlimited budget and no interference. With her finding of No Significant Impact, Kornflint can tear down the clot of warehouses, cedar shacks, docks, and fishing boats, and the goo-goos can sleep at night and the editorial boards won't so much as burp. In writing her report, Brunella's argument is simple: There are no fishermen left on the south side of Salmon Bay; therefore, there is no culture worthy of preservation. To save Salmon Bay as it is would amount to enshrining ghosts and doing so in unsanitary firetraps. But then, this morning she met Duff and found out about the Coulee Kings.

Brunella looks radiant, her shirt unbuttoned three from the top, a short skirt over long legs bronzed by the high-alpine sun of eastern Washington. Just as her presentation is set to begin, she dashes out of the room, past the assembled power brokers and into the bathroom. She stares at her notes, nibbles at her fingernails. Christ. This is truly lame. We can still be the Paris of Puget Sound, *yadda-yadda-yadda*, as long as we respect our past and honor the future. Through the window, she looks at Mount Rainier, a skirt of smoke at its midsection. Five hundred feet below her, she eyes the half-built empire of the city Kornflint is remaking.

She feels something, a jolt, and freezes in place. Is this it? The movement of plates, the shake and relief of crustal slabs, the strain and groan of an aging planet? A sense of sudden horror runs through her.

"Did you feel it?" she asks a friend, as she reenters the room.

"Feel what?"

"Just now. That . . . that tremble?"

The friend shrugs. "You shouldn't go out there showing so much leg, Brunella."

"What, and hide my best asset?" She strolls to the front of the room, one of the most elegant age-encumbered salons in the city: the Chinese Temple Room, a big-windowed attic of collections from across the Pacific, with views over Puget Sound and also east to the mountains, shielded today by smoke. Ethan Winthrop has taken a reserved seat in front. He is scratching his bug-bitten legs.

"You're sunburned," she says to him.

"I'm seeing the dermatologist this afternoon. They're promising clouds later in the week—thank God. Are you ready? You seem a little preoccupied."

"Did you feel something, Ethan, just a minute ago? Some movement?"

"I did not. Maybe we should call this off if you're not ready."

"I'm ready," she says. "I think."

But Brunella's mind is unclear. She goes to the front, faces the mayor, two deputy mayors, most of the city council, Kornflint's aides, public policy lawyers, architects, designers, and a ponytailed bank president. The foundations—Bullitt and Gates, Weyerhaeuser and McCaw, Allen and Boeing—have sent staff members. Television cameras turn on their lights as Brunella introduces herself.

"You can't know who you are," she begins, "if you don't know *where* you are. Where we are today is the top floor of what used to be the tallest building west of the Mississippi. We have memories, those of us attached to this city—call it our sentiment equity—of the times when this building touched the periphery of our lives. The Smith Tower isn't going anywhere, so can you stop looking at me that way. And keep those cell phones off until I'm finished, please."

"Where's Kornflint?" comes a shout from the audience.

Kornflint never makes a public appearance, unless it is on a screen, pretaped. Kornflint never gives interviews. She glances at the row of Kornflint's sweatshirted aides.

"Mr. Kornflint asks the city to condemn several blocks on Salmon

Bay. I have spent the last eight months going over this neighborhood. It has seen better times. Once, you could argue, it was the most storied part of a small corner of the world that has always looked to the sea for life. But now? It is an eyesore. It is polluted. It is—well, I thought it was deserted."

She pauses, moves her lips, but nothing comes forth. She bites her nails. "Ummmm." Silence. The glare of the cameras. A labored moment. She folds her notes and looks straight ahead, trying to hold her hands in place.

"As I started to say, the law requires the city to have a living memory. That means preserving buildings and patterns of life that remind us of our heritage. This is a town sustained by Puget Sound from day one. We don't want to become a city no longer connected to the sea, a city of people whose hands are without blisters. A city that . . . ummmm—"

"Get to the point!" comes another shout. She shields her eyes and tracks the room for the voice of the heckler. In the back, leaning against the wall, his foot on a cooler, is Duff Almvik, still wearing his SPAWN TILL YOU DIE T-shirt.

"Excuse me?"

"I said, 'Get to the point,' " says Duff.

"We—ummm—Duff?"

"Yeah?"

"Could you come forward, please?"

Walking, his cooler in one hand, Duff looks tall, perhaps six feet six inches, with a weathered face and glassy eyes.

Another long silence. The camera lights make Brunella blink.

"Ummmm. . . . Oh, shit, I have—" She begins again. "I have . . . I guess . . . some questions."

Ethan shoots her a threatening look, furiously scratching at his legs.

"Mr. Almvik here—Duff Almvik—is a commercial salmon fisherman. Isn't that right, Duff?"

"You betcha. Third gen."

"And as I've just been informed this morning, he has . . . he's got a permit to take salmon, which he brings home to a pier. Is that correct, Duff?"

He nods in agreement.

"And as we think about this, it seems like it's—well, the very pier Mr. Kornflint wants to destroy for lack of fishermen."

"Got more'n a permit," says Duff. "Got fish." He opens his cooler and removes a good-sized salmon, gutted, the head still on. "Meat's nice and red. Plenty of oil. Caught this puppy last night on a troll line. Tell you what. Four dollars a pound gets this fish out of my hands and into yours."

He holds the fish over the head of Ethan, who turns away in disgust. Duff kisses the fish on the snout and puts it back into the cooler. Then he kisses Brunella on the cheek and offers up a goofy smile, warming to the rare opportunity to entertain somebody other than himself.

Ethan is stunned. Kornflint's aides whisper back and forth. They know Brunella has done an exhaustive search of every commercial fisherman at the pier. She has tracked them down in trailers, in jail, in law firms, in beach houses in Hawaii, in graduate schools, in bars where they picked up their mail. The ones she could find were bought out by Kornflint. The cashouts were generous; in some cases, more than half a million dollars per fisherman. By terms of modern social mitigation, it was nothing. But here is Duff Almvik. Brunella never mentioned him. Where the fuck did he come from?

"Duff may be the last of the line," Brunella continues, her words picking up speed as her hands spring loose, a full flutter of fingers and motion in the air, the Cartolano in her set free. "Or maybe he is the start of a renaissance, a thread to a future where salmon again run through the waterways of our city. But as long as Duff lives on as the sole surviving fisherman on the old side of Salmon Bay and continues to do what the Almvik family has done there for three generations, I'm not sure the Building Department can give Mr. Kornflint his permit."

"What?" From Ethan, a rare shout. "I don't believe what I'm hearing!"

"It would seem to violate the law. Because Salmon Bay *is*, in fact, a living community. If you tear it down, what would that do to Duff? I'm sorry. I didn't know about any of this until just this morning, and I've been trying ever since to process it and do the right—"

Ethan stands and points a finger at Brunella. She has never seen him look so physical, so aggressive. It scares her. A Kornflint aide rises next to him.

"Ms. Cartolano, you are completely out of line," says the aide. "You have violated the terms of your contract, which you can consider terminated as of this moment. We'll be in touch about recouping fees. But more important, to everyone here—you are wrong."

"Tell me."

"The statute says a building permit cannot be issued if, and I quote, *a community* of historical or cultural significance is at risk. I'm reading from your notes, by the way. What you have here with your friend, Mr. Duff, is not a community. As you just said, he may be the last of the line and sole surviving member of his own ethnic subspecies. Fine. Whatever. But he is *solo!* One. Unto himself. Not a community. You have no case." The aide sits down.

A woman, a friend of Brunella's, breaks into the room, breathless, her face downturned and red. "Yes?" Brunella says. "Something I missed?"

"No, no. It's not good. I must talk to you. I must talk to you now. I have terrible news."

The mayor rises and starts to leave, followed by the deputy mayors and several city council members.

"Wait!" Brunella says. The cameras are trained on the mayor, a well-fed man with eyelids at half mast and premature jowls. He pauses for dramatic effect, sensing the sound bite at full ripeness.

"Ms. Cartolano. We'll keep the file open for another six months to see if there is in fact a community at risk—and that means more than one person, just to be clear. But then this forward-looking city must get on with its business. No matter what some people may say about Mr. Kornflint, he is a visionary, and visionaries are not tripped up by phony process. Oh, and Duff: I'll take that fish off your hands."

Ethan is furious. He grabs Brunella by the elbow and tugs her to one side, his bony fingers deep in her skin.

"Why did you flip on me?" Ethan says. "Did you spend a night slumming with the fisherman?"

"Ethan, that hurts. Get your fingers off my arm, and I'll tell you. We're connected, that fisherman and I."

"As I suspected."

"I only met him this morning. Walking to the podium, I realized that we are connected by water. His fish, my father's grapes. The water links us together."

"What, that little half-dead salmon stream?"

"Yes!"

"Then you're doomed."

The woman who has rushed into the room pulls her aside and whispers in her ear. Brunella looks at her as if she is staring at a cipher. *Oh, no. No, it can't be. It can't be. Oh, no.* She collapses on the ground and buries her face.

CHAPTER SIX

T HEY ARE STILL pretty boys. Look at them: the Indians, Sherman and Wes and Joseph and Noflight; the Neds, Dennis and Mack and Wag. Pretty boys at rest. Forever young. The lashless eyes closed. Same with the Pendleton women, the sweet faces of Suzanne and Laura. When they died inside the foil shields, the heat cooked them, like hot dogs in a microwave, but their features are intact. Niccolo's cheeks have a mortician's blush. What a big kid, Brunella thinks. God, he's grown. Niccolo, Niccolo: How did it feel, those last seconds? Dying only one time, yes, not two or three? At least you didn't burn to death, like the Old Man; he died in midstride after the wind took his shelter. What they found of the Old Man was a half-melted wedding ring. His body fat had burned like fuel; his eyes had been sucked out, the cartilage in his nose and ears peeled back, the bones and teeth consumed like dried hardwood. Such details were in the preliminary report. No judgments, no editorializing. Time of death. Cause of death. Condition of the bodies. Identification. An explanation that the melting point for gold is 1,945 degrees, and no documented fire in the Northwest has reached that level since the Big Burn of 1910.

Brunella is done with tears. She is trying to imagine Niccolo's last breaths as a way to bring herself closer to him. Go, sweet brother, to the other side, but leave the burden with me. She does not see the backhand of God swatting down a good man at the start of his life. She has long since given up anthropomorphizing God. The earth shudders. The American prince John F. Kennedy, Jr., falls into the ocean. A kid eats a bad hamburger and dies a few hours after the picnic. There is no order to such events. Randomness is part of nature. Nature is God. The same place where Niccolo took his last breath was under a sheet of ice ten thousand years ago, and fossilized at the edge of the ice was a middle-aged Pleistocene man who stumbled over his own spear point and died from infection. Random.

The church is so full of light this morning it chases away the Gothic gloom. The pews are packed with Forest Service brass in pressed olive green, an honor guard row of people in yellow fire shirts, smoke jumpers, past and present, everyone a Fire God at some point. Brunella is with the other families in the front; most of them snub her. She feels their eyes, the stares of accusation: It was *your* brother who led them to their deaths. How could the government send those jumpers into a furnace? Most of them were just kids. And what did they die for? To save some orchards and summer homes.

The Interior Secretary starts his eulogy. He is the rarest of politicians, a man who admits to ambiguity. He was a jumper himself once, a Fire God. These dead boys, these young women from Pendleton, the Old Man—these smoke jumpers—they will outlive us all, the Interior Secretary says. They will join the heroes who did not make it into the mine shaft in the Bitterroots during the 1910 fire, the young men torched on a flank of Mann Gulch in 1949, the Hotshots who could not outrun a change of the wind in the South Canyon fire of 1994. They are selfless people in a selfish age. We will grow old, crippled, and diseased, cursing the drudgery of waking up. These jumpers will not. They belong to the young American West, he says, to free-flowing rivers and chutes of powder snow, to Butch Cassidy and Picabo Street.

They say it is like drowning. So Brunella tries to imagine suffocation: no oxygen, a blackness, no sound, then a painless final exit. The burning of his skin, the seared outer edges—that had to come after Niccolo was gone. But he must have tried something elemental, some last burst of action in his final seconds; Niccolo would not die with his face in the dirt. He had to kick the firestorm, punch the flames, spit in its face. She wants her father to understand that Niccolo's pain was brief. But Angelo is empty. He never cried when he heard the news. He does not cry now. He was still on the roof with his garden hose, protecting his creation, the three-dimensional glory that he produced from the barren coulee, when word came that the boy was dead. He stayed there, clutching the hose like a sentry, staring upslope, through the vineyards to the smoke. He stayed on the roof through most of a hot night, and only came down when Miguel and two men from the government forced him. Your boy was a hero. He did everything he could. But we have some questions.

Angelo's older son, Roberto, is little comfort. Roberto lives in Houston in a tower where the blinds are always closed, the windows never opened. He is the kind of man who seems to have been born with a scowl on his face, a man whose mirth-smothering personality has long bewildered family friends, a man who never looked more at home than at a funeral. He is research director of a mutual fund, married to his third wife, and has no children. He and Brunella have not seen each other since their mother's funeral, three years earlier. They fought over whether to bury their mother in the coulee or back east, in Baltimore, where she grew up. Roberto threatened to sue if the body was not taken to Baltimore; he won. Since he moved to Houston, he prefers to be known as Bob.

She looks for Teddy. He is one of the living, one of only two. He must know what happened. He must know the details of Niccolo's last moments. She needs him. Teddy Flax was airlifted to the Harborview Burn Center in Seattle. Most of his face was too badly scorched for skin grafts. He was supposed to stay for an indefinite time, but he has disappeared. He walked out, wrapped in his bandages, mummified. A boy saw him unveil his face in the parking lot, and it scared the child so much he could not summon the image without crying. The Flax family is here: Solvan, released from jail for this funeral, Mrs. Flax, three of her sisters. The other survivor, Tozzie Cresthawk, his arm in a sling, is seated up front next to a big Indian man with a brush cut and pressed Forest Service uniform. The big Indian has been put in charge of the investigation, and already the knives of the cynics are in his back. He's a sop, a Forest Service lifer; of course he won't find the true cause of this tragedy.

When Niccolo gave the order for everyone to retreat to their foil shelters, Tozzie did not move. He survived by starting a fire with his fusee and then curling up on the fresh-burned ground, creating a hole in the fire.

The Johnny Blackjack sniffed at his patch of blackened earth and jumped right over him. When Brunella tried to talk to him today before the service started, he said it was bad from the start, a string of shit luck going back to the Suicide Race, when he was forced to shoot his horse. He should have called it quits after he snagged himself in the tree, insisting to Niccolo that they were doomed. He says he remembers nothing else.

"You know what miracles have sprouted from the land watered by the big river," the priest says. "When you see the grapes, the apples, the cherries, the great bounty that God has given us in the Columbia Basin, you know these men and women did not die in vain. They died to protect us all, for we share in that bounty. They died for the Cartolano family. For the Flax family. For the Pickenses and the Hendersons, for the Lopez family, the Castanadas, for all that is good that comes from the irrigated land."

What the priest does not say is that the firestorm was an act of God. To the insurance industry, act of God is a legal term used in American tort law as a way to keep companies from paying for disasters. It means nobody is to blame; nothing could prevent it; it just happened, although there is an implied deliberateness. But in a church, at a funeral, God cannot be seen as acting in such a way.

Brunella knows now that Angelo has lost his faith, that he is hollow inside. Why take Niccolo just as he was ready to bring so much joy to the last stage of Angelo's life? Brunella has no answer, but she struggled with a similar question when her mother died three years ago, killed by a kid in a fortified car. Again, it's the anthropomorphizing that gets people in trouble. Francis saw God in everything around Assisi, most famously in that archetype of animal-kingdom evil, the wolf. She prefers to see good and bad—a forest meadow in full flower and a hillside so charred it is sterile— as one and the same, product neither of blessing nor of curse.

As the priest finishes, she is having trouble breathing. Her lungs are fine, she has never had asthma or allergies, but now she feels like she cannot draw a breath. The air is thin, sparse, and then it's gone, and she feels underwater, panicky. She forces a cough but can't breathe unless she does so very slowly, a mechanical in and out. So maybe this is what she wanted: Niccolo's final moments, choking on the unbearable breath of the Johnny Blackjack, the suffocation; she knows why Francis the nobleman's son, pale and shriveled with open sores, dying in his forty-fourth year, felt such ecstasy when the stigmata finally came. In this struggle to draw a breath, she sees the ghost forest above the coulee as it was on the day she arrived at the family house ten days ago, sees it clearly with Niccolo's pain. She remembers the branches looking arthritic and bony, and the smell, and the sound as the wind pushed through, the clatter of dried limbs—all of it out of place.

After the service, she holds her father's arm tight, accepting the condolences of the Interior Secretary, of other smoke jumpers, of Forest Service brass as they exit the church. Mrs. Flax approaches them, waits for her turn to face Angelo. She moves up close to him and spits in his face; then she stands, without flinching, trying to take in Angelo's humiliation. Solvan escorts his wife away but he does not apologize. Brunella wipes the spit off her father's nose. In the parking lot, Brunella seats her father in the car, gets inside, and starts the engine. Roberto and his third wife are in a separate car. Just as Brunella is leaving, the big Indian from the Forest Service walks up to her window.

The big Indian is about forty years old, with features from distant Asia and the Athabascan north, the nose of a French-Canadian voyageur. He looks Nez Perce, or what Brunella has always envisioned of the Nez Perce, the most handsome people of the West, the Americans whose image seemed to come from the land itself. He cannot be coastal Salish; he is too tall, the nose too prominent, the eyes too deeply set; there is a hint of the face from the Edward Curtis portrait of Chief Joseph. Yes, he is a Columbia Plateau native, she decides. Perhaps Yakama or Umatilla. His eyes hold her face for a moment, and then he leaves her with a note and the only smile she has seen in days.

Two days later, they fly over the skeleton of the Johnny Blackjack fire in the same Sherpa that dropped the jumpers. There are nearly two dozen of them now, mostly family members, pressing the weight limit of the plane. Brunella holds a canister with Niccolo's ashes inside. Angelo does not look out the window. Roberto has stayed behind; he has no desire to see where Niccolo died. Angelo looks straight ahead. You do it, he tells Brunella. Do it and get it over with. They circle the blue ice tops of the big peaks, mounts Fernow and Maude, Glacier Peak and Bonanza, the Sawtooths above Lake Chelan. Out a right-side window is the granite summit of Mount Stuart, site of her father's triumph, but Angelo will not even look at the mountain where he made his Last Man's Club vow. His past has no meaning; it is all gray dissolving to fog.

The Johnny Blackjack has remade the land. Everything is monochrome, even the north sides of boulders, their lichen burned. The plane drops into a valley and crosses a scorched ridge close to where the jumpers died. The fire took every tree. Usually, a burned forest is left charred but upright. This is a horizontal graveyard, with seeps of smoke and smoldering stumps, and only a few standing trees, their thick limbs curled and black. It does not look as if a natural burn, a cleansing periodic sweep of weak trees and dry brush, came through. It looks like the forest was knocked down by a storm of hurricane-force winds or a nuclear blast. From the air, it is clear that the Johnny Blackjack burned right to the edge of the coulee. It did not take out any of the plantings of the 206ers, nor did it touch Cartolano land. The greenest, most fecund center of the coulee is intact, grapes and apples growing as before, an island of sculpted life surrounded by a mass of scarred land.

"Touch him, Babbo," Brunella says. She takes his leathered hand and sets it atop the canister. "Touch him for the last time." The shake in his hand is worse than ever; it looks like a tarantula with Parkinson's disease. She whispers a prayer as she stands, holds a bar for balance, and tosses the ashes out. The winds pick up what is left of Niccolo and scatter him.

At the Cartolano home, the old cherry-wood kitchen table groans under all the food. Lasagna, three-bean salads, blackberry cobbler, cookies, tomatoes and mozzarella, roasted chickens. Flowers fill the main sitting room. One bouquet is from the governor, with a personal note from his young wife. Angelo will not touch the food. Visitors come and go all day. Brunella is the face of the family, explaining why Angelo cannot see anyone. She is relieved to see her friend Emma, a woman with long redwood-colored hair and a raspy voice. They stroll outside.

"You gonna move home?" she asks Brunella.

"I can't."

"You never were one for State B basketball and the apple blossom parade."

"I like being anonymous. You can only do that in the city. How are you, Emma?"

"Fighting with my ex-husband, the creep. Getting the kids back to school. Drindy's sick and the stupid-ass HMO wants a hundred bucks just to take her temperature. I'm broke. I feel trapped in my job at the paper. Every day I call up the coroner and get one of these summaries of somebody's life and write it up in three hundred words or less. You never do them justice. I'm sorry. You don't need to hear any of this."

"Did you know Teddy Flax very well?"

"Same as you, I guess. He was always different."

"He was. You're right, Emma. I mean, he *is* different, still. He seems to have this thing you don't find in a lot of men. He's . . . self-aware, you know what I mean? I'm desperate to see him. His mother thinks it's our fault. What do you think?"

"I think it's going to get worse."

"It can't get worse, Emma. Not for me."

"Listen to me. Some of these people—and this is just scuttlebutt, Brunella—they may end up suing you."

"Suing us? The family? For what?"

"For whatever happened up there under Niccolo's command. They'll sue the government, of course. And then they'll sue you."

"*These people*—you mean the folks who lost somebody in the fire?"

"Yes. And I hear that some of the Two-oh-sixers are talking about getting in on it."

"But those homes were all *saved*."

"Believe me, Brunella, if they think they can take something from Angelo without causing them a hiccup, they'll do it. They're jealous; you know that. They resent him for his success."

"I don't think anything will happen, Emma. This fire was a freak. These are good people who live in this coulee."

"You want to get a drink?"

"No. I want to ask you something, though: You were raised in a conventional Mormon family—"

"I'd call it a prison. We were true believers, the ones who never got over the revelation that threw out polygamy, which means the graybeards have their pick of teenage brides and your job is to shut up and breed."

"But . . . aside from that . . . you had faith once, didn't you, Emma? You believed."

"I still believe. I just don't have faith anymore."

In the evening, Brunella takes the radio to her father's room. The Mariners have lost six in a row, giving up their lead to Texas in the West. Three innings go by without a word from Angelo. When the Ms load the bases, he leaves the room and wanders outside in the dark, up into the vineyards. He does not respond to calls. Brunella and Miguel find him outside the next morning, disheveled and shivering, his eyes swollen.

"Have you lost all common sense, Babbo?" says Brunella. She shakes him, but it is no use. "What's wrong?"

"*Niente.*"

She is talking to a child; soon it will be diapers and shaving him in the morning.

She tends the grapes with Miguel and his crew. They will start harvesting the small lot of white grapes in a few weeks, the Pinot Grigio, the Sauvignon Blanc, some of the fruit used for blending. The Nebbiolo needs at least another month on the vine, maybe six weeks. She has a thousand questions about the harvest, but Angelo waves her off. Wine is immortality, she reminds him, the living link to Niccolo: his words. Doesn't that mean something?

"*Non vale la pena.*"

How many heat units do the grapes need? How do you test the sugar level, the acidity, the tannins? How hard should the skins be? How do you make sure the grapes aren't crushed in the bins? Or is that okay? How much powdery mildew should be left on the grapes? What happens if it rains, do you rush the harvest?

"*Non vale la pena.*"

All week, she sees the big Indian investigator around the coulee, peripatetic with official purpose. Every time she drives past the Flax farm, the big Indian's Forest Service Suburban is there. She spots the Suburban up on the bench, where the 206ers live, next to the main irrigation ditch. At night, the Suburban is outside the Flax home.

Roberto is ready to return to Houston. He sits at the table, tapping his fingers, answering cell phone calls. "This is Bob . . . mmm-hmm . . . mmm-hmm . . . mmmm . . . That's a keeper."

He settles the family in for an announcement, a frown embedded in a face showing the early stages of a second chin. "I think we should sell the place," he says. "Sell it now, at harvest, when it looks its best."

"Are you crazy?" Brunella says

"I've been moving some numbers around, talked to a couple of brokers. This is the premier Nebbiolo vineyard on the West Coast. Mind you, it's not Romanée-Conti or Grand Cru by anyone's standard, but Dad has established a nice little niche up here. In Napa, they're getting a quarter million dollars an acre for a vineyard of this quality. The French are moving into Walla Walla now, buying up everything. We sell the place this month, before the market goes south."

"You just said the vineyard has never been more valuable. Wouldn't it be wise to wait?"

"Who knows how much water is left in the pipeline."

"What do you mean?"

"These Indians, the government, all these salmon people—it's obvious what's going on in this valley. It's a water grab. The irrigator's day is over, Brunella. Why fight the Indians when they've got the government behind them? You're looking at litigation, endless hearings, process crap. We'd probably have to max out contributions to what's-his-name, the old cadaver of a senator. Who needs it? I say we move Dad to residential care—"

"A halfway house to the grave."

He sighs and looks away, as if dealing with a fool. He turns to his father for the first time and speaks in a deliberate tone, his voice loud. "Dad. You are no longer independent. I can find a first-rate place, twenty-four hours of security, all the amenities, games, therapy pool, nurses, people just like you—"

"Stop!" Brunella jumps to her feet. "Roberto, go home. Go back to Houston. You have no connection to this place. You never did."

"And you do?"

"No, I live in the city, just like you. But the Cartolano family does . . . not . . . sell . . . land." She faces Angelo. "Tell Roberto what you've always said. Tell him, Babbo!"

"What time is the game today?" he says.

One day after Roberto returns to Houston, Brunella spots a moving truck in front of the Flax family orchard. They have sold everything: orchard, house, two outbuildings, a barn, a flatbed truck, a half-dozen picker's cabins. Most of the orchard was burned in the fire, driving the value down. Mrs. Flax greets Brunella with the same cold face she presented at the funeral. She is surrounded by cats that curl at her feet like snakes.

"I'm going to die soon," says Mrs. Flax, picking up one of the cats and stroking its head. "And I don't want to see the devil-spawned Cartolano family on my way out."

"Then tell me about Teddy. I thought I would see him at the funeral, but they say he has disappeared. Surely you've heard from him."

"He left us, far as I'm concerned, before he got burned up."

"How can you say that?"

"He never belonged with us."

"I must see him."

"Can't help you there."

"But with the sale of your house, at least he'll have some financial security."

"I wouldn't assume that," says Mrs Flax. "He's not entitled to anything. He wasn't born to the farm, and he didn't stick around. Maybe you can understand that, since you moved away just like him. Loyalty to a place used to mean something."

Her thin lips look harsh and line-drawn, and she narrows her eyes to mere slits of arctic blue. She's rigid, one hand tightly balled, the other clutching a cat.

"The white farmers made this land what it is. We made it ours. And look at it now, look what's happened. Where is our place here? This is the end of our story."

"Where will you go?"

"We have a rental house in town. They'll take in my cats and me while Solvan does his time."

"Who bought the orchard?"

"Some fella from Omak. I don't know his family. He said he wants to make a go of it. Start from scratch. And I say, Good luck, because our day is done."

Two days later Brunella sees smoke coming from the Flax orchard. She races over to the house and finds the Forest Service Suburban out front and another vehicle with a tribal emblem on the side. The big Indian from the Forest Service is watching as a group of natives burn the remaining apple trees in the orchard. Tozzie Cresthawk is helping to supervise the burn. Brunella is horrified. She runs up to the big Indian; he tells her—gently—to stand back. The house is next. At Tozzie's direction, the crew douses the walls of the homestead with gasoline and torches it. It goes up in a swoosh, shingles peeling away, the roof caving in, beams and posts that stood in the coulee sun for more than half a century collapsing in moments. All that's left standing in the smoky heap are the rock chimney and a claw-footed bathtub.

"Controlled burn," the big Indian says. "The new owners feel these structures are too much of a fire hazard. And we agree."

"The new owners?"

"The tribe."

"I thought somebody from Omak purchased this place."

"They did."

"And he was a tribal member?"

"Or an agent, or a cousin. I don't know. It's not my business."

"From what Mrs. Flax said, I didn't think the buyer was an Indian."

"Why? Because he was wearing shoes?"

"And now they're burning it. For what, a new orchard?"

"Nothing. It's going back to the way it was."

"The way it was—when?"

"Before."

"And the water rights? The Flax family had nearly five thousand acre-feet."

"They go to the tribe for their project down by the river."

"What kind of project is that?"

"I'm not sure. You'll have to ask them. I'm a Forest Service employee, Leon Treadtoofar's my name. I approached you after the funeral. You are Brunella Cartolano. I've heard so much about you, your family, the wonderful things that you've done in this coulee. Can you spend some time helping me?"

"I don't think so."

"Let me take you for a walk."

"No. You . . . I don't have anything to say."

In the morning, she finds a dozen sunflowers and a note outside the doorstep from Leon Treadtoofar. He asks her to meet him to talk about the fire, and he includes some lines from Robert Louis Stevenson:

> *Sing a song of seasons!*
> *Something bright in all!*
> *Flowers in the summer,*
> *Fires in the fall!*

It is just cryptic enough to move her. They meet in the Forest Service office in Wenatchee and walk a few blocks to a city park next to the Columbia River, where an army of firefighters has made their encampment. It's a tent city, clothes drying on wires, people sleeping in the shade of the shelters, a long line of ashen-faced yellow-shirted men and women waiting for chow. It smells like defeat, like demobe.

Brunella and the big Indian walk past a circle of people kicking a Hacky Sack, a small foot bag. Leon Treadtoofar tells Brunella about his investigation. It's not an autopsy, he says; the goal is to find out what mistakes were made, to build a record the Forest Service can use, to find lessons for all the people who spend their summers laboring under orange and black skies.

"Did something have to go wrong?" Brunella asks.

"It usually does. There are no pure accidents."

"I don't believe that."

They walk past a group of Indian Hotshots from the Bureau of Land Management, a knot of wiry, muscled men sitting on the grass while they eat. Leon has the slow gait of an elegant big man, his feet soundless on the ground.

"Zunis," Leon says. "They love to fight fire. Probably better than any of the Colville bands."

"My brother had a lot of friends from the tribes: Utes, Navajos, Blackfeet. He told me fighting fires revived their warrior spirit."

"I'm not sure a white man can know what that means, but it seems to me, Brunella, that both you and your brother have stayed out of shallow waters. You seem alive to possibility."

"Coming from somebody who hasn't the foggiest idea who I am, that's a very nice thing to say."

"And is it true?"

"Next question."

White feathery ashes fall from the sky onto Leon's black bristled hair. He wipes them off his pressed uniform. Brunella notices his forearms, thick and powerful, and a Forest Service tattoo on one arm, an emblem of a tree. He is ageless-looking. In profile, she thinks he could pose for a coin minting. He's got to be Nez Perce, she decides.

"Some of these people," says Leon, motioning to the Indians in the circle, "they empty out their village to fight a fire. There's no job on the reservation that pays as well. You want lunch?"

"Sure."

They wait in line for grilled cheese sandwiches, potato salad, and Gatorade.

"What tribe are you from?" Brunella asks him.

"I live in Seattle," says Leon. "Going on my twentieth year with the Forest Service."

"You're not Nez Perce?"

"My father is. On my mother's side, Wanapum and Irish."

"Who are you closer to?"

"My mother. She held us together."

"And she taught you the Stevenson poetry?"

"Got that from the Jesuits."

"Wanapums—are they out by Priest Rapids?"

"You know the tribe?"

"From growing up. I remember they seemed . . . unfriendly."

"Unfriendly. That's what everyone says."

"Why do Indians fight fire?"

"Why did your brother do it?"

"Money. Fun."

"You'll find Indians all over this camp. The Red Hats over there near the river, they're Mescalero Apache. They're probably the best. Nobody is here for fun."

"What do you think happened above the coulee, Mr. Treadtoofar?"

"I'm supposed to ask the questions."

"Then we're done."

"Please bear with me. I'm starting to hear some disturbing things, some patterns. But if I share these things with you, Brunella, I need you to trust me, to see me as someone you can take into your brother's world."

"I don't know you. You're the government."

"You have to get beyond that. Help me understand why Big Ernie got them."

"Big Ernie?"

"The jumpers believe he lives in the wild smoke. Cousin of Coyote."

"The Indian trickster."

"I don't believe in Coyote. I'm not your dream-catcher and pow-wow-dancer Indian."

"You wear shoes."

He smiles at the sly dig. "But I do believe in Big Ernie."

She picks through the potato salad, stares out at the river. The water is gunmetal gray. Barely moving, it looks like a worn-out rug.

"Your brother Niccolo: Was he drunk the night before he left home?"

"What kind of a question is that?" She turns her back to him.

"What did he drink?"

"You want me to trust you, and you start out with an insult."

"Help me understand. What did he drink?"

"What are you going to do with this information?"

"I'm going to find the truth, just as my note said. What did he have to drink?"

"A glass of wine, maybe two. I didn't count. What are you saying, that they found alcohol in his blood—"

"No. But that's what I've been told."

"—and it affected his judgment? That's bullshit. Look at his record. Niccolo was a flawless jumper. How do you think he made foreman before his twenty-second birthday? You should be doing soil analysis."

"I have."

"You insult me, Leon."

"That's not my intent."

"No more flowers."

"Then give me your hand." She holds her hand out tentatively. "An apology, with a grovel. We are trying to make sense of a fire like we have never seen before, Brunella. We know when the Johnny Blackjack blew up it was moving at better than a thousand feet a minute. Nobody can outrun a fire of that speed, carrying heavy packs, Pulaskis, a big Stihl, stumbling over smoky, rocky terrain. Trust me, as I said. I need to take some statements from your father and from you. We'll need a couple of days."

"I'm due back in the city tomorrow."

"Fine. Come see me at my office in Seattle. Or, better yet, I'll take you to lunch. On the government."

"I think I'll just come by the office. You should be talking to the people who pushed those trophy houses out to the edge of the forest with no regard for the laws of nature."

"I have. And I spent some time talking to an old family friend of yours, I guess—Alden Kosbleau. Mostly, he talked to me. Fascinating guy."

"What did he tell you?"

"He said he's going to grow a blue rose."

CHAPTER SEVEN

S HE SINKS into the chair at the far end of the porch, drifting in and out of a sleep brought on by exhaustion, her head falling away and snapping back. The last rays of sun catch the tops of the firs and the peeled skin of the madrona trees, flickering like candlelight across the bay from the home she owns in Seattle. Her house is grafted into the hillside just above the lake. Brunella could never live on flatland. She grew up on the high ground of an ancient coulee and bought this house in Seattle because it seemed to float over the water. She looks across the way at the lights from the construction cranes, the towers planted around one big site on the south shore of Mercer Island, then slips into sleep again. When she opens her eyes it is dark and she is chilled. The phone rings constantly. She can see the coming winter, the backyard smothered in gray. The rains should arrive soon, and she wants to bring it on—the darkness, the low ceiling, the perpetual drizzle, the layers of misted gloom—bring it on heavy.

Voice mail: Three calls from Leon Treadtoofar, the first one perplexed at her failure to show up in his office, the second giving her the benefit of the doubt, the third saying she does not have to talk with him, if that's what she wishes. Two from Roberto. He wants Brunella to reconsider what he said about moving Angelo out of the coulee. He says he is "angry, bordering on hurt," that she lashed out at him. A call from Ethan Winthrop, more condolence about Niccolo's death, need to talk about

Salmon Bay. Another call from Ethan, sounding desperate, please come by for dinner, sorry about being so forceful with her at the Smith Tower. And two calls from the fisherman Duff Almvik, one questioning her motive for suddenly deciding to take on Kornflint, the other asking for a cash advance.

She returns just one call, gets the usual range of robotics, leaves a message. "Don't insult me, Leon Treadtoofar."

She drives across the floating bridge to Mercer Island, down a lane shadowed by big-armed maples, past the construction cranes she has seen from across the lake, and on to Ethan's house. It looks unlived in, beige with white trim, three levels, a guesthouse in the back, a westward view of the city and the Olympic Mountains. In the front, no yard or garden, red gravel around two half-dead rhododendrons.

"You have to water these every now and then," she says, as Ethan greets her.

"They came with the house. I wasn't sure what to do with them. Come in."

Ethan tries to hug her but ends up patting her on the back. He is wearing a down vest over a plaid shirt.

"It's freezing in here," Brunella says. "What happened?"

"I keep it at fifty-seven," he says. "Any warmer and I start to feel clammy."

Her eyes are red, her hair mussed. She blows her nose a lot. Ethan says he went to the cavernous warehouse store at the edge of the city, his favorite place to shop, and bought fifty pounds of yellow goldfish crackers, three hundred rolls of toilet paper, and tonight's dinner.

"But you don't cook," Brunella says.

"With these, you don't have to cook." He shows her flank steak, ready for microwaving, and green beans in a plastic pouch.

"You can stay here, if you want, for a few days. I've got so much room. And I'm not as moody now that the clouds are supposed to return."

"Why did you buy such a big house?"

"For the piano."

"What piano?"

"The baby grand."

"Where?"

"Nowhere. I decided against it. But when I thought I would take up piano, naturally I needed a big enough house to hold my music." He programs the microwave. "Can you eat in two minutes?"

She shrugs. "So you bought a house for a nonexistent piano?"

"Brunella, I know this sounds perfunctory." He approaches her and tries again to offer a hug. His outstretched arm goes to her shoulders before he pulls it back in and quickly scratches his down vest. "I thought Niccolo was a great kid."

"How the hell do you know what he was like?"

"That day at the rodeo. He was very patient with me."

"But you didn't learn anything."

"You never know. How's your fisherman?"

"Needy."

"And?"

"We're doing an exhaustive search now for another fisherman, using some of the money that's just come in."

"We?"

"Some people who want to save the bay. Why should I tell you any of this?"

"Because I feel personally betrayed. You worked for us."

"I did."

"What now? Is this the end of our friendship?"

"I didn't know we had a friendship. You said I was the help."

"I shouldn't have been so aggressive at the Smith Tower. But you threw me. That was a complete surprise, Brunella. Tell me it was just a lapse, a brain warp of some sort."

"It wasn't. I could not in good conscience write off Salmon Bay after we knew there was somebody still working down there."

"Oh, please."

"Believe what you will. That fisherman and I, we are connected by water."

"You said that."

"I suppose I should apologize."

"At the least."

"I'm sorry, Ethan. That's the professional side of me talking. Not the heart."

"You know what this means. You may never get a big job on the West Coast again. We could sue you as well. Breach of contract."

"You paid me to be your conscience, and look what happened. That's not a breach. C'mon, Ethan, we have no past in this city. We erase everything."

"Maybe for good reason. Mr. Kornflint wants to add something better."

"And how authentic will it be?"

"Authentic? I don't see that word in the building code."

"Here we've got this great history, all these Scandies who fled Northern Europe and created a community where people passed on skills that date to . . . to the Vikings, for God's sake! It would be one thing if it was completely gone. But it's not. This guy Duff, yeah, he stinks and looks like a dufus. But he's the real deal, the living link to this terrific past that we're just supposed to junk like an old couch."

"Why keep it going if it can't stay alive on its own?"

Ethan serves the flank steak on paper plates, cuts open the plastic pouch of green beans, and pours water from a container with three inner filters.

"I don't share any of your . . . consuming passions, Brunella. I'm not hardwired for that kind of impulse attachment. You fall in love with things too easily: ideas, people, broken-down piers."

"It gets me in trouble."

"As it should. What you need is a better filter."

"A filter?"

"You know, I'm not without a sense of altruism."

"Oh?"

"After some deliberation, I've decided I'm going to adopt a stream," he says. "In Niccolo's honor. I would endow habitat preservation for perpetuity."

"And what is perpetuity selling for these days?"

"I don't have to do it, if you're offended."

"No, that's sweet of you."

He chews very slowly, eight times per bite.

"Why do you chew that way?"

"I've read three biographies of John D. Rockefeller. He was a stickler for precise mastication. He believed, and I think he was right, that it was a way to keep the stomach settled. He lived to be ninety-seven."

"How much are you worth, Ethan?"

"In money terms?"

This brings a faint smile to her face. "Yes. In money terms."

"I'm not sure. Between twenty and seventy million. Another thing Rockefeller did, he insisted that all his dinner guests chew in the same way he did. I think that's a little odd, don't you?"

She rises, wanders around the kitchen and out to the living room, and collapses on a couch. She sleeps until midmorning the next day.

A week passes in which Brunella tries to disappear within the city. Phone messages go unreturned. When the doorbell rings, she ignores it. She takes long walks in the sunlight that coats Seattle just before the wet season. Still, she craves the rain, the months of darkness, the boiled-spinach greens and metallic sheen of Lake Washington in winter. Bring it on. Hibernation is restorative, time to cook and read and make love, very slowly. She strolls along the lakefront, startled once by a great blue heron that waits until she is nearly upon it before it lifts off, retracting its long slender legs, displacing air with a slow unfolding wingspan the length of a bed. The autumn light has always been her favorite, angled and soft, the air full of hurried purpose. Rowing crews glide across the lake in the morning; sailboats are out riding the northern breezes in the evening. And the birds, the clacking masses following the Pacific flyway south. She hikes around Alki Point in West Seattle to the place where the city's founding party landed in 1851, the women crying at the thought that anyone would try to craft a city under skies so funereal. They huddled in a roofless cabin as the men fed them dreams of tomorrow in this place they wanted to call New York Alki, the last word a bit of Salish Indian jargon meaning *eventually*. She heads for the bistros and condos near downtown. In Belltown, where the hills were leveled, she sees the long-gone cliffs, the old ridgetops, the Victorian hotel that was destroyed a century ago, the Indian camps with their fish-drying poles. Because she knows what came before, she can walk the same neighborhood a dozen times and never see the same thing. She is a tourist in her own town, never bored.

She walks uphill and strolls the length of Capitol Hill, one of the few original nubs the city engineers did not try to shave off during the epic civic face-lift of the early twentieth century. She walks by the body-piercing shops, boulangeries, Thai restaurants, flower stalls, and gay book-stores to the north end at Volunteer Park, where she watches the sun duck behind the Space Needle, brass-tip the mountains, and disappear. In the muddy light, three boys in hoods and baggy pants approach her in menacing fashion. She picks up a rock and hits one of them with a quick throw. They scatter, and she thinks, Not a bad shot.

One night she wants to cook something earthy and rich, with chanterelle mushrooms from the Olympic rain forest and Barolo sauce, reduced and thick so it is like slow-moving blood. She spends a long hour in the organic food store as people with loose-fitting clothes and gray faces float around her in varying states of earnest fussiness. She gets stuck in a long checkout line, behind a woman who questions a teenage clerk about the origin of every bit of food in her cart, and tries not to be impatient, not to curse the dangling earrings, inverted shoes, and threadbare wear as a statement of solidarity with weavers somewhere in a warmer climate. She opens a magazine and gets engrossed in an article on tantric sex, which she imagines is to lovemaking what wheat germ is to dessert. But she is fascinated, reading about closing your eyes to let the other senses come alive, about slow touch, about building and channeling the slow buzz of the orgasm, about a transfer of energy from loin to loin without actually connecting, about men holding and sustaining but never exploding.

She meets a man in a coffee bar who talks about frescoes, telling her how the paint has to settle in with the wet plaster to create the image, but if you do it right the image will live for centuries. She tells him about her father's paintings in the coulee and about the erotic frescoes just uncovered in Pompeii, at least two thousand years old, the oldest surviving depiction of cunnilingus in Europe. She goes home with him, walking up the cleats in the sidewalk to get to his tiny house on the edge of an impossibly steep hill overlooking the distant lights of Husky Stadium. This city, it never fails to take her breath away. She spends most of the night discussing Giotto. She argues that Giotto, credited with the frescoes in Assisi, deserves more praise as the main designer of the campanile in Florence. He is Chinese-American, second generation, with a terrific laugh, hairless arms, and a smell like lavender, and he makes Brunella forget about her prison, though they never make love. In the morning, on the way out, she asks him his name.

She spends one long day at the fishing pier that Waddy Kornflint has already posted with official billboards notifying the public of change. A letter-writing campaign, timed volleys to the newspapers by reasoned citizens, has not moved Kornflint an inch. He does not read newspapers. Her appeals to the museum boards, the arts councils, and the preservation groups has been even more frustrating. All she wants is a chance to make her case, but they will no longer talk to her.

A short path from the pier leads Brunella to the locks, where boats pass from the freshwater of Lake Union in the city to the saltwater entrance of Puget Sound. She takes in a parade of vessels. When the gates of the locks close and water pours in to allow incoming boats to float up to the level of the lake, she crosses over on the footbridge and steps underground to a thick window with a view underwater. She stares at battered coho salmon swimming by, working against the current, oblivious to human eyes, to the three million people turning over dollars in the new metropolis all around them.

She ducks inside the Purple Door Tavern—instant night, circa 1962—to ask about Duff Almvik. The bartender tells her Duff was in for breakfast, and would she like some sausage floating in brine? Duff's boat, the bartender says, is across the bay, in drydock.

She finds him at the marine repair hangar. He takes a long pull from a beer, burps, offers Brunella a sip. She refuses.

"It's only backwash—and a bit warm—so I can see why you wouldn't want a swig," he says. "If I can get set up just south of Whidbey Island by tomorrow night, I should be happy drunk by Sunday night, closing down the Purple Door."

"Can I go with you?"

"No, ma'am, you cannot. I like to free-range when I'm on the water.

And God knows what I'd be like if had to hold my farts in on account of a woman."

"I wouldn't want you doing that. But let me go with you, Duff."

"It'd be wet, dark, and cold, like an armpit in winter."

"That's what I need right now."

"You get me some cash?"

"Just . . . a little nothing." She hands him three hundred dollars. "It's diesel money, I guess."

"That shows you got more than a grandstander's heart, Brunella Cartolano. And I do thank you. I still can't let you go with me. You might spook Loki."

"Your partner?"

"Loki is the Norse god, best friend a fisherman can have, long as you stay on his good side."

"Has Loki done you any favors lately?"

"No, ma'am. But he's gonna grease my passage to other side."

"You mean, help you live a long life and die in your sleep?"

"Fuck that. Norse warriors were ashamed to die of natural causes. It was a chickenshit way to go. These guys would take a knife to themselves tryin' to make the entry guards at Valhalla think they'd been killed in battle. You stroke Loki's back, he'll take you in without your having to carve yourself up at the end."

She takes out an object wrapped in newspaper inside her pack and hands it to Duff. "I got you something. You can offer it up to Loki if it helps."

He opens it and spits by the side, excited. "A sextant! Well, shit shanks!"

"From the late nineteenth century. You'll never get lost now."

"That's half the fun of fishing."

"Duff, aren't you worried?"

" 'Course I'm worried. I miss this run, and I'm drinking Buckhorn instead of Red Hook, and the *SoundGardener* goes another year without fresh paint."

"I mean, about what happens if this line of fish goes extinct because there isn't enough water on the other end. About Svenson's deli and that rust bucket of a dead ferry. About what happens when Kornflint takes over and the fishing sons of Almvik disappear from the water."

"I thought you were going to do the mental whining, and I was going to catch the fish."

"I am."

"Then let's get to it."

"But we have to find someone. Just one . . . other . . . fisherman. Somebody who does what you do. We have to show a community."

"This is some kinda crusade for you now, isn't it? It's personal."

"Your father—he was part of the biggest home port for salmon fishermen on the entire West Coast. Where did they go? They didn't just dry up overnight."

"There *is* one old dude—Tork Tollefson—used to fish outta here, left for Alaska, shit, ten years ago. I hear he's back."

"Where, Duff? Have you seen him?"

"He and I don't get along."

"Why?"

"A long story, one you don't wanna hear."

"I do, I do! Who could hate a fisherman?"

"Another fisherman. Hold your hopes. I'll do some sniffing around, but you keep your distance. I got enemies, lady—mile-back enemies."

Leon Treadtoofar has a corner office in the Forest Service regional headquarters in downtown Seattle. The building is a clump of Art Deco stone, designed to match the color of the rock on Mount Rainier. Leon seems surprised to see Brunella. He stands and extends both arms, a big smile.

"I'd written you off," he says.

"That wouldn't bother me, not one bit."

"You're hostile still. I don't know where that came from. Can I get you something?"

They drink herbal tea but she refuses to sit, prowling his office, fingering the different kinds of evergreen cones that line a windowsill. One of the smaller ones, though charred on the outside, has opened like a rose.

"Do you know what tree that came from?" Leon says.

"Pine."

"Lodgepole pine."

"It's been in a fire?"

"Yes, otherwise it wouldn't open. That cone is from Yellowstone, the big fire."

"The park has recovered."

"Because of fire. Lodgepole pine will not reproduce without it."

"So why have you people spent the last century trying to put out every fire in the West?"

Leon fiddles with a small machine. "Ms. Cartolano, I'd like to run a tape recorder."

"Fine. Strip-search me and videotape me, if you want."

"So you trust me now, enough to invite me to touch you?"

"I don't know you, so I don't trust you. And I certainly haven't invited you to touch me. But I want to believe what you have said from the start: that you will help me—us—find the truth. My family name is at stake. Niccolo's honor."

"You've got honor. I've got honor."

"And something more, Mr. Treadtoofar. There's some liability issues that could mean my family vineyard is on the line as well."

"An Indian doesn't break a promise."

"Oh. You're an Indian now? Not the government?"

"I'm going to start the tape. Someday I'll tell you what it's like to move between worlds."

"Tell me now."

"Will you come to dinner tonight?"

"On the Forest Service?"

"On me."

"Sorry." Brunella points to one of many pictures on the wall, this one a framed black-and-white shot of an Indian man in shoulder-length salt-and-pepper hair, standing next to a white man in a suit, in bright midday sunshine at a dusty locale. "Who's this?"

"That's Chief James with Governor Clarence Martin. The picture was taken in 1933, the day they turned the ceremonial first shovel to build Grand Coulee Dam."

"Look at him, wearing a suit in that glaring desert sun. That land looks like Mars."

"That's what the basin looked like in the summer, the shrub steppe ecosystem of the upper Columbia. Most of it's gone. They turned that shovel, and before long they were digging up Indian graves. Twelve thousand Indian graves. Think there's another cemetery in America where that many bodies have been yanked from the ground?"

"And this picture?" She points to a football player in purple-and-gold uniform, number six, signed at the bottom.

"How long have you lived in Seattle, Ms. Cartolano—ten years, something like that—and you don't know who that is?"

"I'm sorry."

"Sonny Sixkiller, the Washington quarterback. He's the reason why I left the reservation. I came to Seattle, to the university, because of him."

"Were you a football player? You seem tall enough to play any sport."

"Never played anything but the twelve-string guitar, which I learned in Missoula after college, my entry job with the Forest Service. Sonny Sixkiller was the first Indian I ever heard do something great—who wasn't dead. First Indian I ever saw on the cover of *Sports Illustrated*. Probably the *only* Indian. Take away the fact that he was an Indian and you got something else: He was the greatest quarterback in this state. Okay, let's get started, please. Relax. Your hair is very nice today."

"My hair?"

"That's off the record. Here we go: Your brother, Niccolo Cartolano, had a late dinner at the family residence on Sunday the fifth of August, is that correct?"

"Yes."

"And he consumed a quantity of alcoholic beverages?"

"He drank some wine. My father opened a special bottle."

"You had been at the rodeo that evening, the Omak Stampede?"

"Yes, with Teddy Flax. Have you heard from him?"

"I have not. He was badly burned and seems to have left the region. Nobody has seen him since the hospital."

"I know."

"And did you observe your brother consume a quantity of alcoholic beverages at the rodeo?"

"He may have had a beer. Do you mind if I stand while I talk?"

"Why?"

"I need some room. I . . . uh . . ." She unrolls the fingers of her right hand, looking for the word.

"You're very expressive with your hands, I notice."

"It's Italian. I can't fight it."

"Please remain seated, if you will. So by this time it's late, you're at your family home, and he's had how much to drink?"

"Nothing, a couple of beers. And my father opened a bottle, a 1978, I think, which was an extraordinary year for the Cartolano Nebbiolo."

"Nebbiolo, that's a wine?"

"It's a grape, used to make the great northern Italian wines. You've heard of Barolo, also known as the King of Wines? They said you couldn't make a Barolo in the New World. My father pioneered the American version in our coulee."

"What would be the specific quantity that Niccolo consumed that night, Ms. Cartolano?"

"He had two glasses, I would guess, maybe less."

"And then what?"

"And then he . . . and then we sat around the kitchen table and laughed about what it used to be like when we were younger. Niccolo never had much of an appetite as a kid, which is hard to believe now, because he's a such a big vacuum for food. My father would not let him leave the table until he finished the meal. Roberto and I would go off and do our homework, or play outside, and Niccolo would still be at the table. And one time my father put a blanket over his shoulders and set a pillow down on the table, right next to his pork chops. He slept there."

"And did you observe him consume a quantity of alcoholic beverages during this reminiscence? Or, later, pack any bottles into his smoke jumper bag?"

"No. No! This is torture. I observed him laughing, and I saw my *babbo* laugh, and for the first time since before my mother died we were a happy family, and then we all went to bed, and I have no idea how long he slept or whether he slept well. But the next day we went for a walk in the vineyard and he looked fine and then he was gone and I never saw him again and I love him so much that the pain will never go away. So fuck you."

He turns off the tape and grabs her by the arm, forcefully marching her out of the office, past a secretary, several cubicles, to the stairs. They walk to the basement, and he guides her to a locked door. Inside are shovels, chain saws, pumps, all of them blackened by fire and marked by tags. He pulls one pump forward and tells her to stand back as he fires it up. He lets it run, though the sound is painfully loud. He turns it off and faces her, his lip trembling.

"The pump works," he says, all the charm gone from his face, a frightful temper unleashed. "There was nothing wrong with it. You want me to start another one? All three work! And yet . . . those Indian boys cooked to death. Those jumpers cooked to death. This would have saved them. All your brother had to do was be on his game. All he had to do was have his wits about him, be enough of a man, be strong, be enough of a smoke jumper to do what he was trained to do, and those Indian boys would be home with their wives and their girlfriends and their mothers, laughing around a table."

CHAPTER EIGHT

URING THE FIRST WEEK of October the sun holds the grapes in a fleeting embrace, and every grower has a decision to make. Already, the nights are so cold that frost whiskers the vines at the higher reaches of the coulee and the pond is topped by thin ice crystals. A cartwheel of heavy clouds is rolling westward toward the coast and could bring the first snow to the Cascades. But even if it blows north and misses the Columbia basin, the ration of light and heat will soon be gone. Timing is everything in harvesting grapes. Pick early, before the fruit is at full ripeness, and the wine will be tart and astringent. Pick late, when the flavor has peaked, and the must will hint of a wan taste to come later. But pick just right, in the morning after the dew has evaporated, when the skins of the grapes are wrapped tight, the fruit is firm, the sugars are in place, and the acidity has leveled from the big dip in nighttime temperatures, and that convergence of light and chemistry will be embedded in the wine for maybe half a century, holding the epilogue of a story about all the quirks of one year that is never an exact duplicate of another. Someday this grape juice will be described as magnificent and silky with overtones of cedar, or velvety with a touch of cherry, or it will be used as lubricant in a proposal of love or partnership, but in essence it is just one thing—memory in a bottle.

Miguel has two dozen pickers ready to go; he has learned well the details of a perfect harvest and picked up much about the winemaking craft. But he cannot tell his pickers when to start—that job has always belonged to Angelo. There are scientific measures—brix levels, skin thickness, opacity—that most growers use. For Angelo, it comes down to instinct, taste, and superstition.

When Brunella crosses the Columbia after a three-hour drive from Seattle, she sees that some growers are harvesting grapes close to the river, mainly Syrah. The fields are cluttered with workers guiding shaking machines along rows of fruit and moving the grapes to trucks, to separating machines, and on to crushers. The big cottonwoods are holding their gold. She walks among the pickers and samples the grapes. The Syrah is pungent, with purple skin the color of a swollen eye, but the winemaker's daughter does not trust her palate. Angelo has the gift. She can see him walking through the vineyards in early fall, putting grapes into his mouth, crunching the seeds, spitting them out with a shake of his head: *Troppo giovane, troppo giovane.* And when the day comes that he rushes back to alert his pickers that the grapes are ripe and must be picked at once, the flavor has to be captured right now, then he will not stop for days, even to sleep, until all the fruit is in the crushing shed.

Beyond the Syrah vineyard, at the river's edge, three Indians scamper atop a primitive wood platform hanging over the Columbia. Brunella grew up with this image as well, the daredevil boys from the tribe engaged in the oldest human activity along the river, trying to net big fall chinook, the last salmon to come up the river, as much a part of autumn as high school football and Halloween displays. She wanders over to the platform. The Indians are not fishing this morning; their long dip-net poles are on the bank. They appear to be pacing, watching the river as if waiting for a train to arrive.

"Tozzie!" she yells out. "Tozzie, how are you?"

"Hiya," says Tozzie Cresthawk, and turns back quickly to stare at the water from his platform above the river. They search the slow-moving Columbia, oblivious to the grape harvest, trying to find something deep in the river.

"Any chinook?" she asks. "I heard there's a decent run this year of upriver brights."

"Nothing yet."

"So you've taken over the Flax homestead?"

"Not me. It's a tribal thing."

"Well, whatever. We're neighbors, then. I'm helping my father with the harvest this year. You interested in earning some extra money?"

"Do I look like a wet to you?"

"We're paying twelve bucks an hour."

"I don't pick fruit," Tozzie Cresthawk says, "and I don't prune trees. I fight fires and I race horses in the Stampede and I fish."

"You still ought to come by. Visit for a while."

"Yeah," Tozzie says, turning to his friends. "Come by. Look it over. Look it all over. The big land, grapes and apples from ridgetop to ridgetop. One day my dad took me up one of them ridges you got all fancied up in that coulee there. Said, 'Take a look, son.' I looked out. 'Take a long look, son.' Yep. Says, 'One day, none of this will be yours.' "

The Indians laugh and slap hands. Brunella forces a half smile. "Why won't you talk to Leon Treadtoofar? Help him with the investigation?"

"I don't remember nothing, so I can't say nothing."

"Storm's coming on."

"I hope it does," Tozzie says. "Hope it rains hard for days on end. Just a piss pour. That's what the fish need. Sends a signal. They start to move upstream."

"I know the fish need it. But the timing is bad for grapes."

"I don't give a shit about grapes. Rain is good for fish."

Angelo has moved into Niccolo's room. He spends most of the day there and sleeps in his son's bed at night. He has been touring Niccolo's life, rummaging through books, the Boy Scout emblems, the miniature go-cart they carved from a block of spruce, the radio he made by wrapping copper coil around a toilet-paper holder, the baseball signed by Edgar Martinez, the slingshot he used to hit birds, notes from girlfriends, high school pictures, a shot of Niccolo in midair diving from a cliff at Lake Chelan. When Brunella arrives, Angelo is holding Niccolo's mitt, listening to a one-game play-off between Texas and Seattle for the American League West title; they have finished the season in a tie. He is pale, the eyes that once had so much color moist and gray. Brunella sits on the bed next to him and strokes his back, following the game with him, unable to shake the feeling that Angelo has become a very old man in a very short time.

Baseball gives them a shared hope, a three-hour drama into which they have invested the fantasy that their way of life will triumph over the excesses of a bigger, more bulked-up and monied team from a place with different values. The Mariners build an early lead on a walk and three back-to-back singles, but that's it for their offense. In the ninth, Texas loads the bases and brings the American League home-run king to the plate. Brunella can't stand it; she turns the radio off.

"Wait," Angelo says. "Leave it on." The Mariner closer gets the power hitter to ground into a double play for the game; Seattle wins by a run, advancing to the American League play-offs.

"They're better without Griffey and A-Rod," says Angelo. "Niccolo doesn't think so. I told him that when Griffey left years ago. I said, You watch, they will be better. And then A-Rod left, and I said, You just watch, you just wait. They didn't need those guys."

"I'm going to cook something for you tonight, Babbo. *Costoletta di vitelo,* like you used to do it."

"Did you bring any of the big clams over—those goo-ducks?"

"Gooey ducks. I didn't."

"Those clams are something. I love the *vongole grande.*"

"Babbo, have you ever thought of remodeling this room? You might want to push a dormer out, just to keep with the farmhouse theme."

"Theme? I didn't know I'd been living a theme all these years. You think this old house needs a new look, Miss Bigshot?"

"No, I didn't mean that. But you could open the north side as well, let a little more light in during the winter. Something passive."

"You go cook your *costoletta* and leave the old house alone."

In the kitchen, she sips from a Chianti Classico and sings along with Chrissie Hynde, "Gonna use my sidestep, gonna use my fingers, gon' use my, my, my imagination. . . ." She chops onions, tomatoes, throws in hazelnuts and basil leaves, squeezes lemon over it, and sets it aside, all while pleading with her father.

"We have to pick the grapes, Babbo. Miguel can't keep the crew much longer. But I don't know what to do. There's a storm coming."

She pounds the veal cutlets on each side, softening the meat, dips them in an egg batter, and covers them with bread crumbs and garlic.

"Should we pick tomorrow? If we wait, we might lose everything."

"They're better without Griffey and A-Rod. I told Niccolo that, and he didn't believe me."

"Babbo, listen! We have to make a decision! I feel like this whole harvest thing is a giant game of chicken."

"Your pan needs to be hotter," he says. "You only need to fry the meat a few minutes on each side. But it won't be *costoletta alla Milanese* unless your pan is hot. And you forgot something."

"What's that?"

He sniffs. "Smell it."

"I don't have your palate, Babbo."

"Oregano. Use the little flower tops of the herb instead of the leaves. When you pinch and rub it with your fingers, the flavors will be released. People always forget to pinch 'em."

Miguel eats with them. He says he loves the veal cutlets topped with onions and tomato mix. "Like pork." Angelo pokes at the meat, picks it apart, but does not take a single bite. The phone rings, and Brunella answers: a call from France.

"Are you sure? . . . Yes . . . oh, my God! That's wonderful." She scribbles a note down on a sheet of paper. "Uh-huh . . . yes . . . uh-huh. Thank you." She puts down the phone and rushes back to the table.

"You're not going to believe this, Babbo: Your Nebbiolo won a gold medal at VinFaire!"

"Ah." Angelo removes his plate from the table.

"Babbo, do you realize what this means? Yours was the only American red wine to get a gold medal. That's fantastic! It means you have made one of the finest wines in the world from this vineyard of yours. You . . . you have made history."

"I don't want anything to do with it."

"They said—here, I wrote something down real quick, from the critics—'subtle and fascinating, with focused shoe leather on the nose.'"

"What's that, shoe leather on the nose? I don't understand. I want nothing to do with shoes on the nose. I don't make such a thing. I make a *vino rosso* to enjoy, to last, to have a story. Nothing else. The French can have all the shoe leather on the nose."

He retreats outside, where he keeps one old hen in a shed near the pond. Brunella, strolling the grounds, can hear her father talking to the hen, with nothing in return. She goes back inside and sits alone at the big table as the vineyards go dark and the wind kicks at the shutters.

She knows the storm has arrived when the wind goes into a gallop, racing through the coulee and straining the big pines at the edge of their house. The trees groan as their trunks bend, and rain batters the windows in rolling waves. She goes downstairs in the darkness and makes tea. Rainwater squeezes in beneath a windowsill. She sits in the kitchen, sipping the tea, shivering, overcome by a sense of doom with a force like gravity. First the fire, now the storm. How quickly the coulee has gone from an irrigated Eden, bathing in late-summer luminescence, to a battleground for the bullies of nature. The big walls of the scoured-out land no longer seem like shelter. The front door blows open. Brunella jumps back, knocking her tea over, afraid that somebody has invaded the house. She cowers behind the stove, the old Great Western that Angelo purchased for five dollars from a retreating homesteader who didn't believe the government would ever deliver water to the coulee country.

"Go away! Go away!"

She feels again as if she's trapped in the tiny ditch she saw from the plane at age seventeen, the fly-over country, the isolated slit in the earth. She is locked in while the world is out there, beyond the coulee, beyond the storm, a hive of lives, dinner parties at full throttle, the great jostle of ideas, laughter, and drama of the city. After a few minutes, she looks back at the door and sees nobody. For an instant, she feels her mother's presence; the walls are damp and cold with the death chill, the very thing that has kept her away from this house for three years. She creeps forward, bare feet numb in a puddle of rain that has leaked onto the scuffed fir floor. She slams the door shut. Now it is her prison. Back upstairs, in bed, she wants another body next to hers and wonders what Teddy would feel like now.

For most of the day, the rain comes in horizontal sheets, plastering the coulee. She frets as she waits, calling around to her father's friends. Many of the growers have already harvested, and they feel blessed—Brunella detects some smugness—in getting the fruit in before the rain. Again, she asks Angelo for guidance, but he will not leave Niccolo's room; it is his shelter. In late afternoon, she wraps herself in rain pants and shell and goes for a walk. The dahlias, which were erect and full-flowered just twenty-four hours ago, have all been knocked to the ground; some are uprooted and black-spotted. The oranges in their big terra-cotta containers will have to be moved inside to the *limonaia,* or they will lose them. The vineyards are muddy; rivulets of brown water are coursing down the gullies between rows. Many grapes have been slapped to the ground; she can't help thinking of them as roadkill, smudged and squished against the mud. They are going to lose it all, she senses: an entire vintage. She walks to the crest, to the small stone chapel built by her father, stands in the rain just outside the chapel door, and feels the backhand of God—a hard slap. Bring it on. Hit me.

A pickup truck roars into the coulee. Alden Kosbleau steps from the new truck, wearing shorts and a windbreaker. He looks at Brunella, wet and blank-faced, and takes in the battlefield of still-hanging grapes.

"Jesus efffing Christ, Brunella, when the hell are you people going to pick?"

"Alden, thank God. Talk to Babbo."

"Look at these grapes. You wait any longer you're gonna have nothing but raisins. Pick! For God's sake, get the fruit in."

"Talk to Babbo. He's the only one who can give the go-ahead."

A call from Emma—*Meet me in town for a drink at the Windmill*—is Brunella's chance to get away for a night. At dusk the town seems to have closed up, wet and abandoned: a superstore, some minimarts, two drive-throughs peddling food hatched in a chemist's lab in the Midwest, a cop working the same speed trap he worked when Brunella was in high school, and that's it. Except for the Windmill, the special-occasion restaurant, where wedding receptions take place, and the first real date. The closer Brunella gets to the Windmill, the tighter her throat gets. Again, that feeling—she is trapped. In a town without a stoplight, she feels claustrophobic. She pulls her car into the Windmill parking lot but cannot get out. The walls of the town are pressing in on her, and she cannot bear it. Don't bury me here! She drives away, racing back to the coulee. Emma calls, furious and drunk. *You stood me up.*

In the morning on the second day of the storm, Brunella is in the highest part of the coulee when the clouds start to break. She has been wandering for hours and finds herself at the edge of the fire, where Gregory Gorton has put in grapes and a big ornamental garden, forming a line of geometric green against the ashen border of the ghost forest.

Brunella runs her hands through the gray coals of the deadened land. It smells of a sour campfire that has hissed into submission, and it looks odd; there are water bubbles throughout. The rain cannot penetrate the seared soil. She wonders if this ground will ever hold life again. She tiptoes through the spectral forest, remembering all the sage grouse this time of year with their puffed-up white chests, and her father's line that sage grouse were frisky and beautiful to watch, but they were even better grilled. She angles back to the high point of the coulee. From this summit, she sees more dead land in the distance. She recognizes it by the big boulders at the edge of the ridge. This is where the jumpers died; she saw it from the air. She tries to descend but cannot bring herself to move downward.

On the way back home, near the border where the ghost forest meets the 206ers' property, she hears a sound like that of a stream, a gurgling. She follows the sound to the edge of the new plantings, to a talus field, and then beyond, where she tracks it to the source: a small geyser of water, bursting out of the ground, like a spring that will form a river. To the touch, the water is glacier-cold. The water cascades into a holding tank that leads to a large underground pipe, and then it disappears. Brunella has never seen such a thing: a gusher of freshwater from somewhere in the earth that is quickly corralled and directed right back into the ground.

"Hey!" A man's voice, directed at her. She can't see where it's coming from. "You there! What are you doing?"

She ducks behind the talus field.

.   .   .

Back at the house, she rushes in to tell Angelo about her discovery, but he is not in Niccolo's room. Miguel has not seen him either. The door to the old wine cellar is open and the light is on. She hurries down the creaky stairs.

"Babbo?"

A cabinet door is open, with a light on above it. She finds a thick homemade book—Angelo's water charts. There are pencil notations indicating the volume of water used every year on his grapes. Last year, she notices, is a huge upward spike. On the table, she sees his gun, a Luger that he got in a trade with one of the climbers from the Last Man's Club: a case of Nebbiolo for the German pistol.

She fingers the gun; it is still warm, and half the chamber has been emptied. She glances around the cellar, skittish, calling weakly for her father. Miguel appears at the top of the stairs.

"You better come, Brunella," he says, out of breath, "to the new cellar."

She flies up the stairs, runs outside across the courtyard, past the fountain and the rose garden. In mid dash, she slips on the wet ground, falling face first in the mud. The door is open in the stone cellar—the new cellar, they call it—built when Angelo was starting to feel flush. Inside, she sees an ax on the floor with red on the blade, and wine running in a stream, pulled toward the drain. The cellar smells of raw leather and oak, an overwhelming scent.

"What happened here?"

Miguel moves a barrel perforated with bullet holes, slashed at one end. He taps it. "Empty." He does the same thing to several other casks, all of which have been violently ripped open and drained.

"Where are you, Babbo?" Brunella shouts.

"This is the gold-medal vintage," says Miguel. "Somebody has destroyed us. It's all gone. They even took the hen. You know the shed, Brunella; somebody must have broken in. There are feathers all over the floor. We have to call the sheriff."

Brunella staggers outside, her shoes drenched in gold-medal wine, face caked with mud. The clouds are gone, and a heavy wind cleans out the coulee, a dry northerly breeze. The highest flank is burnished by the last light of the day, and it draws her upward. She wanders up to the edge of the coulee, where she looks out over the storm-scuffed vineyards of the Cartolano estate, away to the far west, where Mount Stuart is aglow.

At dusk, on her walk back, a wisp of smoke comes from the house. She can smell it before she enters: sausage blended with garlic and tomatoes. She finds her father standing over the stove, the old man directing a quartet of burners.

"*Ho fame,*" says Angelo.

"Where have you been?"

"*Ho fame.*"

"Me too. Is it—?"

"*Sì. Pappardelle con salsiccia e pomodoro.*"

He makes his tomato sauce the Bolognese way, browning thick spicy sausages in order to draw out the juices that form the stock. He empties a basket of tomatoes into boiling water, rumbling them just long enough so the skins will slide off easily. Then he smashes the peeled cored tomatoes and throws them in a bigger pan, which contains juices from the sausage. Into this mix go garlic, oregano, chopped onions, and a handful of basil leaves.

"It's so simple I could make this blind," says Angelo.

"And this?" She sniffs at a giant pot, stuffed with a large slow-simmering bird.

"My old girlfriend from the shed."

"Not—?"

"*Sì. Gallina vecchia fa buono brodo.*"

"Of course," she says, tearing up. "An old hen makes a good broth. I'm so happy to see the life has returned to you, Babbo."

Brunella points to a bandage wrapped around Angelo's thumb. "I cut myself with an ax," he says.

"An ax? It was you who did all that damage in the cellar?"

"I think I got rid of it all. Two rounds from the Luger, finished off with the ax."

"Why would you ever—?"

"Because I cheated. Don't think any less of me, Nella, but I cheated last year. I took a shortcut. I tried to oak-chip the wine, to do in a few months what should take years because I was afraid it would be weak and not up to my name. We had so little water last year, I got scared, and then I got greedy and used more water than I'm supposed to take—"

"Your charts?"

"Sì. You saw them? Let me explain. I almost flooded the vineyard last year, but you want to know something? It didn't help. It made things worse. The grapes were shit. Today I asked God to forgive me, and maybe he will. I don't know about God anymore, because I heard nothing back."

"You destroyed the best American wine of the year?"

"Says who? The French and those wine people who flock to Bordeaux like pigs to their slop? What do they know?"

"What do they know? Food, wine, and love, for starters, Babbo, but then—"

"They hide the true taste of their food in all that sauce, Nella. You think they would ever cook an old hen like this, just for the juice? Their so-called best wines are overrated and overpriced. Their true best wines are unknown. You give me a little *vino* of the country—I forget what they call them—from the south. *Per amore,* why do you think the French invented perfume? Same reason they cover a decent piece of meat in a blanket of sauce. I'm done with it. It's gone—all of last year's vintage—gone, back into the ground. *Finito. Morto.*"

"That's why you wanted to start fresh, with Niccolo and this year's crop?"

"Sì."

"So this is what, your feast of thanks?"

"My appetite came back. But the reason I'm hungry, Nella, is because I feel like a man again."

A woolen fog holds the coulee air down at night, just at the freezing point, and when it lifts in midmorning the vineyard looks glorious, as if everything has been scoured new by the storm. When Brunella opens the window upstairs she hears a bell ringing from somewhere out in the vineyard and her father singing.

He appears in waders and suspenders, wearing his sweat-salted Mariners cap, with a basket full of grapes. He says it is a morning like fall in the Piemonte, when the fog—the *nebbia* that gives the vines of Barolo its name—rolls out over the hills. Angelo nibbles on little bunches of grapes. Reflectively, he swishes the mash around in his mouth, wrinkles his nose, spits, and takes another bite. He nods in satisfaction. Now he squeezes one bunch at a time, holding the grapes tight, then slowly letting his grip go, testing the resistance. He drops the basket and slaps his hands.

"It's time," he says. "Don't let us waste a minute. It's time. *L'uva è matura.*"

In the Cartolano vineyard, the picking has always been done by hand. Many growers use mechanical sorters, which look like the kind of four-wheeled rig used to shave brush from a roadside and can clean a row of grapes in minutes. But the industrial harvest runs the risk of breaking seeds, which can impart a bitter substance. The Cartolanos equip their pickers with handheld shears and teach them to cut the grapes at a forty-five-degree angle on the stem about three inches from the cluster.

"*Mettiamoci al lavoro!*" Angelo says to Brunella, his call to work, handing her a basket and shears, revved up for the harvest. Perhaps a third of this year's fruit was lost to the storm, but Angelo is anything but heartbroken. The grapes still hanging are robust and flavorful—the survivors. The storm, he says, was nature's way of culling out the inferior fruit.

"And look here," he says, picking a single grape and holding it up to the light, "they should all be this good. No cracks. No leaking juice. No sunburn."

In the course of a long day, the picking crew brings in nearly half the grapes. They are not washed, so that that the powdery resin remains; it contains a natural yeast that helps with the kind of fermentation used in making the great Barolos. Angelo believes there are some very good winemakers with excellent palates, but no great ones—only great grapes. It is the winemaker's job to see that the fruit lives to tell its full story.

Most of the day's harvest goes immediately into the crusher, where the stems, seeds, and skins are flattened into a thick pulp, the *mosto,* as Angelo calls the initial phase of unfermented juice. Nebbiolo's color comes from the skin and is released during the crush. Bees swarm around the fruit; it is a constant fight to avoid getting stung.

Brunella tells her father about her discovery.

"I saw an enormous amount of water, Babbo, coming from underground and then being channeled off somewhere," she says. "Do you know anything about it?"

Angelo shakes his head.

"Right up there on the ridgeline."

"That does not sound right." There is only one natural source of water in this parched bowl, he explains: a small aquifer deep in the ground, which feeds into the little salmon stream at the edge of the Cartolano land and from which the wells in the coulee draw their extra water. The irrigation water that brings everything to life starts with the Columbia River, he tells her, just behind the Grand Coulee Dam. A massive siphon sucks the water three hundred feet up from the reservoir behind the dam and directs it downhill into what used to be the hollowed-out tub of the original Grand Coulee. From there, it goes into several major arteries, moving out in all directions, and then breaks into a series of smaller canals that lead to ditches and ultimately to the coulee.

"Nobody runs water up from the ground and back into the ground, Nella," he says.

"But I saw it, Babbo. Up on the bench."

"Who knows what you saw," says Angelo, poking his hand into the *mosto*. "Take a look at that color, Nella. You may not see that again in your lifetime. God, that's wonderful!"

Alden Kosbleau shows up again on day two of the harvest, ready to help. Angelo is happy to see his old friend, the water king. Kosbleau tells the Cartolanos about his winter plans: He will go to Belize to fly-fish in the saltwater shallows, followed by a six-week cruise of the Caribbean.

"Provided, of course, that nothing holds me here," he says. "You haven't got some trouble brewing, do you, Brunella? I hear you've been talking to the government."

"You hear . . . ?"

"Talking to the government. Let me tell you something, born out of experience: You let a rapist into your house before you let those bastards cross the threshold."

"But you yourself talked to the investigator," Brunella says to Kosbleau.

"Just long enough to size him up."

At the end of the day, the grapes are all in and the *mosto* has been transferred to big open vats. Some vintners add yeast and sugar at this stage, hoping to make slightly more alcohol and produce a bigger, more fruit-forward wine. Angelo prefers to let the juice become wine in the way Italians have done since the Etruscans stored grape juice in terra-cotta jugs. He simply lets the sugars and yeast go at it, making alcohol. The *mosto* undergoes primary fermentation in big stainless-steel tanks and must be punched down by hand around the clock. The tanks are filled to within a foot of the top, allowing for expansion during the most vigorous stage of fermentation. Alden, Miguel, and Brunella take turns punching down the heavy material that floats to the top, but otherwise they leave it alone.

"This vintage will be Niccolo's," Angelo says. "And with this wine he will never leave us."

Now that the heavy work is over, Brunella prepares to go home, leaving the winemaking to her father, with some help from Alden Kosbleau.

"I want to thank you for what you've done, Alden. You are like family."

"I am family," he says. "As much as any non-Italian can be family."

"So, you watch over my father, okay? Don't let him do anything stupid."

"He watches over *me*. He's afraid I'm going to outlive him and get that bottle in your cellar." He moves closer to her, confidential. "Brunella. Tell me what the government is trying to do to you. Maybe I can help. I've given an untold amount of money to a lot of political campaigns over the years, and I'm not without connections in Congress."

"It's all around the coulee. You know the kind of questions."

"They're blaming it on Niccolo, aren't they? Is that what that Indian bastard is trying to do?"

"I'm not sure where he's going, Alden. He's just . . . doing a job. But I will clear the family name."

"So you must. And that's what took you up to the bench a couple days ago?"

"How did you know about that?"

"I sold that two-oh-sixer Gorton a couple thousand acre-feet of water a few years ago, when it looked like the Indians planned to start going after our water. He's a nervous Nellie, like most of these dumb shit heels from the city, so he's always calling me before he lets his brain kick in. Somebody saw you up on the ridge, near his place, and he called me. Said you were snooping."

"Is that what they call a *passeggiata*?" says Brunella.

"I may be like family, but my Italian's not so good."

"I took a little walk. But I know what I saw up there."

"And what was that?"

"Enough water coming out of the ground to flood this coulee up to my father's porch."

"Out of the ground?"

"Yes, and then right back into the ground."

"And you saw this?"

"I did."

"Did you talk to your father about it?"

"Only in passing. His mind's on other things."

"Did you tell the Indian about it?"

"No. What do you make of it, Alden?"

"Wasn't supposed to be much water left up there. But I'm never surprised anymore, Brunella, by anything in the water game. People think it's static, like property. Tell you what: There isn't any such thing as still water. Another thing, what you see ain't what there is. Most of the water in this *en*-tire basin is out of sight, underground. That's how folks get confused. They only see what's on the surface. Did you get pictures, documentation?"

"No. But we can go up there now, if you want, and I'll show you."

"I believe you. Let me look into it."

On the drive out she passes the old Flax homestead. Two teams of Indians are working in the burned-over orchards, dismantling the irrigation pipes that brought water to the apples. At the spot where the family home was torched, some Indian women have set up food next to a big bonfire. They are cooking hot dogs on cedar sticks planted in the ground and placed next to the fire. Brunella stops to chat, asking about their plans for the old Flax farm.

"We don't have any plans," says a large woman, middle-aged, in a

T-shirt that barely covers her belly with LAS VEGAS written over the front. "We have hope."

"For what?"

"Starting something. Giving some water back to the salmon. Getting people to think about the future."

The woman asks Brunella to join them, pointing with open hands to quarts of Diet Coke, pitchers of lemonade, fruit pies, flatbread, corn that's been seared on the fire, bowls of chips.

"As you know, we Indian people come from a long line of Diet Coke drinkers," the woman tells Brunella, and all the other Indian women laugh. "But before that, before the Europeans came, we were Pepsi drinkers."

She stops at the coulee's edge, the asphyxiated stream where she saw the dead fish. This is home, the birthing waters and the grave, for the run of chinooks—the Coulee Kings—that keeps Duff in business. She might be able to save Duff's pier, she thinks, but what about this little ribbon of life? Without water, the fish will return to an arid death. It will be the end of the line. A thought occurs to Brunella: Maybe Ethan was playing her, and the reason he agreed to come to the coulee in August was to check on the stream that might have stood in the way of Kornflint's project. He wasn't curious about the West of rodeos, mountain meadows, and thunderstorms. He wanted to track a salmon run to its source. Or maybe not. How could he have known about Duff and the stream?

Crossing the river, she is puzzled by the expanding foundation of the Indian construction site. The footings cover several acres. Bulldozers are excavating basalt and clay and moving it onto trucks, creating an enormous primitive pit. She detours to a cliff, passing the homestead she saw with Ethan late in the summer, to the dead-end road beyond the fence. She gets out of the car and walks to the high rock perch above the Columbia. She shivers in the wind, looking for the familiar petroglyphs. She touches them, as before, and feels a current, as before, from the etched image of three humans, lively on the rock, chasing antlered animals. But they look flat today, less telling, hiding their story in the stone.

CHAPTER NINE

THE CITY FEELS sleepy at midmorning, ferries tracking back and forth across the impressionist Puget Sound, nobody raising a voice or honking a horn in the filtered sunlight. Brunella is glad to be back in the urban fold. Her routine takes her to Pike Place Market, to banter with the guitar-playing bluesman in front of the brass pig and to trade sex jokes with the fish merchant who sells giant clams, the geoducks that her father craves and that make tourists blush. Walking through the market, she ducks to avoid a fish tossed across the aisle to the counter. And when the salmon are not flying at head level, they are lighting alleys in bright neon, or holding candles in craft stalls, or going uphill, embedded in the sidewalk. An anthropologist new to the Pacific Northwest would find more fish icons than crucifixes.

At lunch, she orders iced tea and shellfish gumbo and tells her friend how good she looks. Audrey Finkelstein is Brooklyn born, dressed in a short black skirt and tights, her hair a cataract of midnight curls. Audrey and Brunella used to share a cubicle at the most promising design firm in Seattle, Tusa & Associates. When it seemed certain that the big public market downtown was going to be bulldozed, the young architects at Tusa led the cause to save it. The firm had gone on to design buildings that reached into the clouds, to draw schools, museums, and summer homes, enclosing dreams in timber and glass for the city's new wealthy class. Their prosperity had made most of the architects flush, paunched, and politically powerful, though they seldom took risks anymore.

Audrey is obsessing about her latest passion, scuba diving. She spent the weekend underwater near the San Juan Islands, playing with octopi.

"They're not that stupid, for mollusks," she says. "Very selective in what they nosh on. The bigger ones, they're like my Uncle Izzy at a wedding."

"And this is somebody, I imagine, whose pants are pulled above his waist—"

"He has no waist. Just three expanding chins and a tush."

"When is the last time you were with a man, Audrey?"

"Why?"

"Forget the question. So here's my pitch for the Yodas at Tusa: Are you familiar with that little hangout called Hat 'n' Boots? It was *the* drive-in for the postwar generation, and now it's a part of quirky Seattle that's slipping away, the Seattle of the Dog House and the Jell-O Mold building and—"

"Brunella, I don't think Hat 'n' Boots—or for that matter, the Dog House or the Jell-O Mold building—would ever meet the criteria for landmarking."

"No, no, and neither do I. But if you folks join me in a show of force in front of the abandoned shell of Hat 'n' Boots, before the television cameras, it's a way to talk about forgotten everyday treasures and what they mean to a city that's in danger of becoming like any other place. That big goofy oversize hat and the twenty-foot cowboy boots—c'mon, it's a classic of retro whimsy. Nirvana shot their first videos down there. You guys bring some clout: the link with the fight to save the market by all the founders of the firm. Then we use that to talk about Salmon Bay."

"Have you been to Cannery Row, Brunella?"

"In Monterey. Of course. And before that I was there with Steinbeck: 'a poem, a stink, a grating noise, a quality of light, a tone, a habit, a nostalgia, a dream.' I'll never forget that opening."

"You know what Cannery Row is now?"

"A theme park, probably. The core has been preserved, hasn't it?"

"But there aren't any fishermen. And there aren't any working canneries. And there aren't any rum-swilling one-legged old souls who inspired your beloved Steinbeck."

"So what are you saying?"

"You can freeze a building. You can freeze a pier, a cannery. But that doesn't keep alive what you're trying to protect. The surface is there, but the soul is gone—isn't that the way you put it in one of those No Significant Impact statements that made you such a high-priced ticket?"

"How do you know the soul is gone?"

"All right. How many working fishermen hang out at this pier you've adopted, Brunella? I'm not talking old salt mannequins."

"There's Duff Almvik, of course . . . and—a lot of rumors. Maybe one other. I'm looking. You're working for Kornflint, aren't you?"

"We have several projects. It's impossible to make a living as an architect in this town and not have something connected to him, as you know. I hear they're incredibly pissed off at you, by the way. A gutsy move."

"Yeah?"

"And a disaster for your career. You're going to be toxic for some time. But do you think I'm saying this because of him—that somehow my opinion has been bought by Waddy Kornflint?"

"I didn't mean it that way."

"You think I need to get laid?"

Brunella laughs. "Don't you ever get this . . . itch? This slow-building oh-my-God-gotta-have-it, and then you grab anything with a middle leg and honest eyes?"

"You're the horny one."

"There was this pretty boy, Teddy. I knew him as a kid. He's a couple years younger. I saw him over the summer, and he'd grown into quite a man and . . . he seems like the rare guy who doesn't take himself too seriously. Do you know how many guys talk about themselves in the third person? They think it's a way to camouflage their ego or something. Teddy had a terrible pull on me. I can't explain it."

"Those are the best kind."

"Yes! You're so right. The ones that fit your image never work out. And then—you know this about me, Audrey—I have this habit of trying to tailor 'em to my tastes, a little refinement here and there. And that always ends in disaster. But here this man Teddy—I mean, a beautiful guy, I realize, and maybe I'm making too much of this now because my life is in the hole—but he was so sweet over this long summer weekend. Then— *bang*—he gets burned in the fire and disappears."

"Nobody just disappears. The world is too small."

"But he did. And since then, with Niccolo's death, I feel disconnected from everything, like I'll never fit. Sometimes—I shouldn't admit this—I even want to be back doing what you do."

"You don't want my life, Brunella. I know you too well."

"But it can fill a void, all that deadline work. Let me ask you something. I'm sorry if this seems like prying—"

"Go ahead."

"Do you believe in heaven? I mean, you're Jewish, and heaven is a Christian construct."

"Heaven? With decent food? And no concerns about excessive facial hair?"

"A place you get to after going through an unimaginable series of horrors. The Aztecs called it Tlalocan; it was eternally warm and comforting. But the only way you could get in was by drowning or getting hit by lightning. It was pretty much the same thing for Norse warriors. If you died of old age, after a good life, it was the low-rent district for you."

"Norse warriors? Where the hell do you get this stuff? Come back to work with me, Brunella. Give Kornflint's people a half-ass apology, say the whole thing was a mistake, and I'll take care of the rest."

"What I love to draw, nobody else wants to build anymore, Audrey. I can't do swervy, and I can't do swooshy."

"And you think that's what I'm doing, fad-driven crap? Thanks for the dis."

"I didn't mean it that way. I'm sorry."

"What about your big life plans?"

"When I left home after high school I was never going to look back. My mother wanted college for me, a year overseas, then a move to New York or Baltimore. Those are the only two real cities in America, she said. And you know what happened to me in New York, with all the shoe closets? My God. One woman wanted an Art Deco suite for her three dozen pairs of pumps. 'Can't you make it more jazzy?' she said. It's a fucking shoe closet! And then LA, that New Urbanist village on Fairfax. It was supposed to be a warren of little shops, the kind of place where I could see people taking their *passeggiata,* even though it's against the law to walk in America because there's a plot to make sure everybody stays fat. It turned out to be a front, like a movie set, for the usual mall suspects. I wouldn't be surprised if they've torn it down to make way for . . . whatever. But the big blow happened in northern California. I spent one afternoon at the home Morris Graves built on the lake. I tell you, Audrey, I close my eyes and I can still see it in all its parts, the way the house seems to drift over the lake, the way the windows open like Japanese screens—house and landscape, one and the same. He and Ibsen Nelsen fought over the thing. They never spoke after it was finished, which is what you'd expect from two masters with excess testosterone. It is perfection. It looks like it sprouted from the earth, like a living thing, not one of these pumped-up trophy houses with the velvet ropes in the living room. I can't begin to describe the effect it had on me."

"I remember you talking about it."

"It paralyzed me. I could never approach that level. And then something else struck me. I was reading about the uncovering of Brunelleschi's tomb under his duomo in Florence, like, five hundred years after he died. So they open the tomb—right—and there's nothing left of him. Nothing! The greatest architect of all time. White dust. Skeleton powder. But overhead, the little guy's marble and sandstone masterpiece is more powerful than ever. He spent his life trying to figure out how to vault that cathedral with a dome at a time when everyone said it could not be done. And the more I think about it, and about Morris Graves's house on the lake, that's sort of like what my babbo has in our little coulee in eastern Washington—perfection, as near as a human can craft such a thing."

"His wine?"

"No ordinary *vino,* kid. Angelo Cartolano made a Barolo in a place where they said you could never make a red wine for the ages. It will outlive him. And what do I have so far? People say, 'Why are you trying to save a loopy fisherman and some wormed-out docks?'"

"Why *are* you trying to save . . . whatever it is that's left down there?"

"Because it's something! Because you can smell it and touch it. Because we just wipe everything clean that came before us unless it's some battlefield or a place where George Washington took a pee."

"Can I get you a beret to go with your rant?"

"I know. I sound like a graduate student, don't I? Who cares. Listen."

She motions for the check. "You'll be there at Hat 'n' Boots with me, Audrey? Please."

"I don't think so."

The cold is starting to gather in her Seattle house, finding the corners. The chill and the longer nights help Brunella sleep, deep under her comforter, deep under the season-changing storms from the Pacific, one lined up after the other. Bring 'em on. More wet, more gray, more night. Hibernation. She has been thinking about Audrey's offer to go back, but to what? A corner office and a third of her waking hours inside an airplane? America in its 24/7 manic mode held no charm for her. She shudders at the thought of another night in a Travel-More Suite, trudging down to the Stairmaster dungeon to join other sullen serfs pedaling a machine while stock quotes blare or meaningless basketball games play on, all to lose enough calories in order to eat a slab of charbroiled expense-account-priced protein. No, thank you. Take those frequent-flier miles and shove 'em.

Sleep is her escape. She visits with Niccolo again in a dream. He is silly, ice-skating on their pond in the coulee, wearing shorts. He motions for Brunella to join him on the ice. She laces her skates while talking to him from her upstairs bedroom window. Hurry, he says, the ice is perfect. Very fast. He starts to sing as he skates, and she tells him, Shush. I do all the singing in the Cartolano family. Her skates are laced but she can't get down the stairs and outside to the pond. Jump out the window, Niccolo tells her. She goes to the window and leaps. But the pond disappears and so does Niccolo. She falls and falls and falls and never lands until she wakes. She wants to get back into the dream, to return to Niccolo. As always, she cannot force the dream to let her in again.

Duff Almvik's boat has not left Salmon Bay. Brunella last saw him ten days ago, when he said he was going to chase a run of coho. Upon his return, Brunella planned to invite television cameras from the local stations to record the seasonal ritual. Even if it was only a handful of fish, it might be enough to excite people. And maybe, she had hoped, the publicity might flush out any fishermen still in the area—enough, at least, to prove that a community of salmon anglers still exists at the pier.

Duff's chipped and frayed boat, the *SoundGardener,* is still at anchor, showing no signs of life. For an instant, she is startled by a displacement of air, a swoosh when an eagle alights from the tallest mast of a neighboring ship. It takes her breath away, the predator with the regal head and moonglow tail plying the city's air currents. Distracted by the raptor, Brunella bumps into a cart full of tools pushed along the dock by a plug of a man with goggles over his eyes.

"Watch where y'going, missy."

"I'm sorry. I—I didn't see you."

"This place has gone t'hell."

"Are you a fisherman?"

"What do I look like, a fuckin' software engineer? Out of my way!"

"If you are a fisherman, then please, give me a moment. I think I know—"

"You're that gal's been looking for me?"

"Oh, my God—Tork. You must be Tork Tollefson!"

"What d'ya want?" His hands are deep-creased and polished with oil. He wears three coats, though the air is temperate. She cannot quite see his eyes through the scratched goggles.

"I want you to help me. Help us save this heritage. You know Duff Almvik, I'm sure—"

"Do I know Duff Almvik?" He sneers. "The last of the Red Finns. I came back here to make him pay."

"The Red Finns? But Duff's Norwegian."

"He didn't tell ya about his mother's side, did he? Didn't tell ya how the Red Finns set the sauna on fire in 1937 and killed two brothers of my grandfather. Yeah, fucking burned them to death."

"I'm not familiar with any of that . . . distant history, Mr. Tollefson."

"Well, you should be, if you knew what was good for ya. If you're gonna muck around down here, you should know what the hell kind of waters you're swimming in."

"I'm just trying to keep Duff fishing so we can—"

"Fishing, is he?"

"Yes, that's his boat." She points down the way to the *SoundGardener.*

"That's his?"

"Sure."

"A fine thing to know. Now get out of my way, wouldja?"

He pushes his cart past her and ambles toward the Purple Door Tavern.

"But wait . . . Tork!"

"Stay away from me. I don't want nothing to do with somebody trying to save a Red Finn."

Game four of the American League Championship Series. Yanks lead two games to one. The Mariners are home; it's the hottest ticket in town, and Ethan Winthrop has invited Brunella to join him twelve rows behind first base. She was surprised at the invitation; he says the brokerage house that manages his money gave him tickets, and he wants to make peace with Brunella. The retractable roof is open, a light breeze is out of the north, and October's retreating sunshine lights up right field.

"It's a pitcher's park," she says, "so we might be able to contain the mercenaries if our starter can get through seven innings."

"Mercenaries?" Ethan looks at her blankly.

"The Yanks. They're not a baseball team, they're a bunch of Hessians in pinstripes. That fireball-throwing ace of theirs, he's been in and out of drug rehab five times. That right fielder, he's been arrested for assaulting three of his five wives. That tub-of-lard first baseman, he's a freak on steroids and Cap'n Crunch. He looks like Mr. Potato Head with all those body parts in the wrong places."

Ethan's face is still a blank; she could have been speaking Sanskrit. "I have no idea what you're talking about."

"Okay, listen, Ethan, I'll explain: The ball doesn't carry well at Safeco because the marine air is too heavy. Advantage to the pitcher."

"And that's supposed to be a big deal?"

"Usually. Unless the pitcher is psycho on the day he takes to the mound: Roger Clemens throwing a bat, Randy Johnson trying to beanball somebody in the head, that kind of thing. You've never been to Safeco Field?"

"I hate sports, Brunella."

"You don't mind if I watch, do you?"

"Not if you're going to talk Hessians and Potato Heads—"

"Off-speed! Did you see that? Piñeiro threw him a sixty-five-mile-an-hour change-up and he missed it by two feet. Here comes that eighty-million-dollar convict the Yanks bought from Cleveland. Hey, felon!"

"Brunella, it seems rude to yell at the participants."

"You should see Yankee Stadium. They throw batteries at our players."

"And here?"

"We recycle them. You want some chowder?"

"I brought a sandwich." Ethan produces a half-squished fold of bread from his coat pocket.

"You're worth seventy million dollars and you brought your own sandwich?"

"Why not? How long is this thing going to last?"

Ethan chews the sandwich very slowly, masticating through two innings of scoreless play. The Yanks put up a pair of runs in the fourth. In the fifth, the Mariners load the bases but the third baseman hits into a double play: end of inning. In the sixth, the Yanks tag on another one. The Ms come back with a leadoff double, followed by a steal of third, but fail to bring the runner home.

"I like the view," says Ethan. "As I recall, there was a parking lot here before it was a stadium."

"Two parking lots, both of them ugly."

"Tell me, Brunella, before this was a parking lot, what was it?"

"Tidelands, I think. Didn't they fill it in with dirt from the lopped-off hills of Seattle?"

"You're the architectural historian, but I believe you're right. Now let me follow on that point: If we had not filled in these tidelands—an improvement, in my mind, as this nation has no shortage of mud—what would we have here instead of this stadium?"

"Water. And clams at the city's doorstep."

"And would you prefer that, Brunella? Or this?"

"I would prefer that this team learn how to stop stranding runners in scoring position."

"Nature answers to its own rules. I heard that from your father, and it rings true in the way that most of those silly rural aphorisms do not. But we're part of nature. And using our intelligence, we craft nature to fit our needs. We are constantly customizing."

"And that's why Kornflint should be allowed to tart up Salmon Bay?"

"I'm just making an argument, one that you—in a more lucid-thinking former life—would have made yourself."

"Only baseball arguments allowed in this park."

"All right. But the least you can do is tell me what's new with the great crusade."

"You're the enemy."

"But an oh-so-benevolent one."

"We are all connected by water."

"Can you be more specific?"

In the ninth, the Ms' leadoff hitter strikes out. The next batter, the shortstop, sends a fastball over the right-field wall, finally giving the crowd some hope. A walk follows, and then a hitter is beaned in the back. Two on, one out.

"Time to go," says Ethan. "I don't want to walk back to my car in the dark." He stumbles as he tries to rise, falling forward in a lurch. Two fans catch him.

"Let me help you. Are you okay?"

"I'm fine."

"Stay. The tying run is at the plate, Ethan."

"Isn't that where he's supposed to be? Thanks for a stimulating afternoon, and the cryptic tip. You see why I still cultivate you as a friend."

She stays. The catcher hits into a double play to end the game. The teams go to New York, where the Yankees close the series with a shutout.

She bangs on the window of the cedar shack where Duff Almvik often sleeps. No answer.

"Duff! Dammit, don't you dare disappear on me."

She calls out several times, walking along the shaky gangplank from the shack to the *SoundGardener*. All the window blinds on the boat are closed, and the hatch to the small living area is sealed. She tiptoes aft from the stern on the starboard side, and there she comes face-to-face with a teenage girl in shorts and spaghetti-strap top, smoking a mint-smelling cigarette.

"Oh my God. Who are you?"

"Cindy."

She looks no older than fourteen. "Cindy . . . who?"

"Cindy who wants to know?"

"This boat belongs to Duff Almvik."

"It does."

"And you are . . . his help?"

She giggles, exhaling a mint-scented cloud of smoke. "Sorta."

"Shouldn't you be in school?"

"I'm only missing two days."

A scratchy voice calls to Cindy from inside the living area of the boat. The hatch opens, and out comes a woman in a bathrobe, her hair up in a knotted bunch, drinking a wine cooler in a bottle, her fingernails bitten to pulp.

"You're looking for Duff," the woman says, draining her drink and chucking the bottle into the bay. "He's not here."

"Where is he?"

"You're the second one to come 'round this morning. Some little guy with goggles was by earlier. Said he had work to do on Duff's boat."

"Tork Tollefson—was that who it was?"

"Didn't get his name. He didn't leave it either."

"What did he want?"

"To work on Duff's boat, like I said. He did jabber at some length about Red Finns. Shit, I haven't heard anyone bring that up since Grandpa was on his last binge. Red Finns this and Red Finns that."

"So where's Duff?"

"Buying lottery tickets," says the woman. "It's a twenty-five-million-dollar jackpot, darling. You know what we could do with that kind of scratch?"

"He should be fishing."

"He should be," says the woman, "but he's been naughty."

"Very naughty," says the girl.

"With both of you?" Brunella says. "Cindy and . . . who are you?"

"I'm Cindy's mother, Nolanne."

Like most forest rangers, Leon Treadtoofar is a biologist by training, five years ending with a master's degree. As he went through his investigation of what happened to the smoke jumpers in the Johnny Blackjack fire, he approached the inquiry like lab work: use scientific method and narrow the possibilities until only one answer remains. He listened to widows, siblings, and parents choke through tears. He asked Tozzie Cresthawk to draw diagrams on aerial photos, so he knew precisely where everybody had been at the time Niccolo ordered the backburn and retreat. He went to the physics lab at the University of Washington and ran different wind speeds and atmospheric conditions through a simulated fire. He tested the soil and the charred stumps to get some sense of what a fire that burned at nearly 2,000 degrees would do to wood fiber and forest compost. He studied hydrology maps and patterns of disease in the trees.

He sits now in Brunella's living room, his back rigid, holding a three-inch-thick file stamped JOHNNY BLACKJACK.

"The Forest Service is not the army—we don't insist that every decision be followed from the top down, nor do we court-martial people for refusing to obey orders," he says.

"I understand that, Leon." She walks around him, sizing up his mood, already sensing a different man.

"So you also understand when I say what I am about to say, that your brother had the right to refuse a command."

"Why are you talking to me like you can't see me? You're so formal. What happened to the gentle face of the Forest Service, the sunflowers and Stevenson poetry?"

"You don't know me."

"Here." She helps Leon to his feet and guides him into the kitchen. "Tea?"

He tries to say something—twice—before getting it out. "I have a temper."

"I saw it, firsthand."

"It's a problem for me. I have to learn to control it. Some days, I'm afraid I might hurt somebody. I apologize for what happened at my office.

It was not professional of me to drag you down to the evidence room. It's a problem."

"We have more in common than you know."

He stares out the window, across the bay to the old-growth forest of the park. "You have a nice view, Brunella."

"The original view. This is what the first whites saw when they canoed along the shore of Lake Washington."

"Were they lost?"

"They were always lost, you know that. This house is from the first Denny plat of the neighborhood. Used to be a farm—an orchard—that sloped to the lake."

"What's this?" He points to a cucumber-shaped mass of aged metal on a display shelf. "It's not what I think it is."

"Yes. From Elba, off the Tuscan coast. The Etruscans were quite the metalsmiths. I found it near an abandoned quarry a thousand feet above the sea on the island. They must have had a furnace of some sort, because all this metal was—"

"It's a penis?"

"Bronze. About twenty-five hundred years old. Question is: Was this the average man or his dream?"

He returns to the living room and opens the file to his summary. Brunella sits next to him, sipping her tea, staring at the perfect shape of his ears, realizing how much she misses the way a man can fill up her living room. He still seems different today, aloof and fresh-pressed.

"I'm speaking now for the United States, Ms. Cartolano, with respect for the dead—"

"Oh, please don't speak for the United States."

"Let me continue. There were three points at which Niccolo made judgment calls: one, the decision to advance on the fire and start a back-burn; two, the fallback to the water pumps; and three, the ultimate retreat to emergency shelters. At each one of those points, the lives of every smoke jumper was in your brother's hands."

Brunella can hear the words, but she becomes more detached as she listens; she senses the outcome and, as she does, Leon shrinks before her.

"You're going to blame my brother, aren't you? Just tell me now! I don't need the throat-clearing, Leon."

"When he advanced on the fire, the Johnny Blackjack had begun to threaten homes and private property. Niccolo was advised to take that advance by the IC, but he could have used his judgment at the scene to refuse."

"You can't blame Niccolo for following orders."

"Number two: In calling for the water pumps, Niccolo acted in concurrence with the IC—a shared decision—again, similar to the first one. We hold him blameless in both those decisions."

"Well, that seems obvious. But thank you nonetheless, and not a minute too soon. These leeches east of the mountains are planning to sue, to take everything—"

"Number three: the retreat, ordered just after eleven o'clock. I'm sorry to interrupt, but it's important that you listen to me, please. Unlike the first two decisions, the retreat was entirely up to Niccolo. He was the Jumper in Charge. He felt his crew to be in imminent danger and acted accordingly. Now we come to the crucial matter. They fell back to a spring where the pumps were in place. But then what happened?"

He pauses, coaxing her with a stare. She holds up her hands.

"Nothing."

"Nothing?"

"Niccolo failed to execute."

"But what about the pumps? They broke down, something—"

"Our postfire tests proved the pumps were in good working order. You saw them in the evidence room. There was nothing wrong with them. Niccolo failed to execute. Had he been able to keep his crew in place, to start the pumps and hold the line, those jumpers would be alive today."

"So what happened?"

"He panicked."

"Panicked . . . panicked! Is that what you wrote in the last page of this file? Is that what we're supposed to tell everyone to ease the pain in their hearts? Oh, Jesus, I'm floored by this, Leon."

She picks up the report, walks outside, and drops it on the porch.

"Goodbye."

"I have gone over what happened in that forest every day since it happened, Ms. Cartolano. Imagine being inside one of those shake-and-bakes when a firestorm is closing in on you. I have. A thousand and one times. I've lived the last moments of those jumpers. Now I must bring order to the chaos of that day. Yes, Niccolo made a mistake. And you did not let me finish. Why did he make a mistake? Why?"

He remains planted on the living room couch while she holds the front door open. When he does not budge, she walks close to him, her face next to his, a challenge. "You tell me."

"Actually, you told me."

"How's that?"

"Niccolo's record as a smoke jumper is superb. In every other fire, his instincts were quick, his decisions first-rate. But this time—this time he was sluggish. He was dulled. What I think happened is this: His dehydration was made worse by the alcohol that was still in his blood from earlier. Do you know what acute dehydration does to judgment?"

"He had a few glasses of wine, days before the fire."

"A few glasses of wine and perhaps something more that he packed in. You say that like it's nothing. I've seen people on the reservation—smart, responsible, good people—become monsters with that much drink."

"He's Italian. Indians don't—can't drink."

"And do we bleed?"

"You know what I mean, Leon."

"Acute dehydration has the same effect on the mind that altitude sickness has on a mountain climber. It turns your brain to crankcase oil, Ms. Cartolano."

"You asked me to trust you."

"I did."

"But look what you've done! You've taken my words, the information I gave you, and you've stabbed my family. You conned me and used me and I feel like I hate what you've become just now. I want you out of here."

He rises, the long legs slow to extend, and walks away from her, outside to the deck, the wind tossing leaves through the air, geese tracking south over Lake Washington, honking. Brunella follows him, her eyes teary.

"In another time," he says, staring at the lake, "maybe a hundred and fifty years ago, they would hang your brother, if he weren't already dead."

She spins him around, slaps him hard on the face, pounds at his chest with her fists. He flinches, but continues.

"Niccolo is your brother. You will always love him. But he made a mistake. As I told you before, there are no pure accidents. This was human error. We will learn from that mistake for as long as there are smoke jumpers—"

"Drop the Forest Service caca, Leon."

"I will make this report public next week. There will be congressional hearings as well. You will be called. Those hearings are meaningless, except to the congressmen. What's important to know is that already we are making changes."

"I don't believe this. I just . . . don't believe this. You're going to blame the soldier for the war."

"No, I'm going to uphold the honor of those dead smoke jumpers."

"Those jumpers did not die because of Niccolo. There's something screwy about that forest. The land was dead."

"We know the forest was stressed by drought."

"No, there's something more than drought, Leon. What if—what if there was some awful human intervention? If somebody caused that forest to die? If somebody, in effect, killed it, and killed all the life that depends on it, all the little springs, and it was tinder, and blew up in the face of those jumpers. You would then have a larger cause—right?— perhaps the real cause. You talked to those people who live up on the bench, the two-oh-sixers?"

"Yes."

"Did you see the water?"

"What water?"

"The water! God, how does everybody miss it? I should have told you about this earlier. Didn't Alden Kosbleau bring it up?"

"He said nothing about it."

"A small pipeline of cold water comes out of the ground right up there at the edge of the burned-out forest. I'd never seen it before. But I saw it during the harvest."

"I'm not sure I know what you're talking about. One of the canals into the coulee?"

"I'll take you there. Do me this favor: Walk that land one time with me before you make this report public."

"What good would that do?"

"You owe me, Leon. You owe the dead. Let's go there together. You must keep looking. You have to keep this report open until . . . until you know what's really going on. You're just touching the surface. I feel it. I have this sense; there's something more. My father is—"

"Your father is not a Forest Service matter."

"He went comatose after Niccolo's death. It almost killed him. He's just now coming out of it. If you make this report public, blaming Nic-colo, you start a process, and you know where that ends up? They take our home. They take the vineyard. They run us out of the coulee. My father is one of the last people left in that part of the Columbia basin still working the land. He will never leave. I'm afraid for my father."

CHAPTER TEN

A FTER THE FIRST blush of pink has dissolved above Cascades, the last of the Salmon Bay gill-netters leaves his berth in the city. Duff Almvik guides the *SoundGardener* past the high-tech campuses along the shore, through the locks, to the open sound, past the homes with great green lawns and roof windows reaching for light, past the restaurants, north at ebb tide. He prods his vessel into a brisk jog, following a hunch that a swarm of late-season kings are massing off Whidbey Island. He cranks the volume on a disk of juggernaut rock as he plows through the inky seas, rolling with the gentle chop. Belowdeck in the fo'c'sle, the hatches are sealed, the windows tight and fresh-caulked, the bunks wrapped in clean linen and topped with down comforters, with flowers in a holder and multi-colored condoms in a candy dish.

He has food for five days, propane for cooking, a fat novel, two cartons of music discs, and a one-liter bottle of Jack Daniel's. His radar, his radio, his depth sounder, his fish finder, and his cell phone are all in good working order. Amidship, the hold is laden with ice. Master of thirty-two feet of floating fiberglass and wood, Duff puts on his fish face, ready for battle. The wheel gives him little resistance. Just off Point No Point, he throttles the engine back to idle—though it chokes a bit, uncertain. He lowers the trolling poles and baits stainless-steel hooks with fresh herring. Trolling will not make him rich, but it is an ancient way to catch the most desirable fish, the clean kings prized by restaurants because their flesh has never been mashed in a pile at the bottom of a net. And if he is skunked, later tonight when he sets his gill nets he will at least have something to show, something to cover the cost of fuel, beer, and bait. With the trolling poles down, *SoundGardener* looks like a big seabird that has just come in for landing. Within fifteen minutes one bell rings, signaling a fish on, and then another and another.

"Shit shanks, I'm feeling it now!" he calls out, as he activates the hydraulic gurdies. *Chanka-chanka-chanka* comes the sound of the in-reeling troll lines. Then the splash, the break of the spiky sea, the emergence from the watery world, the plop on deck, and those beautiful eyes, staring wildly up at Duff. They are gorgeous fish, snouts yet to metamorphose, muscular sides, powerful tails. He holds one at chest level, feeling the last adrenal surge of its life—"Oh, thank you, thank you, thank you"— before he throws it into the hold. Three fish, about thirty pounds apiece, each a hundred-dollar bill. But more than that, Duff has found the vein in the Puget Sound depths. He is locked on.

In the afternoon, winds funnel through canyons in the Olympics and whisk across the water. The *SoundGardener* has trouble holding her position, and when Duff guides her back, she makes a broad turn, unresponsive. It troubles him; she's never acted this way before. He fishes until dusk, taking in another eight kings and two cohos, which are smaller. In a few hours, the real action will begin. He takes a cold bratwurst, slaps it into a bun, and slathers it with mustard. The winds pick up again, blowing at twenty knots, topping off the swells. Duff winches in his trolling poles and steers north out of Useless Bay, around Whidbey's western shore. He is headed for Deception Pass, a deep narrow canyon separating the northern part of Whidbey from Fidalgo Island. During ebb tide, when it seems all of Puget Sound is trying to squeeze through the pass, the water rips through the slot between the islands, creating a roar that bounces off the high rock walls. At peak intensity, when the tidal pull goes the other way and converges with westerly winds, the pass is all froth and turbulence. Duff plans to anchor the *SoundGardener* just outside the entrance to Deception Pass, unroll fifteen hundred feet of nylon netting, and take salmon feeding on the nutrient-rich currents. It will be a tricky series of maneuvers, trying to keep the boat from being smashed against the rocks, holding the net just outside the main current, dodging the flotsam of kelp and driftwood that can tangle a line while making sure his set is just right so that fish swim into the small openings of the net, snagging their gills.

A brief tempestuous sunset frames the Olympics—clouds fevered before they go gray and anonymous. Winds are now blowing at near gale force in the darkness, running in from the west through the Strait of Juan de Fuca. A halo of mist around a squash-colored moon reiterates what the Coast Guard marine forecast has been saying: A seasonal storm is on the way, nothing Duff has not seen before. He cranks the volume. Pearl Jam plays over the diesel strain and a chorus of hissing wind as the seas rise and pour over the stern.

The moon, oh, look at the moon! From the top floor of a tower in Seattle's Belltown neighborhood, the diffused moonlight over Puget Sound is an object of aesthetic wonderment. A party is just getting under way at the home of a man who made more than three hundred million dollars on an Internet graphic tool designed for people with macular degeneration, now used primarily by pornography sites. Brunella has enlisted him to host this fund-raiser for the campaign to save the Salmon Bay fishing community. In skirt, matching top, and heels, Brunella feels overdressed; she stands out among the smooth-faced rich of the Northwest, who are clad in earth-toned, custom-rumpled Seattle mufti, their most expensive piece of clothing a raincoat of exquisite breathing ability. She eyes a couple of pretty boys among the earnestly affluent, and it comes over her again, that sensation of wanting to rub, snuggle, and romp. But she, too, has to put on her fish face.

The apartment seems to have no walls, no ceiling, no linear limits. The central room expands outward to a glimmering pool of water that drops over the edge, a cascade tumbling out of sight. In the kitchen, all burled maple and Italian granite, are glass-blown life-size depictions of all species of Pacific salmon: chinook, coho, sockeye, pink, chum.

When a man with a sprig of facial hair and a smell like licorice bumps into her, Brunella rubs his shoulder with her hand. The touch feels good.

"I'm sorry," he apologizes, in the quick-draw Seattle manner, where no offense is ever intended.

She is surprised to find her father's Nebbiolo, the limited-bottling

1994 vintage, atop a table of inlaid walnut. The young man pours himself a glass and turns to Brunella.

"This bottle got a ninety-three from the *Spectator*," he says. "It's impossible to find."

"Is it?"

"I managed to cellar a case. It was an extraordinary year for the Cartolano Nebbiolo."

"Yes, I know," she says. "The bud was fine, even though there was concern about late frost. Summer temperatures slightly above normal. Harvest was terrific. But it was a terrible year for the family. Excuse me." She backs away to answer her cell phone. "Yes . . . Duff! Oh, fantastic . . . uh-huh, uh-huh . . . Speak up, I'm losing you. . . . That's wonderful news. . . . Wait, I'm losing you again."

They nibble on oysters from a silver tray, milling around this high perch built on ground where longshoremen once slurped bivalves from stools. They sample asparagus wrapped in prosciutto, and Dungeness crabcakes, and then come to attention when the host introduces Brunella. She gives her pitch, more refined than her stumbling first effort atop the Smith Tower, about holding on to what is real in a city, looking for authenticity in the modern age. How could a city by the sea survive without its rituals? As the Sicilians welcomed home their tuna fleet, as the Japanese ritualized the abalone divers, as the Hudson River fishers carried firm-fleshed striped bass to dinner plates in Manhattan, so the gill-netters of Salmon Bay have always had their place in our lives, she says. Most of these people in the room are not from Seattle; many of them arrived with the same missionary impulse that led another group of nouveau Northwesterners to spend thirty years tearing down the hills of the city in the last century. But she needs them, the philanthropists who look barely old enough to drive, the people with money who defy Kornflint only because it's a sport.

The current is going the other way now, with the winds, the big push from the Pacific through the strait. The seas are rolling: eight feet, twelve feet. Two anchors strain to hold *SoundGardener* in place just outside Deception Pass. As Duff lets out the net from the big drum on the stern of the boat, the water takes it and quickly pulls it tight against a narrow opening near the pass. Underwater, it would look something like a big volleyball net: a wall of nylon, with corks on the top and lead weights that hold the bottom down about thirty feet. A marker buoy and small lights show the trail of the net. After all the line is out from the big wheel, Duff goes inside the fo'c'sle for some entertainment. He no sooner gets his pants unhitched than he feels the boat rock and shake—*thump-thump*—like something bumping the boat. He rushes up on deck, wind blowing cold rain into his face. When he pulls on the net, he feels a tug of fortune.

"My sweet mud sharks, I got me the mainline express!" he shouts out, firing up the power reel. Duff works the big wheel with a foot pedal, which frees his hands to shake fish loose as the net rolls in. The old-timers in Ballard used to say that a good gill net set would bring in two hundred fish or more at a time. What Duff sees now is a net so clogged with salmon he cannot reel it in evenly. Fish fill the deck. He pauses the foot pedal to sweep them into the ice hold.

"Must be five hundred of these suckers," he says. "*Whoooeeeeeee!*"

He fills the hold and then slides into the frozen tomb to pack the ice tight against the fish. He flops, wallows, slips among hundreds of fresh-killed coho. He could not be more ecstatic, though his legs have lost all feeling in them.

Back on deck, he unspools the net again for a new set, letting the current pull it out. Even with two anchors, the *SoundGardener* has been yanked closer to Deception Pass, near the high rocks. The rain is turning to wet snow, blowing sideways, pinpricks against the skin. He kicks open the hatch into the fo'c'sle and slides back down into the warm berth.

A few minutes later Duff is back on deck. He calls Brunella on the cell phone.

"Jackpot, baby! Jackpot!"

She tells everyone about Duff's bounty, but the partygoers look at her in silence, not sure what to make of this announcement.

"It's good news," she assures them. "Our gill-netter is catching fish. Lots of them. This is a good thing."

They applaud, tentative at first, then a ripple.

"And there's more good news," she says. "We have a lead on another fisherman, an older gentleman who has returned home. With your help we will not lose this part of our heritage."

Among the oldest human artifacts ever discovered in the United States, Brunella tells them, are scraps of a skeleton and some stone fishing tools that were compacted in a cave in the coastal rain forest north of Puget Sound. The bones were found to be more than nine thousand years old, which means people have been fishing in this part of the world since before men camped along the Nile or built weirs next to the Danube for the same purpose. What followed were winters of brutal efficiency, summers without sun, a small ice age, volcanoes in full fury, earthquakes that brought down five-hundred-year-old trees, and death by toxins in the shellfish or from disease delivered by people with different immune systems. And there also followed—much later—leveling of the hills, cutting down the forests, draining the tidelands, to be replaced by indoor wonders, palaces where a person could satisfy every need without ever leaving a screen.

"Through it all," she says, as some guests start to glance at their watches, "people looked for sustenance from a fish that returned every year to the waters of its birth. Some of these fish, as it turns out, come home to the waters of my birth—a desert coulee in the Columbia basin. I have a special affinity for this run."

"Whatever," she hears somebody say. Brunella thanks the donors as they drop their checks in a bowl and drift away, chatting about vacations over the coming holiday, the drudgery of philanthropy. When Brunella empties the bowl, she finds a check for $100,000—easily enough to keep the Salmon Bay campaign alive for another six months. It is from a foundation she has never heard of. Attached to the check is a note: *Good luck and Godspeed in finding our Puget Sound salmon community.*

She rushes up to her host. "Hey"—she flashes the check—"who's this?" The host has not heard of the foundation. Wet snow hits the wall-sized window and disappears, creating an illusion of movement, as if the apartment were floating in space. Brunella stands next to the great waterfall that flows out of the living room.

"Brunella." The man with the sprig of facial hair approaches. "You doing anything? Some of us are going to this club for body shots."

"Body shots?"

"Tequila from the navel. Join us."

"I have to wait for one more call from my fisherman. And I have an outie."

For the third time that night, Duff works the foot pedal as he hauls in an immense catch. Snow covers his cap. He works the numbers in his head as he shakes fish onto the deck—*plop, plop, plop*—and the volume is so great that now he is thinking Mexico, the beach town of Puerto Escondido, a room with a view of the crashing Pacific for only twenty-five bucks a night, red snapper grilled whole, slathered with salsa and vegetables, washed down with Carta Blanca, and the next day a snooze in the hammock, warm winds rocking him back and forth, babes on the horizon, the topless women from Germany who love the beach town of Escondido.

"Oh, sweet mud sharks," Duff says, shaking in the last of the net—*plop, plop, plop*. And look at those fish, firm with the best color of the year, oh yes, oh yes, oh yes. Maybe three months in Puerto Escondido instead of two. Sure, why not? *Plop, plop, plop*. The engine he uses to reel in the net is smoking, strained to the limit. He is just about done. Now he uses a push broom to shove the fish into the hold, swept away with the bloodstained snow. God, what a mother lode; the hold is nearly full. So, maybe five months in Puerto Escondido, take the whole goddamn rainy season off and stare at topless German babes and sway the days away in a hammock.

"Thank you, thank you, thank you," Duff says, closing the hatch on the fish hold. He tosses his wet snow-covered cap into the sea—the one with the words BITE ME—and sidles into the foc's'cle. He laughs as the *SoundGardener* bounces with the hard current, trying to ride the enlarged seas and the winds from the strait. Duff uses a utility wrench to loosen the lag bolt that holds in place the one-liter bottle of Jack Daniel's and the candy bowl of multicolored condoms. Nirvana busting through the speakers, the saintly junkie Kurt Cobain, poor lovely local kid, the pride of Grays Harbor County.

"A celebration is what we need," Duff says. "A party!" He takes a long pull of the Jack and puts it back in place, his cheeks puckered.

"Ice!" Duff says. "We need ice from the storm. From the sky to us, that's the way it works, ahah! Whoooeee!" He crawls back on deck and walks unsteadily toward the bow. The *SoundGardener* struggles to stay atop the seas, like a horseman trying to ride a bucking bronc.

"Steady, girl," Duff says. "We'll get you home."

The boat lunges with the punch of a big wave. Duff falls flat and laughs. He backs up to the wheelhouse, sets the engine on a steady idle, and crawls back to the bow, where ice has formed around the tip. He knows the idle will hold the boat in place, but still it does not sound right. The *SoundGardener* is laboring. He leans over with a screwdriver and starts to chip a piece of ice for his celebratory drink, his mind on Puerto Escondido again and the topless German babes. The ice slips away. "Damn!" He crouches and edges forward, chipping now at ice on a trolling pole, almost out of reach at the edge of the boat. He chips with one hand, and when the ice breaks away, he reaches out with the other hand to grab it. Just then the boat bucks and lurches. A gagging noise comes from the prop—as if it has seized up or choked on something, as if the prop is snagged and laboring to do its basic function. The lurch throws Duff overboard. He reaches for the thin wire line from the trolling pole, but it does not hold; it sags deep in the water. Duff clutches the line as he thrashes. He is grabbed by the Deception Pass current, and then he's gone, carried into the froth and darkness and high chop as it pours between the two rock walls separating Whidbey Island from Fidalgo. He is tossed underwater, in the grip of the eddy, a hydraulic cyclone. Round and round it spins him, and then another force, the undertow, grabs him and pulls him down to the polished ancient rocks at the floor of the sea, over which fishermen dating back to the late Pleistocene have passed. The *SoundGardener* is orphaned, left without her master, her hull full of fish, serenaded by the sweet heroin addict of Nirvana, the patron saint of all the not-lost young who despair under perpetual gray skies.

CHAPTER ELEVEN

I N THE WINTER of his eighty-first year, Angelo Cartolano feels certain
he can climb Mount Stuart once more, though not by the route he had
pioneered with the Yakima alpine club more than sixty years earlier. There
is another approach, following a long couloir and then traversing over
scree and heather to the final pyramid of granite, a class-four climb at the
end, meaning a fall could kill you or at least snap a bone or collapse a
lung. In the last days of November, a time when daylight falls away like
hair off a cancer victim, Angelo broods over the big mountain to his west,
watching as the knitting of snow extends day by day over its flanks. He is
fired up by the idea of going back to drink once more the potion of risk.
And why not? he tells himself. His legs are oaken, hardened by a lifetime
of clambering up and down the terraced hills of the vineyard. He spends
days by himself looking out the window to the Cascades, letting his
thoughts roam, imagining how he will do it again. Follow Ingalls Creek to
the base of the big couloir. Spend a night there nestled beneath solid
larch trees. Morning, go right up the belly, careful not to grab any loose
boulders, slow, deliberate. Midway up the couloir, track east, find the
bench, and put up the tent. Second morning, on to the small glacier, blue
ice beneath fresh snow. Crampons in the higher reach, where the snow
has not held because of the winds. Walk along its far edge, planting the ax
with every step. Off the glacier, drop pack and ax. Crawl on cold granite,
three points touching rock at all times, to the top. He has made this climb
in his mind now, the complete ascent, at least four times. He knows he

can get himself to the summit of Stuart. He sees himself so clearly, with absolute confidence, on top of the small piece of the earth overlooking the land where he has spent most of his life.

Brunella arrives after a drive that took the entire morning; she was slowed by fresh snow in the pass. On a day when the sun rises just before eight a.m., with a muddy dusk at four, Brunella feels in sync with the moods of the season. The wintering snow geese on the west side, settling in after a long flight from Russia's Wrangel Island, the steelhead trout rushing up thin-veined rivers, the grebes and dunlins, and then a herd of elk just east of the pass in a meadow, chased from the high woods by heavy snow, the diminishing light setting off a hormonal thermostat that causes the males to shed their antlers. She finds Angelo sorting through his climbing equipment, museum-quality gear from a distant era: a wood-handled ice ax, a leather-reinforced backpack, a headlamp connected to a fanny-pack battery holder, and, nearby, a little jar filled with fluid that looks like apple juice. She tells him he cannot be serious; the snow will be too deep, the ice treacherous. It would be suicide.

"You're not Reinhold Messner, Babbo."

"Nobody can be Messner. But once . . . I was as free as Messner."

"Okay, Messner, what's in the jar?"

"Pee."

"Whose pee?"

"Mine. It saves me a trip down the hall."

"So you're going to climb a ten-thousand-foot mountain, but you can't make it to the toilet."

He says he will not be home for dinner; the managers of the irrigation district are holding a strategy session, gearing up for a fight. The hotheads are in control now. Some of the irrigators have fired shots near Fish and Game biologists—warning shots, they say.

"If you can drive me there, I'll get a ride home."

"You can't drive?"

"They took my license. And you know what, Nella? I shouldn't tell you this because it will only make things worse, but it was Roberto who told them I couldn't drive."

"That son of a bitch."

"Your mother was not a bitch."

"I'm sorry. He's driving his own father off the land."

"If it isn't him, somebody else will. The government's turned on us, Nella."

"You believe that?"

"Why are they trying to take back our water and give it to the Indians? When I came here, they told us we could have it all, the water, the land, the fruit, the electricity—come and make something of this land and you can have it all. That's what they told us. They were going to make some salmon for the Indians at the hatcheries. We would all be happy. Now . . . look how they've turned on us. They're going after all the water rights. They can't do that. Once you get hold of some water, doesn't matter how, they can never take it away from you."

"First in time, first in line."

"When I settled in this coulee, Alden Kosbleau told me those very words like it came from the Bible. One of the Commandments. He said, 'This is the West. That's how we do things.' "

"You haven't heard from the Forest Service? I'm expecting a call."

"Is there something new about Niccolo?"

"They're trying to put all the pieces together."

"God took him."

"So now you believe?"

"I have decided I cannot believe that God can order a miracle unless I also believe he can direct a tragedy. This God has many bad moods, and I'm not sure I can live with him."

Brunella sifts through a pile of unopened mail on the cherry-wood kitchen table, pausing over one official-looking envelope. She reads the notice from the sheriff's office: a lien has been placed on the Cartolano land. A lawsuit claims the family is liable because of Niccolo's role in the fire.

"A lawyer's fantasy," Angelo says, waving his hand.

"How could you let this slip?"

"Mount Stuart this time of year: You think it's below zero, with the wind?"

"I won't let them do this. We're going to fight these people. We're going to keep the Forest Service looking until they find the truth about the fire. They will never get this land, Babbo."

"There's something there for you." He points to a small box. Brunella peels away the brown paper to find another box, which is gift-wrapped with a bow. She gasps: Inside is a four-color dry fly.

"Looks like a . . . a mayfly or some kind of stimulator."

"No, Babbo, look closely. It's a royal coachman. I was fishing last summer in one of the lakes above the Methow, using this fly."

"Coachman. Good for catching cutts. Who's it from?"

"No return address. And there isn't a note." She lifts the coachman to her lips, kisses it.

"Make a wish when you do that," says Angelo. *"Esprimi un desiderio."*

"I did."

In the morning, Angelo is in the cellar with Niccolo's vintage. The wine has been moved to the small oak barrels. He is extracting samples, moving it around his tongue, trying to gauge the direction of the wine, sniffing, swishing, and spitting, working the palate through delicate refinements. Brunella walks in with coffee.

"Put that down and try this," says Angelo.

"It's far too early in the wine's life to tell anything, isn't it?"

"Yes, in many ways." He sips and sniffs again; the wine dribbles down his chin. He has his facial color back, the blush of a new father one day out of the delivery room. "See if you can taste where this is going."

She sips, runs the young wine across her tongue, shrugs in frustration. "I can't tell."

"What you taste in the front of the tongue will be different from the back. Now tell me what you taste."

"You know I don't have your gift, Babbo."

"Close your eyes and try again."

"I can't be Niccolo, dammit!"

He looks away, the joy gone from his face. She apologizes for snapping at him.

"Let me ask you something, Nella: What did Niccolo mean at the party when he said he was going to be a winemaker with humility?"

"I think he was talking about listening to the land, not trying to force something."

"Ah, *sì*. And let me ask you something else: Those people at VinFaire, they said the wine was like shoe leather . . . in the face?"

"No, Babbo. Shoe leather on the nose."

"I don't understand shoe leather on the nose. I tasted many barrel samples of that wine before I destroyed it all and I don't remember this shoe in the face."

She takes another sip of Niccolo's vintage, slowly letting some air into her mouth, closing her lips, swishing gently before she spits. "There's a lot of fruit here."

"*Sì. Sì. Molto frutta.* Very big in the front. What else?"

"Tannins are . . . strong."

"*Sì. Sì.* Backbone. Strength. A long life ahead of it. Now tell me about the mouth feel."

She takes another sip and rolls it with her tongue. "It's intense, but it's also a little . . . chalky."

"What's that last word?"

"Chalky. Like the soil."

"Ah, *sì*. Chalky. *Molto bene.* You're tasting the land. You know what I think? Well, I don't know for sure what to make of this wine, Brunella"— he slaps his hands and grins—"but I think, because these grapes were so stressed by the drought and then culled by the storm, what we have left is . . . the best. The strongest. You know what that means, Nella?"

He lowers his voice to a reverential whisper, as if letting her in on a confidence.

"Niccolo's vintage has a story." He claps his hands together again and kisses his daughter. "Oh, I cannot wait!" He does a little dance, a jig up and down the cellar. "I need a woman. *Sono allupato.*"

"What?"

"Your friend you used to work with, I met her at your house in Seattle. Audrey something, with that little skirt. Is she still a woman like the one I saw at your house?"

"Babbo, she's half a century younger than you."

"And that Mormon girl in Wenatchee?"

"Emma?"

"Sì, Emma. Oh, boy, she has the look of hunger in her eyes, and I love that red hair. She must have red hair . . . everywhere! Imagine!"

"Take a nap this afternoon, Babbo. Maybe the lust fairies will pay you a visit. What happened at the irrigation meeting last night?"

"I couldn't listen anymore, Nella. Mrs. Flax was there, leading them on."

"Teddy's mother? I thought she moved into town with her cats and faded away."

"*Acch*—she's gone mad. She's boiled up all the time. Same with everybody. It's becoming a mob that wants blood."

"And wasn't there some counselor there, sent by the government?"

"A doctor with a big fat bag and a bunch of big fat words to go with his big fat bag."

"And what did he say?"

"He wants everyone to take some pills to make us numb."

Waiting for Leon Treadtoofar inside the café, Brunella eats French toast with watery berries and sips from a large glass of tomato juice. She is the only woman in a restaurant full of pink-faced men in baseball hats. Trophy heads of elk, deer, bison, and goat stare back at her from the wall, a glassy-eyed audience. A television with stock quotes blares in the background. The goat looks particularly lost. The waiter slides a petition in front of Brunella while refilling her coffee.

"You a registered voter?"

"Yes."

"Live in this state?"

"Yes."

"You want to save your entitlements?"

"That depends."

"We're talking about our dams, lady. Our water. Our people who are being driven off the land. You want some cheese on that French toast?"

"Cheese?"

"It comes with it."

"What does this petition do?"

"Makes everybody equal." He puts down the coffeepot and leans into her face. "No special rights for Indians. You see what they're building down there on the river, that big construction project, with a goddamn dome of some sort covering the ground? What do you think they're up to? They've been getting our water, sucking the upper basin dry, for whatever the hell it is they're building down there on the river. Some kinda cultural center, huh? They went around buying up water rights, making like they were somebody else, like they were gonna farm. And now they can just tell us to go to hell, 'cause they got the water and they got the government on their side. And they got special rights."

"Treaties."

"Yeah, I got a treaty too. It's called the Constitution."

"That's enough coffee, thank you."

Leon arrives, head to toe in Forest Service green, visibly nervous. The men in the café all turn toward him, no concession in their eyes.

"Let's sit in the corner," he says to Brunella, without greeting her.

"Did you eat?"

"No . . . do you have time? I know you're anxious to show me something in the coulee, but I need something in my stomach."

"You look scared."

"I'm just hungry."

"Don't worry about these people, Leon. They're all talk. Watch." She slides over to a table of pink-faced men, but Leon gets up and pulls her back before she can say anything.

"I've never seen you so unsure," she says to him.

"Let's talk about the water. I want to get this field trip done and still leave enough time to make it home to Seattle by evening."

"What's at home?"

"That water you say is up on the ridge above the coulee, it's not in the blueprints of the irrigation master plan. They got a good-sized aquifer in there, which might be a little low because of the drought and heavy draws from the wells. But the main artery—in fact, the thing that keeps everybody alive—is the spur off the Grand Coulee. Dates to '52, I think, a canal that runs along the coulee. It's been drawn down the last years for endangered species regs. That's it for water in that coulee. Do we have a waiter?" He flags for help.

"You're saying what I saw doesn't exist?"

"There's no record of it."

The waiter arrives but will not look at Leon; he stares at a bison head on the wall as he takes his order. Leon asks for eggs with toast and Coke.

"A Coke?" the waiter says, dismissive. "This early?"

"You'd serve me a Bloody Mary without a question."

"You want cheese on those eggs?"

"Does it come with it?"

"Cheese comes with everything."

Brunella's phone rings and she excuses herself. "Yes . . . yes, I haven't been able to reach him for two days. I'm worried. Uh-huh . . . And what does the Coast Guard say? Okay, please keep me informed, and thank you."

She explains to Leon about Duff Almvik. Nobody has been able to raise him by radio or cell phone. The Coast Guard has been dispatched to his last location near Whidbey Island.

"Apparently they don't serve Indians in this café," he says.

"Leon, of all the things you've said to me in the last four months, there's one thing I can't get out of my mind," she says.

"What's that?" His eggs arrive, scrambled and cold, with a small pond of half-melted cheese atop them.

"About Niccolo: You said a hundred and fifty years ago they would hang him."

"I didn't mean to be cruel." Mouth full, nervous glances back at the table of men.

"You make him sound like a criminal."

"You want some of this?" She shakes her head. "I'm a man of science. I'm very clumsy about people's feelings. I've never been very diplomatic."

"Does that mean the charm offensive is officially over? Look, all I ask—all I've wanted from the start—is for you to be open-minded."

"I'm here, aren't I?"

Three sharp blasts come from outside, like a car backfiring, loud enough to pierce the walls of the café. A truck screeches away. One of the pink-faced men smirks, whispers to the others. Leon gets up slowly, puts money on the table, and walks outside. One of the rear tires in his Forest Service truck has been blown out by gunfire.

A half foot of snow on the upper ridge makes it hard for Brunella and Leon to make it to the crest. They slip back with every step, like walking up a sand dune. Wind is blowing from the north with a bite, scattering snow in horizontal slaps. The vineyards below form distinct rows in their dormancy—scraggly brown vines lined along the broad-sloping shoulders of the snow-covered coulee. The other side of the coulee, the steep river wall, is untouched by sun during the winter. Brunella pauses next to one of the few big trees not destroyed in the fire, a ponderosa pine, its bark scarred.

"Even after the fire," she says, sniffing the air, "you can still smell the butterscotch of these yellow bellies."

"We logged most of these early on," says Leon. "Pine was thought to be a weed by the Service. And then we planted it in fir. As the firs grew, they shaded out the young pines."

He tells her how a century of trying to put out every fire has thrown the natural cycle out of whack. Sage grouse have disappeared. The migratory birds that stopped at the coulee's edge twice a year are a fraction of what they used to be. There is little food for the elk herd that migrates down from the high country in winter to graze during the coldest months. In the summer, beetles prey on weakened trees, aphids choke off the life of perennials before they ever hit their technicolor peak. The conditions are ripe for a catastrophic blowup. But how much of that is the fault of the Forest Service, or the life-killing drought, or something larger?

She grabs his hand and guides him to a flat rock, brushing snow away to make room for both of them. "Sit."

"No, let's continue."

"I want to show you something down below. Get your breath. Relax. Your face seems so stressed; bring that Forest Service butt over here and let me tell you a small story. Do you see our house? We were the first people here. My father came as a boy, a refugee from the internment camp at Missoula, and he built the house in a place where cold never gathers because of the fog. Ingenious to recognize that, I think. And see . . . see where he planted his first vines. He put in windbreaks, the poplars and cottonwoods, up higher, to protect the vines, and topped it all off with a little stone chapel. In some ways this coulee is like a painting that is never finished. He just keeps putting new brushstrokes on the canvas."

"I admire him," says Leon. "But you're wrong about one thing. He was not the first."

"Oh, yes, he was. I've seen the county records. Nobody put so much as a phantom homestead in this coulee until the water came."

"You're lobbying me."

"I'm telling you a small story, the Cartolano story. But yes, if you want me to bare my heart, I'm begging you, Leon. You have to keep looking. You can't close us out with that hasty summary blaming Niccolo."

"There were people here, Brunella, but they were scared of this coulee. The Sanpoil share a myth that Coyote took three women as his wives in here."

"This coulee?"

"Yes, right down there where your father built his house and planted his vines. Coyote would lure them in with the hope that they could be his bride, for he was a handsome man when he wanted to change himself into something. The women, once they made love with him, lost their beauty and had to wander. Harsh, huh?"

"You believe that?"

"In Indian country, every place has a creation myth."

"Italians are the same way."

"You asked me if I believe. The answer is no. I'm a forester, Brunella."

"But you believe in Big Ernie?"

"Every forester believes in Big Ernie."

They hike along the dry fresh snow at the edge of the burned forest, to the highest reach of the coulee, where the new vineyards put in by Gregory Gorton meet the burned-out land. Spindrifts of snow grate in their faces. Brunella picks up the pace. She stops in her tracks, cups her ear.

"Listen."

"I do hear something. Like a creek."

"Not a creek. Follow me, Leon."

She hurries around a big boulder and comes to a stop. She feels triumphant. "See!" Water gushes up from the ground and enters a rusting pipe that channels it back into the earth. Ice has formed around the pipe. Leon is taken aback. The snow is flying so thickly now they cannot see the coulee below.

"Where did this come from?"

"The flow is much smaller than the first time I saw it."

He removes a video camera from his backpack and begins to record the scene.

"Do you know whose land this is?" he asks.

"It's Forest Service, isn't it?"

"No, the boundary is about a quarter mile from here, if my map is right. I think this land belongs to your neighbor. It's vital that we find out. This water is not on any of the hydrology maps. And where the hell does it go?"

She kisses him on the cheek as he videotapes the scene.

"I'm sorry, I'm just . . . excited. Now you believe me."

"It doesn't prove anything."

"In the report, you quote an exchange between my brother and the Incident Commander."

"Yes, Niccolo asked the IC for a bucket drop."

"And you remember what happened: The helicopter never came."

"Smoke on the ground. He couldn't find the reservoir your brother was talking about."

"Reservoir? I'll show you that reservoir." She pulls him by the hand around another boulder and points to a deep depression, covered like the rest of the ground with snow.

"That's your reservoir—bone dry."

"So it's been drained for the season. Most growers do that in the winter. This storm is starting to chew at me."

"It was full in August. I went for a run on the day of my father's party, and I saw it."

"We don't know."

"Leon! What do you mean we don't know?"

"We don't know until we follow the water at both ends. See where it came from and see where it's going, and maybe this tells us something about the bucket drops and maybe it doesn't. But it's a sidelight, Brunella. I can't see how this changes anything."

"You can't? If the buckets had been able to get in here, shit—maybe the fire wouldn't have blown up. Somebody is moving a lot of water back and forth."

"Like who? I'm not real clear on who stands to gain by stealing water from this coulee."

"Don't think like a forester. Think like a thief."

He resumes videotaping, walking slowly around the pipe, but then he plunges suddenly through thin ice covered in snow, falls away, disappears. It looks like the earth has opened up and taken him.

"Leon!"

Bubbles rise to the surface of the ice-chunked water in what appears to be an old narrow well, but no sign of Leon. She drops to her knees at the edge of the water, lowers her hand, and reaches for him. She pulls back his wet Forest Service wool cap. A minute later, he surfaces, choking, his face a fevered red, ice in his hair, spitting, coughing, and flailing. She lowers her leg into the well while holding tight to the side of the old well.

"Grab on!" He continues to slosh and flop in the water, disappearing again beneath the surface. "Leon, grab my leg, dammit!"

He rises and spits out more ice. "Grab it!" she screams. "I've got a good hold."

He clutches her foot, and she pulls her leg up just enough for Leon to reach a twisted piece of rebar on the inside of the well. He uses that to lift himself over the edge and into the snow. He coughs up water, small bits of ice, and stands, trying to regain his dignity.

"Lost my camera. Forest Service bought it new last month. . . ." His words trail off in a low mumble, and he limps a few feet forward before heading off into the teeth of the storm.

"Wrong way, Leon."

His hair, his nose, his neck, his coat, his pants, and boots are iced over from the plunge into slushy water. When Leon's teeth start to chatter, he shakes his head—a snap—as if trying to deny it.

"Can you feel your feet?" She looks into a face contorted by cold. He tries to whistle, his lips purple, not answering her. They fight the frontal force of the windblown snow, slipping often, falling to their knees. Leon's black hair is thick with white flakes caked on ice.

In the whiteout, Leon is disoriented; Brunella senses the panic of a man without any sense of direction. "I know we're going downhill, but I can't tell much else," he says. "I need to call for help."

"You're lost?"

"Yes. Maybe not."

"Nobody's going to help us, Leon. Your backpack and camera are somewhere in that well. Follow me. Breathe easy and keep moving. I know we're close to my father's house, I would guess maybe less than a mile, on the edge of the coulee somewhere, but we might as well be on top of K-Two, 'cause I can't see a thing. How are your feet?"

He slips, falls on his stomach, Brunella tumbling on top of him. She sees the fear again, the man of logic and science without a road map. She helps him up, clutching his hand even after he is on his feet. Each step now is a gingerly reach downhill. He is disoriented from the snow and burning cold on his ice-encased face. He seems to be walking in a circle.

"You must let me lead," Brunella says.

She takes him on a cautious traverse, the snow like a blowtorch on her cheeks. Now it's dark and they can see nothing. The feeling has gone from her toes.

"If we just keep going downhill, we'll be all right," she says.

He is still trying to force a whistle; it sounds choppy, as if he has popcorn in his mouth. His pace has slowed; one leg is stiff and unbending. He stops and falls to his knee, folds, drops facedown in the snow. Brunella slogs on, following a vague outline in the storm. She holds her gloved hand outward, reaching for the image, and feels stone. She rubs the snow, up, down, and across, feeling a wall.

"Leon, I found shelter! It's the chapel." Drifts have piled up at the base of the chapel, obscuring the door. She brushes back snow, working ten minutes to clear it. "Come inside here, Babbo's chapel; we'll be all right." Her words fall away in the blizzard, not carrying in the storm. "Leon?"

She backtracks, clawing at the slope. She finds Leon in a fetal position, his face covered by snow. He has stopped trying to whistle. She falls to the ground and brushes the snow back. "You're hypothermic."

She pulls him up like a boat popping a skier out of the water and leads him down to the tiny chapel, one room with stone walls, stone floor, and rough-cut timber beams arched overhead. He collapses on the floor, shivering violently. She takes the matches that Angelo keeps for his prayers and lights a row of candles. It brings a glow to the frescoed walls, an Italian vineyard scene, transplanted to America, the Columbia River in the background and, behind that, the North Cascades. In the chapel are blankets, water, wine, and wood for the small stove in the corner. She starts a fire, which brings an expanded glow to the room. Leon's eyes are moving back and forth, unable to focus. His entire jaw moves up and down, chattering, and his tongue is bleeding.

"Lie against the wall," she tells him, but he stays on the floor, curled in a ball. She pulls his boots off and strips away the wet socks, pulls down his ice-encrusted pants. His bare legs and butt are as cold to the touch as meat from the freezer. She opens a blanket, rolls him into it, covers him. She rubs the outside of the blanket, moving herself closer, feeling Leon's full-body shiver. She unpeels her own pants and sweater and wraps her nude body around Leon as he rests on his side. She pulls the blanket over them and rolls with her life-giving heat, as the light from candles bounces over the frescoed walls. She tells him again, in greater detail, the story of Angelo Cartolano's journey to America, the trip across the Atlantic, the odd time in Bushwick, internment at Camp Missoula, his discovery of the coulee. If Leon is listening, she cannot tell.

CHAPTER TWELVE

O N THE OTHER SIDE of the Cascades, the clouds cling to the land and the seas are high, with an uneven roll, making it difficult to find anyone in the waters off Whidbey Island. The storm blows freezing rain and wet snow, no breaks between sheets of moisture. The Coast Guard helicopters cannot see anything, and the patrol boats are doing little better. They fight the current in Deception Pass and search along the base of the high rocky cliffs, looking for any sign of the lost fisherman. For three days they look, circumnavigating Whidbey, peeking into the harbors of the San Juans, testing the wall of waves in the Strait of Juan de Fuca to search around Port Townsend, into the entrance of Discovery Bay, off Protection Island. The storm is a weeklong lash.

Brunella is in the bathtub of her home in Seattle, well past midnight on day three of the search, when a call comes from a Coast Guard lieutenant.

"Fishing boat washed up on shore, broken trolling pole on one side, spotted by the watchman at the Dungeness Spit lighthouse. There's a crew on the ground hiking out there now."

Brunella is still awake in the predawn hours when the second call comes in.

"*SoundGardener.* Registered, Washington State, to Almvik, Shepson D., address unknown."

"That's Duff. Oh, Jesus. How is he?"

"He's gone. Lost at sea."

"You mean you didn't find a body? You couldn't tell if . . . he went down fighting? Like a warrior?"

The dispatcher explains that Duff was reported by witnesses to have disappeared late on the night the storm first rolled into Puget Sound. Apparently he fell overboard; he was never seen again.

"Witnesses?"

"Yes. His passengers. Two women, mother and daughter. Cindy Godden, age fifteen, and her mother, Nolanne, age forty-one. They were with him at the time he fell overboard."

"But that's impossible. Duff always fished alone."

Brunella wants a last look at the *SoundGardener,* which has been towed to a Coast Guard dock on the waterfront south of downtown. At midmorning, she finds Duff's boat among a dozen or more vessels behind a fence at the Coast Guard pier. The hull is scuffed and scraped, two windowpanes are broken, a trolling pole has snapped off, but she still looks seaworthy.

"We should hold on to the boat," says Brunella. "It's got historic value."

"It'll be in impound for most of a month," says the duty officer at the dock. "And then they'll probably auction it off."

"Mind if I touch?" she says.

"I don't get your drift, ma'am."

"I want to touch the boat."

"Help yourself. You'd think somebody who'd been fishing that long could keep the prop lugs snug and his main blade sharp enough to give him an even steer."

"What are you talking about?"

"The prop was so loose it's a wonder he made it out there. One blade was folded clear back, like it'd been bent."

"You think somebody deliberately sabotaged it?"

"I can't say that. But that's one guess. Still, even with a mangled prop, he hooked himself one helluva last catch."

"The salmon," she says. "I almost forgot. What happened to all the fish?"

"Those two gals we found on board—mother and her kid—we let them have it. Said they were going to sell the fish from an ice tub at the pier. I think that's illegal."

When Brunella arrives at the dock near Duff's shack, she finds no sign of Cindy and Nolanne. She checks inside the Purple Door Tavern; everybody shrugs. She drops into Svenson's, asking about the other fisherman, Tork Tollefson.

"Popular man," says Svenson the elder.

"Why? Is he in trouble?"

"Far from it. You want to try a herring mini-taco? It's part of the new menu."

"I thought you were going with pocket pitas?"

"They didn't work out."

"Stick with lefse, Svensy. When did you see Tork Tollefson?"

"About a day and a night ago, or maybe it was two nights and a day—it all runs together—two dudes in sweatshirts and briefcases came in here, asking about the same. Old Tork is setting on the side, pulling tabs and taking bets on Dogs and Cougs, when those boys in sweatshirts walked over to him and made him a very happy man. He says, 'Yabba-dabba-doo,' like Fred Flintstone when he gets off work, and he's yammering on about getting a place on the Baja, down the tip, and how there ain't no Red Finns down there—or any of 'em left up here for that matter."

"Red Finns?"

"You know about the Red Finns, don't ya? Everybody in Salmon Bay knows about the Red Finns. They been going at it for a long time with the Tollefsons and his kind. It's one of those powerful feuds stuck in gear that makes no sense to nobody but guys like Tork, who live and die to settle the score."

She feels sick, numb, and stupid. A sequence of random events makes horrid sense now: her telling Tork Tollefson about Duff's whereabouts; the day he showed up to "fix" a nonexistent problem; the loose lug nuts and the mangled prop. Outside, she stares at a billboard-sized draw-ing of Kornflint's French waterfront complex; it shows canals, walkways that match those along the Seine, cafés, patisseries, boulangeries. She wants to hide. How could she see everything in Salmon Bay except for the oldest presence, the ghosts of Red Finns and dead men in a sauna, stirred up by her meddling? She had been trying to save Salmon Bay for the surface charm, the eccentrics and rituals, the lefse deli, the condemned ferry, the live-aboards, the last gill-netter, but not this, not the encrusted hatreds.

She drives to Kornflint's office near Lake Union, about a mile from down-town, running two red lights. She rides the elevator to the top floor, walks into a lobby under a dome of Chihuly glass, and asks to see Kornflint. The secretary, a middle-aged man in a T-shirt, restrains a laugh and explains that Mr. Kornflint is not in.

"When will he be back?" says Brunella. "I can wait."

"You could have a long wait. Why not call one of his assistants?"

"I want to talk to him."

"He won't be in."

"Not today?"

"No."

"Not tomorrow?"

"No."

"Next week?"

"No."

"Next month?"

"Ma'am, I've never seen Mr. Kornflint."

"How long have you worked here?"

"Three years."

"And this *is* his corporate headquarters?"

"Oh, yes."

She drives to the freeway, crosses the floating bridge over Lake Washing-ton, and heads to the south end of Mercer Island, toward the construction cranes, the ones that are visible from her house across the lake. Everyone in the city knows about Kornflint's personal palace, a daily source of fresh-spun rumor and curiosity. The cranes were planted on a site that used to be the home of a Japanese-American blueberry farmer. Kornflint bought the family's single-story home and the houses on all three sides; he tore the houses down, ripped up the two acres of blueberries, and started to build. That was eight years ago. He built a full-size National Basketball Association gym, though nobody ever plays basketball there. He built a gallery, though no one is ever allowed to see the art that hangs inside. He built a cathedral, modeled after the Palace of Popes in Avignon, though no services of any sort have ever been held there. He built a library with forty-foot-high ceilings, but without a single book— it is devoted entirely to electronic media, compact discs and DVDs. After going through three complete design overhauls, the main house is still under construction. Boatloads of tourists on Lake Washington cruise to within video-camera range of the compound, while an announcer thrills them with details of Kornflint's possessions, his sports teams and companies, his artwork, the musicians whose song lists he owns, the ranches in three Western states (one of them half as big as Delaware). The latest version of Kornflint's home was nearly finished last year, but then construction came to a sudden halt and the entire project was torn down. He complained that it looked too much like a manse in the Hamptons.

Brunella follows a lane of tall cedars and Douglas firs to a chain-link fence and a gate at the end of the driveway. A sign points construction vehicles one way, all others to the guard gate.

"Kornflint!" Brunella shouts from the edge of the fence. "I want to see Waddy Kornflint!"

Two guards in baby-blue jogging pants and matching jackets approach the fence. They are smiling, each carrying a palm-sized portable computer.

"Can we help you?"

"I want to see Waddy Kornflint."

"Doesn't everybody."

"He lives here, I know that. Tell him it's Brunella Cartolano. He knows who I am."

"We can't confirm or deny that he lives here," says the smaller of the guards, a cute boy in his early twenties, California-friendly. "But if he did, Ms. Cartolano, I'm sure he would want you to have a terrific day. You can find your way off the Rock, can't you?"

The phone in the cramped office she keeps near Salmon Bay never rings anymore. The fax is quiet. The FedEx truck no longer stops by. The room is just another space without purpose, holding the miscalculating energies of Brunella Cartolano and a complete set of the 1910 *Encyclopedia Britannica,* in mint condition. All the money has dried up; the check for $100,000, written at the Belltown fund-raiser, has bounced. This morning, the newspaper carries a story about Duff Almvik and the mother and daughter found in his boat. They wanted to honor Duff's memory, the Goddens said, and that's why they decided to sell his catch from the dock. The fish sold out in hours. There is no mention of a mangled prop.

Brunella calls Leon. He tells her the snow has been too deep to get back to the coulee and check the water.

"The wind will come through and melt everything and you'll see that pipe, Leon, same as before," she says.

"I'm not sure what we'll see. I lost my camera in that well."

"Did you . . . recover?"

"Allowing myself to get hypothermic, that was a terrible lapse on my part. A weakness. I don't remember much."

"Do you remember anything?"

"Yes."

"And?"

"Thank you."

"Don't worry, Leon, you didn't do anything to dishonor the United States Forest Service. Can I come by?"

"I'm really backed up. I'll call you."

She goes home but never enters the house. She sits on a cold cedar bench out back, soaking in the somnolence of the season. The garden is most alluring now, a time when only imagination can bring it to life. She is thinking a stone path would be nice, lavender on either side, leading to an archway covered by a climbing rose. She is going to drop dahlias everywhere and watch the big flowers stretch for light in the long days of July, and maybe trail some more clematis along a sunny porch rail. The deadest patch of earth is looking today as if it needs columbine, the fine-featured flowers on delicate stems, and a border in the front. She needs to trim back the raspberries and hack and uproot the predatory blackberries. And she will make another try at producing the full Mediterranean raised bed: four tomato hybrids in the rear, basil in front, cukes and zukes spilling out the sides. There were still people who believed it was impossible to grow a good tomato in Seattle, an idea that Brunella always considered both insulting and a challenge. If August and September held up as usual, she would not taste a supermarket salad. For now, it all looks a little sad: the woody fingers of a big fuchsia bush, the lilacs bare and brown, tulip heads poking up through wet earth.

In late January, Brunella closes the office, packs her camping gear, and travels to the desert. She arrives in Las Vegas, wins seven hundred dollars playing blackjack at a casino modeled after the gardens on Lake Como, spends an hour staring at two paintings by Monet in the oddest art gallery on the Strip. She drives north, past still-drying foundations of gated communities named for hill towns in Tuscany and villages in Provence, farther north into the public land, where the Mojave meets the Red Rock country near Mount Charleston. At last, the desert without cosmetic surgery—windy, open, not easy to love, harder still to comprehend. She hikes through scruffy yucca plants at the lower elevations, moves up toward red and white sandstone, a thrust fault rearing its spine in the high rumpled desert like a well-fed dinosaur. "Hey." She slaps the hide of the rock, sixty-five million years old, and sits for a pull of water at midday. There are pockets of snow in shadowed draws, but it seems warm in the dry air. She hikes through a canyon and finds a place to camp next to a spring with a sliver view of the Mojave. The light is clear, and a half-moon gives her some illumination for dinner. She cooks pasta over her stove, mixes it with a sauce of white wine, butter, parmesan cheese, and strips of a chicken breast she picked up at a gas station minimart. There is no wood for a fire, but as long as she is eating she stays warm, rocking back and forth. She is barely twenty miles from the Vegas Strip, from Paris, New York, Venice, and Luxor, but here she is alone, under an infinite ceiling, cold and exhilarated. The next day she hikes a loop, down through a wash where juniper and pinyon pine grow in the margins of seasonal water, and with each step she feels less burdened by the tangle of her life, the failures of the last year, her blindness. Near the end of the loop, she marvels at the Joshua trees, arms crooked in Dr. Seuss fashion, and just before the trail's end she stops and figures out what she has to do.

Brunella calls the Coast Guard to make sure the *SoundGardener* has not been sold and then hurries out to Salmon Bay, looking for Cindy and Nolanne. She finds mother and daughter, late in the afternoon, in the disheveled bar with the six a.m. happy hour and the purple door, now posted with a notice of pending condemnation. She pays the tab and promises Nolanne she will not tell the Liquor Board of her daughter's violation if they agree to help her.

"So listen, cutie. You were with Duff at sea. How much did he tell you?"

"About what?" Cindy asks.

"About fishing, working the net, icing the hold—whatever it is he does when he's bringing in a haul of salmon."

"Didn't tell us nothing, darlin'," says Nolanne. "That's 'cause he didn't have to. I know all there is to know about fishing. Pinks, chums, humpies, kings, silvers—you name 'em, I've slayed 'em. My daddy was a fisherman in Coos Bay."

"Perfect!" Brunella leads them across the street to Svenson's. "I was thinking you two girls—I mean, you brought those fish home."

"In a way, I guess, sorta," says Cindy. "Is this going to take much longer?" And then her cell phone rings, to her relief.

"And you live down here, right?" Brunella asks Nolanne.

"All my life. It's the only place I can afford in Seattle."

"Excellent. Oh, one more thing. Do you have any secrets I should know?"

"Yeah, like I'm going to tell *you* anything," says Cindy.

"No, I mean deep, hidden kinds of family secrets," says Brunella. "Red Finns. Sauna bath wars. Ethnic stuff. I'm Italian. I don't understand people who never emote except with a gun or a knife."

"Me and Cindy, we're open books," says Nolanne.

On Valentine's Day, she surprises Leon Treadtoofar. He looks embarrassed when she walks in unannounced. He stiffens his shoulders, sitting behind his desk, trying to put the Forest Service between him and her. She moves closer to him, a coil of cryptic intentions.

"I brought you something," she says, handing him a wrapped gift.

"I'm . . . not supposed to take anything from the subjects of an investigation."

"I didn't know I was a subject." She edges nearer, whispers, "Open it up."

"I have some news," he says.

"Can it wait?"

He opens the package and finds a liter bottle with light green fluid inside, which puzzles him.

"Olive oil. Cold pressed, sent by a cousin in Umbria. Look at the deep wonderful green of the oil, Leon; it's fruity. You won't believe the taste. This is the only smuggling we still do in the Cartolano family."

He stands, raising his hands as if he has touched contraband.

"It's okay," she says. "Tell me your news."

He unrolls a diagram that covers most of his desk, and his hand brushes her thigh, though she does not move. The paper shows the aquifer, the canals, and the wells drilled throughout the coulee. "Let me show you something. I've been going over these schematics I found. You see here . . . where the water was coming out of the ground and into that mystery pipe. We haven't been able to find the source of that water, but we do know where it's going."

"That's great news."

"The water is channeled downhill—just at the edge of this scheme— through a connection that runs through the crest and down to the Columbia, where it is being stored."

"Stored? Who's the owner?"

"The tribe."

"Jesus. What the hell are they doing with it?"

"I don't know. They've got a construction project on that site, a big development listed on the permit as a cultural and commercial center, and they got a request in for—let me check this now—" He finds another notebook. "Ten thousand acre-feet."

"That's a lot of water."

"A ton. But for my purposes, the big question is: Who was hoarding that much water to begin with, before the tribe got hold of it?"

"I think it's obvious—the same people hoarding it now. You're not going to ignore the tribe?"

"Of course not. The other thing I checked was the reservoir, the one up on the hill that you saw last summer, by Gorton's place. I checked the helicopter pilot from the Johnny Blackjack. He confirmed what he said earlier, about the smoke being too thick to get in there. Then he told me something else. Now, you say that pond was full, yes?"

"On the morning of our party, I went for a run, and I'm sure I saw it."

"And we had the same information; that's why the chopper was sent in there. But this pilot—he said he got a pretty good look at the reservoir, and it was empty on that day."

"Drained! Like I thought! Oh, Leon, this means the bucket drop that could have held down the fire and given those smoke jumpers some breathing room was never made because—" She is pacing when he interrupts her.

"It doesn't mean anything. It's . . . a wrinkle. Very curious, somewhat troubling. We have to find the source of that water now going to the tribe: see who owned it, see what was going on with this—with what looks like a very sophisticated act of hydraulic manipulation."

"A water grab, you mean."

"I have decided to hold back signing off on the report until I can get back there to take one more look and connect the water to a sequence leading up to the fire."

"Thank you."

"I have—uh, one question."

"Yes?"

"What do you do with this stuff?" He holds the bottle like an alien object.

"Olive oil? You bathe in it."

"Seriously?"

She smiles, allowing his imagination to drift beyond the Forest Service office. "Leon, you pour a little bit in some soup. You dip your bread in it. You smell it. You pay homage to—to Sonny Sixkiller with it. Are you doing anything tonight? I'd be happy to give you a baptism in *olio di oliva*."

"I have a meeting. Regional foresters."

"Don't you ever go home?"

"Thanks for the gift."

"You're lonely, but who isn't? If you fill up your life with enough fuss and schedule, you won't have to face the empty—"

"We're done here."

She builds a fire, turns up Sinatra, and sings a duet for the first five songs. She is drinking from a bottle of Valpolicella Classico, the heady *ripassa* from a small vineyard in the Veneto, nothing like the industrial swill sometimes sold under the same name. The wine is dense, earthy, ripe, and lush, and all the flavors taste bittersweet because there is no one to share it with. Her palate is starting to develop; it took some doing, using her nose to identify the pillars of taste, then separating out fruit and texture. She feels a shudder come over her, the start of a dance without romance, leading to the inevitable self-entertainment, bringing herself to climax.

In the life summary that now forces itself on her this night devoted to the Italian saint of the heart, she comes up short. Too many starts, no finishes. A lot of movement and lurches. She follows her spirit, a guide that seems forever lost, prompting so many urges and omens, most of them unfathomable. Acting on impulse, trying to save a fisherman who is now dead, stirring up another one who probably killed him. What an idiot. She never belonged in Salmon Bay.

She loves the story of Valentine and wishes she had someone to tell it to today. In the midst of several military campaigns, the Roman emperor Claudius II banned marriages, decreeing that his armies would be full of single men, unattached by the heart to anything but Rome. Valentine defied him, performing marriages in secret. He was caught and sentenced to death. On the eve of his execution, he cured the jailer's daughter of a terrible disease, but it did not save him. As he was led away to death, he left a note to the woman: *Your Valentine*. It was one of those stories, perhaps no more than half true, that Brunella chose to believe.

Niccolo always said Brunella needed to think more like a man: do a rough draft of her life and then go out and build it. Avoid detours. But she knows she will never be linear and tidy; she could no more stay in the lines than a mountain lion from the Cascade wilderness could learn to love a parking lot. All she really wants is to belong, to see herself in the story, her link in the chain of Cartolanos dating back to an Etruscan feast; to a Roman bath; through years of defying the plague that swept the peninsula like the winter fog of the Po Valley; through the fresh air of the Renaissance to the magnificent chaos of the *risorgimento;* to the hungry years, the ugly time of fascism, to the wanderings of the last century, the leap across the Atlantic, across the continent to the American far corner, digging a toehold in a new land; then only to play her part, to dig in a little deeper on her own and keep the baton of life moving; to have a baby and say, *You are me, and we both belong here. Is it so hard to fit?*

Monday afternoon at Salmon Bay, at the unveiling of Kornflint's final design for the waterfront, the day is clear with a hint of spring. Invisible for the last two weeks, Mount Rainier is out today, beaming off the city skyline like a runway model. Today again Brunella could not look at the city whole and sparkling in late-winter sheen without seeing the Seattle Fault, a basin of soft sediment along a fracture line that must slip, sooner or later, the earth opening and bringing down much of this big new metropolis, making cliffs into beaches, waterfront homes into underwater basements. A string quartet, the musicians clad in running shoes and turquoise stretch pants, plays Vivaldi while waiters deliver café au lait and pastries on a pier where generations of fishermen once mucked about in blood, oil, viscera, and piss. The mayor is here, wearing his Maui tan. A ribbon extends across the pier; behind it is a massive curtain. The promise of an appearance by the hermetic Waddy Kornflint makes for a giddy edginess among the two hundred guests; sentences are half finished as people glance back and forth at the stage, awaiting his arrival.

"I hear he's adopted a school in the central district," says a woman. "Almost all black kids."

A small plane overhead makes three passes before dropping hundreds of tiny parachutes carrying small packages: gifts from Kornflint, each slightly different from the next, as each snowflake is unlike another. They all carry the same inscription, today's date and this line from Goethe:

ANYTHING YOU CAN DO,
OR DREAM YOU CAN, BEGIN IT.
BOLDNESS HAS GENIUS, POWER,
AND MAGIC IN IT.

Brunella is an honored guest with a reserved seat in the front row, next to the mayor, close enough to Kornflint's acolytes to smell the smugness. This city that has never known serious corruption revels in a process where the losers are given applause at the winner's banquet; only a few know they are on the menu. She arrives a few minutes past the designated starting time, with two uninvited guests in tow: Cindy and her mother, Nolanne. The Goddens are flamboyant in heavy makeup, a foundation of leather-colored blush and bruise-purple mascara. Cindy is wobbling on stiletto heels. There's a fuss at the entrance.

"I'm sorry, they're not on the list."

"Oh, they have to be," says Brunella, motioning for someone from the mayor's office. "This is their home you're talking about here," says Brunella. The slight amplitude of Brunella's voice, followed by a head nod from the mayoral aide, prompts the usher to give in. Brunella seats Cindy and Nolanne and then mingles, chatting amiably with her former adversaries. She sees her friend Audrey Finkelstein, clustered with the delegation from Tusa & Associates. Audrey greets her as if at a funeral.

"I'm so sorry, Brunella."

"You look good, Audrey."

"Do you think so? You're sweet. Kornflint is going to do something memorable on this dock, Brunella. He's not going to create another trashy knockoff of those factory waterfront productions you see in Florida. He won't Disnefy the place."

"I'm sure you're right, Audrey. You know my father wants to jump your bones?"

A frail man inside a thick parka taps Brunella's shoulder.

"Ethan, you're not going to give me the same speech?"

"Will you do me a favor and reserve judgment on what Mr. Kornflint is putting together here? And when he's done . . . tell me this is not good for the city."

The string quartet trails off to light applause as everyone takes a seat. The dock is silent, except for the whine of distant traffic and some jets far overhead. Without introduction, a man with a long ponytail and native beads, draped in a shawl of nineteeth-century coastal Salish frog design, walks to the front and turns to the crowd.

"I am Jamon Hearts Afire of the Duwamish. I have a poem."

Nolanne whispers to Brunella, "He doesn't look like an Indian."

"Shhhhh."

"As my people walked this land," says Jamon Hearts Afire, "so must the caretakers who came later learn to tread gently. As my people built their homes here, so must the new stewards shape this land to match our hopes."

"Guy looks familiar," Nolanne says to Brunella. "I think I knew him when his name was Jimmy Hicks. Yeah, that *is* him: Jimmy Hicks. He ain't no stinkin' Indian."

"Shhhhh."

When the poet finishes, he sprinkles cedar shavings on the dock—a blessing, he says—and walks away. A long silence follows. Brunella looks up and spots a bald eagle, perhaps the one she saw on a previous visit. The eagle swoops down in a circular pattern toward the pier. An announcer prances to the front of the curtain.

"Thank you, Jamon, for your prayer, your wisdom, your blessing. Now, please, if everybody will look off to the right side of the pier and see the wood ducks. Mr. Kornflint plans to incorporate many of the native species of this bioregion in the habitat that he will create at this wonderful site in the heart of our city. These wood ducks, which Mr. Kornflint believes to be the most beautiful of all migratory waterfowl, are just the start. Mr. Kornflint will carefully inlay a series of nest boxes near the water. Every year, the wood ducks will return to those places, their new homes, courtesy of Mr. Kornflint.

"Now, before our feature presentation, I would like to thank a special guest. Up front, ladies and gentlemen, please welcome Brunella Cartolano. We thank you for making all of us see the value of the past. Brunella." He tips his hand; the audience claps; she remains seated.

"Now then. I'm afraid I have one bit of disappointing news." The host lowers his voice. "Mr. Kornflint has run into a last-minute emergency. Alas, he will not be here." The wattage dips. "However, we have arranged for him to make an appearance by alternative media. Mr. Mayor, would you come forward, please, and cut the ribbon?"

The mayor takes the scissors and clips the ribbon; as it falls, the massive curtain is pulled back across the broad pier. Murmurs in the crowd turn to gasps—the dry-rotted, oil-stained, slightly listing pier is empty except for one object: a lone purple door, standing like an obelisk of great iconic value. The bald eagle has circled closer to the pier, catching the attention of many in the crowd. People are unsure of what to make of the purple door, but when a single person starts to clap, the crowd follows the cue, two hundred people giving it up for the purple door.

A laser beam shoots down from a corner in the sky; it looks like it's coming from a radio tower atop Queen Anne Hill. At the end of the beam, an image appears, nearly full-dimensional and multicolored: a rumbled, bearded, extremely thin man in a plaid shirt.

"Mr. Kornflint would like a moment of your time," the announcer says, pointing with glee to the laser image on the stage.

"Our little tavern down here is gone, but the Purple Door lives," says the laser-built Kornflint onstage. The image is astonishingly real for broad daylight, a figure formed out of what looks like color and light borrowed from a rainbow. But the vocal quality is odd; the voice sounds manufactured.

"We have taken a bit of history in removing the Purple Door, and we plan to give it an important place in the pantheon of our future. Look for the Purple Door inside our main building."

Applause, a few murmurs.

"Now—as you know—we have lost our fishermen. But they too have a place in our vision. Just across the bay will be a much more sanitary home for the fishermen of the future. When we are fully built out here, I suggest it will be closer in spirit to the sea than what came before. And you just heard about our wood duck restoration project. Wood ducks, what marvelous creatures! Nature answers to its own rules. We respect those rules in our *ruuuhhhh——whooooooo——jigggaaaaaaa . . .*"

The bald eagle has started its downward lurch for prey, circling in and out of the laser. Every time the bird goes through the laser, the image of Waddy Kornflint is splintered and the voice wobbles, rendering it incomprehensible. The eagle is aiming directly for the wood ducks. The charge of the predator creates a panic among the small birds, their bloodred beaks and matching eye circles all aflutter. A burst of feathers and squawking seems a pathetic response. They circle tightly together as the eagle slows its descent, pausing in the middle of the laser. After several moments of screechy confusion, the laser disappears entirely. The emcee returns to the stage.

"I'm terribly sorry about the technical trouble," he says. "It appears we can no longer carry Mr. Kornflint's address. But we will have something on-line later today."

Brunella is the first to stand. She reaches for Cindy and Nolanne and leads them to the mayor.

"Mr. Mayor," she says. "I'd like you to meet Cindy and Nolanne Godden." The mayor does not rise; he looks to an aide for help. "Our fishing community."

Cindy rolls her eyes. Nolanne gives a thumbs-up.

"Duff is dead, God rest his soul. But this pier has life in it yet. These women have fishing in their blood. They've lived down here all their lives, and they helped to bring in the last big haul of salmon to this pier—Duff's legacy. They plan to keep his boat seaworthy. And because there are two of them, they are, in fact, a community."

The mayor stands and waits for an aide to step between him and the heavily made-up fishing Goddens. He whispers something.

"And with this mother-and-daughter community," Brunella says, "we will be seeking a temporary restraining order to keep this pier from becoming another memory hole."

But before the mayor can decide how to respond, either to the lost laser image of Waddy Kornflint or to the sudden appearance of Salmon Bay's unknown fishing community, his attention is drawn to the side of the pier, to the splash and frenzied squawking in the water where the magnificently full-colored wood ducks are cowering in a circle. Now the eagle dives for the hapless ducks, claws fully extended. The big predator makes two runs, missing on both. On the next attempt, the eagle grabs a wood duck by the neck, punctures a vein that squirts blood over the tan-and-white breast, and carts the hapless victim away, off to tall trees near the locks, away from the purple door and the string quartet and the French waiters and the stunned crowd on the pier, waiting still for an image of the civilized Seine on Salmon Bay.

CHAPTER THIRTEEN

I N THE SPRING, the mountains shed their snow early, exposing tree stumps on the floor of the high reservoirs in the Cascades and leaving the land naked. The governor declares an emergency, water rationing across the state, telling people the green will disappear this year and fish will die and the lights may not even come on in some places. The rituals of the season move forward, tentatively, but it's like walking in the dark in a strange room. Brunella holds a party under a full moon for everyone who helped her in the fight against Kornflint. She cooks up piles of ravioli and grills halibut cheeks outside and opens a case of Cartolano wine, the early-release blend that Angelo makes as a *vino da tavola*. She invites Leon, who doesn't show, and she invites Ethan, who does, but he leaves early without saying goodbye. She dances late with people whose names she will not remember in a week and drinks too much wine and forgets to close the grill on the deck, leaving crisp charred hunks of halibut for the raccoons, who cart away every scrap.

The next morning, the sun comes over the Cascades and wakens her in the way that a sheriff with a flashlight can snap to life a sleeper in the backseat of a car. She hears a banging on the door and stumbles downstairs in a woozy daze to find Leon Treadtoofar in pressed Forest Service shorts.

"Ready?"

They follow the Columbia north, new grass fuzzing the hillsides. The river is pregnant with young salmon, millions of fingerlings driven by biological imperative to make it downstream through the desert toward the ocean; they are trapped in a river with little snowmelt, a river that won't move. Clouds of pink rise from the orchards as bulldozers knock down apple trees in midblossom. The bigger trees will yield cordwood; the younger ones will be burned this week. Brunella tries to find a tune on the radio of the Forest Service Suburban, but all she gets are rants from local demagogues. No matter the station, the host is livid, the callers apoplectic. Everybody is going under, their land drying up, their water disappearing, their fruit worthless in a market where money flows to the cheapest producer. They want the government to step in and then step away. They want the Indians to go back to being invisible.

Up ahead, a roadblock, sirens and flashing lights from the state patrol. Somebody has driven a truck and trailer across the width of the road and left it there, stopping all traffic in both directions. The long trailer, the kind used to haul logs, is empty but for a single coffin, over which is draped a banner that reads AMERICAN IRRIGATOR.

In midafternoon they arrive at the Indian construction site. It's a sprawling complex, several stories high, with cement arches out front and workers pouring pavement for a wraparound parking lot, set right next to the backed-up ever-more-cumbrous Columbia. To the side, she sees two canals emptying water into a deep pit covering several acres. As Leon walks to the front, two security men step in front of him.

"Hold on there, chief. You got business here?"

"Forest Service," Leon says, producing a card. "Need to speak to your manager."

The guard runs Leon's business card into a construction shack. Leon and Brunella wait in the sun, watching liquid pavement roll over the crushed brown land. Steam rises from the fresh asphalt; it looks like black oatmeal. Early May, and the heat is already starting to bear down, a hint of the coming months. Two Indian men in hard hats emerge from the shack; Brunella recognizes one of them, Tozzie Cresthawk, and smiles at him. He looks gaunt.

"Help you?" says the older man, gray braids on the front of his shirt beneath his hard hat.

"Need to talk about your water," says Leon.

"What about it?"

"Any of this water come from the coulee up near where we had the fire last summer?"

"You're Treadtoofar. A Wanapum?"

"Half."

"Who's your family?"

"I got a sister at Inchelium. Brother married into the Sho-Bans."

"Your father: he was council president on Bluerock's side, wasn't he?"

"That was my uncle. Long time ago."

"Not to my family. Bluerock has it in for us. What's your business today?"

"Just need to see where your water's coming from. I'm finishing up an investigation of the Johnny Blackjack fire." He motions to the half-sheathed building. "You got quite the Taj Mahal going up here."

"It's gonna get bigger, too."

"You've been buying up a lot of water rights."

"Everything we can get our hands on. The X-O ranch, two golf properties, all the orchards on the east slope—we bought all them water leases, every goddamn drop. It's Bu Rec and Corps stuff, most of it going back to the early fifties. Those boys had some pretty sweet deals. We paid ten times what it was costing 'em. Senior water rights don't come cheap."

"Any of it come from up above, near where we had the fire?"

"You're a Johnny One-Note, ain't ya?"

"You can't possibly need that much water."

"We have plans."

"I'd like to see some documentation of the purchases."

"Fine. It's all on the rez, in Nespelem. You remember how to get to the rez, don't you, brother? Or are you going to need a passport?"

"So this water you've been buying," Brunella says. "How much of it—"

"Who's this?" the man in the braids asks Leon, without making eye contact with Brunella.

"Cartolano," says Tozzie, turning to the older Indian. Tozzie fidgets as he talks, clawing at his arms. "I used to know her brother."

"Ah, Cartolano," says the man with braids. "I've been trying to get ahold of the old man."

"My father."

"I'm Red Thunder. Danny Red Thunder, tribal chairman and general manager. We got an offer standing on your place. You're just about the last holdout."

"We're not selling, thank you very much."

"Every other irrigator has sold."

"My father is a winemaker. We're here forever. What exactly is the tribe building?"

Tozzie looks at her. "Something grand," he says, twitching, scratching at a lesion on his arm.

Brunella detects a mocking tone. "How grand?"

"This parking lot will hold two thousand cars when we're done," says Red Thunder.

"Two thousand cars," Brunella says. "I thought the tribe was building a culture center here."

"We are," says Red Thunder.

"What kind of culture center needs a parking lot for two thousand cars?"

"Culture of blackjack and slot machines."

"A casino."

"Three hundred jobs is what it is," says Red Thunder. He moves closer to Leon and looks him up and down, then holds his stare on the small Forest Service tattoo on one arm. "Casinos are the new salmon, the only way to get back from them a little piece of what they took from us. But you wouldn't know about that, since you wear the uniform."

"What does that mean?"

"Means whatever you want it to mean."

"How deep does the water go in that pit of yours?" Leon says. "Looks like you got yourself a good-sized lake."

"Gonna get bigger," says Red Thunder.

"Why do you need so much water?" Brunella asks. "You trying to duplicate Las Vegas?" She notices that one of the white security guards has his ear cocked to their conversation.

Red Thunder laughs. "Yeah, we should put a couple of neon cowboys out front riding on the world's tallest fountain. That's an idea."

. . .

On the drive to the Cartolano house, Leon ignores Brunella's questions. She wants to know about his family on the reservation, about tribal quarrels, and why Danny Red Thunder seemed so hostile. He shakes his head once, keeps his gaze tight on the road. Now he extends his big right arm and a long slender finger to Brunella's mouth. "Stop. You'll never understand." She thinks Leon is not so hard to comprehend; he is a man who builds his fences to last and lets people in on his terms.

They see dust clouds ahead and hear honking horns; a line of traffic is backing up the single lane of dirt road leading up to Angelo's vineyard. Cars snake all the way to the house. She gets out and starts to trot toward the vineyard. At the head of the line of cars, Miguel is acting like a traffic cop, trying to get people to turn around. He's flustered. Next to him is a big hand-painted sign: SORRY NO WINE.

"Brunella, thank God," he says. "Look at this mess! It's crazy."

"What's going on?"

"Ever since the word got out from France, your father's wine has become a—how did they call it?—cult wine."

"But he got rid of that vintage."

"Yes! Nobody believes me when I say it's gone."

"That's the one he oaked with the wood chips."

"It doesn't matter. The prices people are willing to pay! I've never seen anything like it, Brunella."

"Where's Babbo?"

"Inside. He's . . . he doesn't care. He hasn't left the house in three days. Your brother's been calling, but Angelo won't talk to him. Roberto even called me. He says this French thing—Vin whatever—is huge. Wants me to lean on Angelo. He's got an offer to sell the place. Beeeeeg bucks, he says. But I can't get your dad to pay attention. The bud is just around the corner, and I haven't set the irrigation drip line yet, and smudge pots will have to be cleaned and set, and where is Mr. Cartolano?"

"I'll help you, Miguel. You can teach me."

"But where is the winemaker? See for yourself and then talk to me. Call the sheriff while you're inside. I need help with all these cars."

·   ·   ·

Angelo has transformed Niccolo's room into a shrine to Mount Stuart. On the wall is a blown-up picture of the mountain, marked by Angelo's notations. Piles of climbing gear—crampons, pitons, carabiners, headlamp and batteries, chest and seat harnesses, jumars, and a ninety-foot rope— as well as clothes, gaiters, and packets of sugary drink have been sorted and tagged. He is milling around the room in his underpants, shirtless and barefoot, talking to his ice ax while cross-checking an old notebook. Brunella walks in alone.

He looks up but does not flip up his reading glasses or even seem to recognize his daughter. *"Un momento."* He tells the ice ax to hold on a minute, he is sorry to interrupt. He reads a page with his fingers, walks to the map and big picture on the wall, traces a route. *"Alora.* The glacier is gone."

"Babbo, I need to talk to you. *Adesso!"*

"Oh, Brunella, *mi dispiace.* I didn't see you there. I thought you were Miguel."

"Miguel?"

"Come, find a place to sit. I know it's cluttered."

She notices more jars of urine. "You've gotten worse with these pee jars of yours. Can't you just use the bathroom?"

"Let me show you something." He points to the map. "We climbed it this way. There was a good-sized glacier there. Oh, that was scary, let me tell you. But look at this picture from Beckey's new book. See? Now the glacier is gone."

"Babbo, you can't climb Mount Stuart at your age. This is a delusion."

"A what? Did you bring me any of the big clams?"

"No, but I brought a guest. Who were you talking to just now?"

"My ice ax."

"And how did that go?"

"Fine. Nella, listen to me: I'm going to rewrite my will and give everything to you."

"What's the rush?"

"I don't trust Roberto—my own blood. He's been calling every day, sometimes three and four times. He says he's selling the place. I say it's not for sale. It never will be. He says we have to get out now, before it's too late, before they take it, because we have the big prize from the French wine contest. Oh, how they love the wine that tastes like oak shit. It's caca! I wish I had destroyed every drop. I say to Roberto: A Cartolano does not sell land! Roberto has lost his way in this big country. I knew once he moved to Texas—*acch*, don't let me talk too much about it. But that reminds me of something that is more important now. Bring me my radio. We must hope that God keeps punishing the Texas Rangers."

She makes pasta from scraps in the pantry and refrigerator. Two mounds of measured flour are placed on the counter, one for her, one for Leon. She shows him how to make a hole in the center of the mound, add eggs and olive oil to the well, and slowly work the blend. Leon has trouble keeping the mix from spilling beyond the walls of the flour. She takes his long fingers and works them slowly with the dough, kneading in a deliberate, careful manner, until the surface is somewhat smoothed.

"Cover that," she says, "or it'll dry out."

A half hour later, she takes a roller and smooths out the dough on the counter until it's a thin sheet. She cuts strips, rolls them, and then slices small dollops of pasta, resembling tagliatelle. They let it dry. Outside, she snips off a cluster of chives from a grassy clump and takes sprigs from just emerging oregano. The garden is fragrant with daphne.

"This is my favorite perfume," she says to Leon, running a daphne blossom under his nose.

"You should try sage on that pasta," he says.

"We have some in the corner of the herb garden."

"Not that. I'm talking about wild sage." He pinches off a stem from a scratch of untended land, where mesquite and sage have been left to their own. "Enjoy. I'm not staying for dinner."

"Leon, you have to. You're invited to stay the night, as well."

"Forest Service has a cabin outside Wenatchee."

"No. I insist. Besides, it's bad luck not to eat your own tagliatelle. It's a curse, in fact."

"A Sicilian curse?"

"No, a curse of the Piemontese. Don't you dare test it."

Back in the kitchen, she melts butter, and when it is hot she mixes pine nuts in with the herbs. She stirs for a moment or two while the pasta cooks. At the call of dinner, Angelo emerges. He's wearing pants and a shirt, much to Brunella's relief.

"Needs something," he says, his nose in the blend.

"Bullshit," says Brunella. "Sit down, Babbo. Do you remember Leon Treadtoofar, from the funeral?"

"I recognize the face."

She starts to pour a Pinot Gris, an American version of the Italian Veneto grape that grows well in the Pacific Northwest, but then she remembers what Leon said about alcohol.

"I want you to do as you would always do," he says.

"Then may I pour you a glass of wine? That's what I do for guests."

"No."

"Why can't Indians drink?" says Angelo, sitting down with a massive helping.

"I don't know," Leon says. "Why don't the Cartolanos eat camas bulbs?"

"Eat what?"

"Camas. It was a staple of Indian diets on the Columbia for as long as people lived here. Ten thousand years. In the spring, all the fields were full of blue-flowering camas. You eat it fresh, with elk meat or venison in a stew. Or you dry it and store it for the winter months. My grandmother picked camas. The Nez Perce gave it to Lewis and Clark; it made 'em puke."

"What's it taste like?"

"A sweet onion, or mild garlic."

Angelo stares at Leon; tension has contorted his face. He sets his fork down. "What are you doing to my boy?" Brunella shoots him a look, extending her hand across the table to cover Angelo's, which is shaking.

"I have a report to finish, Mr. Cartolano. We are trying to get to the bottom of what happened last summer. I know Niccolo acted honorably."

"But you're going to blame him," Angelo says.

"Did your daughter tell you that, Mr. Cartolano? Because I'm starting to suspect that the death of our smoke jumpers was the fault of more than one person."

"Really?" says Brunella, taken aback. "And what brought on the change of heart?"

"As I told you, we don't understand why Niccolo couldn't get the pumps to work. Our tests showed nothing wrong with the engines. That's still a mystery, though I have some ideas. I'm sorry, Mr. Cartolano; it points to a lapse of judgment by your son that cost many lives, including his own. But I'm very troubled by what I've been seeing over here. Brunella found something—a pipe, with water emptying out of it up on the ridge. We don't know who owns the water, who would hoard that amount, and for what purpose. We don't even know who owns the land with the pipe. The property records are missing. But we do know where the water's going, and that makes me suspicious."

"So now you think the tribe diverted water from the forest?"

"I didn't say that." He turns to face Angelo, official now, the interrogator from the government, no longer a dinner guest. "And you, Mr. Cartolano, you have people lining up in the dust to buy the wine you make here. So may I ask you one question, sir? How did you produce such a wine during the worst drought in a century? You were under the same water restrictions as everyone else."

The anger reddens Angelo's face; he remains seated, his hand shaking wildly as if under a separate command, and speaks very deliberately. "I make wine from the heart. Everything else is up to God."

"Fine. We'll leave that to God. I have to go."

"Wait." Brunella tries to sit him down. "Dessert. I can thaw some huckleberries."

He thanks them for dinner and leaves the house. After fifteen minutes, he returns, anguished, explaining that he cannot find his car key. "This has never happened to me before," he says. "I'll have to get someone out here with another key."

"You'll stay the night," Brunella says.

"You have an extra room?"

"Three of them."

"Fine. But . . . I had one more question, Mr. Cartolano."

"*Sì, sì.* Have a seat. Brunella will bring coffee and huckleberries."

"No coffee for me. Mr. Cartolano, the IC told us your son was patched through to you on the day of the blowup. Twice."

"Sì."

"And what did you say to him?"

"I told him about . . . our situation."

"What situation?"

"With the fire approaching the vineyard. Are you sure you won't have cappuccino?"

"No."

"I told Niccolo not worry about me. He asked me some questions. I told him about our situation."

"Then what did he say?"

"I don't remember much of it except the end. He said, 'I'll see you tomorrow night.'"

Brunella waits until she hears the purr of her father's snoring before sneaking down the hall to the room they have given Leon. She sees a light under the door, knocks, and enters. He is bare-chested, sitting up in bed, taking notes on a legal pad while going though a thick report.

"Working?"

"I thought you were asleep."

"Let me get you something, some tea or hot chocolate."

"I don't need anything. But the flower is nice."

She sniffs the blossom. "What if we all smelled like daphne."

As she moves closer to him, sitting on the bed, she notices the thin wisp of hair on his chest and the Forest Service tattoo on his upper arm. "The room okay?"

"No cable."

"This was Roberto's room. He kept it perfect, never a stitch of clothes on the floor or a book out of place. He was born with his hair parted."

Her nightshirt is oversize and loose, the tops of her breasts visible when she leans over, the nipples outlined through the fabric. A slight breeze through an open window gives her a shiver, her nipples erect. She crosses her legs and starts to sing in a whispery voice.

"Loooo-chela . . . loooo-chela . . ."

Leon tightens, still holding his pen over his notebook. "What's that you're singing?"

"An Italian lullaby: *lucciola*—it means firefly. A family song for us. *Loooo-chela . . . loooo-chela.*"

"That's nice," Leon says. He sets the book down and listens to her. "We have no songs in our family."

She slides closer to him, spider-walks her fingers down his chest, his stomach, to the edge of the sheets. He puts his hand there to block her. She continues to sing as she stands and slips away. "*Sogni d'oro*, Leon."

Angelo is awake at dawn, talking up a storm in the kitchen, when Brunella greets him. He is in his boxers, carrying a full pot of coffee in one hand and a magnifying lens in the other; he barely notices her as he trails off for the climbing room.

"Babbo? Who were you talking to just now?"

"The coffeepot."

"Does the coffeepot ever talk back?"

"Of course not. Coffee is a living thing, but it can't talk. Nella, I found a key on the counter, near the pasta bowl. Probably belongs to the Indian."

"That's where I left it."

"You hid the Indian's car key?"

"Something like that."

He points to a notepad. "Message for you."

She tries to read his jittery scrawl on a scrap of paper. "Who is this?" Disbelief in her voice. "Teddy Flax? Can this be right?"

She dials the number, waits; there is no answer, not even voice mail. "Four-oh-six. This is Montana's area code. Did you talk to him?"

"*Sì, sì.*"

"What did he say?"

"He said, '*Buon giorno, Signor Cartolano.*'" Angelo laughs as he imitates Teddy's voice.

"What else?"

"He said, '*Come va, Signor Cartolano?*' His accent is terrible, but he's a quick learner, that boy."

She's impatient, takes the coffeepot from his hand. "Babbo, this is important: What . . . did . . . he . . . say?"

"He asked about you. Wanted to know if you had any fishing trips planned this year. Use the royal coachman, he said. I told him about the Indian from the Forest Service, and he seemed to know everything. I told him you looked like a Botticelli painting these days. And he said, 'Botticelli? I'm looking at better frescoes now than anything you ever had in Italy.'"

"Frescoes?" says Brunella. "In Montana?"

"That's what he said. I told him I'm going to climb Mount Stuart. And I told him we're going to crush those bastards from Texas, no matter how many players they buy. He didn't believe the last part."

She follows her father down the hall, to Niccolo's room.

"Babbo, Leon's question last night. You never answered it."

"What was that?" He walks away from the mountain picture and runs his shaky left hand through his climbing notebook.

"How *did* you make a world-class wine in the worst drought in a century?"

"I'll tell you something, Nella: I've made much better wines."

"When?"

"The '86 is just now starting to show. The '94 is better than almost any Bordeaux of that year, if you'll allow me one immodest moment. The '98 is going to live a long time." He turns toward her, looking into her eyes for the first time today.

"How did you do it, Babbo?"

"By accident."

"You mean it wasn't your fault?"

"No, it was my fault. I overwatered the grapes at the end of that summer. I was afraid because of the drought. The grapes came out very ripe, very fat. *Troppo grasso.* But that wine had no story. No life ahead of it. It would do nothing in the cellar, and that's why I oak-chipped it. It's a—how do you say something when it's like a big faker?—it's a lie."

"And where did you get all the extra water?"

He brushes Brunella's hair out of her face and strokes her cheeks with the backside of his sandpapery hand.

"Alden Kosbleau helped me. He saw that my grapes were suffering and he—I will never betray him; he's the most loyal friend I have—he gave me the water."

"Where did he get it? Tell me, Babbo. I have to know."

"No, you listen to me, Nella. That year is gone, no matter what they say at VinFaire. Now, let me tell you something about last fall's vintage. This wine of Niccolo's is different. I did not try to outsmart the grapes."

CHAPTER FOURTEEN

S HE HAS long ago given up trying to find the voice of God inside a church. Better to listen at the margins of life, at low ebb, in desperation, when the soul is famished, or in the sweet moments, the high notes of triumph. But here she is inside the tattooed space of the Saint Ignatius Mission in Montana, and a scratchy voice is filtering down from among the murals. If it's not God, it is certainly familiar. She and Leon left the coulee just after breakfast, driving east across the Coeur d'Alene mountains, through the old silver mining country of the Idaho panhandle, the Bitterroot range. More than 150 years ago, the Jesuits wrapped a frame of timber, brick, and Flathead Valley stone around a piece of the Big Sky near the high mountain walls of the Mission Range. Inside, a cleric spent most of his life on his back, painting fifty-eight murals. Brunella realized after thinking about the phone call that Saint Ignatius had to be Teddy's refuge. It was in the valley where he last lived, the place where he started to build a life just before the fire.

"You found me."

That voice: Where is it? She is afraid to see what he looks like, afraid—mostly—of her reaction. She scans the painted walls, conjuring images of a blackened and scarred face.

"Teddy, where are you?"

"I can see you. I saw the car approaching."

Brunella and Leon walk down different sides of the church, heads back, searching the rafters. She tells herself she will not wince if the liquefied nose, chin, and mouth of Teddy Flax appear. She will not show horror or pity. She will be strong and look through the face and find the man she last saw at camp in the Cascades.

"Teddy, I brought a friend. He's investigating the fire. He's trying—"

"I know who he is. Sit down, both of you."

"Aren't you going to come out? Let me see you, please."

She stands directly beneath the source of his voice. But looking up, all she can see is another mural. When Teddy speaks again, his vaguely amplified voice comes from another part of the church, in a corner. She moves under that space; still no sign of Teddy. And then the voice emanates from a different section, as if it has bounced from one spot to another. Her image of what he will look like changes every time she hears the voice, from monster to featureless polymorph. Maybe he will have softened. She will look for the eyes, make contact, and let nothing distract her. Remember the boy from the coulee.

She wonders how he has kept himself alive, what the burns have done to his immune system, his ability to sleep. She wonders if he has become an OxyContin addict, floating though life on 150 milligrams a day. She wants to know how a man can disappear. What does he do with his time? How does he live?

"I remember what you said about this church, Teddy, and you're right: not your usual bleeding Jesuses and haloed Marys," Brunella says. "Teddy, please come sit with us and talk. We have so much to catch up on."

Lock on the eyes. Lock on the eyes. She will not betray him, not stare at the skin, not dwell on the scars and the hideous surface. She will remember the hike up to the North Cascades, the day at the Omak Stampede, fishing an alpine lake, reveling in his body, laughing at his jokes, the surprise of his humility.

"Have you seen your folks?" Brunella asks.

"I work in the orchard."

"So this is home?"

Damn—now it is starting to piss her off. Where is he? She will put a high beam on that face, if she must, and not wince.

Leon Treadtoofar motions for Brunella to quiet. "We need your voice, Ted," he says. "We need your firsthand account."

"I'm going to tell both of you something, and then you must leave."

"You don't have anything to fear," says Leon.

"You owe it to Niccolo," says Brunella. "Please."

"I owe nothing to Niccolo except a face that looks like it was left in a waffle iron."

"You think it was his fault?" Brunella asks.

"What I think does not matter. Listen to me and then go."

They settle into a pew under Brother Carignano's murals, but Teddy's voice has now left them. They wait in silence for his message. Five minutes pass. Ten. Fifteen.

"He's gone," Brunella whispers to Leon.

"I'm still here." Teddy's voice is now behind the altar, though it no longer sounds amplified or projected. He speaks in low, even tones, strained and reedy. Brunella can see a silhouette of Teddy in this dark corner of the church. He's wearing khakis, a T-shirt. She cannot see his face except for the contours and what looks like a layer or a mask over the front. She tries to find his eyes.

"You came all the way to the Mission Valley to see me. But the answers are just outside your father's doorstep, Brunella."

"I don't understand, Teddy." She rises from the pew and starts to walk toward him, searching for his face in the silhouette. Does he have hair? Were the follicles seared like the ground in the ghost forest? "Let me be next to you."

"Don't come any closer."

Now she can see the covering on his face, like a clear ski mask with silicone gel underneath, holes cut for the nose, the mouth, the eyes. He wears gloves as well.

"What are you going to do, Teddy? You can't live your life as an invisible man."

"I already am."

"Ted," Leon begins, turning on a tape recorder as he remains seated, "the day the Johnny Blackjack blew up, you folks had set up some pumps that were airlifted into that forest basin."

"I have something to tell both of you. But I will not answer questions. You need to go back."

"Back where?" says Brunella.

"To the fire."

"I've been to the burn zone several times, Ted," says Leon. "We have it staked and gridded. We've taken a lot of soil samples, ash content readings."

"You've done everything except the most obvious."

"What would that be, Ted?"

"Go back to the fire. Go and see where we died. Go and walk it. Go and hear me scream when my face caught fire. Go and see the Old Man blow up. And while you're in there, do what you should have done a long time ago."

"What is that, Ted?" says Leon.

"Bring in a pump. Take some water out of that basin. Then you'll know what happened."

They hike toward the ridge the next day. The Cartolano vines, braided with the old hair of seasons past, are starting to show life, the tight-coiled white-and-red buds forcing through the thick wood. The fruit trees are blossoming showy and pink; a swarm of bees holds the morning light; the long curtain of rock on the other side of the coulee is still in shadow. After talking to Teddy, Leon called the Forest Service regional office in Wenatchee and asked them to air-drop a pump into the husk of the Johnny Blackjack fire.

They top the ridge and start to traverse down into the valley toward the burned-out forest. Leon's stride is almost a gallop, while Brunella slows, afraid to enter the place where her brother took his last breath. The ghost forest smells like a burned mattress that has smoldered on for weeks. Nothing has come back, not a hint of green—just dead trees, a black and gray floor. They drop into the draw at the base of a hill, the place where the fire took a leap and swept upward in an explosion. Brunella hears a voice, very low at first, more distinct as they walk over the ashen ground: the sound of Niccolo in her head, the babble of his last words.

"We don't need to go any farther, Leon."

"Of course we do."

"Let's go back. I think we know what happened, don't we?"

"You can go back."

"Give me a moment, Leon. I just . . . have to get clear."

Leon checks a map. Small wooden crosses have been staked into the ground where the jumpers died. Here, the Old Man tried to run through the wall of flames to get to the black as Niccolo ordered, only to be consumed by the fireball. Here, the Pendleton ladies, Suzanne and Laura, held the hoses as long as they could before retreating to coffins of their own making. Here fell the Neds, first-timers Dennis, Mack, and Wag, bundles of adrenaline as the heat took them. Here gasped the Indians, Sherman, Wes, Joseph, and Noflight, tough sons of bitches, cooked without making a sound. And over there, on a spot leveled of soil by his burrowing face, is where Niccolo died. She hears the final beats of his heart, the rabbit pulse as his skin started to boil.

"You ever been in a shake-and-bake?" she asks Leon.

"For training. Never in an actual fire."

"You think you would stay inside and trust it? I mean, it'd be like an oven with the door closed. Or would you run?"

The plane drops a pump and Leon sets it up on the spot where the jumpers made their last stand. He tells Brunella to unwind a hose and then hold it tight, because when the water comes the hose will stiffen quickly and snap around on its own power. He checks a hydrology map, trying to find a seep.

"We know there's water down below," he says. "All the snowmelt from this flank seeps into this little basin. Should be lots of pressure. That's what Niccolo told the IC." He finds a crevasse between rocks and drops the suction end of the intake hose into the crack. He lowers it about fifteen feet. He leans over the pump and fires it up; the dead basin fills with engine noise.

Nothing comes. Brunella clutches the flat hose just as the Old Man and the Pendleton women and the Neds held theirs, waiting for water to inflate, waiting on deliverance from a machine. She closes her eyes. Leon adjusts the valve on the pump, running it at high speed. He checks his intake valve as well, pushing it down even farther.

"Forget it!" Brunella says. "There's no water in this basin."

"There was supposed to be a ton of water under here. A ton."

Leon cranks the engine to its highest level, an ear-straining whine that fills the dead forest land, bouncing over the rocks. He stands back with his hands on his hips, staring at Brunella with the hose, the full-running pump, the connection to the rock. He holds his hand up to stifle whatever Brunella is trying to say, shakes his head, and shuts the engine off.

"Niccolo didn't fuck up," Brunella says.

"Then who did?"

"Why does it have to be somebody?"

"I'll tell you a secret we never let out of the Forest Service. And you must keep it here, in this graveyard: Big Ernie only takes somebody when there's a fuckup."

"Fine, believe what you want. Write what you want. But you can't blame Niccolo. There's no water here, and that's why the pumps couldn't save them. There was never any water, can't you see?"

"There's nothing here now, sure. But there could have been water in here last summer. Would your father know anything about that?"

"I can't imagine how."

"Probably the aquifer is down from all those dry winters when it barely snowed."

"Leon, it's obvious what Teddy is trying to tell us: Niccolo did not fuck up. Niccolo had bad information."

"So why would he ask for pumps when there's no water here?"

"You're too smart by half. All you need to know is that what killed these jumpers—what killed Niccolo—is what killed this forest. It was dead before they came. The fire just finished it off."

He takes notes of two more tests, with the same results. The pumps work fine, but they draw no water from this junction of rock, seared earth, and dead trees. They walk back up to the crest of the ridge, arguing the case. Leon still wants to check the tribal water records and make one more trip to Montana to talk to Teddy. Brunella wants him to close the book and write in the words *Act of God.*

At the ridge, she finds a big boulder, the one they sat on at the start of a blizzard a few months back.

"The well should be somewhere around here," says Leon. "And I thought the pipe was—oh, there it is."

"But it looks empty now," says Brunella. "Nothing coming out of it."

"You don't seem very curious anymore."

"I just think we're at a dead end."

"Our well"—he stumbles around, takes a visual reading across the coulee, stops—"should be right here."

"You're standing on top of it," says Brunella, pointing to a patch of fresh sod, a circle, out of place against the still-brown native grass. "Pull that turf back."

He tugs at the new grass and it lifts away easily from a layer of fresh dirt. He kicks the dirt back until his boot hits a solid surface: cement.

"Capped," he says. "Somebody capped this well."

They pace along the ridge, near the edge of the dead forest and the new homes, to a three-story house with high timbered columns in the front, an entrance of glass, a long curving driveway of limestone. Leon went to Gregory Gorton's house once before, just after the fire, but has not been able to talk to him since then. When they ring the bell, they are met by barking dogs. They try knocking; nobody answers. Brunella walks around the back, toward a garden away from the house, protected from the wind. There she finds Gorton stooped near an immaculately tended row of vines.

Gorton looks up, startled. "You're trespassing."

"Excuse me, I'm Brunella Cartolano, your neighbor. We met at my father's party last year."

He rises, shakes dirt from his gloves, squints at her through quarter-inch-thick glasses, and sniffs. "Ah, yes." He smiles, blinking quickly. "How about that VinFaire? I told you then we had something special going in this coulee."

"Leon!" she yells. "Around back. I found him."

Gregory Gorton has a frozen, almost skeletal smile on his gaunt face, and he blinks constantly, as if he's sending out Morse code with his eyes.

"I hope your father is grateful," he says. He gestures to Leon. "I see the Forest Service is here again. As I recall from our prior conversation, you're an indigenous American of some sort."

Leon studies the single row of vines. He takes out his notebook, flips ahead a few pages, and starts with his questions. "We found water near your place a few months ago, what looked like a spring, going into a pipe."

"That's surprising," says Gorton, still smiling while blinking. "I've had extensive hydrology mapping done of the entire watershed."

"You never saw it?"

"I've been out of the country since late fall."

"The spring, the well, the pipe?"

"You have pictures, something you can show me? Because I have no idea what you're talking about."

"What do you have, five acres up here, Mr. Gorton?"

"Seven, counting the land we keep natural, which is mostly clay."

"And your water comes from . . . ?"

"The tribe. Two years ago they sold me an allotment."

"They didn't have anything to sell at that time, did they?"

"Oh, yes. They were just starting to consolidate some blocks of water, and they agreed to sell me a small portion because I paid a premium."

"Are you telling me the tribe drained that basin?" Leon says. "It's national forestland. Do you have any information on that?"

"I don't know what you're talking about. I'm a libertarian. I think Indians should buy and sell whatever commodity they have, without help from anyone. And I don't believe the government should own any property, which, by implication, would mean your job should be obsolete. With all due respect."

"If that well isn't yours, whose is it?"

"All I know is that I paid a fortune for my water, Mr. Treadtoofar, and made a nice little pile selling it back to the aboriginals. But considering what's about to happen, I missed an even bigger profit by selling too soon. The word is, starting next year, anybody sitting on Columbia River irrigation water can make a claim for permanent market-loss subsidy. If you've got water, and you own land that used to be in cultivation, you've got yourself a significant entitlement. The government is going to make millionaires out of all these sob stories."

CHAPTER FIFTEEN

A FTER TALKING Leon into letting her drive, Brunella steers the Suburban over the swells of brown land east of the Columbia, trying to hold to the lane in the bucking winds. The ground is treeless except for cottonwoods around farmhouses chapped by the dry gusts. Angelo used to tell his children that when he moved to the coulee country the dust storms were such that a farmer would tie a rope to himself and the house just to venture into the backlands of his section; without the cord, the farmer would be lost in a brownout.

The soil no longer lifts itself in great sheets, but the wind remains, of course, especially in the spring. Leon pays no attention to Brunella as she drives; he looks like he is staring into Saskatchewan, his thoughts so far from the front seat.

The river appears at odd turns, flat, moving at a crawl, full of young salmon racing against time to make it downriver, against the biological version of Cinderella's midnight deadline. They must make it to salt water within a few weeks or die, half morphed into something unable to live in freshwater. A few Indians and a biologist mark the passage at a canyon downriver, counting fish and counting days.

Brunella and Leon follow the river past two dams and then head east, into the heart of the Planned Promised Land, a grid of canals, straight roads, and little towns built to transport wheat and fruit, towns now gasping for life. The big irrigation sprinkler systems, aluminum piping set on huge tractor tires, stretching a half mile or more in some directions, spit water on untended fields. Even the large corporate farms are not making money this year, but they still draw their water from the backed-up Columbia and pour it onto the land, because that's what the system is set up to do. The towns have no stoplights, no banks, no grocery stores, just lone silos next to railroad stops, the storage bins stuffed with grain that nobody wants except the government, which has to want it by law. They have no banners highlighting spring festivals or coming opportunities, just the odor of an estate sale at a house where terminal illness still lingers.

Deep into his thoughts, Leon mumbles to himself.

"What?" she says. "Let me in."

"Turn there and follow it to Dry Falls."

The sky is full of drama in the way of spring east of the Cascades, where the mountains pull apart the clouds and the winds rake over the high plateau. They leave the irrigated patches behind and find themselves in the native brown land, with its basalt columns and potholes of water leftover from the ancient flood.

"Stop here," he says, pointing to what looks like a small abandoned garbage dump. The sun is warm on their skin as they step away from the car and walk to a mobile home tilted on one edge. The trailer is peagreen, with the fading legend U.S. GOVERNMENT on the edge. A cherry tree, shaggy but still blooming, stands alone in front.

"They gave these tin cans out to Hanford workers in World War Two," Leon says. "Then they abandoned them."

"Hard to believe anyone could live in something like that."

"Tell that to my mother."

"You mean this was—?"

"Three of us slept in the one room in the back, the one that's partially caved in. Mom had the other room. She was glad to be here. She's Wanapum, both her parents dead of drink. At twelve, she's an orphan, gets sent to the Mountain View School for Girls in Helena. They call her squaw slut and throw bottles at her. She moves back here, meets my father, he's with us for a while and then he goes to the navy, says it's the only way an Indian can get work out of this country, and we don't hear from him for a long time. She has nothing. Everyone says, Why don't you go to the reservation? She's Wanapum, so she can't go to Colville; they don't trust the

Wanapum. The Wanapum never signed the treaty; they had Smohalla. Ever hear of him?"

"Nope."

"Leader of the Dreamers, doomed from the start. Told the Wanapum not to live near whites, eat only Indian food, take nothing from the government. Hard to take anything when they ain't giving you anything, but that's what he said. He says don't be like the Nez Perce; they said yes to everything and the government still sent 'em to Oklahoma. Can you imagine being forced to move there after you've lived in the green mountains? The Nez Perce had a term for Oklahoma, called it *eeikish pah*—the hot place. But the Wanapum don't budge. When the dams came and flooded their homes, they got alcohol training and some land on the Colville Reservation, if they wanted it, forty acres total. Wanapum have to live between the worlds. But one day my mom, she has a change of mind. She says we have to go north, to move to Colville and wait for my father. Along the way, while we're moving, she finds this empty trailer and she takes it. Halfway, she says. We'll go halfway. We lived here six years."

"Who planted the cherry tree?"

"I did. It was a school project."

On the other side of the half-overturned trailer, an aluminum door flaps in the wind, the screen long ago ripped out, the bottom of the door partially peeled back, squawking in the gusts.

"Never did fix that door," says Leon. "We were waiting for my father. He'll fix it when he comes home, that's what my mom said. Fix it when he comes home. And let me tell you about the flies. We had 'em in swarms, from April to October, always the flies; no matter how many you killed, they found a way to get in. Big black flies, the kind that bite. And then"— here he starts to smile mysteriously, walking back to the Suburban—"we took care of the black flies."

They drive away from the last of the irrigated land past narrow lakes, no more geometric fields or big sprinkler systems. Clusters of bright yellow balsamwort, the signature wildflower of the Columbia basin, grow from the hills. He directs her another way, down into a yawning coulee on a dirt road that dead-ends against broad high walls that blot out half of the sky. No wind. He takes her hand and guides her along to a spot he treats as his own. He tells her the story of Dry Falls, where the world's biggest waterfall once roared, forty times the size of Niagara, four miles across. A surge of water equal to ten times the combined flow of all the world's rivers poured through here—four hundred million cubic feet of water per second—thundering down at speeds of sixty miles an hour or more, carving out the cavity big enough to hold Manhattan and all its skyscrapers. A thousand years ago, the last of the water retreated, leaving the rock dry, the falls a phantom. They hear nothing today as they huddle inside the fortress of basalt. Brunella feels she has been allowed into a secret club, as free of any sound as a night sky on the prairie is uncluttered by city light.

"How far to the reservation?" Brunella says.

"We can turn around, go back to Seattle, if you want."

"Are you afraid?"

"The Wanapum don't belong on the Colville Reservation."

"Are you Wanapum?"

"Some days I have no choice."

"So where is home?"

She runs her hand along his face, over the aquiline nose. She moves to kiss him, brushes his cheek, but senses his uneasiness.

"Will you still want to kiss me when I've finished the report on the Johnny Blackjack?"

She acts insulted, pulls back, but at heart she is not so sure of her own motives.

"Your father never answered my question the other night, Brunella."

"I thought he did."

"Maybe you can help me."

"I don't know anything about winemaking."

"Are you sure?"

"He keeps those secrets to himself."

They go past the Grand Coulee Dam without stopping, past the generators sending out enough electricity to power a million homes, past the clock that says LIVE BETTER ELECTRICALLY, past the signs advertising the nightly laser light show, which booms out *I am the river . . . I am life.* The reservoir behind the dam, stretching nearly to Canada, buried ten towns, most of them Indian. The new communities built around the dam, Elmer City, Electric City, Coulee City, are not cities at all but service centers for the Planned Promised Land, oddly retro, frozen in a dream that never advanced beyond 1959. Just like the farm towns, they are dying.

Indian country. The road suddenly turns bad, potholed and uneven, and there is no signage. Rusted mattress springs, tumbleweeds and plastic diapers snagged in the wires, a few cars left where they broke down. Pickup trucks slow as they approach the oncoming Suburban, people staring into the Forest Service car, suspicious, trying to make a connection. The Colville Agency building is like any other government office in Indian country, treated with contempt, peeling paint on the outside, broken steps in front, no landscaping. The reservation was not created out of logic or geography, Leon tells her; it was a casual recipe thrown together as government afterthought. Bands of people, some who got along with one another, some who hated everyone, were given the same homeland, and tossed in with them were a faction of the Nez Perce, the ones who never signed the treaty in which they lost their homeland in the Wallowa Valley, the ones who became Dreamers. They included Joseph, the war hero—at one time, the most famous Indian in America—who died sitting on this wind-lashed ground, staring into a fire, his face heavy with defeat. All these bands had only one thing in common, and when the dams came, the salmon were snuffed out, nearly two-thirds of the river basin drained of a life-giving species with ten thousand years of unbroken ties. After the little towns were buried by the Grand Coulee reservoir, the bands were placed on high windswept ground, just a few miles from the emerald squares and green circles of the Planned Promised Land.

Inside the agency building at Nespelem, Leon settles in with the water records. Brunella strolls outside, gathering stares. Every house in the village has a small satellite dish. Kids ride their scooters. A large banner advertising the Pow Wow competition flaps in the wind. Another group of kids, older, more furtive, lean in the shade against the cinder-block wall of a commodities exchange store, passing a can of hair spray back and forth. One of them covers his face.

Leon walks briskly out of the agency building, a folder of fresh-copied records in his hand. "Let's go," he says, avoiding eye contact with the kids sniffing hair spray.

"What did you find?"

"Get in the car. I'll drive."

A mile or so out of town, he pulls off the road within view of two mobiles with a basketball hoop out front on a shared driveway. Leon opens the folder and points to a line of figures.

"Alden Kosbleau, five thousand acre-feet, sold on the first of February . . . Kosbleau, six thousand acre-feet, sold on the first of March . . . Kosbleau, three thousand acre-feet, sold on the first of April . . ."

He looks up at her.

"That's where the tribe got most of its water—Kosbleau. And look at this: I never dreamed there was so much water still in that part of the basin where we had the fire. Yet . . . the trees in that dying forest, they were so dessicated. The trees wouldn't look like that if there were springs of this magnitude around. He must have been hoarding himself a lake! He must have diverted it all from the original aquifer."

"Why do you say that?"

"Do you know this guy Kosbleau?"

"He's my father's oldest friend. He's the water king, always has been a wheeler-dealer. But this could be a mistake. Alden Kosbleau is an honorable man. You're saying all that water from the pipe on the ridge—"

"Kosbleau."

"And you think he drained the forest where Niccolo died? Sucked it out and redirected it into the pipe, so he could store and sell it later at a huge markup? And that's why we couldn't get anything from the pumps?"

"I don't know the exact time sequence. But he transferred a shitload of water from that entire drainage. He's probably sitting on a fair amount of it now, waiting for the big buyout Gorton was talking about. The rest of it—according to these records—he sold to the tribe."

"Why would he sell to the tribe, knowing there's a buyout on the way?"

"I don't know. The tribe has not been leveling with us."

"With us. You mean, you and me?"

"I mean the Forest Service."

She looks away to the children playing basketball and speaks as if in a trance. "It must be tough for you, Leon."

"For me? Why do you say that? I'm a Forest Service lifer. I'm just doing my job."

"But this looks like the tribe is in pretty deep as well. You must feel . . . conflicted. Imagine if this were your family working that water deal and you knew, if it got out, it would harm your family. What would you do? It's your family, your blood, your home at stake."

"I don't have that choice, so I don't think about it. I worry about what we know. These water transfers never showed up in the hydrology records until now. They were hidden. Those smoke jumpers got bad information when your brother asked for pumps, and it cost them their lives."

"You think this bad information . . ." She trails off, her voice falling away.

"Yes?"

"You think it came from a map? Like a really old hydrology map?"

"I'm not sure why they thought there was water in there. We need to talk to the two survivors. I don't know who would tell them there's water in there when it was barren."

"Tozzie Cresthawk. He's around. We could talk to him."

"But he has no memory."

"So he says. You think he's covering up for the tribe?"

"I didn't say that. We need to interview Ted Flax one more time. He's holding something back. Now tell me, Brunella, and look at me, please, when I ask you this: Do . . . you . . . have . . . any idea what Alden Kosbleau was doing with all that water?"

"It doesn't make sense to me, Leon."

"Would your father know?"

"My father?"

"I can't see your eyes. Look at me, please."

She turns to him, but she will not look him in the face. "I don't know about Kosbleau; he's retired. He's a hobbyist now, grows some cherries and ornamentals, lives well off the subsidies and all his deals. He's no different from anyone else in this basin, except a little smarter."

"Where is he now?"

"Out of town. I told him to look after my father when he returns."

"You what?"

"I left a message. I've been worried about Babbo and this delusion he has about trying to climb Mount Stuart. Kosbleau is family to us. He'll be back in a week."

"What's curious is why he hooked up with the tribe. Look at these payments. They drained most of that watershed together. We'll have to run a clean hydrology test, talk to Kosbleau and Flax. Trace the property ownership on the land that holds that drainage pipe up on the coulee. But it looks clear to me now. I have to call this in."

Two teenage girls catch his eye, shooting hoops next to the mobile. Outside shot—*swish*. Foul line—*swish*. Hook shot—*swish*. They have a rhythm, drawing Leon in. He gets out of his car and walks up to the girls in front of the basketball hoop. A small dog greets him with a scrappy bark. The girls hold the ball, staring at the Indian forest ranger like he's an exotic creature. He says, "Hey, how 'bout a shot?" They toss the ball to him. He says, "Hook shot." He pivots, arcs, misses.

When he returns to the car, Brunella is wiping tears from her face. "I didn't mean to make you cry," Leon says.

"You didn't make me cry."

The biggest house on the reservation sits on a dun-colored hill surrounded by a curve of Ponderosa pines. It is a three-story, three-garage, cedar-shingled home with river-rock chimney, a long driveway, a Grand Cherokee in the front.

"Who owns the starter castle?" Brunella says, as they pull up.

"We do."

"Who's we?"

"Mom, my sister, and her family. You remember I told you about the black flies? Mom came up with a potion. Can't tell you all the ingredients, but it has a couple parts balsamwort, couple camas, some home heating oil. She hardened it all off like a wax. Flies love it, and they die on contact."

"Indian Flykill! It's in every store."

"We got a patent on it. Sold it to one of them petrochemical companies. Bought this house, bought some Cisco before it tanked, got college funds for the boys, lotsa toys for every cousin on three reservations. Hey . . . kid!"

Leon's sister runs from the front door to greet him, her four dogs following her. Esmerelda Treadtoofar is thin-legged, her hair tied back, wearing shorts, Hawaiian flip-flops on her feet. She seems taken aback to see Brunella.

"She's helping me," says Leon.

"But you always work alone."

Inside, a grating sound comes from a large sun-filled room off the main part of the house. A pair of boys with green spiky hair are going at it, fingering controls that direct a big screen where two combatants are trying to lance, bleed, and behead each other.

"Nuke 'em!" one of the boys shouts. "Nuke 'em!"

When Leon pokes his head in the room, the boys look up for an instant, then return to their mortal clashes. On their wall is a signed poster of Sherman Alexie.

"Aren't you boys gonna say hi to your uncle?" Esmerelda asks.

"Hi, Uncle."

"Hi, Uncle."

When Leon is alone with Esmerelda, he tells her the boys ought to be outside, doing something useful, catching fish, chasing rabbits, riding their bikes.

"It's okay," says Esmerelda. "Video games keep 'em off Aqua Net."

"The hair spray?"

"The drug of choice on the rez. They banned inhalants on the Colville, but that stuff is too easy to get."

She serves them steak fajitas, the meat spicy, with grilled sweet onions and peppers, a pitcher of iced tea. Brunella asks Esmerelda what Leon was like as a boy, what kind of teen he was, what he wished for when he was little, but Esmerelda will not give up any of the family stories. She invites her brother to stay overnight, though she does not look at Brunella when she makes the offer. Leon defers. After dinner he tells her he must go, they have a long drive.

"Our house is too good for you?" Esmerelda says, and turns away, not saying goodbye.

At dusk, they drive back through Indian country, stopping at the commodities exchange for gas. A huddle of sunken-faced boys pass hair spray back and forth, sniffing and drifting away from the reservation, in the same spot as they were before. One of them looks familiar.

"Tozzie?" Leon shouts through the wind. The sniffers scatter as he calls out, leaving an empty can of Aqua Net behind.

Inside the commodities exchange, the clerk, a middle-aged man in a Seahawks jacket, scrutinizes the name as Leon signs the credit card.

"Leon Treadtoofar? Son of a buck. We went to high school together."

Leon doesn't recognize the man. "You sure?"

"Sure as shit. What I hear, only you, me, the Get-Me-Home twins, and Sactooth are left alive from our senior class."

"That's something," says Leon, averting eye contact, turning to leave.

"Yeah, that's something," says the clerk, who appears hurt. "I guess what they say about you's true."

"What's that?"

"Nothing."

"Tell me."

"They took the Indian out of you."

Leon bolts for the clerk, grabs his shirt, sticks his nose in his face. "Say that again."

The clerk does not back down. "You heard me."

Leon takes a step back, releases his grip, but keeps his face hard on the clerk. "Just because I left this place doesn't mean I'm any less Indian than you."

As they head toward Grand Coulee, the land is softer in dying light that conceals the scraps of an unhappy place: empty plank houses without roofs, abandoned schoolhouses where grass now grows in place of classroom floors. A few halfhearted thunderheads scoot by.

"Why didn't we stay at your sister's house? Was it because of me?"

"It was because of me. I love Esmerelda, but she probably thinks the same thing about me as that dude at the minimart. I could never live on the reservation. If you leave and make some success for yourself, they won't let you forget it. It's like you did something wrong. What that man said to me—that's the worst thing you can say to somebody who comes from here."

"Is it true?"

"Now you disrespect me as well?"

"Leon, I have at least three thousand years of the Italian peninsula running through my blood. Some days I can feel the Piemonte in my hands. I know the Roman side of my brain. And on days like that, I still don't know where I belong. Have you ever heard of the Ladin?"

"No. It's a family name?"

"The Ladin are the descendants of the last Roman soldiers. After the empire collapsed, they fled from the Visigoths and wandered back and forth across the Alps, hiding in the valleys. They ended up in the Dolomites. My fantasy—well, I've actually thought about it quite a bit—is to go back to Italy and trace the lineage of the Cartolano family, because I'm sure we have some blood link to the Ladin."

"You sure they aren't Indians?"

"Leon, let's not drive straight through to Seattle. Take me someplace that still has magic in it for you."

Leon falls silent for several moments. "I have a place," he says, "but I haven't been there for twenty-five years. Maybe it's gone."

"Take me."

They walk over scablands under a thin moon, and then along a rise, until it starts to drop beneath columns of stacked basalt. Leon appears uncertain but never lost. He smells for sulfur, listens for a sound. A few sandhill cranes, the last to migrate north, lift out of the brush as they approach. Leon spots beer cans and markings on a rock flank—initials—and then stops at a hot spring: a natural pool cradled by rock, steam rising above, the water trickling away as it boils up to the level part of the ground. Drifts of gray ash from the Mount Saint Helens eruption have hardened in one corner against the rock. Brunella unbuttons the top of Leon's shirt, and when he does not resist she pulls down his pants. He slips away, seeming embarrassed, slides into the steaming water, wincing at first, then immersing himself to his chest. Brunella removes her clothes slowly, standing in the silver light. She walks around him naked, tiptoeing on the edge of the rock, her legs beaded in mist. She knows he is admiring her, but he tries to keep some distance. She tests the temperature of the water with her toe.

"What is it that makes hot springs so alluring?" she says. "Something about how the earth opens up to embrace you, don't you think?"

"Are you going to get in?"

She lies on a slab of flat rock next to the springs, on her side, cupping the water with her hand and pouring it over her breasts, her legs. Leon wades over to her, his eyes meeting her body, and she cocks her leg at an angle, opening up, inviting him. He is close enough for her to smell the blend of sweat and sulfur coming off his body. She rubs his neck with the heel of her other foot, and his presence, so near in the hot water, makes her wet and sets her heart racing. Her breathing picks up, and then she slows it deliberately, exhaling with her lips pursed as she becomes more aroused. She closes her eyes and appears to go into a trance, pulling his head in between her legs with her heel. She wants him to bury that Nez Perce nose inside her. But he gets out of the water abruptly, turning his back to her, though she can see he is erect. She tells him to come back, to lie next to her, to relax, to think of floating away.

"*Fare l'amore, per favore.*"

"Speak English."

"Make love to me, Leon. Take your time."

"I can't. You and I could never—"

A coyote starts to howl, setting off an echoing round of other howls, the sound carrying over the scablands.

When they are dressed and walking back over the plateau to his car, he guides her by the hand. She feels close to him in this wordless stroll, wishing they could walk until they collapse of exhaustion. He unrolls two sleeping bags on dry grass next to the Suburban.

"Promise me something, Brunella Cartolano," he says. "Promise me that tonight is off the record."

"I don't know what that means, Leon."

"I'm still the Forest Service."

"You're always the Forest Service."

CHAPTER SIXTEEN

T HE RUMORS started at Forest Service regional headquarters in Seattle, moved quickly across the mountains, trickled out to a talk radio station in taffy pulled from truth, and from there were broadcast as bible into the pickup trucks of irrigators looking for something to blame, into cafés where pink-faced men passed around petitions, into windowless bars where the stories fattened with every new round of beer. By the time Brunella and Leon arrive in midafternoon, a phalanx of sheriff's deputies guards the Indian construction site; they can do little but hold a line at the entrance gate, clutching shotguns. People clank bullhorns of logging trucks, long-beds, and assorted eight-cylinder workhorses, muscle vehicles made obsolete by land that produces little now but government checks. They shout through megaphones and cheer when someone stokes their sense of righteous victimhood. It all makes sense to them now, the swift and spectacular crash of their lives, the dry fields and withered orchards, the recoloring of the land—it makes sense in the way that bad times must lend themselves to a tidy scheme. They hear it on the radio—everyone is talking about it—and here it is in the hot light of the afternoon: a reservoir, still filling, drained from the most productive fruit-growing area in the world. The heart of the Planned Promised Land has been sucked dry by the Indians. Farming is dead. The Indians are hoarding all the water, so the rumors go, because they had a master plan all along, and the evidence is this pit, this graveyard of accumulated water rights. And for what cause have these irrigators lost their water, what new enterprise will replace the people who made the desert bloom? One story making the rounds says all the water is going to be pumped out of the pit and used as a thirty-story hydro show—a Grand Coulee spillway in reverse—an upthrusting fountain that will draw millions to the tribe's new casino.

And so what if the water had been purchased legally from one failing irrigator after another, the tribe taking advantage of good market conditions, buying in a time of panic. Did Solvan Flax or Arnie Petersen know then that these buyers never intended to put another sapling into the ground? Yesterday, the federal government announced plans for the biggest bailout yet. Gregory Gorton was right. Anybody who could prove they owned a farm for at least twenty years, and still had sufficient irrigation water, could set themselves up for a lifetime of "market adjustment" payments. It was said to be temporary, a moratorium. But everyone knew it was the beginning of a lucrative charade. The government would pay the irrigators to pretend, reasoning that this would prop up prices for farmers in other states, while preserving rural culture in the irrigated steppe. This bonanza for the imagined agrarian was coming too late for the majority of the Columbia basin irrigators, who had already sold. And there are few things worse than seeing all the pieces fit together after it is too late to get in on it.

A rumble of mutterings comes from the hot pavement outside the construction site. Sweat drips from baseball hats, the rage ramped up a notch with every incantation.

"Take a look at it," says Mrs. Flax, screaming through a megaphone, pointing a withered finger at the pit, about three acres in size, more than a hundred feet deep. She is draped in cats—around her shoulders, on her lap, around her feet.

"This is rural cleansing!" They bang baseball bats on buckets. They whoop and they drink beer. For most people, what burns is simply the sight of all this water—the liquid nutrients of their livelihoods—drained from the land they transformed and now pooled in one spot.

"They've taken it all," Mrs. Flax shouts. "They are driving us out!"

In every water fight, in every parched and pebbled valley west of the one hundredth meridian, the Indians have never won; even when they seemed to have won, it was temporary, cast aside by senate amendment or executive order. Mrs. Flax reminds the mob of this history now: The Biggest Thing Ever Built by Man was not meant to right an injustice or settle a century-and-a-half-old slight written into treaty. It was built to choke off the River of the West and channel water onto prickly ground, to create something from nothing, to transplant Arcadia to the desert. In the West, they all knew, water flowed uphill to money, not downhill to the dispossessed.

Among the scattershot of suggestions is the idea—which quickly becomes a demand—that the water be given back to the irrigators, that the government force the Indians to stick with fireworks and untaxed cigarettes and cancel all the sales. How the irrigators can get the water back, or how they will reconstruct their lives at a time when nobody wants to pay them at least as much as it costs to grow fruit in a dry land, nobody knows. But government created the Planned Promised Land, and they expected government to restore it.

The Indian construction manager in gray braids appears at the gate, behind the fence, a sheriff's deputy on either side of him. Danny Red Thunder is booed and hissed as he tries to speak into a megaphone.

"Let him talk," Mrs. Flax says. "Then we'll decide what to do."

"I have nothing to say except we will not waste this water—"

"Bullshit!"

"Why are you hoarding it, you son of a bitch!"

"We will not waste it."

"You're lying! Just like you lied when you starting buying up every-thing."

"You sold your water rights to us fair and square," Danny Red Thunder says. "How can you say we have taken it against the will of—"

A teenage boy launches a beer bottle; it hits the Indian construction manager on the forehead, shattering the glass. Danny Red Thunder falls to the pavement, blood pouring from a gash. The deputies scan the crowd, but they do not dare wade among the people. Two other beer bottles follow, and then a full volley of rocks and glass. One man climbs over the fence, storms up to Danny Red Thunder, and throws a handful of gravel into his bleeding face. The deputies try to drag the wounded Indian away from the mob.

Brunella and Leon have been watching from a corner of the parking lot, out of the crowd's view. As they listen, Brunella feels Leon recoil, senses his panic. And she feels as if the bottle thrown at Danny Red Thunder came from her hand. She wants to tell Leon everything, but now it seems too late. Events have passed her by. A force borne on one perception has taken hold and assumed the form of the mob.

"How did this happen?" Leon says. He is sweating profusely, his Forest Service shirt drenched. "These people need to know the truth. They can't just blame the tribe."

"The tribe's got the water, Leon. These people see that, and it makes them mad. They think they were duped into selling."

"No!" He slams his fist against the door of the Forest Service truck, hard enough to make a slight dent. The temper: Here it is again, a flash of violence so sudden it scares her. "That's not it! These people are mad because they can't stand to see Indians have power over their lives."

"You need to have an open mind."

"Open mind!" He raises two clenched fists, tries to catch himself, to exhale slowly and bring this fury down. "I kept this report on the Johnny Blackjack open because of you. I could have closed this thing out last fall. But I kept it open, and look what has happened. Look! This mob . . . who are these people?"

"They're the people I grew up with. That woman with the megaphone, Mrs. Flax—Teddy's mother—you should have known her when she was young."

"She scares the shit out of me."

The man who threw gravel at Danny Red Thunder starts to tug on the wounded Indian, pulling him away from the deputies. He brings Danny to his feet and throws him against the fence. As he holds him there, two other men poke at his knees with a baseball bat through the fence.

"Take the water back!" comes a shout. Several men charge over the fence and break for the pit. They open a valve at the head of the reservoir. Cheers of victory go up, as if a goal were scored in a hockey game. A stream of water—born in the sky, leached through the ground to a deep aquifer, and then sucked from beneath a forest and into a pipe for settlement in a bank of Indian dreams—now leaks onto the hot pavement, where it starts to evaporate.

Tozzie Cresthawk is alone at the river in the last light. He is wearing a headband, nothing else, standing atop a high cliff at the foot of a canyon overlooking the Columbia. The towering rock was deposited in this slot canyon during the last Ice Age flood, and Indians have come here for centuries to check the downstream passage of small salmon, to watch the future pass by, to see the bounty of four years ahead. All afternoon, Tozzie has stood atop this rock, looking for young fish migrating to sea. His dreams through the winter have been of swarms of tiny salmon moving like a steady wind down the River of the West and away to the world. In the last light, he hears the hornet buzz of a pair of jet-skiers, slicing over the pane of the river. He hears laughter and loud chatter from big pleasure boats. No sign of migrating salmon. The fish have to make it here by the end of this week, he knows from the elders, or they will die, unable to live in bodies answering to a growth schedule rooted in ten thousand years of predictability. Since grade school, teachers, priests, elders, and family have all warned Tozzie not to give in to the despair that drapes this landscape. He had diversions and his pride, tied to horse races and smoke jumping and, most of all, fishing. There is nothing to hold him now.

Tozzie moves to the edge of the high rock, stares straight ahead, and mutters a prayer for his soul. He opens his eyes wide. But he can't jump. He appears scared of the height. One more time with the eyes closed, the hands outstretched, the prayer, a move closer to the edge, knees crouched, down, up and—no. He can't do it. A failure, even, at suicide.

Now he crawls back down the rock, cursing himself for his cowardice, loud enough that it echoes across another beacon of rock. Crawling down, not paying attention, he misses a foothold and slips, falls back and tumbles, hits the rock hard, and bounces into the water. One of the pleasure boats picks him up. His heart is beating, but his eyes are closed.

CHAPTER SEVENTEEN

L EON TREADTOOFAR goes to Missoula on the last flight from Seattle, arriving at the small airport in the clearing north of town. On the descent, he keeps his face pressed against the window, taking in the sight of the Blackfoot, the Bitterroot, and the Clark Fork rivers as they converge, noticing the green on the prominent mountainside with the big **M** on its flank above the University of Montana. In the airport he pauses to see if any new stuffed animals are on display in the glass cages; they have added a cougar, to go with the grizzly bear and the bobcat. He walks outside and down the road a few hundred feet to smoke jumper headquarters, picks up a Forest Service car, and drives north to Saint Ignatius. At the mission church, he searches for Teddy Flax, calling into the murals, shouting at the rafters, impatient.

"Where the hell are you?"

An elderly priest in golf shirt and checkered pants tells Leon he will not find Teddy in the church, nor will he find him in the orchard. Teddy is gone, he says. He will not be coming back to Saint Ignatius. No reason.

Returning to Missoula, Leon goes to the jumpers' hangar, moving as if he has run out of time. He is greeted by old friends, men from his rookie year in the Forest Service, still trim and chasing smoke, women who left administrative jobs to dance with Big Ernie. They want to gossip and complain about senators who know nothing of the ways of silviculture. Leon is impatient.

"You won't see Teddy Flax around here," says Hank Shipley, a veteran jumper. "Look for yourself. You won't see him, Leon."

He hustles into a room where three men in running shoes and shorts sit at ancient Singer sewing machines, their bulging thighs bumping up against the bottom of the sewing table. They are running thread through jump chutes, repairing rips and reinforcing weak points. Above them is a poster of Richard Widmark from a movie about the 1949 Mann Gulch fire, *Red Skies of Montana*.

"Hey, Leon. Looking for Teddy Flax, are you?"

"Did somebody put the word out?"

"Everybody knows you're in the endgame."

"And what else does everybody know?" Leon sits down on a stool next to the Singer. "Let me have a rip at this thing." He runs a section of the jumper's suit through the machine, sewing two even lines.

"Now watch me," he says, peeling off his jacket and falling to the ground. He does twenty-five push-ups, stands, gets his breath, and walks over to a bar. He does ten chin-ups, "Three more than required," he says.

"Leon, you don't have to—"

"I'm not done yet." He falls to his back and curls up, elbows behind his head, repeats. Fifty sit-ups.

"Now all I gotta do is run the mile and a half in under eleven minutes. I can do that too."

"You don't need to. I believe you can still qualify."

"I don't want to hear any more talk about hanging a smoke jumper," says Leon, rebuttoning the top of his shirt. "I am one of you, okay? I want to get this thing finished and close it out for all of us. I just want the record to show what happened. Now, where is Ted Flax?"

The jumpers hold up their hands, bewildered.

"All right. One last question: Would you tell me if you knew?"

In unison they answer. "Never."

Brunella follows Leon by a day. After watching the mob outside the Indian construction site, Leon told her he was cutting her loose to finish the job on his own. It was a mistake, he said, to let her help in any way.

She knew he was going to Missoula because that was his only lead. He needed a survivor of the fire to confirm that there was no water in the basin when Niccolo tried to run the pumps. A witness who would take some pressure off the Indians would be even better. With Tozzie in a coma, Teddy Flax was the sole remaining voice.

At smoke jumper headquarters, Hank Shipley guides Brunella around the big hangar, showing her the memorial in honor of Niccolo and the other jumpers who died in the Johnny Blackjack. The dead will remain heroic in this lair of fire gods, joining the pictures of victims from Mann Gulch and South Canyon. As Brunella stares at her brother's image, it strikes her that the Cartolano family story now has a certain symmetry. Angelo began his real American journey in Missoula, at the World War II internment camp with his uncle, and now here is Niccolo's picture in the same western valley, eight thousand miles from the Italian Piemonte.

"Everybody loved Niccolo," says Hank Shipley.

"Now tell me something I don't know," Brunella says, turning away from the wall. "Where is Teddy Flax?"

"He's . . . nowhere in particular."

"Don't bullshit me, Hank."

"I've seen him playing softball," he says, "but then maybe it *wasn't* him. He's been at the bookstore every other Thursday for the poetry slam, but it could've been someone else, you know, with the lights dim and all and his face such a mess from the fire. He's the guy I saw on the ski slope one Monday morning a couple months back, on my day off, 'cause no one else skis like him, with that silly-ass jump-step turn—or maybe not, you know?"

"Hank . . . I'm tired. My father is old and he talks to coffeepots more than to people. One of my brothers is dead; the other one wants to sell the house out from under us. I've got a government agency trying to pin the deaths of all those jumpers on Niccolo, and the guy running that investigation has a valley full of people ready to shoot anybody who's got water. On top of that, I'm trying to keep the fifth-richest man in the world from trashing the fishing culture of the city I love. Or maybe he's third-richest. Please don't fuck with me."

Hank tries to stifle a grin. "God, you're a feisty one. You doing anything tonight?"

"Where's Teddy?"

"He's everywhere and he's nowhere, like I said. Nobody knows where he hangs his hat. And nobody's gonna tell."

In the evening she climbs the switchback behind the university, a brisk jaunt to the big **M** on the mountain flank. At the top, she feels the wind on her wet skin and watches the course of the river as it spills out of a canyon and turns through the center of Missoula. The water is clear enough for dry-fly fishing, and she wonders what the best men of Missoula are using to lure fish to the surface tonight. On the way down, she tries to think like Leon. She knows that he stays in the same hotel chain, that he prefers the ground floor, with views of the parking lot. She knows that he gets up early, skips breakfast, does not drink coffee; that the only thing he will watch on television is the Weather Channel; that he likes Mexican food. He is thorough to the point of being plodding, which means he probably also saw the notice on the wall just below the pictures of dead smoke jumpers, telling Forest Service employees that Dr. Gilbert Pede-cana, the renowned plastic surgeon, was coming to Missoula. Next to that was another notice urging donations to the Intermountain Firefighters Skin Bank.

She stalks the hospital for two days. Some of the nurses know she is part of the Forest Service family, and they allow her to roam the halls. On her third day in Missoula, Brunella corners the doctor in the cafeteria. He tells her skin grafts are painful and sometimes never take, and there is a chronic shortage of donor skin.

"Have you seen Teddy yet?"

He will not divulge anything about the burn victims who have been brought here from all parts of the West for another chance at transforma-tion. "Which one is he?"

"You're being coy, but I'll play along, Doc. The boy with the burned face."

"He's a boy?"

"I always think of him that way. We grew up together. He suffered second-degree burns over more than half of his face."

"Do you know what a second-degree burn is, Ms. Cartolano?"

"Below the epidermis."

"Yes. A skin graft for that sort of burn must be deep. Infections develop. Complications follow, and sometimes the complications are fatal."

She falls asleep on a vinyl-topped bench in a hallway on the third floor of the hospital, a book of Emily Dickinson's poems in her lap. She dozes off with a line in her head: " 'Hope' is the thing with feathers."

In the middle of the night, a male nurse crouches over Brunella and shakes her awake. She is startled by this balding, muscular man in his blue outfit, two beepers attached to his belt. He scolds her, saying visiting hours are over and she must leave the floor. She promises to depart but begs for a moment to go to the bathroom. She stays in the toilet stall for several minutes, then pokes her head out, making sure the nurse is gone. Quickly, she tiptoes past several of the post-op rooms. In one, she finds a long slim figure covered in sheets, an IV tube overhead. The patient looks big enough to be Teddy, but she cannot make out a face. She walks closer, wondering what he looks like now, nearly a year after the fire remade his face. Gently, she tugs at one of the sheets, pulling it back just a few inches.

"Oh, my God!"

She falls back against the sink in the small room, horrified by the sight: the face of an old woman, hairless, lines like a web of canals.

Two doors down, she sneaks into another room, banked with electronic monitoring equipment, a steady beep coming from a digital blood-pressure monitor. She hears a slight high voice come from the bed, a woman. "Something, please . . . I'm so thirsty." Brunella gets a glass of water and puts a straw in the mouth of the patient.

A third room on the floor is meat-locker cold, as if somebody has been trying to drive down the temperature. Brunella shivers as she walks slowly to the bed. The patient smells of antiseptic and pus. She notices two big tubes draining fluids. Most of the patient's face is wrapped in gauze, everything obscured but the nostrils and the mouth. The rest of the body is covered by sheets, except for the right leg, which is exposed. She listens to the labored breathing and sees that, even in the chill, sweat has seeped through the sheets. The patient must have been burning with fever. But when she touches a part of the skin, it feels icy cold. This cannot be Teddy either, she decides; the person looks too slight. On her way out the door, she pauses, returns to the bed, and covers the leg. Then she sees it: the scar, a pink curving line that looks exactly like the Nike swoosh, and she remembers.

She reaches for another blanket from the closet and covers Teddy. She rests her head on his chest, summoning images: the kid racing with him in the coulee; the only guy in high school who didn't look at the world as a hostile place; Teddy at timberline last summer, the West in his face, just the right kind of swagger. She sees him in the alpenglow of that evening after fishing, stripped to his shorts, the son of a bitter woman who had, himself, yet to be poisoned by cynicism or hate.

Hearing footsteps, she dashes into the bathroom and crouches in a narrow space between the wall and the toilet. A nurse enters—the balding man who tried to chase her from the floor. He changes some outer-layer gauze wraps that are yellowed and damp. He checks blood pressure, body temperature, empties one of the drainage containers, puts a drink with straw next to his head. When he leaves after nearly fifteen minutes of adjustments, Brunella has fallen asleep.

She wakes in watery predawn light, her legs cramped, a quirk in her neck from the awkward nap. Back at Teddy's bedside, she notices liquid around the edges of his mouth, in the opening in the gauze. The straw in the drink is damp. But if he is awake, she cannot tell by his face, for his eyes are covered.

"Teddy . . . Teddy, this is Brunella. I'm so glad I found you."

He does not move. She talks to him in a rambling whisper, telling him the story of her last few days in Missoula, about the river running clear and what it would be like to wade into a pool just outside the college campus, a feeder convergence for trout where oxygen bubbles and riffles carry fresh-hatched bugs. He lifts a bandaged hand slowly from beneath the sheets, startling Brunella. She sits back down on the bed, reaches for the hand, folds it in hers, and holds it close to her breast.

"Can you hear me, Teddy?"

She feels life in his hand, a slight squeeze of his fingers around hers. The three fingers that were badly burned when he ran through the fire are pink, like new flesh, but oddly without lines of age or wear. He runs his hand to Brunella's face, contouring over her features, lingering at the mouth, then down, gently, touching the nape of her neck. He drops his hand away and taps on the table.

"Drink? You want to drink?"

She puts the straw to his lips, but he spits the water out, shakes his head, and taps the table again. Beneath the napkin are three books. One of them she recognizes: It is the leather-bound book that never leaves Teddy's side. The cover is scarred from the fire, and the paper edges are blackened.

"Ah, you want me to read?" She opens the book. " 'I am haunted by waters. . . .' " And with those few words she knows Teddy will slip away from the hospital bed to a place in the river where the riffles meet the smooth.

She stays with him for two days, making an agreement with the nurses—even the crank with two beepers—that she can visit anytime during the day so long as she leaves him alone at night. She keeps the room clean, brings smoked salmon for him to eat between meals of creamed spinach and oatmeal, and goes through all the book, though she reads it slowly, knowing how he likes to hear the language. She has brought in some lilacs; the fragrance fills the room, replacing the smell of pus and sweat. He is heavily medicated for pain, which makes him thirsty, woozy, and only periodically coherent, but on the second day he sits up, face still wrapped like a mummy, his chest clean and untouched by fire.

"Why is the food always mush?" he says, in midafternoon.

"They think you're nauseated, Teddy. They think you can't hold anything down."

"I have teeth. They should let me use 'em."

"Will you tell me about Niccolo?"

"Sit closer. I want to touch you."

She sits on the bed, staring into a head that resembles a volleyball. He tours her face with the back of his fingers.

"You're so pretty," he says. "You'll never want to look at me."

"Is that why you fled?"

"When you're invisible, it's a powerful freedom."

"You'll never make a good phantom."

"They're going to take the bandages off my eyes on Thursday, next week."

"What do they expect?"

"*I* expect to look in the mirror and see a face. Not my old face, but a face. I don't know what *they* expect."

"Then what are you going to do with the rest of your life?"

"What are *you* going to do?"

"Maybe I'll run away. Try to be invisible, like you."

"Where would you go?"

"Home."

"To the coulee? That's not running away."

"No, home. The place where the Cartolanos belong, in the Piemonte south of the Alps, or maybe in the Dolomites, hiding in a valley like the Ladins. Or maybe to a village on top of a hill, in a small house of ancient stone, surrounded by ancient footsteps, with grapes sloping to eternity and a festival for every major food group, and a miracle reenacted twice a year in a thousand-year-old church. Away from all the shit—this daily storm."

"Where did you say this place was?"

"Then again, maybe I'll just dig in. Be a stubborn ass and not apologize for it. Maybe I'll become a winemaker like my father. I swore I would never do it. Still, perhaps I was born to the grape. I have a lot of shortcomings, so much to learn. I don't have Babbo's palate. I know very little about viniculture. I still don't know if an oak barrel should be charred or kiln-dried. I never understood when to start a second round of fermentation. Winemaking is a glorious mystery, so much of it. Babbo's got some years left, and he can teach me."

"Like he was going to do for Niccolo. You could take his place."

"And you could come help me."

"For pay? You mean I'd work for you?"

"Or just stay in the stone chapel if you want, make it your temporary home. There's always a place for you in the coulee."

"There's no place for me there."

"Didn't your family leave you something after they sold out?"

"My family? I'm alone in the world, Brunella. And no, Mr. and Mrs. Flax gave me nothing after selling, not a penny. But I didn't expect anything. Could you rub my leg, please?"

"Which one?"

"By the Nike scar. You've been there. It's starting to cramp."

She kneads the muscles in a gentle fashion.

"That's very nice, Brunella."

"*Non c'è problema.*"

"Could you get me my drink?"

She brings the straw to his dry lips; he takes in a long pull, adjusts his body in the bed.

"Describe the day."

"It's wonderful. A few clouds floating past, a light breeze. And I can see snow on the highest part of the Bitterroots. What would you use today if you were on the river, Teddy?"

"Caddis, probably, some garden-variety year-round fly. Too early for the stone-fly hatch. I wouldn't get too fancy with the rainbows of western Montana. They've seen it all. Down a little lower, Brunella, that's where the cramp is." He reaches for his drink but knocks it to the ground.

"Are you hungry?"

"Starved."

"I wonder if they would let me cook. I brought something."

She takes a bag down the hall to the nurses' station. They are reluctant to allow her into the back room where they keep a hot plate, a microwave, and a refrigerator. She walks by without waiting for approval and then starts to entice the nurses with what she's brought.

"*Alora . . . pappardelle con ragu.* Have you ever had a truly rich *ragu,* made of God's own tomatoes, not the hard, tasteless, New World Order things? With porcini mushrooms?" She removes a small sealed jar of tomatoes, a bag of dried *pappardelle,* an onion, some seasoning in a pouch.

"Where did you get these?" the head nurse asks.

"I always travel with the makings of at least one meal. My emergency bag. This"—she points to the jar of Cartolano tomatoes—"and the pasta, I brought from home. Everything else came from the Albertson's on Front Street."

"We can't let this—"

"Please, I'll take full responsibility. Act like you never saw me."

After she gets the *ragu* started, she returns to Teddy's room. He seems to be asleep, though it is difficult to tell with the wrappings over his face. She puts her finger under his nose and feels the breathing. Back in the tiny kitchen, she takes out a bottle of Montepulciano d'Abruzzo, the simple table wine from the mountain region east of Rome. The *ragu* needs only a half cup of the blood of Italy; she sets it aside and begins boiling water on the hot plate for the *pappardelle*. When the thick pasta noodles are ready, she pours wine into two plastic cups and takes the meal into the room with the patient.

The smell awakens Teddy. Brunella is immensely pleased to be able to arouse his senses.

"What is it?"

"Pappardelle con ragu."

"A family recipe?"

"Family tomatoes, well traveled, from Piemonte to Camp Missoula to the Columbia basin to Sacred Heart Hospital. Can you sit up?"

He edges his back slowly into a different position, though it is painful to move his butt and legs, from which skin has been lifted.

"Take a sip." She moves the wine under his mouth and helps him drink. "Montepulciano d'Abruzzo, a wine made for healing."

She feeds him the *pappardelle,* spooning it into his mouth and picking up the pieces that drip on the gauze and the sheets. The light is falling away behind the Bitterroots.

"It's good," he says, between bites. "Keep the wine coming."

"I have to be careful, with your pain medication. All you need is a taste."

He motions for one more sip, then waves off the food. "I know what you came for, Brunella," he says.

"Do you?"

"It was the heat that killed him. He wasn't burned and he didn't die of smoke inhalation. The heat killed Niccolo."

"The heat."

"Yes."

"I suppose that's good."

"No, it's not good. It's worse than anything you can ever imagine.

Worse than flames. Worse than drowning. Worse than being strangled. You see this?" He raises the hand. "Looks like flesh just melted off, the skin peelin' away, but the pain wasn't what you would think 'cause the nerves were destroyed. But Niccolo, he's in that broiler. The air becomes superheated, like—I don't know—four hundred, five hundred, six hundred degrees. Like somebody holding a blowtorch down your throat. But you have to breathe. You can't stop taking in air. You don't have a choice. So what you do is—"

"Stop!"

He reaches out to find her face, pawing the air before his fingers land. "I thought you wanted to know."

"I do."

"You went back to the fire, you and Treadtoofar?"

"Yes. Thank you for the tip. There isn't any water in there."

"That's correct."

"And there wasn't any last summer, Teddy?"

"Bone dry. Those pumps were never going to save us."

"So it wasn't Niccolo's fault?"

"Draw your own conclusions. Nick played it straight with the information he had."

She kisses him very gently, but he still winces at the touch of her lips on the freshly transplanted facial skin beneath damp gauze and silicone. Her eyes are clouded as she whispers a thank-you into his wrapped ears.

"Are you going to tell Leon Treadtoofar . . . what you just said to me?"

"If he asks. There's one more thing. You have to wonder about it yourself."

"Tell me."

"Why did your brother ask for water pumps? Why did he put his trust—and our lives—at risk, if there wasn't any water in there?"

"Well, obviously he didn't know that at the time. He got bad information."

"Did he ever tell you anything about the water in that basin, Brunella, before the fire?"

"No."

"He told me."

"What?"

"He told me about the water."

"Teddy. You mean he told you about Kosbleau and the Indians draining it all for that casino?"

"Is that what you and the investigator think happened?"

"It looks that way."

"Niccolo did everything a fire boss was supposed to do. The reason he was so confident about the pumps giving us relief was that he knew something, Brunella. He knew there had to be water in that basin. Now ask yourself this: How did he know? How could he have been so sure? We're in a humdinger of a drought. Everything's drawn down and caked, and still—still!—he's dead sure there's water in there."

"It's a mystery."

"No, it is not a mystery. Niccolo knew because your father told him."

"That can't be."

"Your father told him on the radio. That's where the bad information came from. I heard him. Angelo told him on the day of the fire. He knew there was water in there. He knew. He told Niccolo to save his life. But obviously something had happened that Angelo didn't know about. The water he thought was in that basin had disappeared."

"Yes, we know that. Leon and I have documents from the reservation, and we found a pipe up on the ridge, and it all leads down to the tribe's casino. But why would my father tell Niccolo there was water in there? How would he know? That's national forestland, not our property. It's been very dry. Everything was dying in there. I don't understand."

"Go ask your father." His lips are pursed, and he makes a sound like wax paper peeling off a piece of meat. "Is there any more of the pasta?"

She spoons another mouthful to him.

"And now I suppose you're going to ditch me."

"Is that what you think of me?"

"You don't need me anymore. I've told you everything I know. When you see my face, you will be afraid. And because a woman like you would never stay with someone disfigured, you won't want to be around me. Remember I told you last summer about the woman I nearly took the big ride with? She had money, and I didn't, and we could never be equal? It's the same with beauty. I understand that."

"A woman like me. What do you mean by that, Teddy?"

"You have a good heart. You may want to stay and see what I look like. But everything you say and do after that will be charity."

"I'll stay until they kick me out."

"No. You don't—"

"I'll stay after they take the bandages off your face."

"You can go."

"I'll stay until I'm—"

"Go, please. That's what I want: Go home and ask your father about the water. Ask him why he was so sure there was water in there. Why did he tell that to Niccolo? Do what I say."

She holds his head in a gentle embrace, rocking slowly, as darkness settles on the Bitterroots and a cooler breeze blows into the hospital room. She rocks him until he sleeps, his head against her chest.

CHAPTER EIGHTEEN

B RUNELLA STRIDES PAST a mound of unopened mail and ignores a flashing phone light. Eighteen new messages, all but three marked urgent. Electronic nannies—can't they ever chill? Nothing is urgent when everything is urgent. And another thing: When did instant gratification become the national anthem? She forgets to close the front door, climbs upstairs, strips off her clothes, and turns on the shower. Here is Teddy once more, the face that followed her west from Missoula, as smooth as newborn skin, pink and dewy, and then mangled and raspberried. She is desperate to hold his face with her eyes and see beyond the surface.

She stays in the shower until the hot water runs out, puts on a robe with the phone in one pocket, and wanders from room to room before going outside. The early evening is warm, sunlight keeping the daylilies open, as she strolls to the backyard and down a path to her cedar bench. The columbine has peaked and gone, making way for black-eyed Susans on one side of her path and Roma tomatoes on the other. Need something to attract hummingbirds. She makes one call, trying to reach Nolanne and Cindy at Salmon Bay. She has not spoken to them since the aborted opening of Kornflint's waterfront compound. Once the injunction was in place, using mother and daughter as evidence of a unique community that would be extinguished by the Kornflint project, Brunella felt secure in leaving. All she wants now is to touch base. When she dials the Godden girls, a robo-voice tells her the number has been disconnected.

The next day she drives to the crumbled fishing pier. The shacks of

Salmon Bay are still standing, tenuously frozen in teardown poses where the dozers came to a halt after the court order. Nothing is stirring. She climbs up the rickety stairs to the office she has been keeping; it smells musty and unused, covered by dust. The newspaper left on the desk from her last day here has yellowed from the sun and looks preposterously old. She opens a window to let in a brisk slice of the bay, a blend of creosote and salt air; the noise is muted, low-industrial. Questions: Why didn't the old vodka-livered Scandies put up more of a fight for their neighborhood? Why did it have to come from her? She does not belong; she is a floater, a tourist, the worst kind of cultural dilettante, she thinks now. Did she bring to life the old hatreds between Red Finns and Tollefsons? Or was it there all along, dormant, and by trying to preserve Salmon Bay she dredged up the ancient toxins? Not for the first time, she wonders if this campaign of hers is simply a ghost dance, trying to hold on to a fishing community in the city when she has her own fight east of the mountains.

Outside, she searches for one active business, a single structure with a pulse. She looks for Svenson's, anticipating lefse just out of the oven. But the deli has closed with no explanation. Just like Scandinavians to leave without comment or emotion, to skulk away—silent, brooding, and blond. Don't these people ever get mad? Brunella drifts around, looking for a familiar face, calling out for Cindy and Nolanne, trying to find something in the abandoned neighborhood. She bangs on the door of a ragged house.

"Looking for somebody?" The voice startles her. She turns to face a stubby man in jogging shoes and hard hat turned backward.

"Where are the people . . . Cindy and Nolanne? And what happened to Svenson's?"

"You mean the people who used to live . . . in that?"

"Yes. This is their home. What's going on here?"

"Let me check." Friendly now. Forced politeness. He calls up a name on a palm-sized computer. "Godden? Is that the last name? We got 'em in the database. Relocated last Tuesday."

"Relocated. Where?"

"It's a free country. And they chose—let me see—Zanesville, Ohio."

"Zanesville? What is that?"

"Can't tell you."

"They've lived here their entire lives. Why would they uproot themselves to Zanesville?"

"Can't tell you. But you can buy a helluva lot of house in a place like Ohio, and with the kind of relocation money they got, why not?"

"What about Svenson?"

"Let me check. . . ." He enters the name into the palm computer, whistles. "This one went to Carefree, Arizona. Can't say I blame him."

"It's a hundred and fifteen degrees down there."

"But with AC you never have to go outside."

"So where does somebody go to get lefse, or aquavit, or lutefisk?"

"We've preserved the John Olerud posters."

A deliveryman is waiting for Brunella on the porch of her home, package in hand. She tells him to leave it with the others in the mound, but he says he cannot deliver it without a signature; it's a legal document. Inside, she rips open the envelope and finds:

LAST WILL AND TESTAMENT OF ANGELO CARTOLANO

She drops the document on the floor and dials the coulee, heart at a gallop, fingers shaking; an interminable time between rings. "Hello?"

"Babbo! You're alive."

"Sì, sono magnifico, Nella. What's the problem?"

"I just got this package."

"My will, entirely rewritten. Hah! Read it carefully, and then you must come home. Roberto is here with some people, and they have so many papers."

She spends the evening going through the material inventory of Angelo's life, his pile after eighty years. He has constructed the will so that all property transfers to Brunella as soon as she signs the document. He leaves her: A premium wine vineyard, most of it in mature Nebbiolo grapes, the remainder in Sauvignon Blanc, Pinot Grigio, and some Sangiovese. An orchard of apple trees, Italian plums, figs, cherries (both Bings and Rainiers), and peaches (whites and Red Havens). The house, built in 1952. Two cellars, one in the main house, with at least a case of every Cartolano bottling except the one Angelo destroyed, and another in the newer detached building, full now with small oak barrels holding the wine dubbed "Niccolo's vintage." Stainless-steel fermentation tanks, six of them. A grape press from the hilltop town of Barolo, circa 1885.

She imagines herself the winemaker, trying to craft a life in that slightly listing house in the coulee, Angelo staring at Mount Stuart in the dying light, nobody from the city to tell her she's been talking to herself too much. What will she do at night, worry about commodity prices, get geared up for Class B basketball, tune in to the local talk-radio demagogue while slurping her Mega Gulp? She would try to lose the city edge, for starters, stop finishing people's sentences, maybe give the talk-radio gasbag a chance.

More stuff: A key to the locker in the cellar that contains the bottle for the Last Man's Club (accompanied by a note in Angelo's barely legible scrawl: *Don't let any of these bastards outlive me*). A pickup truck, in working order, with 127,000 miles on it, and a Taurus station wagon, fifteen years old, in need of a new engine (or a tow). A Marc Chagall lithograph of a harvest scene in Provence, with floating spirits, as usual; one of them, a woman, appears to be masturbating. Jars containing seeds of the Cartolano family tomatoes from Piemonte. A baseball from the 1995 Mariners run—when they came from thirteen games out of first place in early August to win the American League West—signed by the three all-stars of that team: Ken Griffey Jr., Randy Johnson, and Alex Rodriguez. (*Traitors!* Angelo has written in a note attached to the ball.) And a baseball from the 2001 team, which broke the record for most wins by any team in the history of the American League, signed by Ichiro Suzuki.

Included in the will are legal descriptions of the house and land. She studies the boundaries, puzzling over one point. It says the Cartolano property extends to the ridge above the vineyard and coulee, as she thought, but that it also takes in a narrow swath of land on the crest, all the way to the edge of Gregory Gorton's property, bordering the dead forest. And with the kind of fright that comes over a person who looks in the mirror one morning and sees somebody much too old, Brunella realizes that the little parcel of land on the ridge with the pipe draining water out of the national forest belongs to the Cartolanos—more specifically, that she will soon be its owner.

As promised, the irrigators have taken their case to the senator from Idaho who controls Indian affairs and water, and he has delivered. The tribe's water, purchased from the upper Columbia basin and stored in a mammoth pit, will go nowhere pending a federal investigation. The entire casino project has been put on hold, red-tagged by building inspectors. The Indians invoke their sovereign nation status, but they are reminded by the senator from Idaho that Indians are still trustees of the United States. The tribe has countered with an offer: The Indians will give away land across the river, and a modest amount of water, to anyone who wants to start anew, suggesting that they may want to build themselves a golf course. The irrigators are outraged by this suggestion; it's leftover land, windswept and treeless, "unfit for a palsied rattlesnake," in the words of Mrs. Flax. What they want is the water, a ticket to lifetime subsidies. Goddamn right they should pay us, the irrigators say. Mrs. Flax puts out a call for people throughout the West to join her in keeping watch over the Indian water pit.

When Brunella arrives after a sleepless night, several hundred people have set up camp around the fortified gates of the casino project, a make-shift assemblage of tents, trailers, tarps, flags, coolers, guns, generators, dogs, televisions, barbecues in halved metal barrels, fire rings on the asphalt. Mrs. Flax makes the rounds on the hot pavement, a cat in one arm, others trailing her, exhorting people to stand guard round the clock. The Indians have not made a public appearance since the tribal chairman was assaulted. Reports filter into the campsite of Indian moves and intrigue. They've been spotted down the road in a caravan; they showed up at the River-Vu Outlet Mall, couple hundred in one place, and didn't buy anything, just stared at people until they were asked to leave. Upriver from the pit, a dozen or more Indians have gathered around a milling of young salmon, the out-migrating fish trapped in one of the bigger holding pools of the backed-up Columbia. Mrs. Flax distributes white ribbons and instructs people to wrap them around their upper right arms, and she hands out white baseball hats to select deputies. She is hoisted atop a car and delivers a speech about the Constitution and western water rights. The tribe, she says, is a dependent nation, "some would say conquered."

She rattles off the names of all the irrigators who have thrown in the towel, a litany of collapse. Fist in the air, she calls for a citizen's grand jury to investigate the Indians.

"We have that right," she says. "Under the Constitution, all power rests with the people."

As she finishes, a chant is taken up, accompanied by a drumbeat on overturned five-gallon plastic buckets. "Give our water back! Give our water back! Give our water back!"

When Brunella tries to talk to Mrs. Flax after the last speech, she is brushed aside.

"I got nothing to say to a Cartolano," Mrs. Flax says. "Nothing."

"But I saw Teddy, Mrs. Flax. He's had surgery."

"We don't speak no more. He's on his own."

"You should have given him something—some financial help after you sold the property. He's going to have medical bills for years."

"Government should take care of that. I did my share bringing him up: eighteen years of charity. Don't be telling me what I have to do."

"You can't just cut him off."

"Listen, you: He ain't mine."

"You're talking nonsense, Mrs. Flax."

"We raised him, sure. But he's the bastard son of Melvin Gutswag and a little hussy he poked behind the storage shed about thirty years ago. You knew that, didn't ya? Smart girl like you. Teddy knows it. We told him when he was ten years old that he didn't belong to us but we'd try to raise him good as we could. From that day on he turned on us; I think he hated us for telling him. So be it. It's better off if he finds his way with a family of his own. There's some who believe what happened to that boy's face last summer is God's retribution for Melvin Gutswag's sin."

"Surely you don't believe that?"

"Some days I do, some days I don't. Now make yourself useful or get out of the way. We got a new frontier to build here."

The Cartolano vineyard looks healthy at its full-canopied peak, clusters of pellet-sized grapes catching sun on the high south-facing flanks of the coulee. Two cars that Brunella doesn't recognize are parked next to the pond. A surveyor and an assistant line up sites on the ground as Brunella walks toward the porch. When she asks for an explanation, the surveyor says, "You'll have to talk to the man inside. He's the boss."

She walks in to find Roberto going over plans and property documents at the dining room table. He does not rise to greet her. The frown lines around her brother's mouth and nose are more prominent since the last time Brunella saw him, nearly a year ago. She remembers what her mother said about people getting the face they deserve over time.

"I tried to call you," he says. "Don't you ever answer your phone? These men are helping me close on the property."

"The property. What did you do, Roberto? You didn't sell our home."

He rises, making a move to connect with Brunella. He's wearing a pressed shirt, monogrammed on the breast pocket. "We got a good fair price, considering."

She backs away. "Get out," she says to the two strangers.

"Brunella, don't act like an inferior. We need to do something for Father. I told you all along I was taking over his affairs. This place—with the original house, the vineyard and orchard, the two cellars, the stainless-steel tanks— Actually, I got a terrific price, considering the water crisis."

"Babbo will never sell. He's said that a million times. You take away this land, you take away his breath."

"It's done. Sold. A lawyer from San Francisco who wants a different life and says the Columbia basin is the new Napa. He's come up with some nifty legal move to clear the title of liens. I gave him a price reduction for that. Father will have everything he needs."

"You sold this place to a lawyer?"

"He's a lawyer now, but he wants to make premium wine. What changed everything was that one wine Father tried to destroy. After we won at VinFaire, this property became a trophy vineyard. All of a sudden, we're sitting on a gold mine, thanks to one vintage. And I'll tell you something that really shocked me, Brunella: Father doesn't even recognize how good that wine was. Miguel says he tried to destroy it! He's lost it, Brunella, can't you see? He finally makes a world-class wine and what does he do? Takes an ax to it."

"You don't have a clue about this place, do you?"

"I've got several million clues, on the way. So I've had a couple of broad discussions about what the new owner wants to do. With new French oak, he can boost the Nebbiolo rating from Parker and the *Spectator,* get it up in the mid-nineties. Then you tear out half the vineyard and make less wine. A thousand cases—no more. It's a formula for cult-wine status, two hundred fifty dollars a bottle and up, and it makes sense. We keep ten percent for the first five years."

"Did you tell Babbo? He would never go for this scheme."

"Legally—in my view—Father is incompetent. The evidence is all around, but for starters you've got that incomprehensible act of rage against a world-class wine. Under emergency provisions of the law, I'm acting as his guardian. As such, I don't need his acquiescence. But it's important to understand he will have everything he needs when this deal is closed."

"You sold his dream, everything he created, and you didn't even talk to him?"

"It wouldn't make any difference. You know him, he's sentimental. Not a good thing when you've got this kind of coin on the table."

"I hate you," Brunella says.

"I'm going to let that last remark slide, because that's a very hurtful thing to say."

"Then let me say it again in a way that won't slide: You're an asshole. You were born an asshole. You were an asshole as a kid. You were an asshole as an older brother. You were an asshole in college. You became just another asshole from Texas. You've spent your whole life trying to find new ways to be an asshole. No way will you ever sell this place, as long as I am Angelo Cartolano's daughter."

"It's done, I told you. I sold it. We have a deal."

"You can't sell it because I'm the owner."

Roberto sneers, his face falling into the groove of the frown lines, followed by a mirthless laugh. "You're getting like Father. Deluded."

"Well, delude this," she says, throwing the will and property transfer on the table.

"Babbo-o-o." She searches through the shaggy vines at day's end, going up and down the rows of Nebbiolo grapes. "Babbo-o-o . . ."

Above the stone chapel, in the last three rows, she hears pursed breathing and the clank of metal on rock. There she finds her father, with ice ax in one hand, nylon webbing and carabiners wrapped around his chest, his legs scratched, his teal Mariner cap chalky white from dried sweat. He is hiking with slow deliberate kick steps up the hill, forcing his breath out, locking the knees, then repeating the process. Between breaths, he's talking to the vines, this one and that: "You be sure to hold your leaves in when the sun gets too hot, and you there, with the two clusters of grapes, you have to go a little slower or you're going to end up as raisins."

Brunella catches up to him, breathless herself.

"Almost there," he says.

He plants his baseball cleats and kicks another few steps until he reaches the top and falls on his butt. He rests his chin on his knees, removes the cap, and wipes sweat from his face. His crooked-fingered left hand looks like the thin branch of a dead tree.

"I still got it," he says. "I learned that step from an Australian climber who was trying to do all the volcanoes in the Cascades. Ah . . . but my knees are not the same."

"Who were you talking to?"

"The grapes."

She sits next to him, looking out as twilight color floods a flat-bottomed cloud well above Mount Stuart. She realizes her father has been serious all along; he needs to reclaim the summit. He tells her his climb is set for the weekend; he's going to start with the same approach the Yakima boys took long ago but will veer off and take the easier main ascent rather than go up the route he helped to pioneer, the north ridge.

"I'm going with an old friend, an experienced climber," he says. "I will go slow. I won't do anything stupid. And you will say a prayer for me. God willing, I will stand on top of Mount Stuart one more time."

Are all men sentimental about sports and physical challenge, Brunella wonders, or is it something that comes with age, when knees wobble and bellies spill over belt buckles and erections sag instead of salute? Better to climb Mount Stuart at eighty than swap early-bird coupons at the therapy pool.

"I love you, Babbo," she says, wiping sweat from his nose with the sleeve of her shirt. "I wish we had our family together. I feel like it's down to you and me."

"It *is* down to you and me. And you will give me a grandchild someday—soon, perhaps? I promise you something: I will make a better *nonno* than a *babbo*."

"You were a fine *babbo*."

"I failed with Roberto. How can somebody who came from my flesh and soul be such a stranger? I look at him in the dining room and I think somebody has broken into my house, a burglar with my last name. It makes me feel terrible to think such a thought, but that's how I feel. I cannot lie to you. And Niccolo . . . you may never forgive me for what I did to Niccolo."

"What did you do, Babbo?"

"I thought I could play God. I was scared."

"Yes, you've told me that. You were scared for the grapes when everything started to dry up."

"Alden Kosbleau came to me, and he said he had extra water."

"Where?"

"Don't you know by now, Nella? Doesn't the Indian know?"

"I think I understand, but Leon is still in the dark about the big picture. I don't . . . I can't tell him without losing you and the land. Leon believes . . . that there was some manipulation of the aquifer, that Kosbleau and the tribe did something."

"And what about me? *È colpa mia.*"

"It's not your fault."

"Yes. Listen. The sad place where our Niccolo died, Nella—in the forest—there are some empty mine shafts in there. I don't know how he did it, but Alden tapped into some water and he flooded the mine shafts, just below the forest. It was his reserve water, for when things got really bad. For a time, for me, things got really bad. He came to me. He said I could use that water, take a good long drink for the grapes, but we must not tell anyone. Alden said there was plenty of water—enough for the grapes, enough for the forest, enough for fish. That turned out to be the bad vintage, the one everybody wants, the one I destroyed. I should have listened to the earth. And when the fire came . . . ahhhh . . ." He buries his head in his hands, digs one cleated shoe in the ground.

Brunella rubs his back as the coulee slips under the long shadow of the Cascades.

"*È colpa mia.*"

"What happened on the day the fire blew up?"

"Niccolo called me. We talked, two times. I just wanted him to be safe. Those jumpers. They ordered some pumps, and Niccolo asked me about water. I told him . . . I told him yes! Yes! There's plenty of water in there."

"How did you know that, Babbo?"

"Because I had taken some of it myself, like I said."

"But you didn't own it?"

"Hear me, Nella. *Ascolta!* When the drought was so bad it took away my sleep, I was very afraid. I didn't question Alden. He said take the water, and I did. Then I got greedy. I wanted more. I wanted security. I went back to him, and he said I could tap into his big reserve, take all I wanted. He said there was plenty. There was a place in the forest where it seeped up above the ground, up from the mine shafts. Listen, you have to hear all of this, Brunella."

"Go on."

"In the cellar where I keep the Last Man's bottle, next to that is a key. Alden gave me one, and he kept one. You need both keys to make it work. That's how we took the water for the bad vintage. I told Niccolo, '*Non c'è problema,* there's so much water in that basin. Save yourself.' "

"But there wasn't enough water in there to save him. There was nothing; Teddy told me. We tested it with pumps. It was dry. Empty. What happened?"

"Gone! Somehow, I don't know how, it disappeared. Those hot days that never wanted to end, maybe there was no surplus to begin with. *È colpa mia.*"

They sit in silence on the crest of the coulee, each in a corner of their own thoughts. Brunella stands and faces her father, extending her hand. She helps him up, takes him by one hand, while he holds the ice ax with the other. She leads him downhill, through the vineyards, past the stone chapel. Mount Stuart is a black silhouette against the purple sky, barely visible.

"And what about the pipe, Babbo?"

"That came later. After the fire blew up, Alden said we have to do something or they would try to take away everything I own. Alden redirected what was left—deep in the mine shafts, as it turned out—to the Indians. He was trying to cover it up, to make it look like the Indians took the water from the forest. Once they got it, he said we would still be able to get it back because Indians never win. We could go to the senator."

"He did all of this . . . when?"

"After the fire."

"No, he didn't, Babbo. I don't think that's what happened."

"Yes, that is what happened."

"I saw the records. Alden was selling water to the tribe at least four months *before* the fire. Think about it: That's probably why the basin was dry at the time Niccolo ordered the pumps."

"I'm confused."

"Kosbleau was using you to cover his theft. He was using you to steal that water for him. That explains the two keys. You took just a small bit of it, but he was selling big allotments to the Indians. And if anybody traced it back, you'd be on the hook. He didn't do you a favor; you were the pass-through point."

"I am trying never to think about it. It makes it hard to keep living. How does it matter what he did with it? I was a thief! That's what I have to face. I cheated. We thought we could do anything with the water, and it would be okay. We could draw it down, move it around. We could be like our own Grand Coulee Dam in there. We could do anything."

"Tinker with one thing, and you alter the flow of everything."

"What's that you say?"

"Leopold. A good gardener. Who else knows about this?"

"Nobody. Only Alden. And now you. Are you going to tell the big Indian?"

"That makes you responsible for water theft, maybe manslaughter, a conspiracy to withhold information in a federal investigation. How can I tell Leon? You'll go to jail, and we will lose the land—everything."

"That will never happen because you are the owner. You start free and clear, with no sin. I'm just a boy from Alba trying to climb a mountain."

"And what should I do with the land?"

"Make *vino rosso,* Nella. Make *vino rosso* with a story."

With Duff Almvik swallowed by the currents of Deception Pass, with Cindy and Nolanne relocated to Ohio, with Svenson's closed and the old man dispatched with his lefse recipes to Arizona, with the old ferry dragged out to a landfill, and with the purple door of the Purple Door Tavern held in custody, Brunella has nothing left to keep a new carpet from being rolled over the community that was Salmon Bay. She is walking through the rain, a solstice drizzle, worried about her babbo on Mount Stuart and whether Leon will ever look at her again if she tells him the truth about the water. As she climbs the slippery stairs to the second floor, she notices that the door to her office is ajar. She pauses, pushing the door back slowly.

"Ethan." He sits at the desk, the second S book of the 1910 *Encyclopedia Britannica* open in front of him. He's dressed in tight biking togs, with gloves and cleated shoes as well, his skin the color of Sheetrock against the glare of advertisements on his shirt.

"God, you've lost weight, Ethan, if that's possible. And I see you're still wearing a prophylactic whenever you go outside."

"It has a sun protection factor of sixty. Sixty! Isn't that terrific?"

"But it's raining today."

"Yes, and most people don't know that up to thirty percent of UV rays still get through a cloud cover. I came down to see how your fishing community is coming along."

"They're gone. One dead, two moved away. You already knew that. You came down here to gloat."

"You played brilliantly."

"With nothing to show for it. This neighborhood will be completely gone in a few weeks."

"With no significant impact on the lasting culture of the city."

"If only I could believe that."

"I can show you. It says so on the final permit from the city." He looks down at the encyclopedia. "I'm sorry."

"You're not, really."

"Actually, I'm only sorry for you, Brunella. Your enthusiasms are contagious. That's your best quality—these consuming passions. In some ways, I'm envious. It's something I'll never have, not for lack of trying. With me, it just seems sentimental and false. But you ought to learn how to finish what you start, a much more difficult task. Had you just done what you were paid to do and not meddled, we'd still have ended up with the same finding of No Significant Impact and you would have a much brighter future. But no, I'm not sorry for the imminent loss of this huddle of firetraps and dry rot you insist on elevating to the level of cultural heritage."

"Then you're trespassing."

"Technically, I'm not. I've been paying for the office space."

"Bullshit."

"You remember that 'really large check' from the anonymous donor, the one that got your little citizen's action started?"

"You?"

"It was Mr. Kornflint's account. He's a very generous benefactor, if that isn't a redundancy. And a wonderful evening in Belltown, the fundraiser with all the dilettantes. Remember the check that came in at the end—"

"You!"

"Mr. Kornflint, through me, through an acquaintance. We were your biggest boosters." He winces as he tries to rise from the chair and back away, his motions robotic. "And you were our best asset. I'm sorry that check never went through. But Mr. Kornflint had second thoughts. He felt your citizen's group had done everything it set out to do. You found your fishermen, and then you found that delightful mother and her daughter—a truant, I believe. And we found them shortly thereafter. Nothing like success."

"Get out!"

"And just to make sure we had all our bases covered, you showed me the little salmon stream near your father's vineyard. Had we not been able to correct the circumstances here, we would have had to take action on the other end. Your friend Alden Kosbleau was most helpful, drawing down the water table so that your fisherman's run of fish would have nowhere to breed. You were right. We are all connected by water, or something to that effect."

"You're evil."

"I'm neutral. I'm apolitical. I'm asexual. I have no convictions. I don't believe in God and I don't believe in love. I couldn't give a damn what happens to the Seattle Mariners, or if any particular bottle of wine has a good life or not. I care about what is intellectually and logically correct. There are two sides to every story, correct and incorrect. A right way and a wrong way, if you want a moral tone to it."

"Your cynicism is breathtaking."

"Cynicism? Wrong word, Brunella. I'm not cynical. Precision in language is a lost art. I'm agnostic—as open-minded as a man can be. Can you back away a little bit, please? You're standing too close."

"You used me to destroy this neighborhood."

"And you used me to try to save it. There, we're even."

"Get out!"

"Cities have chronological lives, Brunella, just like people. Some are middle-aged and dysfunctional; Cincinnati comes to mind. Some are old and dying; think of Liverpool, one of the premier seaports of the British empire at its peak. And what is it now? A Beatles museum with a surfeit of nursing homes. Your beloved Florence, once the third biggest city in Europe, the fount of new expression in art, poetry, architecture, and politics? Now a renaissance theme park. By contrast, our city is young, still taking shape, without a tether to misplaced and artificial nostalgia. You believe in narrative as it applies to people's lives, maybe even cities. Fine. Well, then the story will always change because the story *has* to change— by definition!"

"And what if the change is for the worse? What if what you do here makes city life more sterile and ugly, makes it harder to live as—"

"So be it. Forty, fifty years from now, one person's city blight will be another's preservation fight. It's a ridiculous cycle of bogus sentimentality. I don't need any Jane Jacobs homilies to know that. Before long, we'll be making national historic districts out of trailer parks in this country, if we aren't doing it already. I was just looking through your excellent reference book here, the *Encyclopedia Britannica,* a superb antique of considerable value in the mint condition you've kept it. And look here; the entry under Seattle—"

"Close the book and get out."

"Let me finish. Here, right after the entry on Sir John Colborne

Seaton, a first baron who took part in Sir Ralph Abercromby's expedition to Egypt in 1801. All these knights. Don't you think peerage has been inflated? I mean, from first barons who whipped Napoleon to Elton John in his funny little beige toupee?"

"Out!"

"Let me finish. Here. I was just reading this—see—Seattle, a city of eighty thousand six hundred seventy-one people after the 1900 census. Two Swedish daily newspapers. Two Japanese dailies as well. How many are there now? If you guess zero, you are correct. Now listen to this: Half the people living here then had foreign-born parentage, and another twenty-five percent were foreign-born themselves. Do you know what that means, Brunella? The city was a stew pot of mongrels from another shore. Tell me about cultural heritage. What happened to the Swedish dailies? They died a natural death as the Swedes became Seattle burghers. What happened to the county almshouse, listed here as one of the principal buildings of architectural distinction? Gone—folded into the American tomorrow."

"I actually thought you were a friend, in your own oddball detached way."

"Don't get personal on me, Brunella. Why can't women stay with the substance of an argument? It's always personal with women. Now recall our so-called Western heritage: cowboys and miners and the like. Do you think anyone in modern times would really like to spend a day in a genuine nineteenth-century frontier town? With the whores and wranglers; the toothless syphilitic wonders, every one of them armed and drunk; the open sewage running through town; the isolation—particularly for women. Of course not. But plenty of people will pay to pan for gold or put on a cowboy hat in a gussied-up version of a Western town. By the same measure, nobody will come to Salmon Bay as long as there are fish guts and what-have-you all over the place. But wait till you see the crowds that will flock to the new neighborhood that will rise here as we re-create the better parts of France. People won't care if the clams come from the East Coast and the salmon are raised on a farm in Chile and the boats are built by cheap labor in China. What's important is that they will *feel* as if they are in France, with the boulangeries turning out fresh bread, the bistros alive with people, and an exquisite little gallery with a courtyard. We'll get some kids from the Lakeside School who speak fluent French to greet diners in the summer. There's nothing wrong with any of that. We Americans take the authentic and smooth it, sand off the rough edges, and re-create its essence better than anyone, so why fight it? As I said—as Mr. Kornflint said, quoting that winemaker from the Piedmont—nature answers to its own rules. We're following the natural rules of this city, rather than trying to fight it."

"That was *you* at the pier ceremony? The laser image?"

"My words, aided by some technical wizardry—vetted by Mr. Kornflint, of course."

"Where is that stick of plaid?"

"Mr. Kornflint? I wouldn't know. He . . . I have never met him."

"What?"

"I speak for him. I mean, he speaks, and I help him translate. He has a problem with verbs—declarative sentences are a particular burden. Our meetings are all virtual, which is okay by me, no exchange of facial gestures or other messy interactions."

"Maybe he doesn't even exist."

"That's entirely possible. Somebody signs the checks. You cashed them. In that sense you've been working for Mr. Kornflint as much as I have. Colleague."

CHAPTER NINETEEN

A T DAWN the tribe gathers for a prayer to Tozzie Cresthawk on a treeless bluff at the edge of the reservation, high above the river. He is still in a coma, paralyzed from the hips down. They meet at a site reserved for the Dreamers, cryptic ground to all but those who shared the philosophy of Smohalla. They talk as if Tozzie were dead, recalling his life as a horse racer and firefighter, how fishing for chinook sustained his pride. Leon Treadtoofar stands off to the side, just outside the circle. He is not wearing his Forest Service uniform. After the ritual is complete and most of the family and friends have walked away, Leon lingers, his eyes transfixed on the little pocket above the Columbia. Danny Red Thunder, his forehead bandaged, his right eye swollen and closed, stays behind as well. He asks Leon what he is going to do about the other Tozzie Cresthawks who stare blankly into a river that won't move, the people who had hoped the tribe could do something restorative with the water but now wonder if they are doomed by historic reflex.

"You have to choose," says Danny Red Thunder. "You are a man who has to choose. Are you with us?"

Leon crouches down and lights a small bundle of sage and sweet grass. As it starts to catch fire, he tosses it atop the ground. "Why?" says Leon, staring into the curl of smoke. "Why do I have to choose?"

"Because you are in a position to save Indian lives. And you have been hiding from your people."

"You think I can make that mob go away? You think I can make the river move again? You think I can free up your water? I'm a GS-Fourteen with the Forest Service. I have a job working with people I respect. I believe in the truth."

Danny Red Thunder laughs at the last word. "We all got a little white blood in us." He turns his back to Leon. "Or maybe that's the Wanapum in you talking. Wanapums eat dog food. I'll tell you about truth: Truth is water that has sustained Indian people for all of time, water that belongs to us as sure as our blood flows from our hearts, water that was taken away when my grandfather was a young man. And just as we are now trying to get some of the water back, we are accused of terrible things. These things are lies. These things are slanders against Indian people. These lies are being used to hold us back."

"Okay, Red Thunder, I will take you at your word, for Tozzie's sake. But tell me how I am supposed to explain how you got all that water?"

"We bought it."

"You bought it from Alden Kosbleau, early last year?"

"Most of it."

"Then I'm going to request that you be arrested and charged—"

"Arrested?"

"You and Kosbleau. That water was not Kosbleau's to sell or yours to buy. It was from National Forest land. The public owns that water. Now, maybe Kosbleau set you up. Maybe he misrepresented ownership, and you were an innocent buyer. That's for the courts to unravel. I answer to the Forest Service, and to the memory of dead smoke jumpers. Four of them, in case you forgot, were Indian boys—Sherman, Joseph, Wes, and Noflight."

"You want to arrest me? For trying to build a future? You're a traitor."

"I'll give you a day to get your things together. A marshal will come by in plain clothes. Make it easy on yourself. I don't want publicity and I don't want the FBI involved. I hate the FBI. A good lawyer can plead the whole thing away with fines."

"You arrest me?" Red Thunder moves within inches of Leon's face.

"I'm not your Indian brother," Leon says. "And I'm not a traitor."

"Why aren't you wearing your uniform?"

.   .   .

The mob at the pit starts to stir as word of Danny Red Thunder's arrest spreads. For weeks, the irrigators have been living on a diet of stale suspicion and innuendo. What they knew for sure was that a formidable amount of water had been transferred from their control to the Indians'. But that transfer, by itself, was not a crime that would hold up in court or even make for sustained grandstanding at a staged hearing by the senator from Idaho. They needed something else, something irrefutable, if they were going to get the water back in time for the government buyouts. Now here is what they have been looking for in Red Thunder's arrest—and what's more, it was another Indian who fingered him. It is enough to spark hope that all the water sales to the tribe can be nullified.

"We got 'em in our sights," Mrs. Flax says, doing a live radio broadcast from under her blue tarp on the hot pavement next to the pit, two cats in her lap. "We want to make sure everyone out there understands: This is nothing against Indians. We irrigators are a lot like the Indians—we've been pushed aside, forgotten. This is about getting back what's rightfully ours."

During a break, a man in a cowboy scarf and straw hat moves up close to Mrs. Flax. The scarf covers most of his lower face, and the hat is drawn down over his forehead.

"What can I do you for, stranger?" Mrs. Flax says.

"Mom . . ."

"Come closer, boy."

"It's me, Mom."

"Show me your face, boy. You're hiding something there."

"It still hurts, Mom. The skin's raw."

"Come closer, Ted. Let me get a look at ya."

She pulls down the scarf and narrows her eyes, staring at the skin grafts patched over Teddy's face. A cat screeches and backs away, tail up, hair on end.

"It's okay, kitty. Come back to Mommy, kitty, kitty. Looks like they made ya a new one, huh."

"They tried. Listen—"

"Where you been hiding?"

"Mom, I gotta talk to you about this campaign against the Indians. It's . . . there's something you don't know."

"There's lots I don't know. But what I know for sure is that we're in the fight of our lives. Put that scarf back up, wouldja?"

The interviewer motions for Mrs. Flax to return to the microphone. She coos for her frightened cat to return to her lap. "Come to Mommy." Teddy removes the scarf, baring his face. He walks away slowly, staring into the crowd, looking at Marvin Heinbeck from East Wenatchee and Lester Thurlock from Brewster and Luanne Lodefest from Electric City. He looks at them all, friends and neighbors once, searches their faces for his place among them, searches their eyes for contact. They see only Teddy's scars, missing the eyes, missing the man, and he knows he is an exile.

The coulee is empty. Not a car anywhere near the house. Brunella walks up the hill, through the vineyard, on a day when the winds are asleep. She expects to hear her father's radio tuned to the baseball game or some sign of his labors. But the air holds none of the familiar groans and wheezes of the Cartolano vineyard—no drip, drip, drip of water on vines, no sprinklers spitting onto the orchards, no motorbikes of the kind that Miguel and his crew use to race from chore to chore. The pond is flat, the shallow water greenish with algae. Uphill, through the vines, Brunella zigs and zags. When she stops to get her breath and her heart calms, she is frightened by the stillness. Here is the onset of death in this coulee, a hint of what would happen if the Cartolanos leave. She flings open the doors of the stone chapel, letting the sunlight in on the wall, her father's frescoes of an idealized Northwest. He saw this image the moment he first entered the coulee, and then he shaped it by sheer force of will and might to fit the art in his mind's eye. Torn from the Piemonte by war and exiled to the edge of the American continent, Angelo cast his dreams into this little slash in the planet and shaped it, day by day, season by season, year by year, until the coulee was the fresco. Now she inherits the dream, but where does she take it? Does she continue making the Nebbiolo of her father? Does she give up a life of the mind to leather her hands, scar her legs, sun-scathe her face, and curl her back until she looks like a walking question mark, like the *nonne* of Italy, humpbacked and dressed in black? Does she do it alone, becoming an eccentric in wooden clogs and straw hat, cursing flies, talking to herself, a Katharine Hepburn of the vine? Does she finally concede that she will never make anything close to Morris Graves's creation on the lake, or even the genius of her father's Nebbiolo? And what about this stone chapel, this cloister of space, transplanting the Catholicism of superstitious Italy to a land of desert salmon and Coyote myths? In darkest confusion, in spiritual dissonance, do you still look for God in this box of homage?

One way out is to tell Leon everything and be done with it. But she cannot see past the confession. He will feel betrayed and probably not even be surprised. How could she be so predictable: Promise and betrayal, what else would an Indian expect from a white woman? Is there no way to explain what happened and still protect Angelo? Tell him, then. But . . . tell him and the Cartolano print on this land will disappear. And even if they could hold on after telling Leon everything, she would have to endure stares of widows and siblings, fathers and mothers, who will always think that in some part of the Cartolano cellar is blood wine of their loved ones, no matter that Angelo destroyed it all. Maybe she does not belong here after all. Maybe the Cartolanos never belonged here. Maybe Angelo's life work no more fits this place than Waddy Kornflint's slice of transplanted France belongs on Salmon Bay. Maybe everything Angelo created is an aberration—he stumbled into this audacious experiment, the biggest river of the West shackled to create the Planned Promised Land, and now he must live with the protracted shutdown, the failure. If God wanted great wine to come from the desert of the Columbia basin, would he not have given this land more than a whisper of rain? She looks away to the high eroded wall on the other side of the chasm, to the scraped-away rock from the Greatest Flood of All Time, the monument to water rushing from high ground to the sea without regard for anything a human being could do.

She runs downhill, flying past the vines, running for speed and release. She reaches the house and dashes up to the porch, this old place, a brittle frame of crowded moments. What is this? A padlock. She bangs against the ancient fir entrance. What the hell is this? She looks in the window, races to the back, and finds another padlock on the rear door, which was never locked. She climbs the maple tree on the side, shimmies up high enough to jump on the roof, and then crawls over to her window. This window, she knows, has no lock. It pushes open, and she falls on her bed. The impulse is to sleep, escape to a dream on a summer afternoon, and wake with her family intact. The house is forever stained with memory, the walls coated with Cartolano struggle and laughter. How dare Roberto think anyone else could live here? The house is worn and shaped to the Cartolanos as a pair of old boots are molded to a person's feet. It slouches. It is scarred. It bends one way to the prevailing winds and creaks another way in a freeze. Walking downstairs, she passes pictures on the wall: the family in a snowbound coulee, Niccolo at high school graduation, a young Angelo and Rita, toddlers on their laps. There on the kitchen table is the wooden globe, showing the latitudinal line drawn from Piemonte to the Columbia. She enters Niccolo's room, the one Angelo has taken over with Mount Stuart fetishes: The climbing gear is gone. The backpack, gone. The ropes and pitons, slings and crampons, helmet, gaiters, and parka, and the wall map, on which he'd plotted his return to the big thumb of exposed granite, taken to their destiny.

She calls Roberto on his cell phone.

"This is Bob. . . . Yes. . . . Yes. . . . Slow down, you're slurring your words. . . . Mmmm-hmm . . . mmmm-hmm . . . I don't have anything to say, really. You can talk to the new owners."

"You locked me out of my home."

"Your home?"

"You locked me out!"

"Easy, Brunella. The locks are always changed in this sort of a deal. It's pro forma, until everything clears."

"How could you do this?"

"Well, I called up a locksmith, that's how. That will—the one you so rudely shoved in my face—it's invalid."

"What happened to Babbo?"

"I couldn't find Father. I've got people out looking for him now, and I've already paid the first six months' rent on a residential care facility."

"He wants this place to stay in our hands. He transferred the whole coulee—"

"Hold it there, Brunella. Take a breath, little girl. As I've been trying to tell you for some time, Father is not altogether with it these days. If you would pay attention, you could see what his real needs are. The man cannot urinate without a diaper. Either that or he collects it; have you seen the jars of pee? He cannot drive without posing a hazard to others on the road. He shows signs of midstage dementia—"

"Of what?"

"Midstage dementia. It's a disease of the mind that eats away at basic cognitive functions, common to octogenarians in a certain risk category."

"A disease. You mean he's old. You call that a disease?"

"I'm going to hang up now, Brunella. Before I go, I need to tell you about the will—that bundle of legal kindling you threw in my face. Father never had a witness. Without a signed witness, a notary, it's no better than a cheap forgery. You own nothing."

"But don't you see what his intentions are? Be a man, Roberto. Be a son. Be a Cartolano! Babbo wants to hold on here. Who cares if he had a witness or not. You're denying him his life request."

"I'm getting him to the last stage of his life."

"No, no! This is a crime against our family. I'm going to get Babbo and bring him to you. He'll tell you exactly what he wants. This time with a witness."

Two old men have set out to climb the high peak in the eastern Cascades, but first they have to shop. Angelo wants fresh food. He wants to stop at the bakery for scones, to load up at the fruit stand with onions, peppers, leeks, mushrooms, and go down to the butcher for a shank of something they can grill over a fire at base camp, and then stop at the Bavarian-style candy hut for white chocolate. But his climbing partner will have none of it. All the food his partner has packed is surplus from the Y2K storage pile he never used, designed to last decades. They nearly come to blows at the cheese counter in the supermarket. Angelo insists on a quarter wedge of Fontina—the cheese from the Valle d'Aosta, where he climbed as a boy—and a small Romano to whittle onto pasta. But his partner slaps the cheeses down, saying he has packets of orange powdered substance.

At the trailhead, Angelo is stymied again. He plans to take one bottle of the Cartolano Nebbiolo to high camp.

"We'll drink this after our victory," Angelo says.

"Are you nuts? That bottle must weigh as much as my stove," his partner says. "We won't make it to the first waterfall. The wine stays in the car."

"Then I'm not going."

"Fine. Bring it. You can carry the rope as well."

The trail follows Ingalls Creek, the footing soft with larch and pine needles. Carrying his heavy pack of postwar climbing gear, the rope, and his bottle of wine, Angelo is slowed by the weight. But the months that he spent going up and down the vineyards under a pack loaded with rocks have paid off; his wind is good. Even then, his body can only do so much; it feels like a blade is tearing at his lower back.

Angelo tells his partner they have nothing but time and should enjoy the approach, take it slow, look at every opening in the forest, pause and listen for birds, smell the wildflowers, watch the mood of the mountains change with the light. He was a jackrabbit long ago, springing up and down the Cascades, often getting lost because he believed it was more important to move fast than to know where he was going; the point was to stay in motion at all times. Now he knows he missed a lot.

His partner takes a different view. "We can't dither," says Alden Kosbleau. He seems edgy, eager to speed things up; he wants to march the three miles to the first camp in one quick pull.

At camp, Kosbleau boils water and pours it into two red aluminum pouches, then stirs and hands a packet to Angelo. He sniffs, nibbles, and gags.

"I can't eat this caca."

"It's beef bourguignon," says Kosbleau. "I got a garage full of this stuff."

Next day they ascend into the higher part of the valley, where Angelo can see the last snow patches on the south side of Stuart. On the other side are the glaciers, bowls of ancient ice. He sits on a salt-and-pepper boulder and takes in the view of Mount Rainier to the southwest, the balding head of the summit with its glare against the hot sky. When they resume, the trail rounds two switchbacks and stops just short of the deep hole of Ingalls Lake, where the boys camped more than sixty years ago. They drop into a small valley, in deep shade, and find a grassy level area next to a fire pit. The pain in Angelo's lower back has intensified. He rubs it and pinches it, adjusting the pack.

At the second camp, a breeze of cool air keeps mosquitoes away. It also could mean the weather might change. Stuart is a magnet for thunderstorms, and Angelo has prepared himself, mentally, for a hit from the sky. He is ready to sit out for days, if that's what it comes to. You're old but you're smart. Use your age, be patient, take time and do it right. Remember, there are old climbers and bold climbers, but no old bold climbers. Your heart is big. Your lungs work. Your legs are still strong. Savor the high country. Look at the rock: this upturned crust of the planet, superb granite, solid and speckled. Carrara itself is no match for this stone haven. He unwinds his sleeping pad and his bag in the tent. Kosbleau is setting up a bivouac sack behind a tree.

"What—now you're too good to sleep in my tent?" Angelo says.

"You fart too much. It keeps me awake."

"It's that powdered caca of yours from dinner."

"I need my sleep," says Kosbleau, "if I'm going to get you to the top."

The arraignment of Danny Red Thunder was supposed to be quiet and routine: a judge, a defendant, a lawyer, a prosecutor, an exchange of bail requests, an agreement, and a release. But word has leaked out to the mob gathered outside the pit, and they decide, on orders from Mrs. Flax, to make a showing. On this hot day the tiny stone courthouse with the Romanesque trim is packed and surrounded by people whose grievance is directed at a bail hearing on the third floor. When Danny Red Thunder is led into the hearing, the room erupts.

"There's the son of a bitch!"

"Thief!"

"Try him here," Mrs. Flax says, which leads to a chant. "Try him here! Try him here! Try him here!"

The judge bangs his gavel and calls for order. There is no air-conditioning inside the stone courthouse, and Judge Kevin Hamilton is sweating under his black robes. When people continue to grumble, the judge orders two sheriff's deputies to remove the more belligerent ones. Mrs. Flax remains, front and center, fixing her blue-eyed stare on the

Indian in orange coveralls. Brunella is sitting near the back. She can see Leon Treadtoofar on the other side of the room, in his Forest Service greens. She tries to catch his eyes, but he will not look her way. Just before the proceedings start, Leon rises abruptly, as if he's going to make a statement, and leaves the room.

Leon makes his way to the casino construction site, climbs over the fence, and approaches the water pit. A pair of elderly men in white caps are playing chess under a blue tarp at the edge of the gate. No one else is on guard; the mob is still down at the courthouse. Leon ducks inside the nearly completed shell of the tribal casino, traipses through a jungle of wires, down a long narrow room where slot machines are wrapped in plastic, and into a second, larger building connected to the first. He slips past half-assembled blackjack tables and a stack of neon-headed clowns awaiting electronic life, through a sports betting room where the seats are in place but the giant screens are not, through all the accessories of the tribal dream for new life, and out a back door. Leon creeps low to avoid setting off any alarms and arrives at a control room. He finds dials and buttons that connect to gates of the pit and monitor the inflows and overall level of the water. He studies the panel hard for ten minutes. Then he presses two buttons, activating the outflow gate of the pit. A buzzer sounds. A floodgate slowly opens, and water spills out.

With a *whoooomphhhhh* the water surges out of the pit, breaking down the gate, cutting away an earthen section that has acted as a dam. Now there is a flood of water heading downhill toward the river, a force strong enough to rattle the card table on the pavement where the two elderly men in white caps are playing chess, strong enough to kick open a second floodgate as water stampedes out of the corral.

The elderly men flee, trying to get out of the way of a side flow of water that swamps the pavement.

The pit empties in a hurry, a tidal-like flush of all the water gathered from high in the Cascades, from north-facing draws and seeps in the granite, from aquifers in the desert and the forest, from canals originating in the backed-up lake behind the Grand Coulee, from streams that died in the taking and farms born in the exchange. As the pit water crashes into the Columbia, a small part of the river changes color and then quickly begins to rise and move in a turgid fashion. For this quarter-mile, the flush jump-starts the river, pushing a sluggish reservoir into the arms of gravity, a current as it takes on its own momentum. And for a short time, the Columbia is a river again.

Downstream, millions of young salmon, trapped in early-stage development by the river that would not move, are now given a brisk nudge, a call to advance. The small salmon scoot down the river and out, out, out to meet a biological deadline, out, out, out to sea and to life.

The prosecutor presents the bail request of $100,000 and says the government believes that Danny Red Thunder, who has lived in the Columbia basin his entire life, is not a flight risk. Danny Red Thunder and his attorney whisper back and forth as the prosecutor talks.

"Okay by you, counsel?" Judge Hamilton says.

"No bail, Your Honor," says Red Thunder's attorney. "My client wants to stay in custody until Your Honor hears our request for a change of venue."

"Coward!" one man bellows. Foot-stomping. Hooting.

Judge Hamilton blows a whistle for silence. "I'm going to conduct an orderly proceeding here, or we are going to start making arrests. Counsel, you refuse a chance to have your client released on bail?"

"That is correct, Your Honor."

Outside, the crowd mills around the front of the stone courthouse under two big oak trees. They don't trust Hamilton; he is a federal judge, appointed for life, who does not have to face the voters in irrigation country. If Red Thunder is allowed a change in venue, they expect it will be a whitewash. What do city people know about the problems of the irrigator? No doubt they'll side with the Indian.

Brunella rushes to find Leon Treadtoofar. She spots him walking toward the river. He crosses the main street and follows a side road down toward the water. Brunella rushes to catch up with him.

"Wait for me, Leon."

He hops over railroad tracks, passes a giant apple warehouse, a windowless cold storage plant with a smiling Indian mural painted on the side, and makes his way down to the river. At the edge of the backed-up Columbia, just above a dam, he turns to face her. His clothes are drenched, his face bruised. "What?"

"Leon." She touches his chest; he backs away. "Leon, what's wrong?"

He hits her in the face. It's a smack, using the back of his hand, strong enough to knock her down.

Leon strips off his wet Forest Service shirt and tosses it in the river. The currents grab the olive-green shirt and drag it under. He removes his shoes, peels away his pants, and dives into the big river. Brunella's face hurts, the sting from the back of his hand more intense. Her ears are ringing. She wonders if Leon hit her out of impulse, an accident maybe, or because he knows now about everything she withheld. But watching him disappear into the fast-swelling Columbia, she realizes she may never know.

"Leon!"

She loses sight of him as he is carried out by the deep-layered currents. He is underwater for more than a minute before he comes up, gasping for air. She cannot tell if it is a trick or desperation. It makes no sense. She kicks off her shoes and wades in, astonished at how quickly the river level seems to be rising, the current gaining in strength.

Leon is on his back, stroking deliberately, as the currents carry him toward the edge of the dam, toward wires and big orange balloons placed as a warning to boaters and low-flying planes. Brunella tries to swim toward Leon. When she catches up, he does a U-turn and heads back toward the shore. She shouts at him. He grabs on to a big timber caught by one of the cables, in the middle of the Columbia. Brunella swims up to him and gets a handhold on the timber next to Leon. She shivers at the chill. Having tested the tug of the river to get to the timber, Brunella is not sure she can make it back.

"What are you doing?"

"I need a swim."

"This is suicidal."

"I need a swim."

Clinging to the timber, Brunella and Leon see a wave of new water just before they feel it. What had been somewhat flat is now churning and hurried, carrying the contents of the pit, the big flush out of the containment hold. The fast-moving water shakes the timber loose from the cable. Brunella and Leon try to hold on, but the wood is moving too quickly. They separate, each flailing in the water. They are carried quickly to the edge of the dam. Brunella turns on her back and tries desperately to slow the ride. She hears the mad flutter of Leon's kicking. It is difficult just to keep her head above water. She reaches for another cable, gets a hand on it, and flips her legs over the line. She hangs just above the river. The current never lets her out of its grip. She holds until the blood leaves her fingers, and then holds longer, though she cannot feel anything in her hands. The river takes another swipe and knocks her from the cable. She is twenty feet from the spillway of the dam and closing. She sees the water drop away into mist and blue sky, into a roar as it crashes downward. Feet forward, feet forward, she tells herself. Here is the dam, the spillway. Her arms are pulled back and the roar shakes her. She keeps her feet down in the fall and never feels the concrete wall. It's a drop of three seconds. At the base, her legs buckle as she is driven down a shaft of oxygenated bubbles and frenzied water. She is conscious of the noise and the cold. She can move. She had not taken a breath before the fall, and her lungs are giving out. Upside down, or downside up? She cannot tell. Her body is hurled forward, underwater still, tumbling, rolling.

Air.

She lies on a slab of river-polished basalt next to the remade shore, alongside Leon. He is scratched and bruised. She thinks her ankle is broken. Her face, where Leon hit her, still feels sore to the touch. None of it matters. Leon's chest is warm in the sun and a place to hide. What do you say when you're given a second chance at life? Just hold me, Leon. She stays with him all afternoon, lying on the rock in the sun, but he is a stranger now. And when she has told him everything about Angelo and the coulee, about how she lost a brother because of a sin of her father, she asks him to forgive her.

"È colpa mia," says Brunella.

"I'm sorry for hitting you," Leon says. "I have a problem."

And then he says he cannot forgive her until Danny Red Thunder is out of jail and Angelo Cartolano is taking his place.

Tomorrow is their summit day. This evening, the two old men lay out everything for the climb to the top. The wind is hard, flapping the tent sides, but that is good, Angelo tells himself. It is the stillness, when the air is fat, that scares him. He does not worry about rain, heat, fog. Only thunderbolts. The old men are on a small ledge surrounded by stunted pine and heather. The ground below Angelo's tent is lumpy, but he does not mind. He lies on his back and thinks of the summit pyramid, the glory of Stuart. All around, the granite is burnished with the fiery light of the end of day. Marmots whistle at one another.

"How did Peter Selworth die?" Angelo says.

"Stroke," says Kosbleau. "On the golf course. The way he wanted to go."

"And McLoften?"

"Cancer. It was all over him. The poor son of a bitch looked like he had a basketball in his chest."

"I still can't get over Wally Simon. Heart attack, wasn't it?"

"Massive. Shut him down entirely. He's the one I expected to outlive us all. Didn't smoke, didn't drink."

"That's what did it," says Angelo. "You can't expect somebody who doesn't drink to be the Last Man. What would he do with the bottle?"

"It's better to die in the mountains, don't you think, Angelo? Better to die up here, as a man, than some drooler in a home?"

"No, it's better to live."

"You kept our secret, didn't you, Angelo? If you want to keep your place, your vineyard, everything you worked for . . . you have to keep our secret."

"I say we get up at four tomorrow," says Angelo. "Just before the light. There's a section up there, very steep. I'm worried. We have to get an early start."

"Did you ever expect to live this long, Angelo?"

"We are not so old. I expect to live some more. Almost thirty years ago the doctor said I was going to die. High blood pressure, a fat heart, some combination of bad things. He gives me some pills, says they will prolong my life, but you can't have sex, and you shouldn't drink anymore.

I laughed in his face. What sort of man wants to live so long without the good things in life? So I took my chance, and I'm still here. What do you think has kept me alive for so long?"

"They've got better medication now, Angelo. You can drink, get an occasional woody, and still live."

"I have to go slow on the snowfield tomorrow. That's the only part I'm not so sure about. Especially when we come down. I'm not so sure about when we come down; that's why we have to start early."

In the evening light, the mountain shadows stretch well over the irrigated steppe. From this distance, high on Stuart, they can see a small stretch of the Columbia and the alternating tables of tumbleweed brown and irrigated green on either side of it. Barely visible in the valley, they see light from another camp.

"We are very lucky men," says Alden Kosbleau. "The government gave us this land for peanuts, backed up the water, told us to take it and make something of it. We started with nothing. Now they're going to pay us to do nothing."

"*Scusi, mi amico.* The Cartolano family is holding on. Brunella will make wine when I'm gone."

"Shit, Angelo, that daughter of yours is one fiery gal, but she's no winemaker, you know that. We're set. Long as you stay quiet, you won't ever have to turn a spade of coulee dirt."

"Nobody else knows about the water?"

"Just you and me. They can't prove anything but that the Indians got themselves into a powerful mess. The water is all out of that pipe now and sitting in that big pit the Indians dug for themselves. That water pit—talk about a smoking gun! Dumbfuck Indians. Think they can play the water game. Our end is clean. The pipe's gone, the well capped. They can't prove a thing unless you say something, Angelo, my boy. You listening to me?"

"I want to see how Niccolo's vintage turns out. And I want to see a World Series in Seattle."

On the floor of the coulee where Angelo Cartolano first spent the night as a young man looking for a home, Brunella spreads a sleeping bag. She thinks of the sky as a blanket, the silvery cover of Milky Way stars. Her ankle is wrapped, swollen. She will never be able to look at Leon without seeing the back of his hand. She still feels the grip of the Columbia as she replays going over the dam in slow motion, holding on to the wire, being pulled loose and dragged over the spillway. The horror at the base of the dam, trapped underwater, then popping up like a balloon. It leaves her with a sense of how little control she has over anything. All these passive, painterly scenes of nature, of rivers flat and sunset-filled, of mountains erect and orderly, of forests green and cool, of inland seas that serve as postcard foreground—they are so deceptive. They only look pretty in repose. The earth is neither predatory nor embracing. It is a heaving, clanking, shedding, burning ball whose only mandate is to keep spinning. Nobody is a spectator, no matter how fortified their lives. She summons the good days the land around her has brought: the forest a wondrous playground for a girl; the mountains that hold the snow that melts into water that fattens the grapes and ends up in a bottle of pure pleasure that will live for a half century or more; the inland sea on the other side of the crest, nursing giant clams and zestful orcas; and the big river itself, still carrying salmon from the desert to the sea while trying to deliver the base nutrients of the Planned Promised Land. But look again and the forest is a furnace that consumed Niccolo, the mountains volcanic and studded with ice daggers, Puget Sound a ragged soup of death for the last fisherman, and the River of the West as life-destroying as it is life-sustaining.

Once more, she feels compelled by a simple desire to belong, to find her place, attach herself to bedrock and move in tandem with the spinning globe. She rises from her sleeping bag and hobbles slowly among the vines, forcing herself to sing *"looo-chela, looo-chela,"* under the universe of stars, forcing *"looo-chela, looo-chela"* and its summers of nonchalance on her, but all she can see is the back of Leon's hand, and she knows that she is falling over the dam again and has no choice but to leave the coulee and probably take Angelo with her.

She is spooked by a sound coming from somewhere near the stone chapel; she thinks a deer is grazing among the vines, despite the eight-foot-high wire fences on the edge.

"Continue." The voice of a man. "I like the song."

"Who's that?" In the dim light, she sees a face of rough contours and, beyond that, the eyes. "Teddy?"

259

"You told me if I ever needed a place to hang, come to the Cartolano vineyard."

"You startled me."

"Does Treadtoofar know about Angelo?"

"I told him everything."

"Everything?"

"Why did you come back?"

"I won't testify, Brunella, not if you don't want me to. I'm the only witness to what happened during the fire, and I can have a loss of memory, if you want me to."

He comes out in the open, walks slowly toward Brunella. She stiffens.

"Are you afraid of me, Brunella?"

His hair is short, as before, and his face . . . is not so bad. She can see where it is going in the healing, the skin new, a face somewhat like the old one emerging. He wears clear silicone gloves on his hands.

"It doesn't matter if you testify or not. It's out. I hope people see that my father is too old for jail and let him keep the place. I hope people can forgive him."

"Not likely, judging by the fever running through this basin."

"Do you know there was supposed to be enough water backed up by the Grand Coulee Dam to last a thousand years?"

"You didn't believe that, did you, Brunella?"

"At one time I did."

"You think there's anything in this country that'll still be around in a thousand years? We're a buncha great ideas in a big land. We're about open space and every race under the sun. We don't hold on to stuff."

"Why did you come back, Teddy?"

"I had to see if there was anything here for me. And you?"

"Same reason." She moves closer to him now, drawn in. "Did you talk to your mother?"

"Tomorrow I'm gone, and I'm never looking back."

"We are the Ladin, Teddy."

"The what?"

"The lost Romans who wandered around the Dolomites looking for one lousy little forgotten valley where they could hide out from the world and start something."

She takes his gloved hand and runs it against her chest, pulling him in. Two of his fingers, unscathed by fire, are ungloved, and she feels a tingle when they touch her breasts. "Come with me."

"Where?"

"To a village on a hilltop, like I said before, to a small house of old stone, surrounded by ancient footsteps, with grapes sloping to eternity—"

"And a festival for every food, and a miracle reenacted twice a year in a thousand-year-old church. I remember, Brunella. After you left the hospital, I had a dream and heard what you said again. But what am I supposed to do, be a kept man?"

"No, you can teach—"

"I won't be a kept man. That will never work."

This night on cold granite has brought only a skip of a dream to Angelo, and now he does not want to leave the womb of the sleeping bag. The chill has made his left hand more of an arthritic mess; he can't even make a fist. He feels like a very old engine trying to crank a tired body, but crank he must, dressing in the dark, joints cracking. The fingers are so stiff, his back all knotted up, one leg numb. So many layers to think about. Long underwear on the chest, topped by a wool shirt, a vest, a parka. What's missing? On his legs, tattered wool knickers, knee-length socks. Angelo spends a long time trying to tighten the laces on his boots; but with only one usable hand, the task is impossible.

"I need you to tie my boots," he says.

Kosbleau boils water for coffee while chomping on hard tasteless biscuits, never offering one to his partner. He stares at Angelo without sympathy. "Jesus effing Christ, you can't tie your own boots?"

"I can't."

Angelo stomps around camp, trying to get the blood moving, coughing in the dawn. He runs through the mental list again: hardware, food, binoculars, his lucky summit cap. The bottle of Cartolano Nebbiolo, which spent the night next to him wrapped in fleece, looks out of place this morning. He holds up the bottle, shining a flashlight on his lifework. The alchemy that makes fruit from a desert coulee into a wine for the ages strikes him as the one great truth of his life.

"You ready?" The call from Kosbleau, like an order.

"*Momento, momento, per favore.*" He kisses the bottle.

Kosbleau has the rope laid out, stretching from their camp to a rise about thirty feet above. He has doubled up the line and tied in advance the knot that will hold Angelo to his carabiner.

"What's the holdup?" Kosbleau says, his new hard plastic boots crunching on the rock as he approaches.

"*Niente, niente.* Are you scared, Alden?"

"Listen." Kosbleau takes the knot and holds it, beckoning Angelo. "Get over here. Now listen to me. You remember this, don't you?"

Angelo attaches himself to the rope, latches his helmet over his wool cap, signals he's ready. He follows Kosbleau. They walk very slowly over hard-crusted snow in a wide couloir. Once they reach the granite where the slope is not as steep, they pick up the rope, so it does not snag on a nub, and untie themselves. They are close to each other, wordless, breathing hard. Angelo's body is starting to warm, all but the toes, which feel dead.

"Rest," says Angelo.

"Too soon. Try to suck it up, old man."

"You suck it up yourself."

They are above tree line, where the snow lives ten months out of the year. The mountain comes alive very quickly with the sunrise, marmots whistling across the face, birds at eight thousand feet, the jays looking for easy food. The Indian paintbrush is deep orange in the first light, a whole flank full of it. Angelo thinks he sees a goat. Now three goats, whiter than the snowfield. They are so agile, bouncing around the good granite of Mount Stuart without a slip; they must have suction cups for feet.

"Rest," says Angelo. "Please."

"Ten minutes."

For Angelo's first time on Stuart, as a man not yet twenty years old, every upward step was a thrill, every nuance of the new day a discovery. He knew in his heart that he would make the summit, just as he knew the coulee would be good to him. He had no fear. He wanted, if anything, to go faster. He didn't need a rope. Gravity was a friend. Death was unknown. He knew nothing of the tricks of the mountain, where to look for handholds, when to duck out of the wind, how to read the clouds. He knew only confidence and adrenaline, the cocktail of youth. Today, he knows so much more about himself, about the winds of the Columbia basin and how to make friends with the granite. But he cannot fool himself into believing he is anything but an old man with a useless left hand and a back compressed by the years.

At the base of the big steep snowfield they sit for fifteen minutes. Sweating, Angelo zips open his parka and removes his wool hat. He's breathing like a fat man, but his heart is good, he says to himself. No chest pains. Kosbleau checks his altimeter. "Another fifteen hundred feet."

After the break, they attach crampons to their boots and retie the ropes. Angelo has to ask for help; the left hand might as well be an ornament. The snowfield is hard, but with the sun it will soften quickly and then go back to ice when the sun slips away. It has a surface like a white-capped lake, the sun cups formed by the pattern of daytime melting and nighttime hardening. Angelo moves very slowly, following Kosbleau's tracks. He slips once—yells "Falling!"—and goes immediately to his gut, clawing at the snow with his ice ax. The ax catches after three stabs. When Angelo gets his footing again, he moves even slower: two steps, rest, two steps, rest. Below them, a climbing party appears at the base of the snowfield, lively, full of bluster. Two men and a woman, in shorts, unroped; they are stripped to their T-shirts. They race by the old men, bantering the whole way, led by the woman with legs that come up to Angelo's chest.

"Morning, boys." The blonde with the legs cuts a switchback over the snowfield. "You guys know what you're doing?"

At the top of the snowfield, long after the other climbing party has passed, Angelo and Kosbleau take their final break before the summit. Kosbleau studies the steep section they have just climbed, looks to the sun, back again at the snowfield. Angelo feels light-headed. He is starting to smell the summit; he thinks he is going to make it. He takes off his helmet and puts on his sweat-stained Mariners cap, the brim chalky.

"Did you see those legs?" he says to Kosbleau.

"Let me take you out of the rope here. It's just a scramble to the top. That's what the book says. Leave the rope here."

Angelo sits against the base of a spire, leaning against the sun-warmed granite, facing Rainier. He sips his water, tips his head back. In two minutes he is asleep and starts to snore. Kosbleau watches him in disgust. After a twenty-minute nap, Angelo snaps awake. As he comes to, he sees a pair of tan extended legs move by him in scissor fashion. His eyes meet the tight butt of the woman as she leads her party down the mountain.

"Summit view is awesome this morning," she says.

"I have a good view already," says Angelo.

The nap has invigorated him. He leads up through the boulders, the scramble to the top. "Where you going?" says Kosbleau.

"*Alto, mi amico.* To heaven."

Using his good hand, he pulls himself over a series of boulders, clambering, strength building with every minor triumph. The final pitch of Stuart follows the ridge, along the south side, where the climbers pick their way through a maze. Several times, Angelo comes up short, his head popping over the ridge, looking straight down to a drop of several thousand feet. He down-climbs and tries again. With trial and error, picking and poking, he gets closer to the sky, leaving more planet behind him. I can do this, he thinks. He can taste the old cocktail again, confidence and adrenaline. He looks up and sees a rock cairn, with a tattered flag poking out, and nothing above it.

"Whooooooo-eeeeeeeeee-oooooooooooooooooo!"

Kosbleau follows in ten minutes. He arrives with a scowl on his face, angry at Angelo for "acting like a goddamned rabbit."

"*Mi dispiace,*" says Angelo. "The summit called."

From the top, alpine lakes spread north, cradled by peaks covered with glaciers, stretching well into British Columbia. The wind is just right. Rainier, Saint Helens, Adams, Hood, Jefferson—all the volcanoes are in splendid formation to the south. But what gets to Angelo's tired heart is the little notch in the potato-skin-colored basin to the east, the place where he made Nebbiolo come to life. He slouches next to the summit cairn, eyes fixed on the coulee, a tired smile on his face.

"I wish . . . I wish I could make this moment last forever."

"Sure. Let's take our time."

"I'm worried about thunder," says Angelo.

"Take our time. Why don't you crack that wine, old man. We'll just have a sip."

Kosbleau looks downslope toward the snowfield, glances back up at the sun, checks his watch. Angelo is having trouble opening the wine; Kosbleau grabs it from him.

"Let me do it."

He pulls the cork and sniffs. "Take a long pull," he says to Angelo. "No hurry."

"But the sun will be off that snow before long, yes?"

"No hurry. Take a pull. You deserve it."

Angelo takes a few sips but makes a face. "It's not right. Too cold up here. Cork it."

"No, let's relax."

"I have to get down, Alden. Let's go now."

"Another twenty minutes."

They leave the summit, moving slowly in a downward crawl. Angelo nearly slips on a lichen-slick boulder, holding to the rock for ten minutes without moving. Kosbleau hurries past Angelo, telling him he will wait at the top of the snowfield and to take his time.

Angelo straggles to where Kosbleau is waiting, looking at his watch. "You want to take another nap?" Kosbleau asks.

"I don't want to go down," Angelo says, the summit glow still in his face. "But we have no time. The sun is on the other side."

"You looked so perky going up, why don't you lead?"

"I'm slow."

"That's okay. You lead. Angle off to the west, in that shade there. The footing should be easier."

Angelo turns on his stomach and kicks a step into the snowfield; in shade, now, it quickly hardens. He turns over on his other side, using his heels to step into the snow, his face toward the sky. After half an hour, he is only a few hundred feet down the snowfield. He lets his mind skip away to the coulee. It has been several months since he sampled Niccolo's vintage, and he thinks that the licorice of the grape must be starting to show. That's the thing with good Nebbiolo when it starts to reveal itself, the licorice. Near the edge of a small cliff, Angelo pauses to look up for Kosbleau, and as he takes his eyes off the snow, he slips. He falls quickly on his butt, slides to the edge. He slashes away at the snowfield with his ice ax, trying to get a grip, but he is falling fast on the sheen on the steep slope. The ax bites at last into the ice. But Angelo is holding on with just the one good hand, and the grip is tenuous. He calls out for Kosbleau. His partner is sitting down, strapping metal crampons to his boots.

"What're you doing, Alden? I need you!"

"Just wait there for me."

"I'm afraid I can't hold for long. Come quickly!"

"Don't do anything. Just wait there for me."

Slowly, digging his metal-pronged boots in the snow, Kosbleau edges toward Angelo.

"Hurry!" Angelo says. His one hand is starting to slip. "You must come now!"

Kosbleau moves even slower, pausing to look around for other climbers, to check the light, to get his footing. When at last he reaches Angelo, he says nothing. Spit and froth cover Angelo's lips. His eyes are wild. The bad hand is shaking; the good hand is numb, clinging to the ax.

"Thank you," Angelo says, in a whisper.

Kosbleau plants his ice ax for a grip and kicks Angelo's ax away from the snow. Angelo looks for a half second into Kosbleau's face and then disappears off the cliff, down the face of Mount Stuart.

Two days later, they find Angelo's body, broken and deflated, more than two thousand feet from where he lost his anchor. The county coroner rules the death an accident, based on an account from Kosbleau, the only witness to the fall. Brunella cannot accept the coroner's verdict, but the county will not investigate further. There is no evidence. Kosbleau was your father's oldest friend, Ms. Cartolano. Your father was an old man on a very big mountain. He fell, he lost his grip, and then the mountain took him. Try to accept this. The body rests for one day in the stone chapel, with Brunella nearby at all times. Down below, Kosbleau gets Roberto to let him into the house; he finds his way to the cellar where Angelo first made wine in the Columbia basin, and he removes an ancient bottle, its label marked by the blood of ten boys who have all left the earth save one.

At dusk on the evening before the funeral, Brunella goes inside and stares at the dead man, the candlelight flickering against Angelo's frescoes on the wall. It is not grief she feels, but love, and it drives her tears. She feels empty and dark and helpless, because the love cannot go with him. The next day, after a small Roman Catholic service in the stone chapel, Angelo Cartolano is buried in the vineyard among his Nebbiolo, honoring his request that he be positioned high enough in the coulee for a view of Mount Stuart on Judgment Day. Brunella stays behind after everyone has left. She tells her *babbo* she is sorry, she has to leave the coulee.

CHAPTER TWENTY

S HE WAKES EARLY in the soft mornings of the Piemonte, when the *nebbia* holds down the light and provides a passage for the last dreams of sleep, walks to the window, and flings open the shutters. It is breathless, these early moments in mid-October, to pull back the curtain of the day and wonder what drama the landscape has in store. The vineyards look like they are pasted against the sky, and then out of the fog will appear the flank of a cream-colored *castello* or some sliver of a cypress. They are fringe players still, she and Teddy, living in a stone barn above the Tanaro River, living day to day, waiting on Uncle Giacomo. But already they have a routine. She rises first, walks two kilometers to the market at Alba, and buys food for the day. It was their great luck to land in the Piemonte when the white truffles are being pulled from the Langhe Hills, though the tourists have caused the market to spike. The truffle hunters and sellers are ruthless, like drug dealers, sniffing the ground at night with their xenophobic dogs and then lording over the market in cartel style. The Mafia are easier to deal with and certainly less menacing. Brunella has cultivated an old man without front teeth who runs an *alimentari* the size of an American bathroom in the shadow of a seven-hundred-year-old church. When he sees her, his face lights up; he opens a drawer and peels back newspaper to show off a pale clump—his *tartufi bianchi*—as if unveiling a rare diamond. She makes him laugh, singing Dino Martino songs for him, Vegas style, like in the movies of his youth.

She only needs one small truffle to last the week; the scent of a few shavings will fill the stone barn. She buys eggs, fruit, *castelmagno* cheese from the mountains, and an oval of *biova* bread before hiking back to Teddy.

The Tanaro is a thin vein this fall, as the rains have yet to arrive. The river has cut a wide path in its epic wanderings from the mountains to the Po; she can see how it has jumped all over the valley. They eat breakfast outside, the *nebbia* dissolving, taking on the colors of the sky. She likes to grate a few flakes of the truffle onto scrambled eggs, add scallions, diced tomatoes, basil, and small clumps of Gorgonzola. After breakfast, it's off to check for Uncle Giacomo. He has been away since they arrived, and she is beginning to wonder if all those Christmas gifts of *panettone* came from a phantom. The caretaker of his house, Marco Provenza, promises he will return for the grape harvest, the *vendemmia,* and yet, with the Barbera ripe and the Nebbiolo almost ready, there is still no sign of Uncle Giacomo. Unlike his brother Angelo, Uncle Giacomo is no winemaker. The baby of the family, never married, he pokes and noodles on his land, spending as little time as he can. He sells his grapes for *vino da tavola* and lives for soccer. Marco says Uncle Giacomo has decided to follow the Milano team around for the Italian Cup. When will he be back? Soon, perhaps. Then, maybe not so soon. Watch the cup. And Marco has some advice for the visitors: Stay away from the Gypsies in town; they will steal from you, using a baby as a ruse to distract you.

The plan is to look for work, while relying on Uncle Giacomo's help in getting settled. They are anxious to shed the label that people stick to them behind their backs: *stranieri,* foreigners. They have yet to register with the carabinieri, as the law requires, but everyone seems to know about the green-eyed American woman and the man with the burned face. Alba is a small town. The stone barn, for all its charms and its placement as a white-noise sleep haven above the river, is not heated. When the chill air moves down from the Alps, the landlord will shutter the barn till spring. As Brunella and Teddy ask around about picking grapes, people scoff at them. The harvest is not for Yanks, unless, of course, they're staying in a tourist *fattoria* and paying to work. (They pay us to do peasant work, some of these Americans!) Nor, it seems, is grape-picking for the Piemontese. Let the teenage boys from Ethiopia pick the crop. Let the Albanians, the few refugees who could sneak into the country, or the Sicilians who can't find work in the factories in Torino; let them stain their hands.

In Alba, lunch is always at a small *osteria* in the piazza near the fountain. Teddy orders foccacia topped by caramelized onions, a plate of olives, and beer, while taking in the movable scenery of shop girls making a *bella figura*. Every day, he orders the same thing. He knows he must learn Italian; grunting, sniffing, and poking while repeating *"mi dispiace, non parlo Italiano,"* will not do if he and Brunella are to make a go of it here. Brunella watches the *nonne* fuss with their boys, always the boys. A baby girl is wonderful, yes, but only a boy can complete your life. And if Italians have the lowest birth rate in the world, in a country that is overwhelmingly Catholic, the worst-kept secret for explaining this phenomenon is the selective womb-culling for boys. The boys can get away with anything.

In early afternoon the town closes up, doors clicking and locking, window bars clanking into place, fruit rolled back under cover, newspapers, shoes, and football jerseys vanishing from display, storefronts putting up blank faces. The men in tailored business suits drain out of offices on scooters; the women hurry home in heels, grandly exiting the *strada*. In the apartments, green shutters close like dominoes falling to a pattern, as every window blocks out light for the communal nap. For the rest of the afternoon, most of Alba and the countryside is on siesta; even the plants, sunflowers and late-blossoming fuchsias, seem to bring in their petals and nod off.

Brunella loves the siesta. She has a little wine inside her, and she's pleasantly tired from the morning exertions. Usually, she makes love with Teddy just before sleep, falling away with his scent all over her body. Teddy does not nap. He is restless. He will not be a kept man. She says he should use the time to learn Italian. But he has found an American friend, a man living near Asti named John Gamont, who tells everyone he is Giovanni Gamonni, somewhat fancifully, as a way to hurry himself to his adopted land. He is an orthopedic surgeon from the Midwest who retired early. Teddy and Giovanni play Foosball, go on the Web to check the baseball play-offs and college football, and run. Giovanni says he will make a real runner out of Teddy. His wife says he would take a thirty-six-minute ten-kilometer race over sex with two women. He says, Not true: I would take the two women on a run and then have sex with them.

On the first night in the stone barn, Brunella made *manzo al Barolo*, marinating the thin beef in the Wine of Kings and garlic, with a side dish of spinach, anchovies, olive oil, and pine nuts blended together. They drank a ten-year-old Barolo for dinner and it was a revelation, even for Teddy, a beer man. She could taste the clay hills and the *nebbia* in this sweat of the Langhe Hills, and he says no wine ever stayed with him longer, but he will not be a kept man.

One morning Teddy wakes early and complains about pain. He is woozy, his eyes unfocused, his lips parched. Brunella strips back the sheets and finds that his leg is inflamed; it looks like an infection in the part of his hip where some skin was lifted for the face grafts. When he tries to get out of bed, he collapses on the floor. By midday, his temperature soars to 105 degrees, and he starts to babble. The bedsheets are drenched.

Teddy is taken by ambulance an hour north to a new hospital in Torino. She cannot suppress the thought that she is going to lose him as well.

"Tay-deee Flox—this man is your husband?" they ask at the hospital, and she nods. "*Sì, sì, un dottore—adesso!—per favore.*"

Over three days, two doctors care for Teddy, one of them a surgeon of some renown who is a friend of Giovanni Gamonni's.

"How are we going to pay for this?" Teddy says. "I have no insurance."

But when they discharge him with a prescription for antibiotics, Teddy is not given a bill. He is told to call if there is any sign of the infection returning. On the way home, Brunella asks him a question. "Who lives better, Italians or Americans?"

One week they travel south to the Ligurian coast, under the mountains to Genoa, along the autostrada and through its endless tunnels—the cars coming to within a few feet of their tail at 120 kilometers an hour—to the sea, the tip of the land where Italy is sliced away to the Mediterranean, to a chin of rock and a town named for the goddess of love. The tour buses are gone for the season, leaving Portovenere to its quirks: laundry hanging from the windows, fishing boats bringing in squid, men arguing over the awful cheaters from the Lazio team, who may well win the cup. They walk to the top of a fortress built by the Genovese when they ruled a corner of the seas, wind their way up through narrow streets to a church of sea-blasted limestone. In a land where extraordinary spaces devoted to God are as routine as sunset, the church of San Lorenzo in Portovenere is an awakening to Brunella. Built of alternating black and white limestone, with a small courtyard, the church has the oddest of ornaments adorning its entrance: Above the green metal doors under a Gothic arch is a sculpture of a man in a loincloth being cooked to death over a grill.

"What happened to this saint?" says Teddy. He cups his hands in the fountain and takes a long drink of the cold clear water from the spout in the courtyard.

Brunella moves back a few steps and stares directly at San Lorenzo, his feet and legs bound as he lies on his back over a metal grill atop a fire. His face is contorted in excruciating pain, a long way from the usual facial bliss of stone martyrs as they transit from this world to the next. Inside the church it is damp and cool, and her eyes take a few minutes to adjust. She approaches a hollowed-out cedar log, dating to 1204, the inscription says, the century after the church was built. Three old people are in a pew up front, near a confessional. Brunella takes her seat near a bleeding Gesu reclining under glass just above her. She goes into the confessional and tells the old priest everything—the theft of water by her father, how he made one fraudulent vintage, trying to fool the elements, how her reluctance to tell the truth hurt many innocent people, and the rage she cannot shake over her father's death, no doubt at the hands of the traitor Alden Kosbleau. The old priest seems confused by her sins and her stories, but she persists. Tell me, Padre, how can you explain the deaths of my brother and father? The priest says he is tired and must go home for siesta.

Outside, standing under San Lorenzo, she stares intently at the face again and feels Niccolo in a way she has not experienced since his funeral. She can sense his presence in San Lorenzo's face, the saint on the grill. Dying once, with superheated air searing his lungs. Dying twice, with the flames.

Giovanni and his wife, Heather, with the willowy legs, arrive in time for dinner. They share plates of tomatoes with mozzarella and sardines and *gnocchi di patate,* the pesto sharp from the cheese, dining in the small piazza at the base of the hill.

"Why does it always taste better over here?" Heather asks.

"Because you are relaxed," says Brunella. "You are letting your senses breathe. You are open to all the small pleasures Italy has refined over the centuries."

"Refined, yes. But tomatoes and potatoes are not native to Italy," says Giovanni.

"Tomatoes came from Sicily, didn't they?" says Teddy.

"They came from the New World. There is not a tomato in all of the Italian peninsula that does not owe its birth to an Indian ancestor across the Atlantic."

"The Cartolano family tomatoes?" Brunella asks.

"Incas, most likely. Same with potatoes. This gnocchi, the polenta that's been a staple in the north for so long, all of it came from Indians, brought back to Europe by the Spaniards. A lot of Europe would have starved without these Indian contributions to diet. But Heather's right— it does taste better over here."

They spend five days in Portovenere. Teddy and Giovanni race up to the top of the small mountain above town, a rock outcrop, timing themselves. Brunella and Heather take a tiny boat to an island just across the water and sunbathe nude on a beach sheltered from the winds. Even in late October, the sun is a warm embrace. At night, they take their *passeggiata* through town and up the hill. One day they hike the length of the *cinque terre,* five villages clinging to the cliffs just north of town. Between the villages, the grapes are nearly falling out to the Mediterranean on the steepest of slopes, and some of the pickers are tied to climbing ropes. They eat *pasta vongole* and whole snapper grilled with rosemary and drink the light dry wine from the vertical vineyards.

"I could live on these cliffs," says Teddy.

"And would you have a better life here than you had in America?" Brunella asks.

"The clams are bigger in Puget Sound."

"I know, but who lives better?"

The moldering pessimism that Teddy developed following the fire has been left behind in America. He is more like the boy of summer that Brunella remembers. He reads, he runs, he makes love to Brunella, undressing her slowly at her command; he has started to tell jokes on himself; he even cooks, but of course, he insists through every chore and every pleasure he will not be a kept man. No, ma'am. She cannot forget that he alone knows everything that happened in the fire; he is a second conscience. But she has yet to believe—even during a low moment after a scrap between them—that he would use it. That life is gone.

When they return to Alba, the stone barn is shuttered for the winter. They retrieve a few possessions from the landlord's cellar and search again for Uncle Giacomo. He owns a tired-looking two-story villa amid a rumpled vineyard on a small hill. He was supposed to be home two days ago, but then Milan beat Parma on a shoot-out and Uncle Giacomo called to say he would be on the road for another month. And how long did you say the tournament lasts? They play though June. Uncle Giacomo says his American niece and her friend can stay in a small apartment on the second floor of his house. It's no problem, *benvenuto, benvenuto,* but try not to use too much heat, limit your baths to once a week, *per favore,* and maybe—if you feel up to it—could you fix the toilet? It has not flushed since Milan lost to Lazio. And when did that happen? During the last Italian Cup.

Noticing the first new snow on the Alps, on a day when the *nebbia* seems to have disappeared for the year, Brunella tells Teddy they must go to the Dolomites before the skiers show up. What's in the Dolomites? Teddy asks.

"The Ladin, Teddy. We have to find the Ladin."

Uncle Giacomo has a boxy Fiat that gets sixty miles to the gallon but sputters like a drunk with bronchitis when forced to run uphill. They are welcome to use it as long as they change the oil, and, say, can you put new spark plugs in as well? *Non c'è problema.* Oh, yes, the heater doesn't work either, but who cares when you're young and in love, right? *Buon viaggio.*

They spend three days at Lake Como, taking the small ferry to Varenna, where they ask for a corner room overlooking the water. As

Brunella has said, it looks like Lake Chelan, albeit with three thousand additional years of cultivation and tailoring. The hotel owner speaks English with what sounds like a Swiss accent and won't let Brunella talk to her in Italian. The owner asks a lot of questions before she gives them the corner room with big windows. Later, when Brunella comes down alone for a stroll, the owner motions her over to the desk. She whispers, as people do when speaking of an illness or death, "What happened to him?"

"He was burned trying to save a forest in the American West," Brunella says. "He is a hero. And can I ask you something?"

"Please, yes, and you're welcome."

"Where are the Ladin?"

The hotel owner does not know anything about the Ladin, but she warns Brunella to watch out for the Africans—they all have AIDS, they are thieves and stalk white women at night—and be sure to keep an eye out for the Gypsies, who will steal your money using a baby as a ruse, and some Albanians are loose in the north as well. You can tell them by their dirty hair, she says.

Teddy and Brunella walk to the eleventh-century castle above the lake and make love on a blanket alongside the ruins. From his runs and hill climbs with Giovanni, Teddy is getting very strong. She loves the grip of his legs around her and she loves having him inside her, and she particularly loves what he does to her when he puts his head under the blanket and tries to imitate a truffle dog. He has learned something already from the Italians: Everything does go better with olive oil.

In the Alto Adige, the summits hold the first snow of the season while the vine-covered lower slopes are still clad in crimson. They stop in Bolzano, the medieval capital, intending to spend an afternoon with the Iceman. On the way to the South Tyrol Museum of Archaeology, Brunella falls for another church door, this inside the fifteenth-century duomo in the Piazza Walther. The *vino porta,* the wine door, is a narrative of people tending to vines in the mountain foothills. It makes her think of Angelo's art in the coulee and then, darkly, the legal letters from home that continue to pile up at Uncle Giacomo's. They look official, menacing, and in need of immediate attention, and she refuses to open any of them. The Iceman was found in a frozen trench near a 10,500-foot pass in the

Dolomites, with an arrow in his back and a copper ax in his belt, wearing shoes of grass and twine wrapped in leather. He died 5,300 years ago and is so well preserved that you can still discern the color of his eyes and the tattoos on his skin.

"He's Ladin?" says Teddy.

"No, he's Bronze Age. Three thousand years before the Romans. Look, they think he was forty years old when he died."

"What was he doing so high up in the mountains?"

In Bolzano for dinner, Teddy orders dumplings filled with meat and potatoes, which makes Brunella frown.

"You're getting *strangolapreti*—that's sacrilegious."

"Why?"

"*Strangolapreti*—it means priest stranglers. Not a lot of Catholics in the Alto Adige."

Teddy grins, summoning the waiter. "And a nun-choking ale to go with it, please." He turns to Brunella. "Why save a priest? They're all child molesters, aren't they?"

"Not over here. Italian priests have mistresses."

For five days, they look for the Ladin in the high valleys of the Dolomites. They start in Ortesei, following the river in the Val Gardena. They hike in early November sun, passing cattle with bells around their necks, grazing on near-frozen grass, and herders with felt hats and cell phones. An amphitheater of peach-colored mountain surrounds them. For lunch, they stop in a hut and eat sausage wrapped in thick slices of coarse bread. They hike another six miles in the afternoon. Brunella is intoxicated; at times she skips through the meadows. Teddy calls her Heidi and tells her to save her gymnastics for night with him. In the town of Selva they find a Ladin craft store, selling wood carvings and costumes, and a clerk who speaks German better than he does Italian.

"Do you not speak Ladin?" Brunella asks.

"Nobody speaks Ladin," the clerk says. "Except in the museum at Vigo di Fassa. You want to buy carvings? The bear is very nice."

"Somebody must speak Ladin," Brunella says.

"Your can hear it on the radio. The Ladin have a station. That's the law. But nobody listens. You want to buy a carving of the chamois? It's authentic."

At dinner they notice immediately that something is missing. The menu is German—sausages, wurst, schnitzel, and heavy beer—and the diners are silent, eating their food without saying a word.

"We've left Italy," Brunella says. "No Italian could ever eat in such deathly silence."

When they reach Vigo di Fassa, they find a woman who speaks fluent Ladin, which she explains is not a dialect but a distinct Romance language, born out of the conquerors' Latin and the natives' Rhaetian. The Ladin lived through many invasions and held on, the woman says, because they could hide in the mountains. This has been their home for almost two thousand years. The hardest time was the Great War, when so many battles were fought in the Dolomites.

"My father lost two uncles in the Dolomites," Brunella says.

"These mountains have seen much sorrow."

"And whose side were the Ladin on?"

"They did not care who won the war, Italians or Austrians. It's all the same. They just wanted to be left alone."

"Do they live somewhere—a central part of a village? Can we visit them?"

The woman laughs. "How long have you been in the Dolomites?"

"A couple of days."

"The Ladin are all around you in these valleys. You have been among them. You would never know unless it was *festa* and they were in costume. Some still grow millet and oats and make cheese. But they are dying out."

"Like the salmon fishermen of Puget Sound," Brunella says.

"I do not know about fishermen," the woman says.

"And what keeps them alive?"

"The government. We have subsidies for endangered cultures recognized by the European Union. It's good for the museum. We buy new computers, and Windows 2005. I can get you carvings of Ladin bear, *Ursus speleus;* it's very rare."

"Where can we find the bear itself?"

"Here," the woman says, with another laugh. "The museum is the only place that can sell the *Ursus speleus* carved by the Ladin. The bear does not live anywhere else. He has been extinct for a long time."

Teddy and Brunella spend their last night trying to get up into the wildest part of the Dolomites. They want to find a place without cable cars, trams, chairlifts, or roads, but they are told it is not possible. They hike nearly ten miles to a hut, a *rifugio* with a close-up view of Marmolada, the highest of the Dolomite peaks on the Italian side of the border. It changes colors with the light, glowing strongest at dusk. They are fed a stew of game and mountain herbs, potatoes and dumplings, which they eat at a table with four other people. The person who runs the hut, an Italo-Austrian named Herman, knows everything about the Dolomites and is a good cook and companion.

"Where is the wilderness?" Brunella asks him after dinner, sipping an Alto Adige grappa in front of the fire.

Herman scrunches up his nose. "What is wilderness, *selva*?"

"No, *selva* is forest." She tries to explain. "Like . . . in the American West, where I come from. The mountains as they always were, a place where you might be the first person to set foot. Wilderness. *Come si dici in Italiano?*"

Herman says there is no word in Italian for wilderness.

They spend the winter in the Piemonte apartment of Uncle Giacomo, trying to build a life. Brunella gets a job teaching English to sixth graders at the *scuola* in Alba, while Teddy tries to learn Italian. The schoolboys are very rough, not paying attention, always up to tricks. One day it's glue on the seat, which prompts a girl to cry all morning. The principal sends the girl home; the boy stays. Ah, the *ragazzi,* you know how it is, Signora Cartolano; their mammas will talk to them. Another day it's a luncheon prank, when two boys put food coloring in the fettucine sauce, turning it blue. The cook is admonished; the two boys are patted on the head. You know how it is with *ragazzi,* Signora Cartolano, just let it be. We have no children left in our country—we're not producing enough to sustain Italy—so you must be lenient. Brunella sits in on religion class, fascinated that the public schools would teach the subject. It is broad and traditional, a snooze. The alternative, the class a student can opt to take instead of religion, has only a handful of children and is taught by a little man from Naples, Lucciano Albertini, who is dressed in a meticulous suit and silk tie at all times. They listen one day to the John Lennon song

"Imagine" and deconstruct the lyrics. Another day the children are taught how to read road signs on the autostrada; the one that looks like men shoveling poop, Lucciano says, means road construction, which gets a good laugh from the students of the alternative-to-religion class. So practical, Brunella tells Lucciano.

The apartment is always cold, but Brunella and Teddy do not complain. They have no phone, but to Brunella's surprise she does not miss it. Uncle Giacomo's calls are routed through Marco Provenza. Everyone in Italy has a phone planted in one ear, talking in restaurants, in church, on scooters. The FedEx packages arrive from Houston and Seattle, always legal documents, the dense, verbless prose communicating liens placed and threats soon to be executed and dire consequences for parties of the second part. Roberto speaks to his sister only through his attorneys, trying to clear the strands leftover so he can complete the sale of the estate to the lawyer from California. For now, the Cartolano homestead is empty except for Miguel, who stays on, paid by Roberto to keep the vineyard going. Brunella waits, with forced detachment, for news from the Forest Service. She is anxious for Leon's final report to see where her father has ended up in the government narrative and what became of Kosbleau. With Angelo dead, there is no witness to Kosbleau's scheming. And the only witness to what happened during the fire is the man who shares Brunella's bed.

Teddy and Giovanni continue to run, even during the winter months. The Alps seem close enough to be on top of them, but the snow rarely sticks around the lowlands. It's cold and dry. Teddy can almost run a five-minute mile. He and Giovanni do sprint work at the indoor track in Torino, alternating that with long runs in the valley between Alba and Asti. After his runs, Teddy returns home as if riding a carpet on helium, kissing Brunella all over. He is beyond pain.

"Those are the endorphins in you speaking," Brunella says.

"I thought you said it was a way to get closer to God."

"Knowledge is the great spoiler of mystery," she says.

Milano, Roma, and Lazio fight it out for the cup in the second half of the season. Napoli was in contention but they have fallen back. Brunella's friend at school, Lucciano Albertini, is crushed when Napoli loses three in a row. Behind his back, the other teachers make fun of Lucciano. He's dark and short, and you know, Signora Cartolano, how the Neapolitans are, a little lazy, a little slow; maybe you should watch your purse. See how he's dressed with the silk tie and the jacket every day, like a pimp. The Neapolitans, some of them, are as bad as Gypsies, Signora Cartolano. You must keep your distance. You've seen the prostitutes along the road. They are Neapolitans or Africans. You can tell by the smell.

The first hint of spring arrives at the end of February, with the almond trees pink-flowering and fragrant, and the hated Lazio team on top in the standings. Teddy and Brunella become soccer fans, in part because hatred of Lazio has seeped into them by sports osmosis, and in part because they are not looking forward to Uncle Giacomo's return, should Milano not make the final. They have their unfinished projects. The toilet is an ongoing disaster. First, they had to unblock the pipes, then fix the pump. And a septic tank dating to the Great War has split a seam and come gurgling to the surface. In a rage one day, Teddy pulls at the chain and it breaks off a ceramic piece at the base of the overhead toilet tank. He throws the piece at the wall and it bounces, shattering the window.

"Now what have you done?" Marco Provenza says.

"It's only a window. I'll go into town. It can't be hard to fix."

"You must get a permit from the government first. They can arrest you if you go ahead without the permit. And the carabinieri; surely they will be called. You are on the edge of some very serious trouble, my friend. Take a nap. Take many naps. And then forget about it. You can always shit in the woods."

Brunella spends three days in five permit offices in Alba, showing progressively more leg as she moves through the Piemonte bureaucracy. Uncle Giacomo's house dates to 1682, she is told in the historic preservation office. It has Savoy influences, some touches from the Napoleonic era, a room added during the *Risorgimento*—the rebirth. You would think all of Italy's glorious past was coursing through Uncle Giacomo's dump. It cannot be altered in any way without grave consequences, Signora Cartolano.

"*Signorina, per favore,*" she says, hiking the skirt even more, "are we talking about the same place?"

"*Sì, sì,* it's all here in the books."

"I just need to replace a window."

"It is not a window you are replacing, Signora Cartolano; it is a fragment of history."

"Signorina, per favore."

They hammer plywood over the opening and wait, all spring, for a permit to come through on Uncle Giacomo's bathroom window.

She opens the latest FedEx envelope and finds a single page—handwritten—from Roberto. This time, no legal papers, no lawyerly summons, just a simple note:

Brunella:

    I remain deeply hurt by your insinuations and your overt hatred of me, but we have some business that needs immediate attention. The buyer has withdrawn. He could not wait out the uncertainty of Father's estate as it winds though the legal process. In his place we have a new buyer from Seattle. I have yet to meet him, but he has offered to pay twice what our gentleman from San Francisco offered. That's right, twice! Our senior water rights are now worth a fortune because of a new government buyout program. In fact, the water on Father's property may be worth more than the vines, or so I'm told. I can't imagine how you're getting by or what you're doing over there with Flax, or if you even receive my many urgent summons. But this offer is nothing to walk away from. It would make you financially secure for life. I've enclosed a clipping about the Indian from the Forest Service. Most interesting!

Cordial regards,

Bob

The clipping is from the Wenatchee paper, headlined FS INTERNAL PROBE OF FIRE INVESTIGATOR HEATS UP. Leon Treadtoofar is under investigation, the story says, because his work on the Johnny Blackjack fire may have been compromised by his closeness to one of the subjects.

In the late afternoons, home from her teaching job, Brunella walks the Barolo vineyards, knocking on doors, introducing herself, trying to pry some secrets of the grape from the clannish men who make the wine. Always the men. She becomes friends with Matteo Rudolfo, a thickset vintner with dancing eyes. His family has been making wine since the 1870s, when Barolo came of age in the courts of Europe, which he says is not very long in the story of wine. In Pliny the Elder's natural history, he tells her, the Roman wrote of a climbing vine in the Piemonte that grew in the fog. He places his hand over hers, tightens it.

"And I know of your father," says Matteo Rudolfo. "From what I've heard, Angelo Cartolano has done great things in America."

She cannot help but like Matteo, for no one else among the Piemontese has shown respect for the Cartolano name. They know only the old bachelor, Giacomo, the roustabout with his untended vines and ramshackle villa; few connect Brunella to the Nebbiolo from the American West. On Matteo's land is a catch-basin pond, just like the one Angelo built in the coulee. Matteo says his grapes rely on water from the sky and the pond—nothing else. To force a Barolo by any other way would be cheating, he says. Sipping Dolcetto late one afternoon in Matteo's courtyard, Brunella tells him her father's story. Matteo jumps up several times at key moments of the telling, once spilling his wine. His grandfather as well considered sending the children off to America after Il Duce used the poisonous gas in Ethiopia, the bastard. And how did Angelo make his wine come to life in the New World? Surely, Nebbiolo could never find a home in such a faraway corner of the world.

"We have a long growing season, longer than any other place in the States. The sun sets at ten o'clock in July. You know how Nebbiolo won't ripen if it does not get the long days. And Babbo has done a lot of experimenting. He innovates, following his palate."

"We had our innovation already," says Matteo, his face stern. "Now we have perfection, based on decrees dating to 1758, passed by the town of Alba and strictly enforced. I know my friends in Bordeaux and California disagree with me, but I know in my heart I am right. We have been making the greatest wine in the world for some time now, and one big reason is because we set standards."

"You say 1758, Matteo? Do you know what was going on in 1758 in the American West? They thought there was a river connecting one ocean to the other. The Rocky Mountains had not been charted. And many people still thought California was an island."

"If you'd let the Genovese continue to map your New World, you wouldn't have had that problem." He pours more Dolcetto for both of them. "You look so lovely in this light, Brunella. I can see the face of the Piemonte in those green eyes of yours. You belong here, yes?"

She returns to Uncle Giacomo's house woozy from the Dolcetto and ravenous for Teddy. He is lying in the overgrown grass shaded by chestnut trees, reading A *Soldier of the Great War,* when Brunella crawls toward him. She uses her teeth to pull down his running shorts, though he continues reading. She works her way past the Nike scar and brings him slowly to arousal. Then she mounts him and rides in the last of the Piemonte light, bouncing and rocking, until she falls atop his chest, exhausted. Her eyes closed, she listens to the gallop of his heart and takes in the aroma that fills Uncle Giacomo's fields, down from the Langhe Hills, strongest at the end of the day: jasmine.

"Does all of Italy smell like this?" Teddy asks.

"Only in the spring."

She craves big breakfasts, lots of extreme cheese, aged taleggio and Piemonte robiola with the musky tastes, loud and over the top. She also visits the *gelateria* every day, sneaking out of school during the mid-morning break, waiting for the shopkeeper's gates to slide back, and then pouncing on fresh-smoothed ice cream. The cantaloupe-flavored one is her favorite. Her senses are alive like no other time. In the middle of teaching about common English adjectives—not so hard to learn, you don't have to match gender, as a beautiful table is never anything but asexual—she rushes from the classroom and hurries down the hall to the bathroom to vomit. It is like this for weeks, the need for extreme cheese and gelato, the nausea at some point in the day. And in the late afternoons—Teddy. She wants him all the time. She wants him standing, leaning against the ancient rock wall outside. She wants him upside down. She wants him in the bathtub, glistening like a seal. She wants him in the middle of the night, when he is softly snoring. Nothing makes her full.

She will not drink more than half a glass of wine anymore, even the light Soave and Pinot Grigio.

"Are you—?"

"Yes! I mean, I think so." Face flushed, green eyes lit. "Yes! Eight weeks, about. I saw the doctor today. A bambino is on the way, Teddy."

"American or Italian?"

When school is out they count the days till Uncle Giacomo's return, making the most of every hour alone in the Langhe Hills summer. Another note arrives by FedEx from Roberto:

> Brunella:
> The estate has finally cleared. You should be getting formal notice of this soon. I have become sole owner by default. As I predicted, the will from Father that you produced was ruled invalid because there was no witness. You can't say I did not give you fair warning. You ignored everything that was sent to you and missed all four court appearances. The judge was extremely tolerant of your intolerant behavior. I have gone ahead and closed the sale with the second buyer. It turns out to be a holding company in Seattle for Waddy Kornflint. I believe you know of him from your work there. They paid us $3.7 million. I will try to make sure, despite your obstinacy, your continued absence, and your overt hatred of me, that you receive a share of the proceeds of this sale. Please see the enclosed clip on the Forest Service investigator.
>
> Regards,
> Bob

The second clip from the Wenatchee paper, headlined: FS TO TRANS-FER FIRE INVESTIGATOR, reports the results of the internal investigation of Leon Treadtoofar. The Forest Service found he had erred in his investigation, allowing one of the subjects to influence the outcome, and in the process overlooked key facts. As a disciplinary move, he would be transferred next summer to another unit of the Forest Service.

They watch the Italian Cup finals with Marco Provenza and root for Milano. Uncle Giacomo calls just before the final. They can barely make out his words, he is so excited. "If Milano wins," he says, "it will be the greatest day of my life." And how old are you again, Uncle Giacomo? "I will be seventy-five in November." Lazio gets an early goal on a stunning header, a setup pass from midfield that ricochets off the bald head of their multiply pierced star. The lead holds until late in the game, with ten minutes to play, when Milano ties it up. Regular time ends with the teams still deadlocked. In makeup time, a Milano player is clipped from behind and rips up his knee. The injury seems to inspire the team. They score on a penalty kick, and it holds. The cup is Milano's.

Joy fills every crag, valley, and village of the Piemonte. In Alba, people spill into the streets honking horns, pouring Prosecco over heads, strangers kissing strangers. Brunella and Teddy parade down the town's medieval alleys, eating dessert four times, singing the Milano song until the sun comes over the hills and touches the Tanaro River with the color of victory. Their late sleep is broken by a bang on the door in early afternoon. It is Marco Provenza, pale and breathless.

"Giacomo is dead!"

"Are you sure?"

"They found him wrapped in Milano banners, early this morning."

"Killed?"

"No, they think heart attack."

Brunella smiles. So many ways to die, and every man finds his own route to heaven. She makes sure that Uncle Giacomo is buried with the front page of Milano's newspaper, *Il Giornale*—the entire cover taken up with words and pictures of the team's victory—and dressed in the team's colors. The service is small, attended by only a handful of people. For as long as the baby of the Cartolano family lived in the Langhe Hills, it is surprising to Brunella how few friends he has. She is happy that Lucciano Albertini, from the school, has made it to the funeral.

"You are a gentleman," she tells him.

"For you, Signora Cartolano, I would do anything," the little man from Naples says.

As they walk away after the burial, Brunella takes Lucciano Albertini's arm and kisses him on the forehead.

"I won't be coming back to school in the fall," he tells her. "I'm moving home to Napoli."

"Moving home? Lucciano, you cannot. You are my best friend in all of Italy. Why?"

"I don't belong here in the north. I know what they say about me at school. Do not think I cannot hear them. They don't like Neapolitans. They think we are like monkeys. I know. My only consolation, if I can be immodest, is that you should hear the way they talk about the Sicilians."

"You must stay, Lucciano. Who will teach alternative-to-religion?"

"I'm too far from home."

"Too far? Naples is just a day's drive south. I am eight thousand miles from where I was born."

"Americans are different. I never should have left Napoli."

In the fall, four months pregnant, Brunella is told to come down to the Law and Justice Center in Torino at ten o'clock in the morning and to bring an *avvocato*—an attorney. The carabinieri know about the window, Teddy says. They will kick us out of Italy. They know we never checked in with them, have stayed past the length of a tourist visa, and are getting ready to bring a bambino into Italy without sufficient evidence of long-term employment. They will deport us, surely. Maybe jail.

When Brunella and Teddy arrive at the Law and Justice Center without an *avvocato,* the magistrate is angry and Brunella thinks now they will surely be deported. We have a saying here in Italy, the magistrate tells them: He who has himself for an attorney has a fool for a client.

"We have the same saying in America," Teddy says in English, and she tells him to shush, she will talk to the magistrate. She riffs for five minutes in Dante's Italian on the perfect symmetry of Italian law, particularly how it protects old houses.

"Then you will appreciate what I am about to tell you. We have here the will of your uncle, Giacomo Leonardo Cartolano. He owed back taxes in excess of one hundred seventeen thousand euro. We have taken the back taxes. Otherwise, his will is very clean. Let me ask you something under oath. Sign here, please." She gives him her signature. "You are Brunella Angelina Cartolano of the United States?"

"That is my name."

"Then you are now the owner of the estate of Giacomo Leonardo Cartolano."

She gasps.

"He left everything to you. And might I ask, Why no mourning dress? In the south a woman dresses five years in black for an uncle."

"What am I supposed to do?"

"First, you pay additional taxes. Let me advise you of something, Brunella Cartolano: Do not try to dodge taxes, the oldest of Italian sports. You may have to sell some of the land, or you may be a rich American with money. Either way, it's not my business. One more piece of advice: Be a good steward of your land. Remember, you are only a caretaker, no matter how long you live. We are done here. *Buon giorno.*"

The new owner of the villa dating to 1682 and the unkempt vineyards that produce a *vino da tavola* of unknown quality spends the first month doing nothing. She wants to fix the window. She and Teddy buy Venetian glass block and stack it to make a small unobtrusive window in the bathroom.

"Now you must wait for amnesty," says Marco Provenza, who has been kept on because he knows all the secrets.

"Amnesty?"

"Every few years the government lets you declare your illegal house modifications. You declare, and you pay a fine, and then the window has the full protection of our cultural preservation laws. In that way, you are no longer a criminal."

They get married on a Saturday in November just after the last of the Nebbiolo has been harvested and the Piemontese have started to slow down for the winter. The wedding is a small ceremony in San Lorenzo, the twelfth-century church in Portovenere. Brunella is well into her second trimester, but she looks radiant in a silk dress as white as the chalk cliffs south of Barolo.

"Memorable cleavage," Lucciano Albertini says to her, and the comment fills her with pride. The children from her English class sing at the wedding. Lucciano plays the John Lennon song himself, on a cello; the alternative-to-religion anthem never sounded as good as it does now under the limestone shelter that honors the saint on the grill. Glancing at the burned saint, she feels Niccolo and cries that her brother cannot be here. She wishes Babbo could her see her now and wonders about his honor and what will happen to his creations in the coulee now that Roberto has sold it to a holding company owned by Waddy Kornflint. Of course, everyone wants to know about the baby: Do you have a boy or a girl or don't you know: and if it's a boy—ah, well, you are one of the chosen ones, and if it's a girl you can always try again. And your baby will be Italian, yes? We need babies in Italy. There are no children. We have become too selfish. America is too violent. It's all about money and fat people. You do not want to raise a child there, please. On their wedding night, Teddy curls up behind Brunella, careful not to shake the baby. He is no longer a kept man, he says, but the owner of a four-century-old estate.

Every winter the winemakers of the Langhe Hills hold a Christmas tasting and contest in the big *castello* at the end of the cobblestone road in the village of Barolo. This year, Matteo Rudolfo has invited Brunella and Teddy to be his guests. She wants to bring an entry of her own.

"I'm sure your uncle Giacomo left you a very quaffable *vino da tavola*, but we have only one rule at this tasting: It must be Nebbiolo."

"*Sì*, Matteo. I have something."

Miguel has sent Brunella a case of the Cartolano Nebbiolo. His note explains that this was the one Brunella's father called Niccolo's vintage, the last wine Angelo Cartolano ever made. The grapes grew on nothing but well water and hose extensions from the pond. The wine has been in oak for two years and has just been bottled. Let it settle, the note says, and then enjoy a long life with a taste of the coulee. When they try the wine, Teddy is unsure what to make of it, but he likes it. "This rocks," he says.

Brunella holds a glass to her nose, trying to find the elements as her father taught her. Earthy, yes, as Angelo's wines always were, though nothing like the truffle hint of the true Barolos. Tannic as well, but surprisingly settled for a Nebbiolo from such a ripe vintage. And for wine that has been in wood for two years, the oak is subdued. She sips, sloshes it around, runs it from the front of her tongue to the back, and then holds her fist in the air.

"Babbo was right, Teddy, Babbo was right! This wine . . . has a story."

On an icy evening in December the winemakers march behind a banner down the winding main street in Barolo, past Christmas lights and shopkeepers who applaud the masters of the Wine of Kings, to the *castello* that holds many of the secrets from centuries past. The village is tucked snug into the hills, like a midwinter sleeper. Following a trumpet's blare, they enter the building and make their way down three flights of stairs to a high-arched stone-walled basement. Off to one side is a room full of leather-bound books and boxes stacked to the ceiling with notations of vintages past. There, records are kept in meticulous detail—rainfall, monthly temperatures, time of harvest, volume of grapes—so that a winemaker generations later can find an account of what worked in a particular year. Then comes a blessing from the bishop of Torino, the most solemn moment in the ceremony. When Europe's great vines were destroyed by the scourge of phylloxera in the nineteenth century, Nebbiolo alone survived. The Piemonte winemakers believe the fact that the grape lived while the plague wiped out almost everything else was a miracle, though they continue to debate if Bacchus or Jesus was directly responsible. For that reason, Angelo chose Nebbiolo when he started his vineyard in the coulee; perhaps he would not be able to craft a great wine, but he knew the vine itself would never die.

Three wooden tables are stretched, end to end, in the center of the tasting room in the *castello*. On the tables are the wines, each covered to the neck in a paper bag and marked by number. The vintners are to choose the ten best wines. This is the first year that an American has been allowed to enter a wine, and Brunella's presence has generated backbiting and complaints. One of the best-known of the Barolo masters, Romeo Alettino, a twelfth-generation winemaker, scowls throughout the tasting. Allowing the American wine into the contest, he says, cheapens the event. He is a massive man, with four chins, a red face, and swollen fingers that look like little hot dogs.

The winemakers work their way through the samples, sniffing, sloshing, and spitting. They scribble notations on pads, exchange information, argue and cajole, speculate and harrumph. Brunella feels tired, carrying a baby now in its seventh month. She sits off to the side and watches the masters at work. After two hours of tasting, the winemakers begin their presentations, a chance to show how refined and developed their palates are.

"This wine," says Matteo Rudolfo, who leads off the discussion, pointing to a bag marked by the number 18, "is from the 1990 vintage. It is powerful, and still very much in its youth. I give it my highest score." He invites the other winemakers to join in the discussion of bag number 18. Most of them agree with Matteo, though Romeo Alettino says it is not a 1990 at all but probably much younger.

They unveil number 18 to find that Matteo got it exactly right—it is Barolo Cannubi from the spectacular '90 vintage.

"Bravo, Matteo!"

The winemakers discuss three more bottles: a Barbaresco, a Nebbiolo from Langhe but not within the Barolo D.O.C., and a fifteen-year-old vintage that fooled everyone by the strength of its fruit. Brunella is starting to fret. Teddy is angry and can barely restrain himself. "These weenies," he says. "What do they know?"

Matteo calls for attention. "Now I want your picks for the American Nebbiolo," he says. The winemakers make apologetic faces to Brunella, some patting her on the head, saying *"Mi dispiace"* just before they proceed. The most vocal is Romeo Alettino.

"This, clearly, is the American wine," says the three-hundred-pound Barolo master, his eyelids half closed, his stubby fingers wrapped around a bag-covered bottle with number 72 on it. "It tastes of too much oak. It has a juvenile quality, really. And there's a cheapness. Almost a tawdry cheapness. Very American."

"Sì, sì," another winemaker says. "Romeo is right. *È vero*—there's a cheapness, I'm sorry to say. The fruit is far too aggressive, like it's been hurried along. Typical with the Americans, always in a hurry. *Mi dispiace,* Signora Cartolano." Others join in, piling on the insults, some of them sneering. Only Matteo and two very old men pick a different bag.

When at last the brown paper is pulled away, the grand tasting room falls silent. The wine that Romeo Alettino and his colleagues have dinged with a slew of insults is not the American Nebbiolo but a Barolo from one of the newer Bordeaux-influenced winemakers. The *Spectator* had given it a 95 rating.

"Impossible," Romeo mumbles. "And where is the American wine?"

"Here is my guess," says Matteo, hoisting the bag chosen by him and two elderly men. "You can taste the *terroir,* but it's not our land, not the Langhe Hills. It is fresh and original, with much life ahead of it. Bring it back in five years, and I would be worried about the future of Barolo. A wonderful finish, some licorice in there. All in all, this wine has a story."

"Matteo!" Brunella bolts from the chair, her belly so extended it looks like she could give birth at this moment. "*Grazie, Matteo!*" She kisses him, and he laughs while stripping away the bag to reveal Angelo Cartolano's last wine.

"*Congratulazioni!*" says Matteo, kissing Brunella in return. "Gentlemen, our Nebbiolo has found another home."

"A home?" says Brunella.

"*Sì, sì.*"

In bed as a light snow falls outside the villa, Brunella cannot sleep. The baby is kicking at a furious pace, but that is not what keeps her awake. She nudges Teddy, trying to engage him in conversation.

"Is it time?" he says, sitting upright, glancing around the room. "I'll get the car."

"No, no, Teddy. Something else. We have to go back."

"What?"

"We have to go back to the coulee."

"I'm the owner of an Italian villa with a baby on the way and free medical care. I cannot go back to America, Brunella. I have nothing there."

"We must. Don't you realize what happened tonight with Niccolo's vintage?"

"Now owned by a holding company of Waddy Kornflint."

"That Nebbiolo of ours—it was not forced. It is authentic, Teddy. Didn't you hear Matteo, the way he described it? It tastes of the land.

What my father started, when he had just the pond for water, and this wine, which was made after he returned to basics—we cannot let that die."

A seven-pound three-ounce girl is born on the twenty-fourth of January, three weeks early, in a fifteenth-century *ospedale* in Asti. As there are so few babies born in Italy, Brunella was given a large suite to herself and, during labor, was helped by three attendants, along with the *dottore* and Teddy. The infant is healthy, as ripe as fruit, the *dottore* says. Brunella can see Teddy's face in the baby, the face before fire reshaped his features, and also the Cartolano nose. It will take some time to see if the eyes burn green. She asks the *dottore* for a small vial of her baby's placenta. They name the girl Angelina Tedea Cartolano and make plans to take her to America in the spring.

CHAPTER TWENTY-ONE

S HE SLIPS into a room stripped bare of pictures and stacked with boxes. It feels cold and anonymous, like government space. She stares at the empty windowsill—where Leon Treadtoofar once kept his lodge-pole pinecone from the Yellowstone fire—and looks around for a place to leave a note. He has not returned her phone calls. Staring outside, she tries to phrase her words, to get it right, but the city distracts her. After their year and a half in Italy, Seattle looks new, wrapped in green and so temporary, everything made of wood and glass, oversize, under construction. The cars are big. The people are big. It feels like a city not far removed from the wild, with something growing from every crack in the sidewalk, the rhododendrons luminescent. It does not take much to remember why she put up with the rain.

"Help you?"

Leon fills the room at once. She moves toward him in the doorway, forgets what she was going to say in the note. She wants to touch him.

"I thought you left the country."

"And I thought you were fired."

"They don't fire you in the Forest Service. They just send you to a place without trees."

"So where are you going?"

"I'm being transferred to Oklahoma."

"What's in Oklahoma?"

"Grasslands. National Grasslands run by the service."

"Aren't there a lot of Indians in Oklahoma?"

"Not by choice."

"Why not leave the Forest Service?"

"It's family. I could never leave."

"È vero."

"What that?"

"Italian: 'So true.' " She touches his face, the Nez Perce nose. He stares back, no reflex to respond, stares hard.

"I heard you had a baby."

"A girl. You want to see a picture? She's beautiful, Leon." She starts to retrieve a photo.

"You never said goodbye, Brunella."

"Why would they send you away?"

"We all share some of the blame. I accept mine."

"What about Kosbleau? Didn't you have enough, with what I told you and the water records, to go after him?"

"No witness, not after your father died. And with no water left under the burned forest, I have no physical proof."

"Are you reading any poetry, Leon?"

"I always read poetry."

He moves past her as if she were a cleaning woman, gathering the last of his office possessions.

"Leon, I have an idea. You need proof in order to show what really happened in that forest. My father told me about a key. It was something, I never gave it a second thought because things were moving so fast in the last days in the coulee. It's a key, he said, to a valve that controls movement of the water in that basin. Kosbleau and my father each had one. You could not move the water without using both keys."

"Like sharing a crime. I'm sure the keys are long gone. Kosbleau covered his tracks well."

"But what if I could draw him out?"

"With what?"

"They had a club, my father and the old men who climbed Mount Stuart a long time ago. A Last Man's club. The winner got a bottle in our cellar. That's where my father kept his key. Kosbleau is the last man, which means he must have both keys."

"And how do you get him to use them?"

"I don't know. But if he did, if you could search his home, if you could find them, it would show his intimate knowledge of all the water thefts. You could use that. It would be huge."

He says nothing.

"Leon . . . ?"

"Is it because I hit you?"

"What?"

"Is that why you never said goodbye, Brunella? Because I hit you?"

"I see that in a man—I'll be honest with you, Leon—and it scares me. You never look at somebody the same way afterward. All you can see is the back of the hand."

"I have a problem. It scares me too."

Leon hefts a box of his belongings and turns to walk out. "Are you moving back to America?"

The drought is over. The rivers west of the Cascades—Stillaguamish, Skykomish, Snohomish, Skagit, and Nooksack—all the frothy drainages named for the people who used to live at their mouths, are running near flood stage in midspring. Even in the arid country on the other side of the mountains, water is waking gravel beds that have not felt such a rousting since before the dams were built. On city streets and in the countryside, on boat decks and Little League fields, people look skyward, without umbrellas, and let the rain hit their faces. Brunella detects joy, as if a long plague has just ended and it is safe again to go outside.

On her way to the coulee, Brunella gets stuck in mud just outside the entrance and tries not to see it as a bad omen. Miguel greets her and takes Brunella on the back of his three-wheeler to the vineyard.

"You want to see the house, Brunella?"

"Don't go near it," she says.

"It's nothing to be afraid of."

"Don't go near it, Miguel."

"Just a drive-by. Okay?"

"No!" She will not look at the house. But the vineyards, now starting to leaf, and the balsamwort flowering at the base of the basalt columns, and the light against the wall of the North Cascades—it draws her in and makes her feel disloyal for being gone so long. Look at the pond; she cannot believe how full it is, brimming with rainwater. She cannot let herself go soft or sentimental. Try to make it neutral ground, hard earth, photosynthesis. The place has been sold. It's gone. Over. She has a home in the Old World, a man she loves, a *bella bambina*. This life is over. She motions for Miguel to take her up through the soft green of the vines, as fast as he can, until they are high on the coulee ridge.

"Everything seems so lush."

"A wet spring," says Miguel. "I've seen things I haven't seen for twenty years."

"You've kept everything up."

"I don't know nothing else."

She jumps off and waves him away. The winds carry heavy clouds, the low edges ragged, threatening. It takes most of the morning to hike down into the ghost forest, the way slippery on slick clay and still the smell of smoke like she remembered it from before, burned mattresses. She finds the Forest Service markers. To her surprise, Niccolo's last stand is covered by water; where the ground was hard and seared there is now a shallow pond. She hears moving water, gurgling up, filling the basin. She slops around in the chill depth, talking to Niccolo, telling him about her baby and the grilled San Lorenzo, surely Niccolo's soul mate today. Her teeth are chattering. God, where did all this water come from? Yes, it has been raining a lot this spring, as Miguel said, and maybe people are seeing things that have not been seen in the Columbia basin for decades, but this section is supposed to be drained and dry. There is still no vegetation, nothing to hold the runoff and the rainfall, so where did this swamp come from? She looks closely, following the sound; it appears that the water is seeping up from below, but how could this be? Didn't Kosbleau suck it dry?

She listens with great care and discerns another sound, distinct and familiar; now she knows that water has been coursing through here for months.

Zeee-eeet! Zeee-eeet! What could dippers find to like in this haunted ground?

When she goes to Alden Kosbleau's manse on the hill above Lake Chelan, she expects to be turned away by dogs or alarms. Instead, the water king himself ambles down the driveway to welcome her. Arms outstretched, wearing a loud T-shirt, baggy shorts. Why do older Americans dress like ten-year-olds?

"My prodigal friend—Brunella Cartolano!"

"Hello, Alden." No smile from her, a cursory hug. Such a bullshit artist, how could she not see through him years ago? He looks sunbaked, the skin on his face furrowed and leathery, covered with age spots. A Palm Springs winter, he explains. Though bruised clouds coast low over the wet land, Kosbleau's automatic sprinklers are spreading water over his acreage, all the exotic trees sloping to the lake.

"Come up to the house. Where's the baby?"

"You heard?"

"I would never let Brunella Cartolano leave my heart. Remember, I'm like family, you once said."

"I can't come in. I don't have time. We—I have some legal papers to close. I'm meeting someone later. The new buyer."

"Bob kept me informed about the sale. You're in my tax bracket now, kid. You must come inside. Have a drink. I've got some single malt—eighteen-year-old stuff—it'll make your heart burn peat."

"I went into the dead forest yesterday, Alden, and I found something."

"Yes?" Hand on his mouth, eyebrows arched. She notices Kosbleau's hand, with its brown spots and gold watch.

"I found water."

"Well, no shit, it's been raining for two months or more. Wettest spring I've seen in thirty-seven years."

"This water didn't come from the sky. It came from the ground."

"Yes?" Hand still on the mouth, no expression. "Are you a hydrologist now? Why do you tell me such a thing?"

"I know what the government is paying for water."

"Yes?"

"And I know how much you value it."

"Yes?"

"That's it. I just wanted to let you know."

"Do you think I lack for water, Brunella? Do you think I need to squeeze another dime from this land? Do you think I don't have everything I want? Look around this place. Your old man had a good thing going in the coulee, but he only took it so far. Look around here. Tell me if you think something is missing."

The clouds collide, darken, and spill, and when the rain falls hard Kosbleau stutter-steps up the driveway. "Come quick. I want to show you something."

"I don't have time."

"This will just take a minute." He guides her up the hill and around the back, behind the manse, where delicate canes are planted in a raised bed of loamy black soil, positioned under the retractable glass roof of what looks like a crystal greenhouse. The soil is tilled like finely ground coffee, and a thin electronic fence surrounds it. The lower parts of the canes are wrapped in white cloth, and the tops have sprouted new growth. As soon as rain touches the glass, the roof automatically covers the raised bed.

"Behold the blue rose!" Kosbleau says, his face red from the exertion. "This year, I will get my flower, the one color that is unobtainable. This year, everything is in place for the blue rose."

"Why the glass roof?"

"For protection. The blue rose will not tolerate rain without getting black spots. I control all water, all nutrients, the hours of sunshine— everything! What do you think? Your old man would have been proud of me, huh?"

"I don't know."

"What's wrong? You don't seem very impressed."

"I have to go."

His lips are trembling, the rain splattering his glasses. "You think you're better than me, don't you?"

He slips to the ground a few feet from the electronic fence. She extends a hand to lift him. He gets up without her help, mumbling to himself, and wipes the mud from his glasses.

"You think you're better than me."

"No, I—"

"Say it, bitch!"

"What happened to the bottle, Alden?"

"The bottle?"

"From the cellar. The Last Man's Club bottle."

"It's with me. Where it belongs."

Kosbleau rummages around the house, trying to remember everything. He grabs his pistol, a heavy raincoat, a phone. In the closet of the master bedroom is a safe. Inside, the bottle. Next to the bottle, two keys. He sets the bottle on a table and takes the two keys.

He drives south to the coulee and guns his Bronco forward. The rain makes the clay slide and fold, like great mounds of dough. He has been warned by Miguel, who greeted him in the driveway, not to go into the ghost forest. The way is unstable and it smells like death. He drops into first gear, four-wheel drive, and goes deeper into the burned woods on a slight way trail never intended for cars, the tires sinking in the mud and the rain falling so hard there is no visibility. The Bronco bounces into a rut and spins, one tire in the air, still moving forward. Kosbleau's face is clenched.

"Here!" he says to himself. He stops the car and gets out, cursing now. Goddamn Mexicans, afraid of a little rain. Slop, slop; the charcoaled mud is horrid, hard to get any footing, and the smell—the Mexican was right—is indeed the smell of death. These wets know a thing or two about superstition. But look here, Cartolano is on to something; it's a god-damn mother lode. Look at all this water. Christ. It's coming from deep down, no doubt, just like the Cartolano girl said. He wades through, look-ing around for a source, doused by the torrent. So he didn't get it all. Most of the water was moved to the Indians, but here is a small fortune left behind. It eats at him to think of all the water the Indians let go, the pit, emptied into the big river. And for what? The rain must have recharged some springs in here, must have flushed the deepest part of the aquifer to the surface. Well, now it belongs to the water king. All he has to do to send it back to storage in the mine shafts is gin up the pumps. Can't let this chance slip by. One last bonanza. Water is always moving. Some-body's going to lose it; somebody's going to get it. It's finite, the most con-sistent shaper of destiny on the planet.

He walks to a pile of boulders at the base of the hill, next to the water, searching the rock for a particular entrance. Here it is, the opening. He tugs at a small boulder, reaching to get inside at something, but it will not move. On his second attempt he falls backward into the water. He gags and coughs, spitting out the cold mouthful. Now his chest hurts, shooting pains. He staggers to his feet, soaked to his skin, shivering uncontrollably. He removes the pistol from his coat pocket, steps to the side, and fires a round at the small rock entrance. It chips away enough that he can get a grip and pull back the rock. Behind that, the big valve. Okay, now the two keys. Get both of them. Hands steady. First one; yes, of course it fits. Now the other. Perfect. He wrestles with the rusted valve handle, trying to make it budge. It starts to move. There must truly be a fortune in this deep well, an untapped gusher born of the wet spring, and all he has to do is get this big rusted wheel cranked just enough to activate the link under-ground that will move some of this water into one of the mine shafts—storage, for now. He completes his task, gasping for breath, the chest pains worse, his mind feverish with the numbers.

Back at the manse, Kosbleau draws a bath in the marbled Jacuzzi. He pours himself three fingers of Scotch on ice, the eighteen-year-old single malt. Oh, that's fine. Oh, that burns peat. With every sip, the mud and cold water dissipate. He pours himself another three fingers, and sips, sips, sips; oh, shit, is that fine, the taste of the good life. His Scotch buzz on, he stumbles to the great room, full of trophy heads: the last cougar to roam the Columbia basin, shot in November near the Safeway parking lot; a six-point trophy elk; a big-chested mountain goat from uplake, got him with a single shot from the boat. He grabs the Last Man's bottle. Time to put this thing away as well. Probably tastes like shit, but it's a tri-umphant chaser. He puts the Last Man's bottle on a counter next to the Jacuzzi tub and turns on a small television with a remote. One more belt of the single malt, then slide into the water and forget about the chill, the mud, and the memory of the Cartolano bitch. Two fingers this time. Two fingers for the last water conquest in the Planned Promised Land. Scotch in one hand, he steps into the tub but loses his balance, falls sharply against the marbled corner edge, cuts his head, and drops headfirst into the tub, unconscious. Water fills his lungs. With a jerk, his body trembles, an upward foot snagging a wire of the television from its nook, pulling it into the tub. The shock runs through his body, shorts out the electricity in the house: all the pumps, the lights, the wire fence outside. Within the hour, a deer crosses over the lifeless wires to a raised bed on the open-air side of the greenhouse and munches on the tender young shoots of a well-manicured blue rose.

The rain is still falling when Brunella arrives at the new tribal casino along the Columbia River. The parking lot is stuffed with SUVs and minivans, every spot taken. A tour bus from the city takes a load of gamblers to the front entrance, where ponytailed natives greet them with open arms. It's a flow of money and people, at times like a stampede, all going one way.

Brunella has arranged to meet the new buyer of the vineyard at a restaurant in a quiet corner of the casino. She gets a window table in an area cantilevered over the river. She looks at the wine list and finds the Cartolano Nebbiolo, with a star next to it to show it's a local product. But when she asks for a bottle, the Indian waitress frowns. "I'm sorry, we're all out."

Brunella asks the woman about herself, and she says she is a full-blood member of the tribe who moved to Los Angeles but returned when the casino opened. The tribe has full employment.

"We do have some of the Cartolano table wine," the waitress says. "I can bring you a glass of that."

"How would you describe it?"

"Well"—she flashes a dimpled smile—"I don't drink. The reservation is dry, except for the casino. But I can tell you it's a full-bodied red, not very tannic, with a nice finish from an excellent vintage."

"How do you know?"

"They made us take a class on wine in Yakima. The casino paid for it. Should I bring you a glass of the red?"

"Please."

The River of the West is bigger than Brunella ever remembers, swollen and running fast. The wine arrives. Brunella can taste the pebbles of the coulee, the stony imprint from the ancient flood, and it draws her back to the last afternoon with Angelo and Niccolo, high in the vineyard. What her father's Nebbiolo has over the same grape in Italy is the struggle, she decides. As Angelo said, the roots in the coulee have to reach far down to find moisture, and in the process they carry the taste of the pebbled ground from the deep cleft in the earth upward to the grape. The deposit from the Greatest Flood of All Time has nurtured this cup of velvet. And she understands why the only vintage her father never liked, the one he destroyed, did not have a story. No struggle, no story. *In vino veritas*, of course, as the Romans knew from the beginning, unless you cheat. The new owner will never understand this. The new owner is buying a rating, a brand name.

She waits half an hour, ordering a second glass of the Cartolano table wine, her mind adrift as she stares at the river. How can she live with herself if she lets this sale proceed? It was a betrayal of her father's life wish. Can the soul of Angelo Cartolano be free if his body remains in ground owned by someone else?

"The water is so high," Brunella says to the waitress.

"Good for fish," the waitress says. "Everyone's very excited. Two years ago, somebody emptied out this great big pit of water the tribe had stored . . . here, right outside the casino. We never found out who did it. But they say it was a miracle, as if Chief Joseph came back from the dead to give the river life again. You see, it was a horrible drought, the river so low the little salmon were stuck; they couldn't move. Then all the water poured out of the pit like a big hand of God. And that flush carried a lot of baby salmon to the ocean. There's supposed to be a great big run when they come back as old fish ready to spawn. My dad and his friends, they talk about this as the creator's miracle of salmon and the new casino. Can I get you something to eat?"

"I'm still waiting."

A thin man with a hesitant gait makes his way to Brunella's table. Ethan Winthrop looks much older, his hair on top nearly gone, his eyes sunken. He always seemed helpless and papery, but now he looks to be a step removed from life itself. He is swaddled in a heavy winter parka; when he takes off his gloves, his fingers are white, the blood drained away.

"I'm sorry I'm late. This thing"—he shows her a palm-sized Global Positioning System—"was supposed to get me here with pinpoint accuracy, but I ended up at a Wal-Mart in Wenatchee."

"What are you doing here?"

"We have business to settle."

"We?"

"I'm the new buyer."

She rises from her chair.

"Please," Ethan says, extending a hand with chalky fingers. "Don't walk out. Oh, waitress, can you bring me some hot water for tea?"

Ethan keeps his coat on as he removes a stack of documents from his briefcase. His hands move slowly, without fluidity.

"Your father's wine?" he says, pointing to her drink.

"Yes."

"How is it?"

"My father always said his wine would make him immortal."

"And?"

"He lives in this glass. So does Niccolo."

Ethan turns to the legal papers in his folder. "I had thought of structuring this as a straight gift."

"A gift?"

"The way people with old money pass something on to their ultimately inferior and typically ungrateful children. But I have no ultimately inferior and typically ungrateful children, as you know. I have no siblings. Both parents are dead. I decided to pay your brother for the place, exactly as outlined in the deal memo, and then sell it back to you for one dollar."

"One dollar?" Her face is blank. "Sell it back to me?"

The hot water arrives.

"What happened to your voice, Ethan? I can hardly hear you."

"But then I thought, No, that won't work. For tax purposes, it's a drain. I'm trying to speak up. . . ."

"What's wrong?"

"Will you pour the tea for me? What I came up with was a sort of trust, another trick of the rich; I'm learning these things, though I'm still nouveau, of course. It's like a conservation easement, if you will. Are you familiar with those? I'm sure you are, with all your preservation work. People do this when they want to keep a ranch from becoming another strip mall. So, here's what I've put together: The Cartolano vineyard will stay as it is, a working vineyard, for eternity. It can be sold upon your death, but it must stay as a working vineyard, no matter how many hands it passes through. What do you think?"

"I don't know what to think."

"There is a catch. One condition, only: You would have to stay on the land."

"Stay on the land?"

"Yes. You can make wine. You can pay somebody to make wine. You can spend your winters in—I don't know—wherever, but you have to make the coulee your primary home."

"I . . . I . . . you say it will always stay a vineyard, as long as I live there?"

"Yes. I know it sounds like a form of indentured servitude. But you would never hear from me again. I promise. I can put it in this document, if you want. It would be yours, basically."

"Are you okay, Ethan?"

"I'm sick. Can't you tell?"

"I didn't want to say anything."

"Surely, you knew something was wrong with me long ago. Our hike almost killed me. And remember when I stumbled at the stadium? I didn't think I would make it up those stairs."

"I just thought you weren't very physical."

"Not my choice. It's . . . this is embarrassing, Brunella, because I hate sports. I have amyotrophic lateral sclerosis—"

"Lou Gehrig's disease."

"They're making progress at the degenerative neurological institute on Lake Union, but I don't have ten years to wait for the research. Anyway, that's the way I structured this deal. Do you accept?"

"Why are you doing this, Ethan?"

"It's cheaper, for tax purposes."

"I understand that part, but why—?"

"Oh, I suppose that's a complicated palaver for another time. But let's say I envy you your consuming passions."

"You said I fall in love too easily, with too many things."

"And I don't fall in love with anything. But listen: Will you accept?"

"I live in Italy now, in a valley not far from the Alps, where they've been making wine for three thousand years. I have a farm, an old villa, a husband I love, a baby girl, and some grapes."

"But where is home?"

She holds the glass of wine, raises the blood of the coulee, and looks at the color, a *vino rosso* with a story. Could she ever make such a thing?

Brunella has no trouble finding her father's grave, a small mound of dirt at the crest of the coulee. The pond is so full that water spills out three over-flow ditches, the primitive canals that Angelo dug by hand when he first moved here and had no other source of water. She watches it trickle out and flow evenly into the vineyard. She kneels over the grave, claws away the top layer of soil, the pebbles Angelo loved, one parent of his magnifi-cent *vino*, talking all the while, telling the story of Uncle Giacomo and his place in Italy, describing what happened in Barolo, the rude man with the swollen fingers, the insults, and how the Cartolano wine proved itself in the end when judged against the Wine of Kings. She tells him that she knew—in that instant—that the Cartolanos belonged to this coulee because Nebbiolo belonged to the Columbia basin. And yes, it's true, as her *babbo* always said, you could tell you were home when you could look at the tangle of grapes, the flowering orchards, the blushing walls of gran-ite to the west and say, *È bello da mozzare il fiato.* It did take her breath away—still. She scrapes at the wet pebbled ground, takes the small vial of her baby's placenta, and buries it, smoothing the soil over Angelo's grave. Mount Stuart is veiled, but on a clear day this is the best view.

ACKNOWLEDGMENTS

Through the years, this story was sustained by fresh enthusiasm when it was most needed. The smoke jumpers of the United States Forest Service have answered more questions than government service requires, while opening their doors as well. My Seattle manuscript readers, especially Anne Hurley and Michael Knoll, tried to make sure the illogic of fiction stayed consistent. My thanks to Ash Green, Luba Ostashevsky, Kathleen Fridella, and Sonny Mehta at Knopf, and my agent, Carol Mann, for literary matchmaking. In the art of living well and the craft of winemaking, I owe much to the late Angelo Pellegrini, whose philosophy is best distilled in his book, *Lean Years, Happy Years*. Also, *The Wine Project: Washington State's Winemaking History*, by Ronald Irvine with Walter J. Clore, is an excellent resource. John and Cora Picken, at Lake Chalan, know the irrigation country better than anyone. In Italy, Sergio and Rina, our neighbors one floor below, revealed some of the timeless secrets of Chianti Classico, even while tolerating our feeble Italian. And finally my deepest gratitude to Joni, for three dimensions of support.

A NOTE ABOUT THE AUTHOR

Timothy Egan, a third-generation westerner, is the author of *Lasso the Wind, The Good Rain,* and *Breaking Blue.* He has been a writer for the *New York Times* for the past fifteen years and was part of a team that won the Pulitzer Prize in 2001 for national reporting. He lives in Seattle with his wife, Joni Balter, and their two children. This is his first novel.

A NOTE ON THE TYPE

This book was set in Fairfield, the first typeface from the hand of the distinguished American artist and engraver Rudolph Ruzicka (1883–1978). In its structure Fairfield displays the sober and sane qualities of the master craftsman whose talent has long been dedicated to clarity. It is this trait that accounts for the trim grace and vigor, the spirited design and sensitive balance of this original typeface.

Composed by Creative Graphics, Allentown, Pennsylvania
Printed and bound by Berryville Graphics, Berryville, Virginia
Designed by Robert C. Olsson